ONE WEEK IN WINTER

Sheila Norton

Copyright © 2023 Sheila Norton
Image: iStock: Evelyne Herbin

All rights reserved

ABOUT THE AUTHOR

Sheila Norton lives near Chelmsford in Essex, and part-time in Torquay, Devon, and has been writing avidly since childhood. Her first published works were short stories, having had more than a hundred published in national women's magazines before her first novel was published in 2003. Since then, she has had over twenty more novels published, most of which have been with major publishers.

Married, with three daughters and six grandchildren, Sheila worked for most of her life, prior to retirement, as a medical secretary. When not writing she enjoys spending time with family and friends, reading, music, photography, and walking in the beautiful countryside around her Devon and Essex homes. She also enjoys the company of her two Ragamese cats, the latest in a succession of much-loved dogs and cats over the years.

Sheila enjoys hearing from readers and can be contacted through her website: **www.sheilanorton.com**, where you can also sign up for quarterly email newsletters.

For my daughters, who are such lovely sisters to each other.
And for my sisters-in-law, who are like sisters to me.
I love you all.

A Saturday in January

Julia

'This must be the place,' I say, winding down the car window and leaning out to stare, in the beam of the headlights, at the rusty-looking sign by the enormous iron gates in front of us.

'Well, I hope so,' Lauren grumbles. 'I've just about had enough of these ridiculous narrow country lanes. I wouldn't have minded if your Sat Nav had been any help –'

'It's hardly the fault of the Sat Nav,' I point out with a sigh. Lauren has done very little but grumble during the entire four-hour journey from London. 'The whole area is obviously completely off the beaten track, and –'

'So if this is the place, how are we supposed to get in?' she interrupts me impatiently.

'I presume there's a bell to ring, or something like that. I'll get out and have a look.'

'No, don't worry, I'll do it.'

She turns on her phone's torch and slams the door as she leaves the car. You'd never guess we were here to enjoy ourselves. Well, that was the theory, anyway. A holiday, of some sort – a winter break in the countryside. So far, it's not exactly going well. The difficulty of finding the place hasn't helped, but perhaps the whole idea was doomed from the start. I'd been hoping that, now we're here, things might start to improve, but it doesn't look like it.

Just as I'm thinking this, Lauren turns back to look at me and, even in the darkness I can judge from her stance that things are definitely not yet improving.

'The sign says *Deepcombe Manor*,' she calls out as I wind down the window. 'I thought we were booked into Deepcombe *Lodge.*'

I get out of the car and go to stand beside her, reading the sign myself.

'Deepcombe *Manor*,' I repeat. 'Perhaps it's . . . I don't know, just another name for the same place? Are you sure the booking said *Lodge*?'

Lauren passes me her phone, where she's already got the booking confirmation email open.

'I've been staring at it most of the way down here,' she says in a resigned tone.

'Perhaps it's just a mistake – on the booking,' I suggest hopefully.

'Well, look, there's an intercom thing here anyway. It says press for entry.'

We look at each other and I shrug. 'OK.' I press the button, and we both wait.

'Press it again,' Lauren instructs, and I'm just about to do so when there's a loud crackling sound from the intercom, and a disembodied ancient-sounding voice hollers:

'Hello? Who is it?'

'Um – my name's Lauren Chandler. We've got a reservation. Two of us, for a week –'

'Reservation?' croaks the voice. Then there follows a cackle of laughter that makes us both flinch. 'Not 'ere you 'aven't, my lovely. This is the Manor. The holiday cottage is The Lodge. Another two hundred yards down the lane, see? The gates are open down there. Drive straight in. Key's in the door.'

'Well, it would have been nice if that information had been –' Lauren begins indignantly, but she's wasting her breath. The intercom has already crackled itself into silence.

'Come on,' I say. 'At least we're nearly there.'

'Key in the door?' she's still complaining as we get back into the car. 'What sort of arrangement is that? Anybody could have gone in and helped themselves to . . . whatever there is. How do we know there isn't somebody actually *squatting* in there when we finally arrive?'

'They'd have had to find it first,' I point out drily as I start the engine again and concentrate on negotiating the single-track lane without veering into a ditch. And within a minute or two I add: 'Right, I think we're here now, anyway.'

I slow down as we approach another set of iron gates – open this time, as promised. 'Look, this sign says *Deepcombe Lodge.*'

'Well, thank God for that,' Lauren says.

Then we both fall silent as I pull up in front of our holiday home. It might have been called a Lodge, but if first impressions are anything to go by, it looks more like . . . a ramshackle old hut. In the light of the car headlights, I can see that there's ivy growing rampantly over the place, even encroaching over the front door. The ancient whitewashed walls look wonky, the windows are grimy, and it looks like there are tiles missing from the roof.

'This can't be it,' I say in a hoarse whisper. It's cold, with sleet in the air, half past four now and already dark. I'm tired from the driving and desperate for a hot cup of tea. The thought of getting back in the car and trying again to find the right place is suddenly more than I can bear.

'It is,' Lauren says. There's an edge of horror in her voice. 'Look. *Deepcombe Lodge* on the door.' To be strictly accurate, the wooden sign is hanging *off* the door. 'And – yes, the key's in the lock.'

She walks up to the front door and turns the key to open it. I follow cautiously behind her.

'Well, it looks a bit better inside than it did from the outside –' I begin, and then stop in surprise as two cats run up to us, meowing a friendly greeting. Or possibly a furious warning. How does one tell, with cats? 'Somebody's in here!' I whisper urgently. 'You were right!'

I look around, half expecting to see an angry family coming down the stairs, accusing us of trespass, of entering with intent to steal their cats.

'Hang on,' Lauren says. 'There's a note on the table here.'

I follow Lauren across the room and peer at the scrawly writing on a page of paper that looks as if it's been torn from a notebook. We contemplate the message in silence for a moment, and then begin to read out loud, more or less in unison:

Welcome to Deepcombe Lodge. No smoking. TV signal is best on BBC South West. WI-FI works most days unless it's raining. Cats might come in through cat flaps, please don't close the flaps or they will mess on carpets. Nothing down the toilet please or it will block.

We look at each other for a moment. I feel a bit like laughing hysterically, but I'm very much afraid my sister might actually cry.

This was, originally, supposed to be her dream holiday, with her dream man. The dream man has buggered off. And it's hard now to imagine that this is going to be any sort of dream holiday either. Possibly more like a nightmare. To my own surprise, I find myself enveloping her in a hug. We're not the kind of sisters who hug. Then again, we aren't the kind of sisters who go on holiday together, either. But there's a first time for everything, I suppose.

Lauren

I could just sit down and cry. It's all very well for Julia; she didn't even want to come here in the first place. OK, to be honest, neither did I. I wanted to go on the dream holiday Carl had promised me, and this wasn't it. But I didn't want to go anyway after he walked out. Why would I?

It was Julia's idea for us to come on the holiday together. Well, strictly speaking, her original idea was that I should come on my own. *Stick two fingers up to Carl*, she said, when she called me a few days ago to wish me a happy birthday. *Go ahead, enjoy the holiday, sod him, he's the one missing out. You don't always have to have a man with you, to have a good time.*

She wasn't sounding particularly sympathetic to my situation, frankly. But then, she's never been particularly sympathetic when I've been through relationship break-ups. We're not close, and we don't often even speak to each other these days. Over the years, I've got frankly fed-up with being patronised by her, spoken to like I'm still a child, when in fact she's only five years older than me.

'You didn't mind having a man with you, all those years you were married to Phil,' I reminded her. 'Or was it only because he was rich and successful –'

I could have gone on . . . gone on over the same old ground again, leading to the same kind of weary argument we've normally ended up having whenever we've spoken. But I stopped short because, for once, I was secretly quite glad she'd called me. I didn't want a row, I didn't want Julia to hang up on me, I was still feeling too emotionally wrecked about Carl.

'Sorry,' I conceded. 'Let's not fight.'

'I didn't want a fight,' she said calmly. 'I called to wish you a happy birthday.'

'I know. Thank you. But it doesn't look like it's going to be very happy now, does it?'

She started, again, to give me her usual lecture about how we shouldn't need a man to fulfil our lives, how we need to make our own happiness and how, by my age (forty the following day), I should have grown out of my adolescent fantasies about finding *the one.* But she stopped, mid-sentence, and apologised too.

'OK, I know, I suppose I'm not helping, am I?' she admitted. 'I *am* sorry about Carl. But as for the holiday, Lauren, you really are being a bit pathetic. Come on, seriously, you say Carl's left you all the details of the place he's booked, and it's supposed to be his birthday present to you – so you owe it to yourself. A spot of R and R.'

'*You* have the bloody holiday, if you're so determined I shouldn't waste it!' I snapped back, on the verge of tears now. I wanted sympathy, not a lecture, from her. 'I don't want to go on my own. I don't want to go anywhere without Carl.'

I thought for a moment Julia had hung up on me, but no, I could hear her breathing.

'Don't be silly,' she said eventually. She was talking softly now, gently, like I was a hurt child. 'Carl's gone, I'm sorry you're upset, obviously, but you need to think about yourself now. Can't you take a friend with you? Go away, enjoy it, forget him.'

She really had no idea, did she? I'd just lost the love of my life, and she was talking as if I'd mislaid a pair of gloves or something.

'Where is this holiday, anyway?' she went on. 'Somewhere exotic? If it's abroad, you'll need to change the name on the plane ticket –'

'I haven't even opened the envelope,' I admitted. 'He gave me the booking details in an envelope, with my birthday card. I was waiting till tomorrow to open it.'

'Open it now,' Julia said. Taking charge, as usual. 'If the booking is for next week, you're going to need to organise things quickly.'

I sighed. I supposed it didn't make any difference, now. If I opened it the next day, on my ruined birthday, I wasn't exactly going to feel any better for knowing which destination I would have been flying off to with Carl if he hadn't decided to finish with me.

'OK,' I said. 'Hang on.'

I put down the phone while I found the envelope and opened it, glancing out of the window as I did. It was late, after eleven o'clock at night, and raining outside. On these rare occasions – usually birthdays and Christmas – when Julia called me, it was always late at night. She was too busy with her important career, of course, to think about her sister during the day. Looking back now on that moment, I think everything might have felt different if it had been daytime – mid-morning, say, on a bright sunny day. I'd been sitting on my own with a consolatory gin and tonic, feeling as if my life was over, but in the daytime the disappointment might not have felt quite so catastrophic. I might have even laughed about it.

'It's not somewhere exotic,' I told Julia as I started to read the booking confirmation – printed out on a single sheet of A4 paper, no doubt on my own unreliable home printer, as indicated by the ink smudges halfway down the page. 'It's not even abroad.' I sniffed back the first few tears. 'It's not a hotel. It's –' And here I burst into proper, uncontrolled crying. Wailing. It felt like the last straw, that's all I can say. Like Carl had not only left me, he was mocking me. 'It's some self-catering bloody *cottage* in *Devon.*'

For a few minutes there was silence at the other end of the phone. Or perhaps I just couldn't hear Julia's reaction because I was wailing so much. Then she spoke, very firmly, very decisively, and I felt so wretched I just nodded in response, as if she could see me.

'OK. Look: Devon's lovely. It'll be great, Lauren. Perfect. A winter break in the countryside. Is there a phone number? It's probably a booking agency. Call them and change it to your own name. Is it for this Saturday? It's too short-notice to book anything different now. I'll drive. I'll come and pick you up early in the morning and –'

'You want to come with me?' I sobbed, too far gone with my crying by now to even register the full extent of my shock. 'But you won't be able to get the time off work, will you, at such short notice?'

'Lauren, I'm a partner in the company,' she said. 'I take off whatever time I like, whenever I choose.'

Rub it in, why didn't she? Successful career, nice home, independent woman who didn't (now) seem to need a man in her life. Everything I *wasn't*.

'I'll see you on Saturday,' she went on more gently. 'Try to have a nice birthday tomorrow. Do something nice after work. Treat yourself – some shopping, or . . . a film, and a meal out.'

'OK,' I said, although I knew I wouldn't. I'd probably sit in front of rubbish on the TV with a takeaway.

I felt such a failure. I'd failed in everything, all my life: firstly in my ambition to become some kind of lawyer, ending up instead as an *assistant* to a legal secretary – not even good enough to become the actual secretary; and then, ever since, with my succession of failed relationships.

Yes, I know, I admit it, I was totally absorbed in my self-pity that day.

'I'm sorry you're so upset, Lauren,' Julia went on in her new, gentle, patient voice. 'But I have to be honest with you: Carl wasn't the love of your life at all. Frankly, he was an arse.'

That was all very well for her to say. But I loved him.

Julia

I have no idea why I feel guilty. It's not Lauren's fault, of course, that the so-called self-catering cottage has turned out to be such a disappointment, but it certainly isn't mine either. But I sometimes feel like I've gone through most of my life feeling guilty about my sister. Guilty because she's clearly so unhappy. Guilty because I've got over my divorce, emerged from it stronger, and made something of my life whereas she . . . has just never managed to find a man who's hung around, or a job that's satisfied her. Guilty because I don't give her enough of my time, because when I try to – if I'm honest – she wears me down with her negativity.

'Did you look the place up on-line before we came – after you'd opened the envelope?' I ask her, as gently as I can, once we've got over our initial shock. 'Weren't there any pictures of it?'

'Yes, I did!' she retorts angrily. 'And there was a picture of a lovely old house – a big house! – with, well, with big chimneys and lots of windows and a huge front door, and –'

'Perhaps that was the Manor House,' I suggest. 'No pictures of this . . . um . . . *Lodge*, then?'

I nearly said *dump*, but I didn't want to upset her any more than she already is.

'No!' Lauren says. 'I assumed the picture was of the place we were booked into. Well, you would, wouldn't you? It's . . . it's *misrepresentation*, that's what it is. I'm going to call the number on the booking, and complain. We can't be expected to stay *here*.'

'Well, perhaps it'll be OK,' I say a little doubtfully. 'It looks all right inside, doesn't it?' One of the cats is circling around my legs and I bend down to stroke it. 'Perhaps we should look upstairs before we decide.'

To be honest, I'm worried Lauren will be even more depressed if there turns out to be no alternative and we end up having to go home – quite apart from the fact that I know I'm too exhausted now to drive back again.

'Look, the cats are very friendly,' I add, as if that matters. They're quite cute cats, to be fair. One black with white paws, the other ginger with a rather wonky tail.

'It's not all about cats, Julia,' Lauren says firmly, beginning to dial a number on her phone. 'We shouldn't even have to put up with having cats here. Just supposing we'd brought a dog with us?'

'But we haven't.'

She's ignoring me. She's got through to someone now, and is launching into her complaint. I can hear the voice of the person on the other end of the call, trying to be placatory.

'But it's just not acceptable!' Lauren interrupts them crossly. 'No, I didn't read the caption under the picture that said it was of the Manor. No, I didn't see the part that explained the Lodge is in the Manor's grounds! Do *you* read every tiny little word of small print on every website you look at? Well, it's still not acceptable. There was no picture of this place, and the accommodation is . . . well, it's not up to the standard anyone could expect, to put it mildly. And there are *cats,* and the Wi-Fi might not work, and . . . yes! Yes, I *do* know it's in the middle of the countryside; yes, of course I'm aware that it's on Dartmoor –'

'Lauren,' I say quietly. 'Leave it. It's OK.'

'Look,' Lauren goes on regardless, turning away from me, 'this holiday is supposed to be a special birthday present. Yes! Well, thank you but that's hardly the point – it's a present from my . . .' Here she flounders for a moment and has to take a deep breath before going on. 'It was a special present. And on first impression, I'm afraid it's just not up to a suitable standard. I'm afraid I'm going to have to insist you to find us an alternative accommodation, or issue a refund.'

'Lauren –' I try to warn her, putting a hand on her arm, but she shakes me off.

'Well, yes, I know we're still at the end of the Christmas holiday season,' she continues. 'Right, well, obviously if there's nowhere else available –'

'I'm *not* driving back again today,' I interrupt her firmly.

'– then we'll have to stay here tonight, but we'll leave tomorrow and you'll have to give us a refund.' She pauses, listening to the response, frowning. 'What do you mean, refunded to the card of the person who –? You can't –? Well, that's ridiculous. It's a present! If someone bought me a jumper from a shop for a present, and it was coming apart at the seams, I'd take it back and get a refund, so surely you should –? Of course I realise a *cottage* is different from a jumper, but nevertheless it's falling apart! Oh, really, this is *just* not good enough. Put me through to your manager. Oh, you are the –? Well I'm going to make a formal complaint. What? The owner? No, of course we haven't met him – OK, *her*, whatever – we've only just arrived here. She lives in The Manor? Well, yes, absolutely we'll take it up with her, but you haven't heard the end of this, I promise you. Good *night*.'

'Lauren,' I say gently as she hangs up, 'we haven't even looked around the place yet.'

'No, and I don't particularly want to!' she snaps. 'I'm going to find the owner of this so-called cottage and tell her exactly what I think of it.'

'Oh, come on, let's not be melodramatic, let's at least leave it till the morning,' I say. 'I'm tired, we're both upset, we can put up with it for one night.'

The more I look around, now, the less I think the place is actually as bad as we first thought. OK, so from the outside it looks a little . . . neglected. But inside here, there's no sign of dust or decay, and there are some nice, homely touches. A huge brick fireplace with pictures of Dartmoor scenes on the chimney breast. A big solid oak table, with a jug of fresh flowers in the centre. Two comfy-looking sofas, piled with brightly-coloured patchwork cushions. A grandfather clock with a soothing gentle tick-tock, and heavy-looking curtains to pull across the latticed windows. Through the open doorway into the kitchen, I can see a range cooker, the type that pretends to be an ancient Aga but is, I'm sure, a modern electric replica. And a surprisingly large fridge freezer. I walk through into the kitchen – it's bigger than I first thought – to find another, smaller table, covered by a blue-and-white check cloth, on which there's a tray set with two mugs and a complementary packet of biscuits. Above the deep porcelain sink is a wooden shelf displaying an assortment of things: a big brown teapot, a couple of jugs, caddies for tea, sugar and coffee, washing-up liquid, some old photos, and some china cat ornaments. Several more mugs are hanging jauntily from hooks beneath the shelf, and a clean tea-towel and hand-towel are folded over a towel-rail under the sink. The navy-blue and white floor tiles look sparklingly clean, and in fact nothing I've seen so far *inside* the cottage could be accused of being of an unacceptable standard.

'I think someone keeps the interior of this place cleaned regularly,' I tell Lauren as I walk back into the living room. 'Seriously, it's much nicer than it looks from outside.'

I look at my sister more closely. She's sitting on one of the sofas now, and I can see she's been crying.

'Oh, come on, love.' I sit next to her and put an arm around her, thinking again how long it might have been since I've had this kind of physical contact with her. 'Don't be upset. Honestly, I really think this is going to be OK. I'm going to have a look upstairs.' I get up and head for the staircase. The cats have already run up ahead of me.

Lauren stays where she is, wiping her eyes and looking sorry for herself.

'Put the kettle on?' I suggest.

Perhaps she'll feel better if she has something to do.

The stairs are polished wood, with a little half-landing on the way up. More old pictures decorate the wall beside the stairs; I'll look at those later – I want to check out the bedrooms, and as I arrive upstairs, I can already catch a glimpse of the one at the front. I guess it's the bigger one, as it has a double bed and what appear to be fairly newly-fitted pine wardrobes. The bed's covered by a warm-looking forest-green duvet which matches the curtains. I go to look out of the window, but apart from some lights in the near-distance which I realise could be from the windows of the Manor, there's complete darkness.

The second bedroom, at the back of the house, is a good size too, but has twin beds, side by side – a cat now comfortably snuggled down on each. There's a small wardrobe, and a tier of shelves fitted into an alcove. Two of these have been left empty, presumably for the use of the holiday renters, but the others house a display of books, and a pile of board games.

'Oh, that's good,' I say to myself. 'They'll keep us occupied during the evenings.' I realise I already seem to be forgetting that we weren't going to stay here.

Between the two bedrooms there's a bathroom – smallish but well-fitted, with a decent-looking shower, washbasin and loo, bright white tiling on the walls and a blue and white blind at the window. I honestly don't think even Lauren will be able to find anything to criticise up here. I go back downstairs, gasping by now for that cup of tea, and I'm pleased to see Lauren has roused herself to go into the kitchen and make it.

'Let's open those biscuits,' I say. 'Or shall I get the fruit cake out of the bag?'

We've brought groceries with us for the first day or two, as we've got no idea how far we are from any shop, and the food bags are the only ones we've brought inside so far.

'OK,' Lauren says. She looks round at me and I can see she's trying to force a smile. 'I suppose we'd better try and make the best of it. For tonight, anyway. But there's no point unpacking our cases. We're leaving tomorrow, right?'

I don't bother to respond. She's made up her mind.

Sunday morning

Lauren

I must admit, I felt a bit better last night after we'd had a cup of tea and a piece of cake and I'd had a look around the place myself. I shooed the cats off the beds. Not that I dislike cats, but I didn't want their hair all over where we were going to be sleeping, even if it *was* only for one night. I told Julia she could have the double bedroom and I'd have the twin, but she insisted that it was, after all, *my* holiday and I should have the best room.

We'd only brought the bags of food in from the car, so we went back for our cases, but I only unpacked my night things and one change of clothes. I was still anticipating leaving after we'd spoken to the owner in the morning. To my surprise, everything in the kitchen was clean and tidy, and we cooked some sausages we'd bought when we stopped halfway down the motorway, and ate them like hot-dogs, in rolls, with salad and crisps on the side. A lazy meal but an easy one, and we both cleared our plates – it was the first time I'd really felt hungry since Carl left. Julia settled down with a book and I managed to get the TV working, not that there was anything remotely interesting to watch on the one station that seemed to be available. By ten o'clock we were both yawning and agreed to turn in for the night.

I shut the kitchen door so that the cats – if they decided to come in through the cat flap during the night – wouldn't be able to come upstairs. They seemed friendly enough cats, especially the black one, who sat on Julia's lap and purred while she was reading, but you have to draw the line somewhere. I mean, whose cats were they anyway and why would they be allowed here in the holiday let? It seemed ridiculous.

When I wake up this morning it's already light. I put on my dressing gown and pull back the curtains. It's a better day; overcast but not raining, at least. My room overlooks what I presume is part of the grounds of the Manor, because the house itself is clearly visible in the distance, with the tall chimneys I saw in the website image. The grounds between the two properties look completely unkempt, the grass uncut, broken branches hanging from trees, the trunks of them swathed in creepers. Obviously there's no gardener, or groundsman, and the owner doesn't seem to care.

I go downstairs, to find Julia already up, dressed, and boiling the kettle for tea.

'Morning!' she says chirpily. 'The rain's stopped, and it doesn't feel quite so cold out today.'

'You've been out already?' I squawk in surprise, looking at the clock on the wall. Nine-fifteen. 'What for?'

'Oh, just to have a look around. The grounds are beautiful, Lauren. And the Manor looks such a lovely old house. A bit neglected-looking – like this Lodge – but probably full of history.'

'I just looked out of the window,' I say, taking the mug of tea she passes me, 'but the grounds look completely overgrown, to me.'

'But that's what *is* so beautiful,' she insists earnestly. 'We're in the middle of the countryside, here. I'm just blown away by how lovely nature can be when it's left alone to do its own thing. Far more lovely than a neatly manicured lawn and flowerbeds in a city park, don't you think?'

'Huh. I think it could all do with being cut back a bit.'

'Well, I'd love to see a place like this in the spring, when there are bluebells and wild daffodils growing around the trees. Or in the summer – I bet there are loads of wildflowers then – and maybe berries, and nuts, and mushrooms in the autumn.'

She sounds a bit hyper about it all. Almost unhinged, in my opinion, considering our situation – stuck here in the middle of, frankly, a jungle, in a tumbledown little shack, however nice it might be inside. Going on like this about the wonders of nature – as if anyone would come on a winter break hoping to find anything other than a lovely five-star hotel with thick, fitted carpets, log fires burning and a fabulous restaurant and bar! And a loving boyfriend to share it all with . . . but if I think about that too much, I know I'll just start crying again.

We've brought some packets of quick porridge with us – just right for a winter day stuck in the middle of nowhere – so we breakfast on this, followed by some hot toast with honey. I must admit I'm feeling a little bit better now I've had a good night's sleep and a good breakfast. But far from being fired up with enthusiasm about nature like my sister suddenly seems to be, I'm now working myself up to the confrontation I'm determined to have with the owner of this property.

After breakfast we set off to traipse across the grounds to the Manor. Julia's marching ahead through the tangle of roots and twisted mass of bracken, bindweed and ivy, swinging a stick, like a country girl out for a hike. I have to keep calling out to her to wait for me and be careful; there are holes, muddy patches and fallen branches everywhere. Either of us could trip and break a leg at any moment, and God only knows where the nearest hospital might be.

'What a mess,' I say crossly, picking my way carefully through the overgrown gorse bushes. 'This place is in sore need of a gardener. The grass hasn't been cut in a generation, by the look of it. These ferny-things in the undergrowth are completely out of control. They're weeds, and they need culling.'

'Weeds are only plants that didn't need a human to put them there,' Julia says cheerfully.

Nice to know she's so happy, I suppose, but she's beginning to seriously get on my nerves. I just want to make our complaint and get this over with.

We both fall silent as we approach the massive front door of the Manor. The place looks just as decaying and neglected from the outside as the Lodge does – worse, if anything. It could easily feature as a haunted house in a ghost story or thriller. I reach up and pull the old-fashioned doorbell chain, and we wait, glancing at each other, wondering if anything's going to happen – so that when the door finally creaks open, we both jump.

'Yes?' says the elderly woman standing in the doorway – and I recognise her voice straight away as being the one that answered the intercom yesterday.

Actually, to call her *elderly* is just being polite. She's old – as old as the hills. Bent, haggard-looking, dressed in a black dress and a threadbare black cardigan, her thin grey hair piled on top of her head and fastened with what honestly looks like a bone. Her hands are like claws, her feet encased in grubby brown slippers that look as if the soles are hanging off them, her stick-thin legs wrapped in wrinkled grey socks.

'Um – excuse me,' I begin. 'But are you the owner of the Lodge?'

'Yes,' the woman says. 'And who are you?'

'We're your *guests*,' I tell her, a little impatiently. 'At the Lodge. Your *paying* guests.'

The fact that it was in fact Carl who paid for the accommodation is neither here nor there.

'Yes?' says the woman. 'And what do you want?'

I'm getting riled by her tone now.

'Well,' I begin – but then I stop, feeling suddenly confused. What exactly *do* we want? I was planning, of course, to make a complaint, to demand some sort of recompense for the state of the accommodation, possibly to cancel the booking. But now I realise I'm not really even sure about that. Last night, despite feeling irritated by the situation, we cooked in a well-stocked kitchen, relaxed in a pleasant, airy living room, and slept in warm, comfortable beds. We had good hot showers, with clean towels, and enjoyed our breakfast while the cats waited politely under the table without bothering us. To be perfectly honest, I know Julia's right: we'll be unlikely to find alternative accommodation at such short notice. And I suddenly realise the last thing I feel like doing is going straight back home. But there's a little spark of irritation in me that's still making me feel the need to complain.

'Well, we just wanted to say –' Julia begins, trying to help me out, 'the outsides of the windows –'

'Yes, they are completely unacceptable,' I finish, grateful to have been reminded of something that's actually unsatisfactory. 'Absolutely filthy, with ivy growing all over them.'

'I'll get Nathan to chop it back and clean them,' the woman says calmly.

'And the grounds –' I go on, glad I've remembered to mention this too, but the woman interrupts me.

'You're welcome to walk around them.' She waves a bony hand in the direction of the wooded area we've just ploughed through, and her face suddenly breaks into a crooked smile. 'You just enjoy yourselves, my lovelies, that's what you need, I expect, when you're stressed out from life in that damned city.'

'Oh, well, thank you, I'm sure we will,' Julia says, sounding a little uncertain and glancing at me, as if for approval.

'And you can use the pool, of course,' the woman goes on. 'It comes with the booking, see? Use of the pool. I told them, at the agency, to put that in the words. On the computer-thing. You'll like that, my lovelies, won't you?'

'Um, the *pool*?' I say in surprise. The agency certainly didn't mention this in *the words* – or if they did, I missed it during my quick glance.

'Course you can! It's heated, see? Nathan sees to it.' She opens the door a little wider. 'Come in and I'll show you.'

'Oh, well,' Julia says, sounding a bit alarmed now. 'I don't think . . . I mean, we haven't even got any swimming things with us. It's fine, we'll just –'

'Come in for a minute anyway.' She gives a little cackle of laughter. 'It's all right, I don't bite. Come in while I get the key.'

'Key?' I'm beginning to wonder if she's not quite the full ticket. 'We've already got the key, it was in the door –'

'Not the key to the Lodge!' She laughs again. 'The key to the pool.'

Julia and I look at each other. Key to the pool? Do pools have keys, and anyway, haven't we just told her we won't be using it?

'Come on, in you come!' she insists, as we're both just standing here, gabbling something about not troubling her. 'Never mind if you don't want to swim, I'll get the key and show you anyway.'

She turns away, leaving the door wide open, and shuffles off from us down the passage.

'Well, we can't just walk off now –' Julia whispers. 'Better humour her.'

We follow the woman along the passage and into a huge kitchen. It's as old-fashioned as she herself is: flagstones on the floor, big cream-coloured tiles on the walls, many of them cracked, and adorned with swirly patterns depicting jugs and teapots.

'Come on, come on,' she repeats, leading the way surprisingly quickly to a rickety-looking back door that leads out to . . . an astonishingly large conservatory.

'Oh!' I find myself exclaiming out loud.

'Yes, this is a surprise,' Julia says.

And we both stand, open-mouthed, staring around us, as the old woman cackles with laughter beside us.

'Didn't expect this, did you! It was Nathan, see? Nathan had it built – to house the pool. When he moved back in with me, see, when that ridiculous marriage went to pot.'

Of course, we have no idea who she's talking about, but I guess the mysterious Nathan must be her son.

'The pool was here already,' she goes on. 'But it wasn't covered, it was open to the elements, all green and slimy, more of a pond than a pool really.' She chuckles again. 'But Nathan wanted to swim, he likes to keep fit, so he had it all cleaned up and properly lined, and had this conservatory built over it. Nice and warm in here, isn't it, my lovelies!'

'Yes,' I have to agree. 'It is.'

It *is* really nice, too. There are modern heaters on the walls, and along one edge of the pool are two little cane tables with six matching chairs. There's a rack with towels on it, and hooks presumably for coats or discarded clothes. And all around the room there are huge pot plants, obviously thriving in the warm, damp atmosphere, climbing up canes towards the glass roof, making the whole place resemble a little watering hole in a jungle.

'Here you are,' our hostess says, handing me a large brass key. 'It's for the outside door over the other side – see? You can get in that way – saves you coming through the house. Not that I mind,' she adds with a grin. I'm finding her grin quite infectious now. It completely belies her original stern impression. In fact, the more she talks, the more I begin to wonder about my first impression of her age. She might be dressed like someone of about ninety, and she has the croaky, ancient voice of a long-term smoker, but I'm now thinking she might be a little younger than she looks.

'Thank you,' I say. 'But as I said, we won't be swimming, we haven't got –'

'Costumes? You can swim in your undies, can't you?' she says. 'Nathan won't look.'

I have no intention of letting Nathan, whoever he might be, see me in here in my bra and pants, whatever she thinks!

'Well, I suppose we might just come and sit in here for a spot of relaxation, mightn't we, Lauren?' Julia suggests. 'It's so light and warm in here – we could bring a book or a magazine over and just enjoy it for a while?'

'Course you can, my lovely,' the woman says. 'Give a knock on the back door here, when you do, and I'll bring you out a nice hot drink each. How does that sound?'

'Oh! Well, no need for that, obviously –' I begin, but she waves my protest aside.

'I'm on my own here, see? While Nathan's at work. Nice to have people here. I wasn't sure how it was going to turn out, if you want to know the truth, when Nathan suggested it – letting the Lodge out for holiday rentals. He did it all up, ready, but I said to him: *I don't know, Nathan. I don't know about people coming here, strangers, they might not be nice people.* But I'm glad he talked me into it now. You two young ladies seem very nice.'

'Are we the first ones, then?' I ask in surprise. 'Your first guests?'

'You are, yes.' She smiles. 'Sorry if I seemed a bit unfriendly when you knocked. I was nervous. Worried you were coming to complain about something.'

'Oh, no, not at all!' Julia says quickly, avoiding my eyes. 'Well, only the . . . er, windows.'

'Yes, I'm sorry about that. We had a terrible storm the other night, see? That's probably what's happened – the wind and the rain will have brought down all the ivy, and the muck out of the trees. I hope there isn't any damage to the roof or anything. I'll send Nathan out to check it when he gets home. He's out looking around a potential job.'

'Well, thank you.' I still don't like to ask who he is, or what job he might be *looking around.* 'And yes, it'd be nice to come over here sometimes and sit for a while.'

What am I saying? I glance at Julia. Have I now actually decided we're going to stay here, despite everything I said? Well, if we are here for the week, we'd definitely better get some more food in.

'How far is it to the nearest shops, Mrs . . . um . . .?' I ask the woman.

'Oh, I'm Mrs Lennon. But you can call me Betty.' She cackles again. 'My name's Beatrice, but I started calling myself Betty many years ago, to stop my friends calling me Beatle.'

'Beetle?' I repeat, puzzled.

'*Beatle* with an *A*,' she says. 'With a name like Lennon, back in the Sixties, what else could I expect? Not that I minded, at the time. I was a fan, like everyone else. I actually saw the Beatles performing live, once, when I was young.' She pauses, looks down, and adds more quietly, 'That was an exciting day.'

'You'll have to tell us all about it,' Julia says. Seems like Mrs Lennon – Betty – has decided she'll be our new best friend for the week. Well, I suppose it might liven things up a bit. 'I'm Julia, by the way, and this is my sister Lauren.'

'Um – the shops?' I remind her, as that subject seemed to have been overlooked in favour of the legend of Betty and the Beatles.

'Oh yes; the village – Deepcombe – is just a mile or so further down the lane. Pass the church, keep going, you'll come to the shop next to the pub, opposite the village hall.'

'Thank you. Just the one shop, is it?' Julia asks.

'Of course. They sell everything,' she says with a shrug. 'But they're only open from ten till twelve on a Sunday.'

'Thanks,' I nod and turn towards the outside door. 'We'll let ourselves out of that other door, then, if that's OK. To save walking through your house, Mrs . . . um, Betty.'

Then I stop, suddenly remembering something else I'd intended to ask about.

'Oh – by the way – the cats?'

'I hope you don't mind them. They come and go, see? They're no trouble. They get fed over here, mind, so don't let them talk you into giving them anything. Greedy little beasts, cats are.'

'But whose are they? Are they yours?'

'Yes, of course. My babies. But cats don't have much loyalty – it's Nathan they love best. So he put the cat flap in, when he was living in the Lodge. He thinks we should block up the cat flap now, although they'd still probably be running in there as soon as you opened the door. But if you don't like cats, then of course –'. She suddenly stops and puts a bony hand to her mouth, eyes wide. Oh, you're not allergic, are you? Nothing like that?'

'No, no, we're not allergic,' Julia says. 'And they do seem lovely cats – and well-behaved too.'

'I'm not having them on the bed, though,' I put in quickly. I feel the need to reassert myself, somehow – as if I'm in danger of losing some kind of battle. With myself, if nobody else.

'No, fair enough.' Betty nods enthusiastically. 'Throw them off, they won't be offended. See you soon, then, my lovelies, I hope.'

Julia and I don't talk much on our way back to the Lodge. I think we're both just too bemused by the way things have turned out. We went over there – well, at least, *I* certainly did – to complain, demand recompense and tell her we were leaving. And instead, the visit somehow turned into an invitation to hot chocolate and a cosy chat by the pool!

Betty

I feel strangely excited after my little chat with the two young ladies – my first guests in The Lodge. I was very wary when they knocked on the door. Nearly didn't open it, to tell the truth. I'd looked through the window, you see, and when I saw them standing there, I didn't know who they were. The agency told me it was a young couple who were going to be coming, and – stupidly, I know, in this day and age when we should all know better, and none more so than me – I assumed a couple to mean a man and a woman. So I didn't know if these two girls were troublemakers of some sort, selling something, or trying to talk me into taking out life insurance or something equally daft – at my age! I'm not so old and stupid that I haven't heard stories and warnings about strangers doing this, knocking on doors, trying to trick old people out of our money. As a rule, you see, I don't get people knocking on my front door. People who know me, people from the village, always come round the back of the house, past the greenhouses, and knock on the back door.

So when they told me who they were, my first thought was that they were going to complain about something. They *looked* like they were going to complain. Not that I could imagine what they could find to complain about; after all, Nathan's done the place up lovely, all nicely painted, all good furniture, comfy beds, thick carpets. Nothing missing, I went through it all with him, made sure there was clean bedding, clean towels, fresh flowers on the table, tea and coffee and so on in the kitchen. When he took me in to show me after it was all ready, I said I felt like moving in there myself!

Anyway, it's just the windows – dirty after the storm. Nothing that Nathan won't be able to sort out in the blink of an eye. And they're not a couple at all, they're sisters. One tall and blonde, in an expensive-looking coat, her hair very neat, wearing make-up even though she's on holiday in the middle of the countryside, the other one shorter, pretty but tired-looking, her face a bit puffy as if she's been crying for days on end. Both of them so pale you'd think they've never been outside their homes or offices before in their lives. Sore in need of some rest, pampering and good Devon fresh air, I can see that already.

Well, they've come to the right place. I can feel myself smiling with satisfaction as I walk back into my kitchen. I'm glad, after all, that I agreed to Nathan's plan. I've never liked to admit to being lonely. I *shouldn't* feel lonely. I might not be able to get out and about now, but people do call on me, people from the village who come here to do business and then sit and chat to me, mostly about themselves and their problems, to tell the truth – but at least it means I keep up to date with what goes on beyond my four ancient, crumbling, walls. And I've got Nathan living here now, dear Nathan with his youthful energy and strength, so good to have around, although God knows I wouldn't have wanted him to go through that dreadful marriage break-up, such a lot of upset, poor lad. But he's so keen, now he's here, to take care of me and help me survive. He can't be with me all the time, of course, and I wouldn't expect him to be; he has to work. So yes, although I don't like admitting it, and even with the benefit of my cats to keep me company, I do sometimes feel lonely.

I know, of course, that these two young sisters aren't here for my benefit. They're on holiday; they'll want to go out, drive across Dartmoor, see all the places in the tourist guide books. They won't want, in the slightest, to be bothered with an old woman like me – why would they? But I've given them an option, if they have a rainy day, if they want a quiet afternoon. If they decide to take me up on it, I won't get in their way, or cramp their style. But just having them here, knowing they're staying over there in the Lodge, is already, in a strange way, making me feel less lonely. I've always been interested in people, their relationships, what makes them tick. And already I'm feeling that there's a lot of unhappiness going on between those two girls. I won't be asking any questions, of course, even if they do come over for a chat, but I'll be trying to work them out, the way I always do, just by watching, and listening.

If nothing else, I hope Deepcombe is going to help them somehow. That would, in a funny kind of way, help me to feel better too; because I've loved the place my whole life, and I don't want it to feel like a place of sadness now forever.

Julia

I'm amazed how quickly Lauren's mood changed while we were talking to Mrs Lennon, and looking at the pool room. I don't quite know what to say to her now, as we walk back through the tangle of branches and bracken, avoiding the slippery areas of red mud underfoot. She'd been so determined to make a complaint about the accommodation and possibly even to go home, and yet within a few minutes in *Betty's* company, she brightened up and seemed to change her tune completely. She didn't even try to disagree when I suggested it might be nice to go and sit in the pool room sometimes. She'd obviously backed down and decided to stay. I'm very relieved, to be honest – I really couldn't have faced the thought of just getting back in the car and driving home again, with Lauren even more depressed than on the way down here. So I don't even mention her change of heart as we walk back, and she's so quiet too, that I reckon she might be surprised at herself. She doesn't say anything until we're back at the Lodge and I've put the kettle on to make coffee.

'Well,' she says, plonking herself down on one of the kitchen chairs, 'It looks like we're staying put, then.'

'Are you sure you're happy to stay?'

She sighs. 'Yes, I suppose so. I think I lost the will for the fight once I saw her – the old woman. And to be fair, in the cold light of day I suppose there isn't much wrong with this place apart from grubby windows and a couple of loose roof tiles.'

'All of which Nathan – whoever he might be – is apparently being sent to fix,' I remind her.

'Yes. Her son, I suppose.' She sighs again and goes on in a shaky voice, like she's on the verge of tears, 'Anyway, I'm just so tired, Julia. So tired and so fed up with everything going wrong in my life, fed up with crying, fed up with feeling depressed, even fed up with complaining.'

'So let's just give in and have a relaxing week here,' I say, putting two mugs of coffee down on the table and sitting down opposite her. 'I actually think this place might turn out to be exactly what you need, you know: somewhere quiet, with nothing much to do except rest and recharge your batteries.'

'Yes, you're probably right,' she says in a little voice.

'OK. So when we've had this, we can go and find the village shop, stock up for a few days, and then just chill out.'

'Sounds good,' she agrees. She looks up at me, a little sheepishly. 'Thanks.'

'For the coffee?'

'For all of this. Coming here with me. Driving us. Putting up with . . . my bad mood. It's – well, I didn't expect it. It's not as if we –'

'It's all right,' I say quickly, cutting her off before she starts talking about how little we normally see each other, talk to each other, care about each other. I don't want to hear it, don't want to have to admit to any of it. Not while we're here, thrown together by my own sudden and unexpected inability to bear listening to her crying on the phone about Carl and his pathetic offering of a holiday. Talking about our normal state of estrangement is hardly going to help either of us. Better to skirt around it for now. Or probably forever. 'Let's just have this week together, OK? And get you back to . . . well, feeling better, hopefully.'

'Yes. Sorry, yes. I'll try not to be such a misery.' Her eyes fill up with tears even as she's saying it. 'It's just that I *loved* Carl, Julia! I loved him so much, and he ended up treating me like shit.'

'Come on, don't cry.' I manage somehow to keep the impatience out of my voice. I wouldn't mind if this was the first time it's happened, but I heard Lauren saying exactly the same thing a year or so ago about Tom. And before him, about Ian. And before *him* – well, you get the picture. She's a serial victim of the world's love-rats. I find it hard to understand how anyone can continue to let this happen to her so many times, and still not start to question whether she might have contributed to the problem in any way. I'm not saying she *has* contributed to it, that it's her fault – it wouldn't be fair for me to say that, as I don't know enough about her these days to judge. But surely, if things like this keep happening to you, you need to at least ask yourself some questions, don't you?

'Sorry,' she says again, sniffing and trying to smile. 'OK, I won't cry anymore. He doesn't deserve my tears, does he?'

'No, you're right, he doesn't.' I smile, and leave it at that.

Although this whole thing isn't about me, I can't help reflecting that a week here at Deepcombe Lodge might turn out to be what I need too. I've been working flat out, and worrying more than I want to admit about things I'm not sharing with Lauren – in view of her broken heart – and I suppose I'm beginning to realise I'm probably in need of a spot of rest and relaxation myself.

We go out to the car and I put *Deepcombe* into the Sat Nav even though Betty's told us the village is just a mile or so down the lane. And as it turns out, I'm glad I did, as we've only gone a few yards beyond the Lodge gate when we come to a fork in the road, with no signpost, so I could well have headed in the wrong direction. As it is, we're soon passing the church and then, there's the pub, The Duck and Partridge, a small thatched building with its sign swinging in the breeze and wooden benches outside. I slow down, not that I'd felt inclined to drive at anything much above twenty miles per hour down the narrow little lane anyway, and sure enough, the shop – Deepcombe Community Store – is right next-door.

'It used to be a post-office and proper full-time shop,' the woman at the till tells us, leaning on the counter and chatting to us at full volume as we make our way around the shelves. 'But when the Pritchards retired – they ran it for more than forty years – it was going to be closed down. So we stepped in and saved it.'

'You did?' Lauren asks.

'All of us did – the villagers. We bought the shop between us and we run it on a rota basis. We open seven days a week but only for a few hours each day

– that's plenty of time for local people to get their shopping in, and it serves as a meeting place too. Some of the volunteers even do deliveries to housebound people.'

'What a great idea.' I give her a smile as I put our shopping on the counter for her to ring up.

'It's kept the village alive, that's the thing,' she says proudly. 'We've seen other villages lose their shops and . . . well, the shop is the heart of a village. Without it, the village dies.'

'That's very moving,' Lauren says.

'You're not from round here, obviously,' the woman observes. 'Visitors, are you? From up-country?'

'Yes, we're on holiday,' I say.

'Welcome to Deepcombe, then. I'm Janice. Anything you need while you're here, I can get it ordered in if we haven't got it in stock.'

'Thank you, Janice, that's nice to know –'

'And where might you be staying?' she goes on, fixing us with a curious stare.

'At Deepcombe Lodge,' Lauren says. 'Just up the lane –'

'Oh, Betty's finally done it then, has she?' Janice nods to herself and smiles with what looks like satisfaction.

'Done what?'

'Started renting the Lodge out. Nathan's talked her into it, then. She was worried about it. But Nathan's done it all up – took him a while, of course. It was in a right old state, I can tell you that.'

'Well, it's very nice now,' I say quickly, feeling a sudden surge of loyalty towards Betty.

'She probably needs the income. Living up there in that great old place, keeping it going, just with the veg and stuff –'

'Veg?' I query, but she doesn't even pause for breath.

'She must be mad, if you ask me. She'd be better off moving into a nice little what-d'you-call-it, bungalow, somewhere. Crazy.' She shakes her head. 'I sometimes wonder why they call her the Wise Woman of Deepcombe, I really do.'

'Do they?' Lauren asks, sounding as astonished by this as I am.

'Oh yes. I don't know how it started.' Janice begins to take items out of our basket and ring them up on the till. 'She did used to be a teacher, fair enough, but people round here act like she's some kind of what-d'you-call-it, *guru.*'

'Guru? Really?' I chuckle.

'Yes. People say they feel better, they know what to do about things, after they've been to see Betty.' She sniffs. 'Huh! Some people around here are so gullible.'

'Well, if it helps them to talk to her, I suppose . . .' I say with a shrug.

'Huh,' she says again, ringing up our total with a flourish. 'A fool and his money are easily parted, that's all I'm saying on the subject.'

'They *pay* her for her um – wisdom?' Lauren exclaims. I give her a warning look. I'd already decided not to pay any attention to this woman's gossip.

And as it happens, Janice has now pursed her lips as if to say she's decided, rather belatedly, to keep her opinions to herself. But then, just as I'm handing her my card for the payment, she goes on in a rush, like she can't help herself:

'They pay her for what they *buy* from her. The so-called wisdom is what you might call an added extra. Along with the hot chocolate she doles out for nothing. Makes me wonder what the hell she puts in the chocolate, that's all I can say. But I'm saying nothing,' she adds, to contradict herself. 'It's nothing to do with me.'

'Right,' Lauren says faintly.

'Well, thank you very much,' I say as we're leaving. To be honest, I can't wait to get out of there now. Janice's veiled criticisms and hints at – what? I hardly like to guess! – are a bit disconcerting to say the least.

'You're welcome. Enjoy your holiday,' she says with a strange little laugh.

'What do you make of all that?' Lauren is asking me as I turn the car round to set off back down the lane.

'I think she's a gossip and we shouldn't take any notice.'

'But what is it that people are paying Betty for? – never mind getting free *wisdom*!'

'And never mind what she's hinting might be going into her hot chocolate!' I add.

'I'm not sure we ought to sample it!' Lauren agrees, laughing.

At least the nonsense the silly woman was spouting has made Lauren laugh. For that, I almost feel like running back into the shop and thanking her!

Janice hasn't put us off enough to stop us discussing, after lunch, whether to take ourselves over to the *Wise Woman's* pool room for the rest of the afternoon. But before we've made a decision, both cats – who've been snoozing on the kitchen chairs, noses tucked under their tails – suddenly sit up, ears alert, staring towards the front of the cottage. The black one jumps down and runs towards the front window, followed by the ginger one, and by the time I've come after them, they're both on the windowsill, meowing in unison. There's a ladder propped against the front wall, and from where I'm standing, I can see two large feet in heavy work boots on a rung near the top of the ladder, and above them, a pair of jeans-clad legs. Beyond that, I can only assume –

'It must be Nathan,' Lauren says from behind me. 'Betty's son or whoever he is. She said he'd come over and check the roof, didn't she.'

I open the front door and we both step outside, shivering in the cold, and look up at the guy at the top of the ladder. Even at this angle it's plain to see he's too young to be Betty's son, unless she gave birth to him at an exceptionally mature age. And he's . . . not to put too fine a point on it. . . heart-stoppingly beautiful. His hair is dark, thick-looking, wavy and long enough to frame his face; and – as I can't help noticing now that he's glancing down and has caught sight of us watching him – he has a smile to take your breath away. Not that I'm interested in beautiful men with breath-taking smiles, of any age and certainly not of the kind of age that would make me feel like his granny.

'Hi!' he calls down. 'Sorry, I didn't want to disturb you by knocking. I'm Nathan. My gran sent me to check whether the storm's dislodged any tiles.'

Ah. His gran. That certainly makes sense. I'd guess he's not much more than twenty.

'Well, thank you for coming so quickly,' I call back. 'We'll let you get on. I don't want you falling off the ladder!'

He laughs. 'I'm all right, I'm used to it. I'm a builder and handyman. I did this place up for Gran when she finally agreed to use it as a holiday let. The roof was pretty sound when I'd finished all the work, but the storm we had the night before you arrived has shifted a couple of tiles so I'm just sorting that out now. I'll come back tomorrow afternoon to cut the ivy back a bit and clean the windows, if you don't mind. It's looking like it's about to rain again any moment now, so –'

'Oh, please don't worry about that, Nathan,' Lauren says. 'If it's going to be bad weather this week anyway, it'll hardly matter if the windows aren't sparkling clean.'

He laughs again. 'There's always bad weather threatened on Dartmoor, unfortunately. Not that we don't get lovely sunny days – we do – but you can't trust the sky up here. It can change in seconds. That's what catches so many hikers out, up on the open moor.' He lets go of the ladder with one hand as he says this, gesturing widely over the back of the cottage towards the distant countryside. 'Have you ladies ever visited this part of the country before?'

'No,' we both say together.

'But we're looking forward to exploring Dartmoor,' Lauren says.

I swallow back a retort of '*Oh, are we?*'. This is the first I've heard of it! So far, her few remarks about this area we've found ourselves staying in, have been along the lines of *back of beyond, boring* and *where are all the shops*?

'Well, there's plenty to see, and it's a good time of year for it,' Nathan says. 'Much better without all the summer visitors clogging the roads up. You can climb some of the tors and see for miles around if you manage to get a clear day. Let me know if you want any advice about where best to go.'

'Thank you,' Lauren says. I can't help thinking she's sounding a lot more cheerful and positive while there's a good-looking young man to talk to.

'But we'd better let you get on now,' I repeat, more firmly. 'Especially if it's going to rain.'

'OK.' He treats us to another of those lovely smiles. 'Have a nice afternoon, ladies.'

'I think maybe I'll just stay here for the rest of the day after all,' Lauren says casually after we've gone back inside. She plonks herself down on the sofa where she's got a direct view of Nathan's legs.

'Lauren, he's just a *child*,' I say warningly, my irritation levels soaring. 'And anyway, you've only just –'

'Did I say anything?' she retorts. 'I'm not interested. I've just had my heart broken, Julia, in case you'd forgotten.'

'*I* hadn't forgotten.'

'I'll never get over the way Carl's treated me. Never.'

'OK.' I sigh. 'All I'm saying is, Nathan looks about the same age as Simon. My son, your nephew. He's a boy. I mean, sure, a very . . . nice-looking boy, but –'

'It sounds like you're the one who's interested,' Lauren interrupts me drily. 'I'm *not*. I'm just watching him. It's something to do. Can we drop it now?'

I go back to the kitchen, shaking my head. The trouble is, I've known this to happen before. All right, not with someone the same age as my son – that's a first. But how many times have I known Lauren to have her heart broken, only to fall in love with someone else within weeks, if not days? It's what she does. I should be used to it. But actually, all I feel right now is a kind of exasperated weariness. I felt really sorry for her about bloody Carl, but already – however much she's denying it – she seems to be ready to eye up a handsome young lad. Well, at least it might cheer her up, I suppose!

Monday

Lauren

I was so annoyed by Julia's attitude, yesterday, the way she virtually accused me of flirting with Betty's grandson, when nothing was further from my mind. As if I don't realise how young Nathan is! I happen to *like* men; I like looking at them and talking to them. It's only natural, isn't it? I'm not like her, married to her job and probably forgotten what it's like to find men attractive. She probably hasn't even had sex since she and Phil got divorced. Just because I looked at Nathan, doesn't mean I'm going to run off with him or anything. And she admitted herself that he was good-looking!

We watched something excruciatingly boring on TV during the evening. I fell asleep halfway through, and when I woke up, Julia had turned it off and was reading her book. We ended up having another early night, barely speaking to each other.

This morning I decided that at least one of us needs to be the grown-up around here and move on. I mean, just because we hardly ever see each other these days (which frankly is her fault more than mine, she's always so obsessed with her career) doesn't mean we have to behave like we used to when we were children – always either bickering or refusing to speak to each other. And it's a shame to be like this, when we seemed to be rubbing along OK so far this week.

'I *was* hoping we might be able to go for a walk or something today,' I say brightly while we're getting breakfast ready. 'But not in this weather.'

As Nathan warned us, it started raining soon after he finished the roof tiles yesterday, and carried on all night and into the morning. Everything looks dark, sodden and bleak outside now.

'No,' she agrees. She sounds like she's relieved that I've broken the silence between us. 'Not exactly the weather for going out and exploring, is it.'

I sit down at the little table and start buttering some toast. 'Well, how about we go over to Betty's pool room this morning?' I suggest. 'Perhaps the rain might stop by lunchtime, then we can –'

'OK,' she says. She sounds a bit strained, like she's got a headache or didn't sleep much. 'But you go on ahead. I'll join you in a bit. I . . . need to make a couple of phone calls. I'd better do it while I've got a half-decent signal on my phone, in case it disappears completely if the weather gets any worse.'

'Work, I suppose?' I say with a sniff. Typical! Can't she ever leave it alone? 'You're on holiday, Julia. Can't they manage without you for just one week?'

'Of course they can,' she retorts. 'But something urgent has come up. I won't be long. Go on – just be careful of the hot chocolate!' she adds, obviously trying to make a joke of it.

So I go over there on my own. If she wants to make a martyr of herself for the business her *ex-husband* still runs, the business he so kindly made her a partner in when they got married, despite the fact she'd had no special skills or qualifications to offer at the time – well, that's up to her, I suppose.

'Julia *says* she'll come over later,' I explain to Betty when we're sitting together in the warmth of her pool room. I've insisted she should join me, since she's been kind enough to make me a drink. I've decided to sample a mug of her famous chocolate; I take a cautious sip of it now. It's lovely, and doesn't taste of anything weird. 'She's literally obsessed with her work. I can't understand how she can still work for her ex. I mean, if you hate each other enough to get divorced, how could you still run a business together?'

I know I shouldn't talk like this about my sister to a virtual stranger. It's disloyal, especially after Julia's been pretty good to me really, bringing me down to Devon like this, at the drop of a hat in the middle of winter. But I'm feeling grumpy. She acted all superior to me yesterday just because I cast the tiniest glance at Nathan, and yet I've forgiven her and tried to be nice this morning. But here she is, putting her work before me again, as always.

'Sorry,' I admit when Betty doesn't respond. 'I shouldn't be landing all that on you, but when you asked me why she's not with me this morning . . . well, it just kind of burst out of me. It was pretty rude.'

'Not to worry, my lovely, you needed to get it off your chest, and I'm the soul of discretion,' she says calmly. 'I'm a good listener, see.'

'Oh yes, of course,' I find myself saying before I can stop myself. 'The woman in the village shop said everyone comes to talk to you about their problems. She called you the *Wise Woman*.'

What the hell's wrong with me? It's like my mouth has suddenly got a mind of its own, opening up without my permission and spouting the most indiscreet stuff possible. Luckily, though, Betty's laughing: that rasping cackle that makes her sound like a forty-a-day smoker.

'Ha! I know all about that. *Wise Woman* indeed! I'm not wise at all, my lovely, I've just lived a hell of a lot longer than most people. Eighty last birthday, I was. But I don't give out advice. I just listen, that's all. I like listening to people.'

Eighty. She might look even older, but the more I see of her, the more I'm realising that her mind is probably as sharp as that of a much younger person. Her pale blue eyes are lined with wrinkles, but they're lit with humour and – despite our first encounter with her on her front doorstep – kindness.

'So: Nathan's been over and fixed the roof tiles, then,' she says. 'He's coming back to do the windows later if it's not raining, all right?'

'Yes – thank you.' And then, after a pause, during which I can't help swirling my mug around and staring into the drink, looking for something – what? – that she might have added, I go on: 'So Nathan's your grandson, then?'

'He is. Didn't I say? Nice boy, despite what happened. Helps me out a lot around here. Doing the place up a bit – although that's a job for an army, to be honest. He gets his dinners cooked for him in return, of course!'

I don't like to ask what *despite what happened* might mean, although I'm guessing she's referring to the marriage break-up she mentioned before. And after a brief pause, she continues more quietly, turning to look at me with some sympathy in her eyes: 'Maybe this little holiday might do your sister some good, if she's a bit of a workaholic.'

I sigh. 'Yes, maybe. Perhaps this was what we both needed.'

I take a couple more mouthfuls of my drink and lean back in my chair. It's stopped raining now, and the sky's beginning to lighten slightly, a few rays of weak winter sunshine finding their way through the clouds. It's warm in here, and the hot drink has soothed my irritation slightly. I've been feeling so annoyed with Julia that I've almost forgotten to feel sad about Carl, but now, suddenly, the cloud of loss and despair that's engulfed me since he left, sweeps over me again like a treacherous fog, filling my eyes with tears so that I have to turn my face away, blinking and swallowing desperately.

After a moment, I feel the touch of a hard, bony hand on mine. When I turn round, Betty's looking at me with such gentle compassion that I can't help letting out a strangled sob.

'Cry, my lovely, if you need to,' she says gently. 'I'm sure you can sort things out, with your sister. If you both want to.'

'It's not about her,' I mutter.

'Oh, I see.' She doesn't go on, ask the inevitable question, but for some reason I feel obliged to explain.

'A break-up. Probably my own fault, as usual. At least, I'm sure that's what Julia thinks.'

She doesn't even respond to this, and when I look back at her she's just nodding to herself thoughtfully. I feel bad then, and go on quickly:

'But of course, it's been good of her, coming here with me, doing all the driving. It's been a surprise, to be honest, considering we . . . haven't been close. But I know what she thinks of me. She makes it obvious.'

'Well, you know, I find it's always worth looking for the good in people.'

Really? I close my eyes, suddenly irritated again. This is ridiculous. I didn't come here to listen to platitudes about finding good in people! I don't even know this woman, and anyway, didn't she just say she doesn't try to give advice? What am I even doing here, sitting in her conservatory, drinking her hot chocolate, talking to her about Julia like this? It's not right. We might not be close, but Julia's my sister, and Betty's a complete stranger. I seem to have got lulled into sharing these confidences with her by her quiet West Country accent, her lack of fuss, and her apparent sympathy, but at the end of the day, she's probably just a nosy old bat who likes knowing about other people's business. I'm going to keep my thoughts to myself from now on. I'll just sit here and relax, and watch the pale sunlight forcing its way through the clouds, dancing and sparkling on the water of the pool.

In fact it's only another ten minutes or so before Julia arrives to join us, full of apologies but looking worried and distracted. I immediately feel even more guilty for thinking the worst of her. I suppose people with powerful important jobs need to make the occasional work call when they're on holiday, and get stressed about it – what would I know? That must be the price they pay for having that kind of responsibility, even if their ex-husband *is* there to, presumably, shore them up.

'Everything OK?' I say, and she sits down heavily next to me, sighing, before seeming to straighten up, pull back her shoulders and give me a fake smile.

'Yes, fine. Sorry – hello, Betty. Oh, don't get up on my account, it's your house, for heaven's sake –'

'I was just going to make you a drink,' Betty says, 'If you'd like one? Chocolate? That might relax you a little bit, my lovely.'

'Oh. Well, that's very nice of you, thank you. I'd love one.' Julia turns back to me as Betty goes into the kitchen. 'Are *you* having a nice relaxation?'

'Yes, I am, thanks. We've just been sitting here . . . chatting.'

She nods. 'It *is* nice in here, isn't it. With all the plants, and the views out over the grounds, and – oh, look!' She laughs suddenly. 'One of the cats has followed me here. He was brushing against my legs while I was coming out of the Lodge.'

It's the ginger cat with the wonky tail. He's meowing pathetically outside the outer door of the conservatory.

'That's Rosie,' Betty calls from the kitchen doorway. 'The black one's Basil. You can let Rosie in, if you like – if you don't mind her.'

'I hope she won't fall in the pool,' I say to Julia as she duly gets up and goes to let the cat in. 'I'd forgotten, you used to like cats, didn't you?'

'We both did,' she corrects me, over her shoulder. 'Don't you remember the one we had when we were kids?'

She walks back with Rosie trotting happily behind her, and when she sits down, the cat jumps straight onto her lap. I feel a childish pang of jealousy, and reach across to stroke her.

'Yes, of course I remember our cat,' I say. 'I loved her.'

'You wanted to call her Ermintrude,' she reminds me, laughing. 'Daft name for a cat!'

'Because of *Magic Roundabout*. I liked it. I was only little.'

'But Ermintrude was the cow!'

Here I am, forty years old, and still being mocked for being the silly one, the baby!

'So?' I shoot back. 'Was your choice really any less daft? *Smoky*, for a white cat? It made no sense.'

'It was ironic. You were too young to understand that. Anyway, Mum and Dad agreed, and the name suited her.' She shakes her head at me. 'Why are we arguing about that *now*?'

'Because that's what we seem to do, what we've always done,' I say wearily. I close my eyes and listen to Rosie purring on Julia's lap. 'Have you ever had a cat, since?'

'No. You?'

'No. Although I'm thinking it might be nice. Company. Now I'm on my own again.'

'Good idea. Perhaps I should get one, too. We could message each other pictures of our cats, like people do, on Instagram.'

I don't bother to reply. We both know perfectly well we'd never message each other pictures on Instagram, of cats or anything else.

'Here's your drink, my lovely,' Betty interrupts us, passing a steaming mug to Julia. 'Want another one?' she adds to me as I'm just draining my mug.

'No – thanks, Betty, it was delicious but I couldn't manage any more. Very chocolatey!'

'No point having hot chocolate – or anything else in life, I always say – and doing it half-heartedly, is there? I can't understand all this business, these days, of having things with *less* – less sugar, less fat, less caffeine, less calories – less bloody fun, if you ask me.'

'It's all about healthy living, isn't it,' I say gloomily, thinking about the hundreds of calories there must have been in that drink, and how tight my jeans are feeling already.

'Pah! People should eat and drink what they like, and just get off their backsides a bit more, that's all they need to do. Go for a walk, move around, get out in the fresh air.'

'You're probably right,' says Julia – who has, I'm pretty sure, never had to diet or exercise in her slender, blonde, beautiful life.

'Ah, well, it's easy for me to say, isn't it,' Betty says. She sits back down with a huff and a puff as if the exertion of walking from the kitchen has taken all her strength out of her, and I feel a pang of conscience. She shouldn't be waiting on us, at her age. 'I'm all skin and bone these days,' she goes on. 'Like the skeleton I'll be turning into before much longer.'

'Oh, don't say that!' Julia and I both protest together.

'Why not?' she laughs. 'It's true, and there's no point denying it. Ah, at your age you've still got half your lives in front of you, you don't need to start thinking about turning into skeletons yet. It's not till you're old like me that you realise it's true what everyone says – true and inescapable: *Life's too short.* And mine's nearly over, and I'll tell you what, it's been a good one. There've been plenty of sad bits, of course, but I don't dwell on those. I haven't really got any regrets.'

I feel myself gulping, partly in distress at what she's just said: *Mine's nearly over*! – and partly because I just don't know how to reply. Julia's silent too.

'I wish I could say that,' I find myself saying eventually. 'That I don't *dwell* on things. That I haven't got any regrets.'

I feel, rather than see, Julia looking at me, and I turn to meet her eyes.

'Me too,' she says softly. 'I've got regrets, all right.' She pauses, then goes on in a rush: 'Some of them are even about you.'

40 years previously

Julia

My earliest really clear memory is of my first day at school. Back then, we started school at the beginning of the term following our fifth birthday. I'd been going to playschool for the previous two years, four mornings every week, and although I'd enjoyed it, I was now one of the oldest children in the group, and it had started to feel babyish. After the November when I turned five, my parents started talking to me about all the interesting things I'd be doing at school. *After Christmas,* they said, smiling at my excitement. *You'll be going to school after Christmas.* So once December had turned into January, I started asking Mum every day if this was finally going to be the First Day at School.

When the big day finally arrived, I was up early, dressed in my new school uniform and anxious to get going.

'Can we go to school straight after breakfast?' I said as soon as I went downstairs.

I was going to have a packed lunch, in a special blue lunch box, and I'd be eating in the school dining room with my classmates – lots of whom I knew from Playschool. Lunch, I'd decided, would be one of the highlights of my new life, together with Playtime.

Mum laughed. 'We mustn't go too early, Julia, or the teachers won't even be there!'

My mum was massive at the time. Of course, I'd been told all about the baby in her tummy, told about it over and over for so long now that it was becoming boring and I'd stopped paying much attention. It had been exciting at first, learning that I was going to have a baby brother or sister. Quite a few of my friends had brothers or sisters, some older, some younger, so I had an idea of what it was like, from when I'd been to play at their houses. Sisters were obviously preferable to brothers, who seemed mostly to be loud and annoying, but I thought it would be quite fun to have a little baby of some sort, like one of my dolls but *actually alive*, so that I could perhaps push it around in my doll's pram and dress it up. And I'd be able to show off to my friends about *my baby sister* or *my baby brother*, like I'd heard some of them doing. But I hadn't realised how long it took for babies to be born.

'It's not due until the end of February,' Mum kept reminding me.

'Can't we get it out quicker?' I'd asked, and my parents had both laughed.

I was far more excited now, though, about starting school. I'd got used to Mum being enormous now, and nothing could have been further from my mind, that cold January morning as we set off together to walk to my first day at school, than the baby that everyone kept on about.

It was a day full of new things, and by the end of the afternoon I was tired, but bursting with excitement to tell my mum everything as soon as she came to meet me. The parents of all the new children had to come to the classroom door to collect us, and I was one of the first ones to have my coat buttoned up, my hat and gloves on, and be ready in the line at the door. Miss Broom, the teacher, called out each child's name as soon as their parent stepped forward to ask for them. I watched as my friend Amy was whisked away by her mum, then my friend Gemma, then David – the boy who'd cried all day and wet his pants at dinnertime – followed by Peter, and Karen, and Tanya – and eventually, there was only me, standing at the open classroom door behind Miss Broom, staring out at the empty playground.

'Is your mummy coming for you, or somebody else?' Miss Broom asked in a kind voice.

'Mummy,' I said. I had a funny feeling in my tummy, like I might be sick. 'Where is she?'

'I'm sure she'll be here in a minute. Perhaps something has held her up. Why don't you sit back down at your table and look at a book while we wait?'

I did as I was told, but I couldn't see the pictures in the book properly because my eyes were starting to fill up with tears. Mummy had *promised* she'd be here, at the classroom door, when it was time to go home! Why wasn't she there? I sat at the table, without moving, feeling like I could hardly breathe, for what felt like ages. The school secretary came into the room and Miss Broom talked to her very quietly, and I saw them both glance at me quickly and then look away again. And then finally – just as I felt like I wouldn't be able to stop myself from crying really loudly and really messily – there was somebody outside the classroom door – somebody waving at me, smiling at me, somebody who was ushered in by Miss Broom, with another very quiet conversation between the two of them. Somebody who wasn't my mum, but a neighbour across the road who I only knew as Mrs Peachy and had never even said hello to before. I covered my face with my hands so that I didn't have to look at her. My mum had told me never to go with strangers. Was Mrs Peachy a stranger? I was frightened because I didn't know.

'I want my Mummy,' I said in a shaky, nearly-crying voice as Mrs Peachy approached me across the classroom. 'Where's my mummy?'

'Julia,' Miss Broom said gently, coming to stand beside me, 'Mrs Peachy is going to take you back to her house to wait for your daddy. Your mummy is fine, but she couldn't come to collect you today. She's got a super-special surprise for you, though!'

I looked back at Miss Broom through my fingers.

'What surprise? Why couldn't she come? She promised! I don't want to go with Mrs Peachy,' I added in a whisper. 'Is she a stranger?'

'Of course I'm not a stranger, poppet!' Mrs Peachy said, laughing. 'You know me, I live across the road. Your mummy knows I'm taking you home.'

'I know you're upset,' Miss Broom said. 'And I know Mummy will be very upset too that she can't be here to take you home. But Mrs Peachy is going to stay with you until your daddy gets home, and he'll explain everything. All right? And I'll see you tomorrow and you can tell me all about the special surprise then.'

'I don't want a special surprise,' I said, feeling trembly and weak with fear. 'I just want Mummy.'

'Of course you do, sweetheart,' Mrs Peachy said. She tried to hold my hand, but I wouldn't let her. 'Come on, dear, let's get you home and I'll get you a nice drink and biscuit. What sort of biscuit is your favourite?'

I just shook my head. I knew I shouldn't be rude, but I couldn't bring myself to talk to Mrs Peachy, who was old, and wore a silly pink hat, and smelt a bit like the stuff Mummy sprayed the bathroom with. When we went into Mrs Peachey's house, I sat in silence at the kitchen table, sipped the orange juice and nibbled the biscuit she gave me, while wiping tears away with the back of my hand and refusing to speak.

It felt like hours and hours before there was a knock at the door. It was dark outside, and I was struggling to stay awake. Mrs Peachey had offered me soup, or sausages, or toast with jam, but I didn't want to eat anything because I felt sick. She'd suggested I should lie down on her sofa and have a little sleep, but I was scared that I might never be able to go home if I fell asleep there. I might end up like Cinderella who fell asleep for a hundred years. Or Mrs Peachey might decide to keep me, or do something horrible to me like the witch in *Hansel and Gretel*.

'Daddy!' I said when I heard my father's voice – and I ran out into the hallway, finally crying properly: huge noisy sobs, my chest heaving, my nose running. My dad was talking quietly to Mrs Peachy, and he looked . . . different. Tired, and worried. It made me feel even more frightened. 'Where's Mummy?' I asked him, as he held out his arms to me for a hug. 'She didn't come to get me.'

'I know, darling.' He stroked my hair, lifted my face to talk to me. 'Mummy's really, *really* sorry. But something happened, and she had to go to the hospital.'

'*Hospital*? What's wrong with her?'

'Nothing.' He smiled – with his mouth but not his eyes. 'It's the baby, Julia. Mummy's had the baby this afternoon.'

'The *baby*?' I wriggled out of his arms and stared at him in disgust. 'The baby shouldn't have come today! It could have waited till tomorrow, or next week – why did it have to come today? Today was my first day at school, and Mummy *promised* to come to take me home, she shouldn't have let the stupid baby come today!'

'Darling, it wasn't Mummy's fault. Babies come when they want to come.'

'Well, that's not fair! *I* didn't want it to come today! I had lots and lots to tell Mummy about school, and now I've forgotten it all, and I had to sit and look at a book for *ages and ages* all on my own, everyone else had gone home and I had to try really hard not to cry.'

'I know. It must have been really scary and horrible for you,' Dad tried to soothe me. But I was tired and cross and wasn't about to be soothed.

'Where's Mummy now?' I asked sulkily.

'Still in the hospital. The baby came much too soon. She's very tiny, and she has to stay in hospital for a while, and be looked after, so Mummy has to stay with her –'

'Why? *I* want Mummy! I want her to come home and be with *me.*' I was working herself up into what my parents always referred to as a *proper strop*, and although I wanted to stop, to be nice, be good, behave myself and try not to mind about Mummy suddenly seeming to prefer this annoying new baby to me, I just couldn't. I'd been too scared, too disappointed and now it had gone too far to stop it. 'I don't even *want* a stupid baby!' I finished, stamping my foot.

'She's your little sister,' Dad said, still managing to sound quite calm although his face had stopped smiling now, and his eyes were really sad and really tired. 'I know you're cross now, but you'll be so pleased, once everything's settled down and she can come home with us. We're calling her Lauren. Do you think it's a nice name?'

'No. It's horrid, and I *won't* be pleased, I'll hate her.'

'All right, Julia, I know you're tired. Let's get you home to bed,' Daddy said quietly. He thanked Mrs Peachy, took my hand and led me across the road to our own house, where I was in bed and fast asleep within minutes, without even being properly aware of it happening.

In the morning, when I remembered how cross and bad-tempered I'd been with my dad, I felt ashamed. But then I remembered that my mummy still wouldn't be coming home, that she'd chosen instead to stay with the baby, who could surely have been left at hospital to be looked after by the nurses – and I felt cross all over again, and refused to feel excited about my dad taking me for my second day at school. When Miss Broom asked me, with a big smile on her face, to tell the class about my *super-special surprise*, I just shook my head and wouldn't speak.

'I think you've got a new baby sister, Julia,' Miss Broom encouraged me. 'Isn't that right?'

I shrugged and scowled, and Miss Broom finally took the hint and moved on to talk to the class about something else. All I knew was that my mummy had obviously decided she liked the new baby more than she liked me, because otherwise she would have known how important it was to hear about my first day at school, left that stupid baby with the nurses and come to meet me like she'd promised. As far as I was concerned, baby Lauren could stay in the hospital for as long as she liked. I didn't want her.

And if you think I don't regret having had those feelings, Lauren, then you really don't know me at all. I've regretted it every day, ever since!

Julia

I feel slightly spooked about the whole thing now. What the hell came over me there? I've never talked to Lauren about all that. After all, who admits to their little sister that they resented her arrival? I can't believe I've come out and told her that, at the age of five, I was convinced I'd always hate her. But now I have, and she doesn't seem surprised. When I finished pouring all that out, she just nodded calmly and said:

'I know. I always knew that.'

'But I did love you,' I said. I was already looking around me, taking in my situation – the pool, the warmth under the glass roof, and Betty, who'd got up while I was talking, and had been watering some of her pot plants behind us, pretending she hadn't been listening. I felt like I'd been talking in my sleep. It unnerved me. 'I think I *wanted* to hate you, but as soon as I first set eyes on you – when they were finally allowed to bring you home from hospital – I loved you. Whatever you might think.'

I loved her, but resented her at the same time. I was too young to understand my own feelings or put them into words. Even before she was brought home from hospital, when my dad sat me down and tried to explain why she was having to stay there for so long – because she was too little, and her heart wasn't working properly, so she needed the doctors to do an operation to make it better – I felt the weight of my guilt for the first time, because although I did feel sorry for this too-small baby sister of mine for having a poorly heart, I still resented her for stealing my mum away from me.

Betty has come to sit down with us again now, slopping some water over the edge of her watering-can as she does. Some of it splashes over Rosie the cat, who's been lying by my feet half-asleep – and she jumps up, meowing in protest. Betty laughs and reaches down to stroke her. She doesn't say anything, doesn't comment at all about my outpourings of guilt.

Lauren and I both sit in silence now; she doesn't even seem shocked by what I've said. As soon as I've managed to pull myself together, we say goodbye to Betty and make our way back to the Lodge. Nathan is outside, cleaning the windows.

'Thank you, they look much better now,' I say. 'You've trimmed the ivy too.'

He grins. 'It did need doing – sorry, it must have put you off a bit when you arrived.'

'Not at all,' Lauren says, lying through her teeth. 'But yes, thank you.'

'Been out exploring, have you?' he asks.

'No.' I say. 'As it was raining earlier, we've just been sitting having a chat with your gran, over in the pool room.'

'Ah! She can chat for England, my gran can!'

I smile, but in fact I'm quite aware that it wasn't Betty chatting, most of the time, it was me, rambling on about my childhood memories.

'Well, I'm glad the rain's stopped now, for you both,' he goes on. 'Tomorrow's forecast to be a good day. Sunny but cold. Good day for exploring the moor, if you want to.'

'Yes, that'd be good, wouldn't it, Julia?' Lauren says, and then turns back to him without waiting for my agreement. 'Is there anywhere you'd particularly recommend we should go?'

He scratches his face thoughtfully. 'Well, there are a whole lot of places worth visiting. Some of them, though, you wouldn't want to drive to in a nice car like that.' He nods at my Mercedes, hesitates for a minute, then goes on a little diffidently: 'I could take you out to Foxes Brook Bridge and Wolf Tor tomorrow if you like. I drive an old four-by-four. She's used to the moor and puts up with whatever comes her way.'

'Oh, we wouldn't want to trouble you,' I say, although I can't help smiling at his use of the feminine pronouns for his car. 'You'll surely be at work, anyway, won't you?'

'Nothing on, at the moment. Last job finished before Christmas. I went out to look at a big job the other day, but I've only just done the quote for that work. So unless anything else comes up . . .' He shrugs. 'Well, it's the quiet time of year. That's why I've been helping my gran here.'

'Well, if you're sure you don't mind, that would be –' Laura begins.

'– too much trouble for you,' I interrupt her.

Nathan laughs. 'No trouble at all. I'd enjoy a day out on the moor. Promise I won't get you lost! Pick you up here at ten?'

'That'll be great,' Lauren says, ignoring the looks I'm giving her. 'We'll bring lunch.'

'Don't bother with that. We'll stop off at Widecombe. Nice pub there. And no tourists crowding it out at this time of year, like they do in the summer. Apart from you two, of course!'

'But –' I try to protest, but Lauren's already thanking him and tugging me indoors.

'Apparently it's easy to get lost on Dartmoor,' she says after we've closed the door behind us. 'So it'd be silly to refuse the offer of a local guide, don't you think?'

Despite the irritation I feel with her about it, I can't help laughing. *Local guide*? She's making it sound like we're going trekking in the Himalayas, rather than for a gentle drive across the open Devon moorland!

'And it sounded like he's a bit bored,' she goes on. 'Probably glad to have a reason to get out for a few hours.'

'OK, OK.' I give in, if only to stop her coming up with any more excuses for her eagerness to be in the company of the young Mister Heartthrob.

I might be putting up more of a protest if it weren't for the strange way I'm feeling after my confessional outpourings earlier. Over lunch, I try again, clumsily, to apologise for what I said.

'I didn't mean to come out with any of it,' I admit. 'It . . . was like I was dreaming. Talking under hypnosis or something.'

'I wonder what Betty *did* put in that hot chocolate!' she jokes.

And I know she's only teasing me. I'm grateful that she didn't take offence or feel upset – it would have made the rest of the week here even more difficult. But at the same time, I feel a little shiver of apprehension. Of course I know it's nonsense, what that Janice woman in the shop was implying about Betty and her hot drinks. Chocolate's well known for its sedative qualities. It was warm in the room. I was feeling anxious about the phone conversation I had earlier, and the chocolate soothed me. But . . . it actually did almost *feel* like I'd been drugged!

I try to put it out of my mind during the afternoon. It's started raining again, the trees outside dripping fat droplets through their bare branches, rainwater cascading down the outsides of the windows. We decide to play a game of Cluedo, and we laugh together about the weapons and the murderer, companionably, as if we we're those kinds of sisters who enjoy each other's company. Lauren doesn't mention Nathan anymore for the rest of the day. But more to the point, she doesn't mention Carl either.

Tuesday

Lauren

Nathan was right: today's going to be a better day, I can see it as soon as I open my bedroom curtains, despite the fact that daylight's only just dawning. The wind's dropped, the rain's stopped, and there's a stillness and emerging brightness outside.

Julia's got the Dartmoor tourist map spread out on the table before I've even come downstairs for breakfast, and she's studying it carefully, looking for the places Nathan suggested taking us to see.

'Wolf Tor seems to be a viewpoint,' she says. 'And Foxes Brook Bridge is . . . well, a bridge. There doesn't seem to be anything else there.'

'The viewpoint sounds interesting,' I say, shooing Basil the cat off a chair and sitting down opposite her. 'Nathan was right, it looks like being a nice sunny day. It might be our only chance to get a view of anything.'

Julia's still being a bit tight-lipped and prim about Nathan. She tried, yesterday, to refuse his offer of taking us out, but I can't see the harm in it. If she still honestly believes I'm lusting after a young guy like him, she can think what she likes, but the truth is, he might be very good-looking but I'm not interested. And anyway, I know perfectly well that Nathan wouldn't be interested in *me*.

It'll be good, though, to see some places on Dartmoor, places off the beaten track that we might not have found on our own.

'It was very nice of him to offer,' I tell her as we eat our breakfast. 'We could always buy him lunch to thank him.'

'I suppose so,' Julia says.

We're outside, ready, in plenty of time for meeting Nathan. We've brought walking boots with us, and warm coats, hats, gloves and scarves. We're not going to take any chances with the weather; it might be a brighter day, but it's very cold outside. I feel cheerful and quite excited about our day out; and at the same time, I'm a bit worried about the fact that I can even begin to feel cheerful, in the circumstances. I've just had my heart broken; I've got no right to be cheerful. Or perhaps Julia's right, after all – as she always seems to think she is? Perhaps I'd never really been in love with Carl, at all? I can't begin to ask myself that kind of serious question yet; it does my head in, even to think about it, to contemplate the idea that I might have been fooling myself about the relationship. Again.

When Nathan pulls up in his jeep, Julia climbs straight into the front passenger seat next to him. She probably thinks I can't be trusted close to him! She's brought the Dartmoor guidebook with her and as Nathan drives, she reads a couple of bits of it out loud for my benefit.

'Apparently Wolf Tor is one of the easier tors to climb,' she says. She pauses and adds, to Nathan: 'What exactly *is* a tor?'

'An outcrop of rock. Some of them are huge, others not very big at all.'

'I see. So this one is described as not very high, but a great viewpoint. How's that possible?'

'Ah well, the road climbs up high before we actually get to the tor. You'll see.'

'OK.' She goes back to reading the book in silence.

I'm watching the scenery, fascinated by the way the road winds its way across vast open landscapes of brown and green and purple, broken up occasionally by a sudden bend, and a narrow bridge over a stream. We climb slowly towards the distant horizon, passing the occasional isolated stone cottage, a group of ponies huddled together by a wind-bent cluster of trees, a clutch of sheep here and there, and, as Nathan negotiates one bend, several of them ambling across the road in front of us.

'According to the book, there's a legend about this place,' Julia says as, eventually, we pull up next to a signpost for Wolf Tor. 'Something about a wolf that killed people in revenge for its family. Sounds a bit grizzly.'

'Yes, I know the story.' Nathan gets out of the car and pulls the passenger doors open for us. The final part of the journey here has confirmed his explanation about why the view from the top should be good: the road climbed steadily higher and higher, so we could already see for miles around, without having even approached the foot of the tor. 'There are legends about a lot of these places. I'll tell you about it as we walk up.'

I pull my hat down over my ears. The cold wind is whistling around us already and I'm sure it's going to get worse as we go higher.

'The story goes,' he goes on, raising his voice against the wind as we set off to climb the small rocky hillock, 'that long ago, some villagers from nearby killed a she-wolf at this spot, and its cubs had starved to death by the time the male returned to their den. In revenge, the male went into the village every night to hunt for a human baby. Whenever it found one, it brought it back here and killed it. Every time people heard the wolf howling from the top of the tor, they knew they'd lost another of their children.'

'That's horrible!' I exclaim. 'Do you know what was supposed to have happened in the end?'

'No. But you can bet your life a crowd of them came out here and killed the male wolf too. Or, maybe the villagers who killed the vixen had to sacrifice themselves to the pack, to stop the babies being killed. Something gruesome like that.'

I shudder. 'There aren't wolves on Dartmoor anymore, are there?'

'Not that I know of, apart from in the zoo!' he said. 'But I've heard there are plans to reintroduce them. Part of a rewilding scheme, apparently.'

'I don't know about wolves – it's cold enough up here for polar bears,' Julia puts in. 'Come on, let's step it out a bit, the exercise might warm us up.'

It's not a particularly strenuous climb to the top of the tor, but it's made more difficult by the rocky terrain.

'You'd think they'd have made a proper footpath up here,' I complain as I stumble for the third time.

'Lauren, this is nature!' Julia scolds me. 'You sound like such a stereotypical city girl.'

Nathan's laughing, but he slows his pace a little so that I can catch up.

'Well, I still think the council could have –' I begin. Then I stop, straighten up and add 'Wow!'

We're almost at the top, and the view is amazing: a three-hundred-and-sixty-degree panorama of moorland, broken up by outcrops of rock, with a haze of purple in the distance. In one direction, a small group of cottages and a church spire glint in the winter sunshine, looking, from here, as tiny as children's toys.

'Well, it was worth the climb,' I say quietly.

'Yes, it was.' Julia smiles at me. 'And thank God, no wolves!'

The freezing cold wind is whipping around all our faces, and Julia's cheeks have turned pink, making her look like a healthy outdoor girl. Me, I just feel like my eyes are watering and my nose is going to run. We both take some photos of the view, before following Nathan back down to the car again, slipping occasionally on the loose scree underfoot.

'Glad I didn't wear my heels,' Julia jokes.

Nathan turns up the heater in the car for a few minutes while we take off our hats and gloves and try to warm up.

I stretch and sigh. 'Thank you for bringing us here, Nathan. And showing us that view.'

'You're welcome. I always love being out here on the moor.'

His own cheeks are flushed and healthy-looking from the wind. As soon as we got back to the car, he shrugged off the green Barbour-type jacket he'd been wearing, and he doesn't seem to be shivering like we are.

'I guess you're used to it,' I say as he starts the engine and pulls back onto the road.

'The weather? Well, it can be pretty harsh up here, and we get snow fairly often. It's forecast this week, as a matter of fact.'

'Oh!' Julia says, and falls silent.

I guess she's wondering whether that might make it difficult for our journey home – but I don't want to think about that. The first few days here have gone so quickly, and – unbelievably, considering how it started off – I'm actually enjoying myself. I don't want to think about the end of the holiday, going back to my lonely home, back to my boring job and my boring life without Carl.

'OK to go on to Foxes Brook Bridge?' Nathan's saying. 'Nothing much there – it's just known as a beauty spot. A pretty little bridge and a couple of cottages by the stream. It's a bit off the beaten track, which is why I said you're better off in a four by four.'

'Sounds good,' I agree.

A mile or so further along the road he turns off onto what I'd have thought was just a track. *Unsuitable for most motor vehicles* says the sign on the junction. *No passing places for two miles.*

'Not unsuitable for *this* vehicle,' Nathan reassures us, glancing in the mirror and smiling at the look on my face.

'So what happens if we meet something coming the other way?' Julia asks.

'Unlikely.' He chuckles.

Fortunately, he's right: we don't see another soul – not along the so-called road, which is barely wide enough for us, let alone the suggestion of another vehicle – and not when we finally pull up on a grassy verge at the bottom of the hill. As Nathan opens the car doors, I can already hear the gentle burbling of the brook. We walk towards the sound. It's sheltered from the wind down here, and the sunshine makes everything look clean and bright. When we turn a slight bend in the lane, there's the little hump-backed stone bridge, and beyond it, two pastel painted thatched cottages: one pink, one cream. We walk onto the bridge, where I lean on the parapet and look down at the clear, fast-flowing water below. The sun's glinting and reflecting off the ripples, and I feel something inside me shift and start to melt as I look up and stare around me.

'It's beautiful here,' I whisper. It feels like it would be wrong to speak any more loudly – like shouting in church.

'Yes,' he agrees simply.

'Who lives in the cottages?' Julia asks. 'What an earth do they do for a living – out here in the middle of nowhere?'

'I don't know. They might work at one of the sheep farms hereabout. Or commute out to one of the towns or villages just beyond the moor. Or these might be holiday cottages,' he adds with a shrug. 'But at least the houses aren't being allowed to fester.'

Fester. I smile. It seems such an apt word for how these lovely cottages could have ended up looking if they'd been abandoned or neglected. We passed a couple such broken-down little houses on the drive here. I can understand it, in a way – it seems almost impossible that anyone could live out here.

Julia and I take photos of the bridge and the cottages, and Nathan offers to take a picture of us together on the bridge. We pose with our arms around each other . . . and I don't even stop to think about how strange that is, until we're back in the car, warming up again. We've *never* been the type of sisters to put our arms round each other. It must just have been the photo opportunity that made us do it.

'Ready for a lunch stop now?' Nathan asks as he starts the engine. 'We're only a short drive from Widecombe. You city girls will like it – there are a couple of shops there!'

'Really?' Julia says, and he laughs.

'Only a couple, and they don't sell the sort of things you might hope for. But if you'd like a box of fudge with pictures of Dartmoor on the lid, or a tea towel with the words of *Widecombe Fayre* on it, or a book of Devon recipes –'

'I get it,' I say, laughing too. 'As you said, it's a tourist place.'

'Yes. But very pretty. With a couple of nice pubs.'

'Sounds good,' Julia says.

Before long we've parked up and got ourselves settled at a table in a cosy corner of the pub in the centre of the village, with a hot drink each in front of us and Ploughman's lunches on order.

'It's been great today – thanks so much, Nathan,' I say.

'Yes, we're very grateful,' Julia agrees.

'Not at all, it's my pleasure. I've enjoyed it too. I don't often get the chance to have a day out, like this. Since I moved back in with Gran, I've been pretty busy.' He shrugs. 'I don't see myself always wanting to work on building sites or doing odd jobs; I'd like to have my own business someday – something completely different, I'm not sure what, though. But for now, it gets me by. And when I haven't been working elsewhere, I've been doing up the Lodge ready for guests.'

'And we're the first ones, apparently,' Julia says. She pauses, then goes on, 'Your gran was very kind, making us hot chocolate! We wondered what on earth she puts in it that makes it so . . . delicious.'

'Nothing,' he says, with a smile. 'She's got a bit of a reputation for it, though. Gran just loves to chat, you see. So when people come to buy produce from her, she makes them a hot drink, to persuade them to sit down and spend a bit of time with her. She gets lonely, that's all. When I'm not there.'

'I see.' Julia nods, and glances at me. 'So you say she sells produce? Home-grown?'

'Yes. Have a look in the greenhouses. Round the other side of the house. Green-fingered, is my gran! But I've been helping her with that too, of course, since I've been back. She finds it harder, these days, to be on her feet for too long.'

'That's interesting, we'll have to have a look – see what she's growing –' I start, but Julia's already moved the conversation on, giving Nathan a sympathetic smile, as she tells him gently:

'We were sorry to hear about what happened – you and your wife –'

'My *wife*?' He says, stopping with his coffee mug halfway to his mouth and looking at her in surprise. 'Um –'

I shake my head frantically at Julia, but she goes on regardless:

'Sorry, I'm sure it's a painful subject, it's just that your Gran mentioned –'

'Oh, trust Gran! She can't help herself – she *has* to get in a dig about my marriage whenever she gets the chance.' He's shaking his head but looks amused about it. 'She was against it from the start, and to be fair, it turned out she was right. But I didn't have a wife. I had a husband: Ben.'

'Oh.' Julia draws the word out, a long *O – o – o h* of realisation. 'I'm so sorry. I didn't –'

'Don't worry,' he says, smiling. 'I don't exactly walk about with a sign round my neck, and even in these enlightened times, people still tend to assume most marriages are between a man and a woman. I'm not offended.'

'Well, we were sorry to hear about it anyway,' I say.

'It was my own fault. I didn't know him well enough. I rushed into it. He . . . wasn't who I thought he was. I'll get over it, but I'm not in a hurry to repeat the mistake.'

'I don't blame you,' I say. 'I've just broken up with my boyfriend, and I feel the same way.'

Julia's gone silent, sipping her coffee, looking at me almost accusingly. I suppose she thinks I should have told her – but although I suspected Nathan was gay, I wasn't completely sure. And despite what she thought, it didn't matter to me, either way.

'I gave up the flat I was renting in Ivybridge, to move in with Ben,' he's saying now. 'But I grew up at Deepcombe, with my parents, and Gran. So when Gran suggested I move back, it seemed a good idea. She needs help, these days.'

'And your parents don't live there with her anymore?' Julia asks.

He shakes his head, and I notice his hand shaking slightly as he puts his mug down on the table.

'My mum passed away two years ago –'

'Oh, I'm so sorry,' Julia and I both say together, but he waves this aside.

'Yes, it was . . . a difficult time, obviously. She'd been ill for ages, so . . . it wasn't a shock. But Dad moved up-country afterwards. He couldn't bear to be around Deepcombe without her. He'd brought her home there as a bride and, well, her presence is everywhere there – you can imagine.'

'That's so sad,' I say softly.

'Well, life *is* sad, to be honest, isn't it? In between the happy times, there's always something sad lurking there, waiting to jump out at us! But look, here's something to cheer us all up,' he adds with a grin. 'The ploughman's lunches here are fantastic – look at those huge chunks of cheese. And warm crusty bread! God, I didn't realise how hungry I was.'

So, taking this as our cue to drop the subject of his personal losses, we tuck into the delicious lunches right away. The fresh air has made me hungry, and eventually – having cleared our plates and paid the bill – we take a few minutes to browse the little gift shop, where I feel strangely obliged to buy the

Widecombe Fayre tea-towel, and Julia buys a book about the legends of Dartmoor.

'Why didn't you tell me?' Julia hisses at me as soon as we've arrived back at the Lodge and closed the front door behind us. 'I could *see* you knew he was gay –'

'*Suspected* it,' I correct her. 'But what difference does it make? Are you disappointed?' I add with a grin.

She throws her Dartmoor Legends book at me. But at least she's laughing.

Wednesday

Julia

I suppose, to be honest, that now the initial embarrassment about my *faux pas* yesterday with Nathan has faded, I realise it was my own fault. I did pretty much accuse Lauren of fancying him. I felt cross and exasperated with her about it, and ignored her denials, her insistence that she wasn't looking for another relationship yet. With her track record, though, I couldn't really be blamed for that.

But it was a good day yesterday. I enjoyed being out in the wild open countryside, despite the cold wind. It took my mind off . . . well, off everything. Even the phone conversation I'd had the previous morning. But after we were back at the Lodge, I started worrying about it again.

'I just need to make a call,' I told Lauren. She'd put the kettle on as soon as we'd got back and taken off our coats and boots. 'I'll go upstairs.'

'Work again, I suppose?' she said, raising her eyebrows.

I wanted to retaliate, to tell her not to take that tone, to wipe that sneer off her face – that this was serious, and furthermore, the whole world didn't revolve around her and *her* problems. But I didn't. I didn't want an argument. I just nodded and said it wouldn't take long.

When I finally came back downstairs, Lauren's mood seemed to have changed. Perhaps it was something in my expression, something she read in my eyes.

'I'll make your tea,' she said. 'Sit down.'

'Thanks.' I sank onto the sofa, leaning back, closing my eyes – and I think, when she brought my cup of tea, she might have thought I was asleep. But I sat up and made an effort.

'Shall we have another game of Cluedo?' I suggested.

'Good idea. I'll get it out.'

'And *I'm* Miss Scarlett this time, OK?'

Distraction. Sometimes it's the only way to carry on. Besides which, I really don't want to talk to her about it. It wouldn't do to have two of us crying, would it?

After breakfast this morning, we decide to go and have a look at Betty's greenhouses, as Nathan suggested. It's colder than ever outside now, the sky pewter grey, the wind whipping our faces cruelly as we make our way through the undergrowth towards the manor house. Squirrels scamper up trees in front of us, the grass and fallen leaves underfoot rustle with the movements of unseen small creatures, and in the freezing currents high above us, birds swoop and dive, and call out to each other unhappily, as if warning of some kind of imminent doom.

'A magpie,' Lauren points out, as it takes flight from an old bare tree in front of us. 'Oh no, we need to see another one now. One for sorrow, two for joy –'

'Three for a girl, four for a boy,' I finish for her. 'Yes, I know that one too.'

'But that's not all of it. Then it goes: Five for silver, six for gold, seven for a secret, never to be told.'

'Oh.' I look at her in surprise. 'I didn't know that bit. I don't think I've ever seen that many magpies together at the same time, though.'

'No, me neither.'

But regardless of seeing seven magpies – we all have secrets, don't we.

We pass by the outside door of the conservatory and continue around the corner of the manor house. We haven't explored this part of the grounds before.

'There's a patio round here!' I say in surprise.

'Of sorts.'

It's crazy paving, and looks like it was laid at least fifty years ago. The weeds have pushed between the stones, moss has grown across their surface, and the little wall separating the paving from the grass is crumbling in places.

'I think Nathan's got his work cut out here,' I comment.

'Perhaps he'll have it broken up and completely re-laid.' Lauren sighs. 'The whole place has got such a sad air about it, hasn't it? It's a shame – this was probably a beautiful house at one time.'

'Yes, I'm sure it was. Oh, there are the greenhouses.' I point across what was probably once a lawn, with a path of stepping stones – now overgrown, like everything else. 'Let's have a look.'

Of course, we've got no idea what we're looking at. I've never been into gardening, and although I don't know much about Lauren's life these days, I've noticed that her small garden consists of a neat little patio and a tiny lawn. No flower beds and certainly no vegetables. But it's clear, even to me, that the plants in the greenhouses, whatever they are, look healthy and are being tended carefully.

'I think they might be tomato plants,' Lauren says somewhat uncertainly, pointing to one shelf near the door of the first greenhouse.

'Possibly.' I pause, wondering whether or not to voice what I'm thinking. 'And how would either of us know if . . . well, if Betty was growing something here that she might actually put into hot drinks?'

'Oh, come on,' Lauren scoffs. 'Nathan's already assured us his gran doesn't do that. And I thought we'd both agreed, that what's-her-name, Janice, in the shop was talking rubbish? It's just gossip. What – you think she'd crush a chilli pepper or something, and stir it into –'

'No. You know what I was wondering about, and so were you – don't pretend it didn't cross your mind. A . . . herbal, um, derivative, of some sort –'

'Cannabis? I bet you don't even know what it looks like?'

'No, I don't! I've never indulged. Have you?' I challenge her.

She's laughing at me. It annoys me. I haven't exactly led a sheltered life; I've just stayed away from drugs, and I don't think that's anything to apologise for.

'Only in a cake,' she says, smiling to herself at the memory. 'In Amsterdam, when I went there on a hen weekend years ago. It's what everyone does, over there. It was disappointing, to be honest: I didn't notice any effect from it whatsoever. Anyway, this whole conversation is ridiculous.' She raises her eyes and turns away. 'Come on – let's go back to the conservatory, it's freezing out here.'

I follow her, feeling silly now. Of course the elderly Betty wouldn't be growing cannabis and selling it to the villagers – I know Lauren's right, it's a ridiculous thought. What's wrong with me? We unlock the conservatory door and the warmth hits us immediately.

'Phew, that's better.' I undo my coat as we walk round the pool to the chairs at the far side.

Suddenly there's a ripple and a splash – and a head and shoulders emerge from the water, making Lauren and I both hold onto each other, gasping with surprise.

'Oh!' I exclaim as Nathan hauls himself onto the side of the pool, dripping and laughing at our shock. 'We didn't see you in there!'

Knowing he's gay doesn't take anything away from the fact that he's extremely easy on the eye, in his swimming trunks. Like a hero from a rom-com film emerging from the ocean onto a soft white beach. Not that I'm feeling particularly romantic at the moment. Perhaps I'm just practising distraction again, to prevent myself from thinking about more worrying things.

'Sorry, I was doing lengths underwater,' Nathan says casually as if it were a perfectly normal feat. Perhaps it is, for him. He doesn't even sound out of breath. He walks over to the towel racks and grabs a large green towel, with which he rubs his hair quickly. Then he drapes it around himself, pushing his feet into a pair of flip-flops. 'Have a seat and relax, ladies. I'll go and tell Gran you're here.'

The two cats are lying in the nearest seat, and rather than disturb them, we move to some other chairs, and a couple of moments later Betty comes out of her kitchen door. I pull a third chair across.

'You're going to join us, aren't you?'

'I will, if you don't mind? But I'll get the kettle on first and make us some hot drinks. What would you like, my lovelies? Tea? Coffee? Or chocolate?'

'Well, your hot chocolate is to die for, Betty,' Lauren says quickly. 'Especially in this cold weather.'

'Coming up, then.'

She soon arrives back with a tray bearing three steaming mugs, plus a cake tin. Putting the tray down on the table, she removes the lid of the tin with a flourish and announces:

'Special treat today, my lovelies. I've made some of my seed cakes for you.'

Immediately my thoughts fly straight back to Lauren's description of her experimentation with the cakes in Amsterdam.

'What kind of seeds?' I ask, trying to sound casual. Are there any seeds that have hallucinogenic properties? I have no idea.

Betty looks at me in surprise. 'Sunflower seeds. And a few pumpkin seeds. Are you allergic, or something?'

'No.' I look away, trying to avoid catching Lauren's eyes. I've heard her sighing as if in exasperation. 'They sound lovely, Betty. Thank you.' I take one and take a large bite, smiling at her as I'm munching. 'Mm, delicious.' The cake's still warm, and so light and moist, it's melting in my mouth.

'Sorry about the crumbs, Betty!' Lauren says, looking down at the tiled floor after we've all finished our cakes, but she laughs and points at Rosie, who's already hoovering them up enthusiastically, and Basil, who's watching from his chair, flicking his tail in disapproval as if he'd like to join in but is too comfortable to move. Well, if the cat doesn't fall into a trance after eating the cake crumbs, then I reckon we're safe too!

'Did you both have a nice day yesterday out on the moor?' Betty asks.

I've been watching her, without trying to make it too obvious, as she absent-mindedly brushes her thick grey trousers down with her hands, trying ineffectively to remove the cat hairs. I don't suppose she knows, and good for her if she doesn't care, but her hand-knitted navy-blue jumper is even thicker with their hair. She looks up and catches me watching, and chuckles.

'Bloomin' cats!' she says. 'I brush them every single day. I don't want them leaving their fur in the guest accommodation. You don't want them shedding it all over your things.'

'Don't worry, Betty,' I say, smiling. 'We both like cats. And yesterday was great. It was really kind of Nathan to drive us.'

'Oh, he enjoyed himself too. I'm glad. He deserves a day off now and then. He's always working, either here, or out on a job for someone else. Still, I suppose it takes his mind off things.'

'We were sorry to hear he lost his mum last year,' Lauren says.

'Yes. Janie was my daughter-in-law, but you know, I loved her like she was my own daughter.' Betty sighs and shakes her head. 'Bloody cancer, it took her far too young, and far too slowly. My son won't ever get over it. Had to move out, he did. Moved up-country to start afresh. We were hoping he'd come home for Christmas, but . . . he called, said he couldn't face it. Without Janie.'

'So sorry.' I reach across to touch her hand. Poor Betty, it must feel like she's lost her son now, in a way, as well as her daughter-in-law. 'Life can be so unfair.'

'Well, yes, it *is* unfair. It should've been me the cancer got, shouldn't it? Eighty years old, and a heavy smoker for most of my life – I should've been the one to go, not her, sweet little soul that she was. Didn't even drink, bless her heart. Didn't deserve it.'

Lauren's eyes are filling with tears. Betty looks up, notices her wiping them away and shakes her head again, apologising.

'What a miserable old bag I'm being! Sorry, my lovelies, take no notice of me. You're on your holiday, you should be enjoying yourselves, I should be giving you happy memories of this place, not making you bloody cry!'

'That's all right, Betty,' Lauren says, sniffing. 'It's just me, feeling a bit emotional at the moment.'

'Ah, well, there's nothing a nice warm cake and a mug of hot chocolate can't put right. Drink up, I can make some more if you want it.' She pauses and looked at Lauren more closely. 'And what is it you're feeling emotional about now, on your holiday? The break-up you mentioned when we were talking before? Of course, you don't have to tell me if you don't want to,' she adds quickly.

'Oh, it doesn't matter, Betty, it's no secret,' Lauren says. 'I was supposed to be having this holiday with my boyfriend. Partner. It was his present for me, for my fortieth birthday. I'd . . . kind of anticipated a really posh hotel somewhere abroad, somewhere in the sun, so it was –'

'– disappointing to find yourself on Dartmoor in the depths of winter,' Betty finishes for her with a chuckle.

'Sorry, I don't mean to be rude. But yes! It . . . just added to the whole misery of the situation, really.' She glances at me. 'I wasn't going to come. But Julia talked me into it, and said she'd bring me. And I'm very grateful for that, because being here has helped to take my mind off it . . . off *him*. Some of the time, anyway.' She pauses again, and then goes on suddenly, in a rush: 'And it's been such a surprise, because, let's face it, Julia – we've never got on, have we?'

'Well . . .' I frown, feeling awkward. 'I wouldn't say that, exactly.'

'Oh, come on. We were never close, even as children. You were only saying the other day, how much you resented me being born.'

'I was *five*!' I protest. 'And yes, I might have resented the way you came along – the timing, the fact that my nose was put out of joint – but I never resented *you*. I've told you: I loved you as soon as I set eyes on you.'

'So why don't we ever see each other now – normally, I mean? Why don't we spend Christmases and holidays and things together, like other families? Why don't we call each other, apart from the odd dutiful phone call on birthdays? Why don't you ever make *time* for me, Julia? Can't you spare any time from your so-important job that's more important than your sister?'

'It works both ways,' I shoot back. 'When did you last call me? Or visit me? Or your nephew, for that matter? Simon's forgotten what you look like. *You're* always too busy with your latest man! It's always the same – every time, you let them take over your life, you always think they're *the one* – you never bloody learn!'

I stop, shocked at myself. Arguing like this in front of Betty – it's awful. We're behaving like children, like those squabbling kids we used to be, when we both lived at home with Mum and Dad. Betty's looking the other way, talking softly to the cats, pretending not to be listening.

'Not everyone has the good fortune to meet a perfect man – a perfect, *loaded* man, lined up to inherit his father's business – when they're barely into their teens,' Lauren hisses back, her voice shaking slightly. I start to reply, but she holds up her hand to stop me, going on in a calmer, quieter voice: 'You really have no idea, Julia. No idea what it was like, growing up with you – the big sister who had everything. Always the pretty one, the clever one, the popular one, the *healthy* one. The favourite.'

'That's ridiculous! The favourite? You must be joking. That was you! The spoilt baby, who got all the attention!'

'Because I had a fucking heart condition, that's all, for God's sake! Sorry, Betty, for swearing.' She raises her eyes as if she's counting to ten for patience. 'Do you think I *enjoyed* all those hospital stays, all those consultations, medication, operations? Of course our parents fussed over me – I nearly died! But they didn't love you any less, if anything they loved you *more*, because you were perfect. And I wasn't!'

Her voice has risen to nearly shouting again. I just stare at her, shocked into silence.

'You nearly died?' I repeat.

I supposed our parents kept that from me. Wanted to protect me from too much detail, perhaps. I knew she was a sickly baby, of course. I always thought she enjoyed all the fuss and attention, and probably made more of it than necessary. Even now, purely out of habit, I'm wondering if she's exaggerating.

'OK,' I say quietly. 'Tell me about it, then.'

Forty years previously

Lauren

Like most premature babies, I had problems, of course. I was obviously a low birth weight, and together with multiple other issues, my lungs were underdeveloped and I had a serious heart defect. I was kept in the neonatal intensive care unit to try to stabilise me, and eventually Mum was asked to consent to them giving me heart surgery. I can imagine how traumatic it must have been for her and Dad – apparently, I was still so very tiny they could hold me in one hand. Mum told me that several times after the operation, the beeps went off on my monitor and the doctors had to run to resuscitate me. They warned my parents that there was only a twenty percent chance I'd survive. Then, slowly, over the weeks, it grew to fifty percent, then eighty percent, and at long last I was allowed home. I was nearly four months old, and still very small, but brea!thing unaided and feeding OK. And I was going to need more surgery when I was bigger and stronger; they'd only risked doing enough, that first time, to give me a chance of life.

I was told all of this as I grew up. My parents didn't spare me any of the details; they wanted me to be aware, they said, of the reasons why they were overprotective of me. They wanted me to understand why I had to miss weeks of school for two more heart operations at the ages of five and eleven, and why I so often got ill. I think they also wanted to make it clear to me that I couldn't be like the other kids – healthy, robust, normal kids who played a lot of sport, who ran around in the playground without getting out of breath and weren't teased for being a namby-pamby, a weakling, a wheezy, sickly, girl who had to sit out of PE and games. I think, in a way, they encouraged me to think of myself as an invalid because they worried about me so much and didn't want me to *strain myself.*

'Don't run, Lauren, you'll strain yourself,' they'd say. 'Sit down, Lauren, you'll strain your heart.'

After I'd recovered from the final cardiac surgery, I was twelve years old. Plenty old enough to understand everything the doctors were saying.

'I'm OK, now, Mum,' I tried to convince her. 'The doctor said my heart will be as good as anyone else's now. He said it would be *good* for me to have more exercise. He said swimming would be –'

She held her hand out to stop me, her face creased with concern.

'And will that doctor be there, watching you, while you're swimming?' she demanded. 'Will he rescue you if you get into difficulties in the pool, or God forbid, in the sea? Will he run along beside you if you start racing with other kids – healthy kids –'

'Mum, I *am* healthy now! He said –'

'Lauren, you don't know what your father and I went through,' she said, her eyes filling up with tears. 'Watching you, day and night, for all those weeks while you were connected up to all the tubes and wires; watching the doctors struggling to bring you back to life after you stopped breathing! If you think we're going to stand by and let you kill yourself now –,'

It was hopeless. Every time I tried to talk to her about it, she'd get upset, and OK, I understood, I knew it must have been awful for her, watching me nearly die, having to nurse me and pray I'd pull through, I got it and I didn't want to upset her. But how could I help comparing my sheltered, protected life with that of my sister? Not only was she allowed more freedom than me, naturally, because of her age, but she was able to do all the things I was barred from because of me being *special*, as Mum insisted on calling it. And what made it worse was that Julia didn't even seem to appreciate her luck! She was clever – she always had her nose in a book – but she didn't work hard enough at school and left as soon as she could, whereas I became obsessive about keeping up with the other kids, the ones who hadn't had to have time off sick and fall behind. I worked so hard at keeping up that eventually I overtook them all and usually got the best marks, which didn't help my popularity one little bit. Not only a physical weakling who wasn't allowed to do anything fun, but now also the class swot! Added to which, because my parents had pampered me and overfed me from babyhood due to my underdevelopment, it had become a habit. So as I grew older, I never achieved a normal height for my age but I continued to overeat. I know why I did it: to cheer myself up when I was sitting at home on my own with my homework, no friends, and a sister who made it clear she resented me. I piled on the weight, which became a problem I've lived with ever since.

I'm short and plump, while my glamorous big sister is tall, slim and beautiful.

OK, I know I'm sounding pathetically sorry for myself now, as well as being jealous. But I suppose that's become a kind of habit too. I nearly died as a new-born baby, and presumably nobody told Julia, because they wanted to protect her from it. Pity they didn't do the same for me. By the time I was a teenager, believe me, I was sick of hearing about my infant brush with death. Julia was then eighteen and had already been going out with Phil, who'd been in her year at school, for at least three years. He lived in a nice big house, and he'd left school at sixteen, to work at his father's car dealership. He'd had his own car since he passed his test at seventeen, took her to lovely restaurants, bought her clothes and shoes and all kinds of presents. They were already talking about getting engaged, and my parents seemed totally thrilled about it.

I couldn't imagine any boys ever being interested in me, so I set my sights on having a good career. I was predicted to fly through my GCSEs and A-levels, and I decided I was going to go to university and do a degree in law; the rigorous study required for it appealed to me. It would keep me from thinking about how different my life might have been, if I'd been born healthy.

But I reckoned without what happened when I was eighteen. And I presume Julia remembers all about that, so I'm not going into it – I'm going to shut up now, as I can see I've ruined a pleasant morning with my saga of self-pity. Sorry, Betty.

And sorry, Julia – but you did ask. Now I've told you, so let's drop it, shall we? Honestly, I do appreciate you bringing me on this holiday, and yes, we've had some nice times together this week and you were right, it's been better than sitting around at home feeling miserable about Carl. But we never had anything in common when we were children, and we still haven't, now. So let's just enjoy the rest of this week away together, without trying to fool ourselves that it means we've suddenly become close after all these years. I think it's too late for that – don't you?

Betty

Oh dear. She really has got some hang-ups from her childhood, hasn't she, that one? As usual, I've pretended not to listen, just got up and pottered around, tending my plants. And I won't say anything, it's none of my business. Of course, she feels sorry for herself – it's not nice to listen to, all that self-pity and comparing her lot with her sister's. I can't blame her for feeling like that when she was young, but surely by now, for God's sake, she should have pulled her socks up and got over herself, especially as she says she's in good health these days.

But then again, she said something else happened when she was eighteen. Maybe her first broken heart? She's already hinted that that's happened more than once. Seems like she's unlucky in love, on top of everything else. I don't know why. She keeps comparing herself to her sister, but frankly, I think the older one is too thin – like a lot of young women these days, if you ask me. And I doubt whether her hair's naturally blonde. She looks good, of course – *groomed*. But the younger one looks more natural. She looks nice to me, not overweight, just right. It's a shame she hasn't got more self-confidence – that's probably all she's lacking.

I'd like to be able to fix the pair of them; they've obviously both got *issues*, as people insist on calling it now. And it's so sad to hear this one saying it's too late, that they'll never be friends now because they've never got along together before. I want to tell them that's wrong: it's *never* too late to mend things. They both seem to be enjoying their holiday here; if they really hated each other, they wouldn't be telling me what a nice time they'd had yesterday, out on the moor together with Nathan. I saw them walking past here earlier, to look at the greenhouses, and they were chatting together, smiling, looking up at the magpies in the trees – they looked *companionable.* That counts for a lot, in my book, if you can be companionable with someone, even if they're not your most favourite person.

The two girls are sitting here in silence, now. Julia's looking at Lauren with a horrified expression on her face. She didn't know her sister felt so strongly. They're so jealous of each other, for different reasons, and they both think the other one was their parents' favourite. I'd like to tell them to grow up, that life's too short, that they're lucky to have each other. But I can't do that. Instead, I sit back down and, if only to fill the very uncomfortable silence now, I tell them what I know about jealousy myself.

I know what it's like. For instance, I know it can make people jealous if you inherit something – like Julia's husband apparently inherited the business from his father. Believe me, it can even make you feel uncomfortable yourself, especially if you've only got it because of a much-loved parent passing away. It's a mixed blessing.

I only inherited Deepcombe Manor because both my parents died within a year of each other. I'd been living in London since I left college. Like a lot of young people, I wanted to get away from the countryside, from a boring small Devon village where everybody knew me and watched my every move! London was where real life was going on, where people didn't judge each other by the morals of the Victorian era. That's how I saw it at the time, anyway, although the shine wore off London for me after a while. But it wasn't London itself that kept me from coming back to Devon, it was somebody *in* London. Oh, I started missing Deepcombe long before I eventually came back. Missed it the way you'd miss your arm if it was cut off, to tell the truth. But it's hardly surprising that when I came back to live here again, in my thirties and pregnant with my son, local people didn't take too kindly to me at first. They saw me as a traitor, I suppose, and now an outsider – one of their own who'd abandoned the village in favour of city life up-country, and had the temerity to become the owner of the manor. Why should someone like me come to live in this big old house as soon as my father had passed away? What did I do to deserve it?

It was several years before they started to accept me again, but even now there's a few who view me with a kind of suspicion. It's like that, around here, if you go away from them. They hold it against you, find it hard to forgive. Forgiveness is a tricky thing, you know. It's hard for people to give it, and sometimes it's hard to accept it, too.

Julia

We walk back to the Lodge in silence. I haven't got my gloves on, and the bitter wind is biting at my fingers as I push my way through the frost-bitten bracken, my nose and eyes stinging with cold. The sky is a dark, sulky grey, and every now and then, flurries of sleet wipe across my face as if the clouds are spitting their angst at me.

I don't understand Lauren. I thought we were starting to get along better this week. I even thought it might be the beginning of a better relationship between us, but it feels as if she's just slammed a door in my face. I'm sorry, really sorry that I didn't know she nearly died as a baby, but honestly, is it my fault? Is *all* of it my fault? OK, so I suppose I was sometimes guilty of thinking she enjoyed all the fuss our parents made of her, and I accept that I got that wrong. But come on – when she had her last heart surgery at eleven or twelve, I'd have been seventeen. Yes, I was already seeing Phil, I was in love, I was happy. Probably I was a bit selfish, but who isn't, at that age?

'I'm sorry if I didn't take enough interest in you when we were younger,' I say, finally, when we're back in the warmth of the Lodge, but she just shrugs her shoulders, her back to me as she peels her coat off and flings it over the back of a chair. 'And what were you saying about something that happened when you were eighteen? I don't remember . . . remind me.'

She turns and stares at me, looking aghast, making me feel even worse. I guess she broke up with a boyfriend or something, and fair enough – if it was her first love, I can understand that, at that age, it would feel like the end of the world. But how does she expect me to remember now, after all this time?

'Oh, don't worry about it, Julia, if you don't remember. It doesn't matter now, does it,' she says. 'I wish I'd never mentioned it, never brought all that stuff up. Like you said, sitting in that conservatory, drinking Betty's hot chocolate, it seems to lull us into saying all sorts of stuff that should probably be left unsaid. Forget it.'

I want to push her into talking it over. I want us to be OK together – if not exactly *close*, because as she says, perhaps it's too late for that – to at least be able to chat, and have a few laughs together the way we've been doing over the last couple of days. But the set of her shoulders, the tone of her voice, tell me she's not going to be up for it.

'Cheese on toast for lunch?' I suggest, to change the subject. I go through to the kitchen, and she comes in after me, nodding agreement, getting cheese out of the fridge and cutting it while I put slices of bread under the grill. We eat in silence.

After we've eaten, I decide to make another trip to the village shop; I ask Lauren if she wants to come, but she pretends she's in the middle of reading something interesting in one of her magazines. Janice is in the shop again, and is just about to close up when I walk in.

'You'll have to learn the opening times, if you're staying here,' she admonishes me, handing me an A5 leaflet with the shop's hours printed on it.

'We're only here till Saturday,' I say. 'But thanks. Is it OK if I just grab a couple of things, or am I too late?'

'Go on, that's all right, I make allowances for outsiders,' she says without any rancour in her tone. She watches me as I whizz round the shelves as quickly as I can, dropping things into my basket. 'Got enough? You might not be able to come back for a couple of days. Heavy snow forecast.'

'Really?' I put the full basket on the counter and shake my head. 'I know it's cold, but –'

'Sleet in the air. Snow by nightfall,' she says, nodding with satisfaction. 'Sheep and ponies are all huddled together out on the moor. Always a sign of snow coming, that is. How's it going with the Wise Woman?' she adds with a little smirk.

'Betty's lovely. We were with her this morning, having a nice chat.' I hesitate over the *nice chat*, but she doesn't seem to notice.

'Watch out she doesn't put anything funny in your drinks, that's all I can say,' she says, laughing.

I stop putting items in my bag and stare at her. 'You mentioned that before. What exactly do you mean?'

'Oh, I don't rightly know. People have said they come over all *trance*-like after they've drunk a mug of her hot chocolate. It gets them talking about things they didn't mean to. Like they're under hypnosis, that's what Harry Dunn down the lane says.'

'Probably just the warm room and the warm drink, don't you think?' I counter. I'm trying to take a sensible stance, to remind myself what ridiculous gossip this is, but still, the memory of how I prattled on the other day, and how Lauren did the same today, nags at me. *Hypnosis.* Yes, that's exactly how it felt! Almost like some kind of . . . magic spell.

'Maybe you're right,' Janice says, unconcerned, as she rings up my final item. 'Anyway, stay warm and safe tonight, won't you, my lovely, it's going to be bad, mark my words. That's thirty-seven pounds, sixty-eight, please.'

'Janice in the shop says there's heavy snow forecast tonight,' I repeat to Lauren as I unload the shopping. 'She made it sound like there's going to be ten-foot-high snowdrifts, and polar bears sniffing around the place by morning.'

'Yeah. There's a red warning for snow in the West Country – it came up on my weather app.'

'Did it?'

'They always exaggerate, though, don't they? Anything rather than get caught out again like that year with the hurricane.'

I smile. I remember that day so well. Nineteen-eighty-nine. Lauren would only have been little, but I was twelve and at secondary school, and more excited about school being closed for the day than anything else. There was a huge tree down across our street, and an ambulance which had been called to take an old lady opposite to hospital had to stop the other side of the blockage, while the paramedics carried the patient on a stretcher down the road and climbed over the tree with her. My mum ran out into the street to ask if she could help. Our front fence had blown down too, and on the way back from talking to the paramedics she picked up the broken fence panels, one under each arm, and put them somewhere safe so that Lauren wouldn't cut herself on them. I suppose, looking back, that if it had been me that was seven years old at the time, I'd probably have been allowed to play with them, never mind the jagged edges, never mind splinters. I know Lauren has a point.

'I do get it,' I tell her, suddenly wanting to try again to breach the gulf between us. 'I know you were overprotected.'

'You don't get it at *all*,' she retorts. 'As I said, Julia, let's drop it and just try to –'

'But it wasn't my fault!' I insist, putting a packet of biscuits down on the kitchen table with such a thump that they've probably all broken. 'I was a teenager, I was probably a bit selfish, but come on –'

She gives a little snort, as if she'd laugh if it was even half-funny.

'Julia, it wasn't only when you were a *teenager* that you were selfish,' she says.

I turn to face her, startled. Where are we going now?

'What's that supposed to mean?' I demand.

'Well, where *were* you, all those years, after Dad left? When Mum and I were on our own? Mum could have done with some extra help sometimes, a bit of support, but were you ever around for her? Were you around when she got ill and needed some love and care? No, it all fell on me – not that I minded; after all, I was the unmarried one, the one who still lived at home because no rich man with his own business had wanted to marry *me* –'

'Oh, for God's sake, Lauren, enough of the bitterness!'

'Enough? No, it's not nearly enough! And yes, of course I'm bitter, why wouldn't I be? Don't get me wrong, I never minded looking after Mum. I nursed her through her cancer, I visited her in hospital, you came – what? – once, twice? And still she stuck up for you. *She's got her little boy to consider*, she said. *She's got the business to worry about.* As if that was any excuse for not coming to see your sick mother! And then, the final insult –'

She pauses, standing facing me, her eyes looking into mine, and I know exactly what she's going to say next. I feel myself actually shiver, because once this has been brought up, there'll be no going back, no glossing over it the way it's been glossed over for the past fifteen years.

'Let's drop it,' I mutter, looking away from her, picking up the biscuit packet again.

'No, let's not. *You* insisted on bringing all this up. Even when our mum was dying, Julia, even on the day I called you, leaving you messages at home, at your office, on your mobile – even *then* you couldn't tear yourself away from your own so-important life, to come and see her before she passed away! Is it any wonder I'm bitter? Any wonder I say we can't ever be close? Why don't you just piss off, Julia? This holiday was a mistake, I should never have let you talk me into it.'

I mustn't cry. I can't let her see me cry, because she's right, absolutely right, I was a bad daughter to our mum and I've had to live with that ever since. Of course, there's so much she doesn't know, doesn't understand, but I can't even begin to tell her that. She's stormed out of the kitchen now, and when I look back into the living room, I see her putting on her coat and her shoes.

'Where are you going?' I ask in a small voice.

'Out. Just out. I need some fresh air.'

'It looks like it's started snowing.'

'So what?' She opens the front door. The sleet, as I saw from the kitchen window, has already turned to snow – huge flakes of it, billowing across the doorway in the wind. She slams the door behind her. She surely won't stay out long in this weather. I bet she's going back to Betty's, probably to pour out more of my failings to her.

Is she right? Was it a stupid mistake to come on this holiday together? Until today, I thought we could make it work, even maybe try to repair our relationship a little. Perhaps I was mad to even think it. Too much water under the bridge.

I finish unpacking the shopping, make myself a cup of tea and sit down with my book, but I'm not reading it, the words are dancing about on the page, my mind is too full of the past, of regret and angst and shame. Lauren would never understand, even if I told her, and I couldn't blame her.

I think I must have dozed off for a little while, because when I wake up, my book's on the floor, my forgotten tea is cold in the cup and it's dark outside. It's past six o'clock. Lauren's been gone for nearly three hours, and when I look out of the window, I feel a jolt of shock. In the light from inside, I can see the snow's settled quite thickly, covering some of the fallen branches, and is still coming down fast. I'm annoyed with Lauren now. OK, I know she was cross, I know I shouldn't have pushed her into it, should have kept quiet and let things tick over the way they'd been doing, the way she suggested, for the rest of the week. But now, she's just staying with Betty to annoy me and get me worried. Betty won't want her there all this time. I'm going to have to go over there, if only to apologise and try to get her to agree to draw a line underneath today and try to start afresh tomorrow.

I pull on my coat and boots. Hers are standing inside the door – I sigh with exasperation as I realise she's gone out in her ordinary shoes. I'd better take her boots with me so that she can walk back in them. And her hat – I grab it from the hook as I put mine on and open the door. Snow blows inside on the wind, and I step out, turning on the torch on my phone as I take the first couple of steps towards the Manor. Then I stop, staring in horror at where my car should be parked.

I open the front door of the Lodge again and look across the room at the place on the dresser where I put my car keys. They've gone. She took them without me noticing. She's taken my bloody car. The stupid, stupid girl has driven off in my car, to God knows where, across Dartmoor in a snowstorm. I close the door again, find her number on my phone and press Call. No reply. What the hell? I don't know whether to be angry or frightened or both. What am I supposed to do – run down the lane looking for her? She could be anywhere by now. She could even be halfway back to London, except that she hasn't taken any of her things with her. Would she do that, is she really that angry?

It's only because I honestly don't know what else to do, that I open the door again and trudge through the snow to the Manor. I can't sit on my own, worrying, waiting for her to come back. I need to tell somebody.

Lauren

I'm all right now. I'll stay where I am for now – all night, if necessary. I'm just relieved to be safe and warm. I know I've been stupid. I had no idea where I was going when I walked out of the Lodge. I was so angry, I just needed to get away, and taking Julia's precious car was, in some childish, spiteful way, making me feel better. I didn't even care if I crashed it, I thought it would serve her right.

All I could think, as I started the engine and drove out of Deepcombe, was how the hell she dared to tell me not to be bitter? How would she feel, if she'd been the one left at home, left there because her life was already a mess and a failure, and on top of that, had to take on one hundred percent of the care of our mum? OK, Julia visited occasionally. Once in a blue moon. I actually remember her telling me once that she was only doing it out of duty. I know how *that* feels, too, because that was how I felt about visiting our dad. I think I went twice, during the entire time after they split up.

Thinking about this again now, a little voice of reason in my head starts whispering something to me, something I don't want to hear. It was trying to get through to me while I was driving, but I blocked it out by concentrating on controlling the car. I didn't get very far; it was impossible to drive at more than about ten miles per hour in the weather. To be honest I could hardly see where I was going, the snow was falling so heavily, swirling in giant waves across the windscreen, accumulating along the bottom and sides of the screen where the wipers were shovelling it up. It got dark soon after I left Deepcombe, sooner than it normally does even at this time of year, because of the thickness of the snow clouds. I ploughed on along those awful little narrow lanes, feeling sure that eventually I'd come to a main road, but I didn't. The roads got worse, the snow got deeper, I kept thinking I was going to end up going into a ditch or hitting a tree. Eventually I stopped, turned off the engine and cried.

I sat there for about half an hour, but it only took a few minutes of that time for me to pull myself together again. I spent the rest of the time giving myself a stern lecture. This was no good, I told myself. I was completely lost, and the longer I stayed there, the worse it would be, the worse the conditions were going to get. I'd end up having to call Julia and getting her to send out a helicopter or something to look for me. I was *not* giving her that satisfaction. I had no idea how to use the Sat Nav in her car; mine didn't have one, so I normally just used Google Maps to direct me. It would probably be quicker that way, than fiddling about with all the controls in this ridiculously techie car that I didn't understand. I put *Deepcombe* into Google on my phone and managed a splutter of laughter when the familiar voice directed me to *Turn around when possible.* It was never going to be possible to turn around, in a single-track lane bordered by hedges and covered in snow! I started the car again and crawled forwards slowly for another mile or two, until I came to a junction with an even smaller lane, where I managed a frighteningly precarious reverse turn, and headed back the way I'd come.

Forty-five heart-stopping minutes later, the headlights picked out the Welcome to Deepcombe sign by the side of the road and I nearly burst into tears again, in relief. The next thing I saw was the light from the window of the Duck and Partridge pub. On an impulse, I pulled into the car park. Now that I knew I was only five minutes from the Lodge, the sense of euphoria I felt was eclipsing everything else. I needed a hot drink, something to warm me up and soothe my rattled nerves. What I *didn't* need was to go straight back to Julia.

In view of the weather, I expected to find the pub more or less empty. I couldn't have been more wrong. It's crowded with cheerful people holding mugs of beer or glasses of wine, some sitting at the bar, others huddling around the big open fireplace, chatting and laughing together.

So I'm OK now. I'll stay here for a bit and then carry on back to the Lodge. Or not. Either way, I'm not worried anymore, and I'm just trying not to think about what I've done. Driving Julia's car, without her permission, without insurance, without knowing what I was doing or where I was going. She's never going to forgive me. I'm not sure I can really even forgive myself.

'What can I get for you, my lovely?' the big, florid landlord asks me as I grab a vacant bar stool and lean on the bar.

I'd intended to ask for a coffee, but seeing the woman next to me lift a large glass of red wine to her lips, I nod at it and say, without stopping to consider it:

'I'll have one of those, please. And a packet of crisps.'

The woman drinking the wine turns to smile at me. She's about my age, with cropped, bright red hair, an eyebrow piercing, nose piercing and a tattoo of a dragon – breathing fire – on her neck.

'You from London?' she asks.

'Yes. I'm on holiday here.' I find myself smiling back as I take my drink from the landlord and pay with my card. Lucky that I had it inside my phone case. I've come out without my purse. 'Some holiday!'

'Well, the weather's only to be expected this time of year,' she says, reasonably enough. 'I'm from mid-Wales,' she goes on, not that it would be hard to work out from her accent. 'The snow can be worse than this up there. Where are you staying?'

'At Deepcombe Lodge.'

'Oh, up at the Manor?' She grins. 'With the Wise Woman, is it?'

'So people say.' I really don't want to get drawn into another discussion about Betty. 'Oh, sorry – that's my phone.' I pull it out of my pocket, and it should, of course, be no surprise that it's Julia on the caller display. The fifth or sixth time she's tried to call me, but Mrs Google Maps' voice was the only one I was interested in listening to while I was in the car.

'Aren't you going to answer it?' my new Welsh friend says, a little too intrusively for an acquaintance of only a few minutes.

'No.' I take a big gulp of the wine and settle myself more comfortably on the stool. Julia can wait. I'll be back soon enough, and already I'm dreading the lecture I'm going to get. Not that I don't deserve it.

'Boyfriend? Husband?' she persists, grinning at me meaningfully. 'Had a row, is it?'

'Sister. And yes, we have.' I crunch a mouthful of crisps and wash them down with some more wine. 'And I took her car, and drove it through the snow like a lunatic. And got lost.'

Why the hell am I telling this to a complete stranger? She's still grinning, like it's hilariously funny.

'Don't talk to me about sisters,' she says. 'I've got four. And a brother. Couldn't wait to get away from them, that's why I've moved down here. Families can be hell on earth, can't they?'

I nod, but don't reply, because I'm thinking: she's got all those siblings, and she doesn't realise how lucky she is. Then I take the thought one step further: I've only got one sister, and no, we don't appreciate each other. I drink some more wine, to dull the shame that's slowly creeping over me. It isn't *all* Julia's fault. I know that, but I don't want to admit it. I can't. To admit it, would change everything, all our history, all of our parents' history, the way I've always thought of her. How I've always thought of *myself*. Or pretended to think?

I finish off the crisps, tipping the packet into my mouth to get the final crumbs out, and take a greedy further gulp of my wine.

'Anyway,' the other woman goes on. 'I didn't *only* move here to get away from them – my family. I was moving in with my girlfriend. I'm Fern, by the way. I live in the farm cottage, just over the road.'

'I'm Lauren,' I say. I wonder why she's here on her own. Perhaps she's had a row with her girlfriend. She seems to be somewhat focused on people having rows.

'Nice to meet you, Lauren. Andy – my girlfriend – is at home with our baby.' I glance at her, to see her face completely transformed by the mention of the baby. I feel something shift and soften inside me. 'Andy doesn't mind me coming over here for a quick drink, I've been working all day on the farm, and she knows what it's like. We're both farm workers, that's how we met. She's on parental leave at the moment. We adopted our little girl, Ella, a couple of months ago. She's nearly two.' She fishes in her jeans pocket for her phone, and scrolls through some pictures. 'Look. She's lush, isn't she?'

Dark haired, with big brown eyes, the toddler is sitting on a rug surrounded by toys, smiling at the camera, obviously as contented and loved as any child should be. My heart actually hurts. I smile and hand back the phone.

'She's beautiful. You and Andy must be so happy to have her.'

'We are. The adoption process is tortuous, though. Still a few more stages to go through before we can actually say that's it, she's completely ours, for ever. That'll be cracking. We love her more than anything.' Fern looks at her watch and finishes her wine. 'If I go back now, I'll be in time to see her before she goes to bed. Nice to meet you, Lauren. Enjoy the rest of your holiday – I hope the weather doesn't wreck it.' She gets down from her stool, gives me another smile and adds more quietly: 'I'm not the right one to say this, with my past history. But if you've come away on holiday with your sister, things can't be that bad between you. Go back and see if you can make it up?'

I don't reply. I don't even know this woman, she's broken up with her entire family, and yet she's gone on to get a girlfriend and a gorgeous little kid, and she thinks she knows what I should do? I'm not going to admit, even to myself, that she might be right. I drain my glass and ask for another. I won't be able to drive now, but what the hell? The snow's probably too deep anyway. Maybe the pub's got rooms; I'll stay here tonight, worry about it tomorrow.

'No rooms, my lovely, sorry,' the landlord says when, another hour later, I finally finish my third large glass of wine and ask him if I can stay. 'Can I call someone for you, to get you home? Where've you got to get to?'

'Only a little way down the road,' I tell him, getting up unsteadily. 'Not to worry. I'll walk.'

'Dressed like that?' he says, his face creasing with concern. 'It's like Siberia out there, you know.'

'I've got a coat,' I say, looking around for it, before remembering I took it off as soon as I got in the car, back at the Lodge, because despite the weather, my anger was making me hot. 'It's outside. I'll get it.'

'Be careful, lovely, the snow is –' he tries to warn me, but I'm already on my way out of the door. A blast of freezing cold air blows snow into my face as soon as I set foot outside. Heading for Julia's car in the car park, I sink into the snow halfway up my shins. One shoe comes off, and I nearly overbalance, trying to stand on one leg while I bend down to fish it out.

'I'll be all right when I've got my coat,' I tell myself out loud through chattering teeth. I'm wearing a warm jumper but the wind is so cold, and the snow is falling so fast and thick that it already feels as though I might as well be wrapped in a wet sheet. Pushing my feet forwards awkwardly in an attempt to keep my shoes on, I finally reach the car and shake the snow from my hair as I struggle to get the car key out my jeans pocket and unlock the car. Except that the car won't unlock.

'Come on, you bastard,' I mutter at the key. 'For God's sake. What's the matter with you?'

'I reckon the lock's frozen,' says a voice behind me.

I wheel round, losing both shoes this time as well as my balance, sitting down inelegantly, almost up to my waist in snow, my arms flailing, dropping the car key and swearing in a way I normally try not to. 'For God's *sake!*' I say again, trying and failing to get onto my feet.

'Sorry,' says the man looking down at me. 'I startled you. Here.' He holds out a hand to help me up, and reluctantly I take it, as I think, otherwise, I'd be sitting here in this snowdrift all night. I give myself a shake and wipe about half a ton of snow from my clothes. They all feel cold and wet, even my knickers.

'I've dropped the key,' I say, staring at where I dropped it. 'Oh God, I'll have to find it, it's my sister's car.'

'Here,' he says again, bending down and flicking a little of the disturbed snow to one side. He holds the key out to me. 'But I think the lock's frozen. You'll need to warm it, unless you've got any de-icer handy?'

'Not on me, no,' I say a little sarcastically. I'm shaking with cold now, every part of my body feels like ice and I think there are icicles hanging off my nose. My feet, still buried in the snow in just my socks, have gone completely numb and I'm wondering how long it takes to die from frostbite.

'I've got one in my jeep,' he says, starting to turn away and head towards a snow-covered vehicle I can see on the other side of the carpark. Then he stops, looks back at me and says a bit diffidently: 'But . . . um, I'm not being rude, but are you sure you're OK to drive?'

There's something familiar about this guy. I can only presume he was in the pub, although I didn't notice him. I guess he saw the way I was downing the red wine. Well, he's not wrong, to be fair.

'I wasn't going to drive,' I say. 'I just want my coat. It's on the passenger seat.'

'So how were you going to get home?' he says, staring at me as if I'm mad. 'You can't walk, in this weather.'

'I've only got to go a little way down the road.'

I want to ask him to stop talking and go and get his bloody antifreeze. I try to lift one foot out of the snow to avert the risk of dying from frostbite, and he looks down, noticing my socks. Blue, with pink spots, not that it matters – they're so wet I might as well not be wearing any. I see his eyes widen with surprise.

'You're not even wearing any shoes!' he says.

'I was. They've come off. They're down here somewhere –' I try to fish around in the snow for them and nearly overbalance again. He grabs my arm and doesn't let go. 'OK, that does it. Come on,' he says, tugging at my arm.

'What?' I feel a frisson of panic on top of the shivering and shaking I'm doing. 'Let me go, I just want to –'

'I can't let you walk home, it's ridiculous. Look,' he goes on, stopping for a moment in his attempt to drag me after him through the snow. 'I'm nearly fifty, I'm cold and tired myself, miserable and hungry and just want to get where I'm going and have a hot meal and an early night. I promise you nothing could be further from my mind than any dastardly deed you might be imagining –'

'But I've only got to go as far as Deepcombe Lodge,' I insist, shaking myself free from him. After all, no rapist or murderer ever admits to be planning dastardly deeds, do they. 'I'll be OK to walk once I've got my coat –'

'Deepcombe Lodge?' he says, staring at me. 'You're staying in the Lodge?'

'Yes.' And if I don't get going soon, I'm not going to be able to move. I think I'm slowly turning to ice.

'So you must be my mother's first guest,' he says, with a little chuckle.

'Your *mother*?'

'Betty. She told me she was expecting her first guests this week. My son's talked her into it. He's been doing the place up for her. Oh, for God's sake!' he goes on impatiently. 'Come on, get in the jeep, you know who I am now, I'm expected at the Manor tonight, I'm hardly likely to abduct you.'

I allow myself to be helped along again, abandoning my shoes to their fate. I'm too surprised to argue any more. He's Betty's son? Nathan's father? Suddenly, I realise exactly why he looked so familiar. His eyes, the shape of his mouth, his facial expressions, what I can see of the colour of his hair, even his build and the tone of his voice – they're all exactly like Nathan's but older.

'Betty didn't say –' I'm shaking so badly now that my speech comes out kind-of high pitched and staccato. 'She didn't say you were coming . . . Nathan said you moved away . . .'

'Don't talk,' he says, his voice gentler now as we reach his Jeep and he opens the door and helps me up. 'God almighty, you feel like ice; your clothes are soaked through. You're going to need to get yourself into the shower when you're back indoors. You've got to thaw out slowly, OK? There's no way you could have walked back. You'd have collapsed with exposure. What on earth were you thinking?'

'I don't know.' He's put the heater on, and I feel dangerously like either bursting into tears or falling asleep. 'It was stupid. I was cross with my sister –'

He pulls out onto the road, slowly but steadily ploughing through the snow. 'Thank God I was passing,' he says as we bump along the lane. 'I caught sight of you, standing there shivering by the car, with no coat, up to your knees in the snow, stumbling about, and I thought you must be drunk and I'd better help –'

So he wasn't even in the pub. He just stopped to rescue me. I feel tears threatening again, but they'd probably freeze in my eyes or form icicles on my cheeks so I swallow them back.

'I was a little bit drunk,' I admit. 'I wouldn't have driven. But I think the cold's sobered me up.'

He laughs. 'Seriously, don't fall asleep in those wet clothes.' He's already pulling into the entrance of The Lodge. How easy it seems, in the right kind of vehicle. He turns to look at me. His eyes are full of compassion, as if he knew me, as if I were someone he cared about. 'Promise me you'll get straight under a warm shower. Warm, not hot. Then wrap yourself in warm clothes. And have some soup, or a warm drink.'

Warm, warm, warm. The word rolls around in my brain, soothing me. I want to sleep, more than anything I can think of. Curl up and sleep.

'Don't sleep,' he repeats, 'until you've done all that, OK?' He gets out and comes round to open the passenger door. 'Have you got your key? Did you say you're with your sister – will she be there?'

'I expect so.' I hadn't thought about this. I haven't got the key, of course, I left in too much of a temper to think about that. 'Unless . . . oh God, I hope she hasn't gone out looking for me.'

He helps me down from the Jeep and takes my arm to lead me, shaking from head to toe, up to the door of the Lodge.

'I'll wait,' he says, knocking on the door for me. 'If she's not here, I'll take you over to my mum. She'll look after you.'

But almost immediately, Julia opens the door. Without a word, she grabs me in her arms and bursts into violent, noisy crying. And I faint.

Thursday

Julia

We didn't really talk last night. Lauren collapsed on the floor as soon as she came through the door, and when I tried to strip her freezing cold, wet jumper off her and run upstairs to get a duvet from one of our beds, she came round again, muttering about a warm shower.

'Warm,' she kept saying. 'Warm drink, warm shower.'

I didn't know who the man was, who'd brought her home. When I tried to thank him, he just waved it aside, asking if I needed any help getting Lauren upstairs, and repeating the advice about a warm shower.

'I'll come and check on her in the morning,' he said, making me wonder if he was a doctor.

I didn't even ask where my car was, what had happened to it, until this morning. It didn't seem to matter. I helped Lauren up to the bathroom, ran the shower for her and stripped her out of her wet things. Her skin felt like ice. Her feet – God knows where her shoes had gone – were blue.

'I'm staying here in case you faint again,' I told her.

But the warm water did seem to revive her a little. Once she'd warmed up enough, I wrapped her in a towel and, while she dried herself, went downstairs to make her a hot drink. And after she'd drunk her tea, I got her settled in bed, with the duvet pulled up to her chin and the heating turned up. Basil was lying across her feet on top of the duvet and she didn't even try to push him off.

'He's keeping my feet warm,' she said. 'It's nice.'

I went back downstairs to call Betty. I'd told her about Lauren driving off in the snow, in case Lauren might take it into her head to go there instead of coming back to me. Betty had been worried, of course, and offered to call the police, but I said we probably should give it a while before we panicked. Not that I wasn't panicking already. Betty and I had exchanged phone numbers and she asked me to call her and let her know as soon as Lauren came back.

But to my surprise, picking up my phone, I saw I'd already missed a call from her.

'I'm so relieved to hear your sister's back,' she said when I returned her call.

'Oh – how did you know?'

'Stuart told me. He's with me now. I didn't even know he was coming until this afternoon – such a lovely surprise!'

'Stuart?' I asked, frowning. But already, I was remembering how familiar I'd thought the face of the stranger had been, when he'd brought Lauren to the door. Like an older version of Nathan. 'Oh, is he your son, Betty?'

'Yes. It's the first time he's been back here since . . .' she stopped, tutting at herself. 'But never mind that, I called to ask how your sister is. Stuart says she was wet through and blue with the cold. I hope she's had a warm shower?'

'Yes. And a hot drink, and she's in bed now. I don't know what happened, Betty – I won't talk to her about it until the morning now, obviously, but it seems your son must have found her somewhere.'

'Yes.' There was a pause, and now – now that I know the full story – I realise Betty wouldn't have wanted to tell me Lauren had just been drinking at the village pub. It sounds bad, put like that, but I know, now, that there was more to it. That she'd got lost, frightened herself badly, and then lost her shoes, couldn't open the car door, couldn't get her coat, and, well, there's no point in making it any worse than it is. I'm too relieved that she's OK.

'I'm really very grateful to your son,' I said.

'He was worried about her. I hope she sleeps well and that she's quite recovered in the morning.'

'Thank you. Perhaps we'll come over and see you tomorrow. If the snow isn't too deep!'

I sat on the sofa for the rest of the evening, with the TV on, the sound low, and not really watching it. Lauren hadn't said much at all, apart from 'Sorry, I'm so sorry,' a couple of times. But there was just one thing she did say, just as she was on the point of falling asleep, which I can only dismiss as the trauma and exhaustion having taken its toll.

'I've never told you, Julia,' she muttered, her eyes closing, her voice faltering with tiredness, 'But there's one thing I really, really want, and it's not a husband or a boyfriend. I just want a baby.'

This morning, Lauren looks better, back to her normal self, but full of apologies and full of gratitude to Stuart.

'Your car's safe, it's in the pub car park in the village,' she says. 'I am *really* sorry, Julia. There's no excuse, you must be furious with me.'

'It's OK. Let's draw a line under it. I don't think it would be helpful to go over what we were arguing about yesterday.'

'No, you're probably right. But I did realise, as I was driving, that I was wrong to blame everything on you. I mean, I do know you took our dad's side when they divorced, so it was inevitable –'

'Lauren, let's leave it, please.'

'OK.'

We eat our breakfast in silence for a few minutes. Then she puts down her spoon and goes on:

'I only stopped at the pub because I was so relieved to be back in Deepcombe, knowing where I was, and feeling safe. I was going to get a coffee, but instead, I –'

'It doesn't matter. I doubt whether I'll be able to get the car back yet, though.'

It's still snowing; not as heavily as last night, but the snow is lying thick on the ground outside. I'm worrying about the fact that we're due to drive home in two days' time – but hopefully it'll thaw by then.

'And then, in the pub,' Lauren goes on, 'I met a girl – a woman – about our age, and she was telling me how she and her girlfriend have adopted a baby. A little girl. She showed me some photos. She's gorgeous.' She pauses, taking a mouthful of her porridge, and suddenly I know where this is going. 'I've decided that's what I'm going to do. You don't have to have a partner. Single people can adopt. I'm going to look into it. It's what I want.'

'Lauren, you had a bad experience yesterday, then you chatted to somebody in the pub who was happy with her own life – it doesn't mean it's right for you to do the same,' I tell her reasonably. 'I mean, good for her, but she's presumably in a happy, stable relationship –'

'Yes, and that's what I've been trying to do for years! *I* wanted that, Julia, I wanted that for myself – a happy, stable relationship, someone to have a family of my own with – but it's just kept going wrong. Every time, every man, they turn out to be all wrong for me, and now I'm forty and it's probably going to be too late now if I don't meet the right man really soon. And what if I never do? So I'd been thinking seriously about IVF –'

'What? What *are* you talking about? You've never mentioned IVF, you've never even mentioned wanting a baby before!'

'When did we last talk to each other about what we wanted from our lives?' she shoots back. 'When did we ever talk properly to each other at all?'

She's right, of course, and it shuts me up for a moment.

'Look, I really think this is all a bit too sudden,' I go on after taking a swallow of my tea. 'And just because you talked to someone in the pub, you can't suddenly decide –'

'There's nothing sudden about it. I've always wanted a child of my own, ever since you had Simon in fact. It's why I've been such a crap auntie to him. I was so jealous, so horribly jealous, I just kept thinking *When I'm a mum too, we can get together with our children.* I kept hoping one of the guys I've dated would turn out to be the one I could have a baby with. I came off the Pill so many times, but I never got pregnant.'

I stare at her. 'You tried to get pregnant? Did any of the men you were with even *know* what you were doing?'

'No,' she says quite calmly. 'I didn't tell them, because I was never sure if they'd stick around. It was my own decision, and if I got pregnant and they didn't want the baby, they could just bugger off and I'd bring it up on my own.'

'Oh my God. You realise you're making it sound as if you were just using your boyfriends as sperm donors, Lauren? But you were so devastated each time you went through a break-up! You told me Carl was the love of your life.'

'I thought he was. And I really thought, at the beginning, he'd stay with me if I got pregnant, that we'd bring up a baby together. But I know – I do know, now I've had a chance to think logically about it – that he wasn't right for me at all. I haven't met the right man for me yet, at all, and I'm forty now and perhaps I never will. So I'm just going to concentrate on having my own child, and forget about having a man to help me do it.'

I shake my head. I can't believe I'm hearing all this. But at the same time as feeling exasperated by what I can only think of as Lauren's naivety, I feel something strangely like admiration for her. If she's telling the truth – if this is really something she's been wanting, for all these years, and not just a ridiculous flash-in-the-pan of an idea based on the girl in the pub showing off her baby photos – then how can I not agree with her that she'd be better off going it alone, rather than continuing to have boyfriend after boyfriend in the hope that one of them will get her pregnant while she pretends to herself that she loves them? I can't criticise her. I've barely even known her for the last half of her life. Perhaps now I'm finally finding out who she actually is.

'Don't rush into anything,' is all I can say. 'Please, think it over really carefully before you do anything.'

'I'll have to. From what I've heard, the adoption process takes ages, and they go through everything with you: your motives, your lifestyle, your background, your home – it's very rigorous, and so it should be. I *have* thought about adoption already, obviously, but listening to Fern talking about it last night has decided me. It's better to give a new life to a child whose parents couldn't keep it, for whatever reason, than to try for IVF just so that I can have a new-born with half my own genes. That's not important. I just want to be a parent, Julia. To bring up a child, myself, before I'm too old.' She looks up at me, and I see the honesty in her eyes. 'Is that wrong of me?'

'No,' I say gently. I take her hand, across the table, and hold it in mine. 'It's not wrong at all. It's the most natural thing in the world. And I hope it works out for you, I really do.'

She holds my gaze for a moment and I get the oddest sensation. It's as if nothing that's happened to us, between us, over the past forty years has really happened, and we're just two sisters, like other sisters – sharing confidences, being each other's best friends, caring for each other. It lasts for all of two minutes before it becomes too much for me and I know I have to say something to break the spell and get us back to normal, or one of us is going to cry.

'But I still think you're still a complete prat for driving my car through that snowstorm last night and getting yourself lost,' I tell her, with a laugh to show I'm only partly serious.

'I know,' she concedes. 'I was a total idiot.'

And then there's a knock on the door – and it's Stuart, stamping his feet on the doorstep to shake the snow off his boots, brushing it off his hair, and smiling that smile that's so like Nathan's as I invite him in.

'Mum didn't want to be out in this weather, so she sent me to find out whether you're feeling better this morning,' he says to Lauren, and then adds quickly, 'And I wanted to find out myself, too, obviously!'

'I'm fine, thank you,' Lauren says. 'I'm so sorry to have been such a bother to you last night. Thanks so much for bringing me back.'

'Don't be silly. I couldn't leave you out there in the cold.' He turns to me. 'She thought she was going to walk home. With no shoes, and wearing wet clothes in the freezing cold! She'd have probably died from exposure and hypothermia.'

I gulp. I think I did realise how serious it could have been – but hearing it spelt out like this has made me feel, suddenly, quite sick. Just because we had a stupid row yesterday – a row about our past, about our mother – my sister went and put herself in so much danger, I could have lost her. I glance at her now, and she's looking back at me. I imagine she's thinking the same thing.

We can't ever let anything like that happen again. And even by deciding this, I realise I'm also deciding we're going to maintain our new relationship from now on. It's taken a snowstorm to bring us back together. There are still things she doesn't know about me . . . things that could change everything again. But I'll just have to carry on keeping them to myself.

Betty

Stuart's back fairly quickly from checking on Lauren.

'How is she?' I ask him immediately. I've been worried about her all night. They might be strangers to me really, but over the last couple of days, chatting with them and listening to their problems and arguments, I feel as if I've got to know these two sisters a little bit, and it was awful to see how worried Julia was last night. Awful, but at the same time, kind-of reassuring. Perhaps there's hope for them after all.

'Fine,' he says, and smiles. 'They've both walked back with me: they're waiting for you in the conservatory.'

'Oh!' I hurry out through the connecting door and find the two of them taking off their coats, hats and boots, padding over to the chairs in their socks. 'Are you warm enough?' I ask them. 'Would you like blankets or anything?'

Lauren laughs. 'We're not invalids, Betty!'

'Well, from what Stuart told me, you were pretty poorly last night. Are you feeling completely better now?'

'Yes, honestly, I'm fine. I'm just sorry I caused everyone so much worry.'

'We're very grateful to Stuart,' Julia adds. She still looks a bit shaken, to be honest. 'I dread to think what would have happened to Lauren if he hadn't been there.'

'It must have been fate,' I tell them. 'I wasn't even expecting Stuart to come, until he called me yesterday.'

He'd told me, when he called, that ever since he opted out of coming down for Christmas, he'd regretted it. It's been hard for him, obviously, to imagine living back here without Janie. But at the same time, it's been just as difficult for him being away from us – from Nathan, and me. But he had a few days off work, and suddenly decided to just get in the car and drive down, before he could change his mind. It's so lovely for us to see him. Nathan's missed his dad. On top of losing his mum, and of course, his marriage breaking up – that was hard for him too, admitting he'd made a mistake. I liked all his previous boyfriends, but that one – Ben – I never took to him. He was older than Nathan and I felt like he put too much pressure on him to get married. It was too sudden; I knew it wouldn't work out, not that it gives me any pleasure to say so.

Stuart and Nathan are heading towards us now out of the kitchen, Stuart carrying a plate of biscuits and Nathan holding a tray of steaming mugs, which are sliding precariously on the surface of the tray as they nudge each other, joking together about something. My heart does a little dance of happiness, seeing them together like this. Perhaps Stuart isn't finding it as difficult as he'd feared, being back here.

'Oh, I was just coming in to do that!' I protest, getting up to take the tray from them, but Nathan shoos me away and carries it to the table. 'I was going to put a little something special in the girls' hot chocolate.'

'Stop fussing, Gran, I can do that now if they want it,' Nathan says with a grin.

There's a moment of silence before Julia asks: 'Um . . . what kind of *something special*?'

I turn to look at her. She's looking startled, as if I'd sworn in church, and Lauren's eyes are wide too.

'A spoonful of brandy – to warm you up,' I say. 'I keep some in the kitchen specially – it's perfect for a day like this. But if you don't like it, don't worry, we won't put any in. Or . . . oh, oh dear, I hope you're not alcoholics or anything like that? Sworn off it? Or . . . it's against your religion or something? I wouldn't want to offend anyone.'

But Lauren's already laughing, and Julia's shaking her head.

'No, don't worry, we're not offended,' she says. 'But the drinks are fine just as they are, thank you!'

'How long are you staying here for, Stuart?' Julia asks as he and Nathan pull up two chairs and join us – along with the two cats, who've suddenly realised where everyone is and have come out of the kitchen too, to lie at our feet, purring.

'I'm only off work till Monday,' he says, and I notice he sounds quite regretful. 'But now I've done it – come back, got over the . . . *impact* . . . of being here again, realised how much I've missed the place, well, I'll be back again as soon as I can.'

'I'm sure your mum, and your son, are pleased to hear that,' Lauren says with a smile.

He turns to give me an apologetic look. 'Well, I'm just sorry it's taken me so long,' he says gently, reaching out to touch my hand. 'It was selfish of me to stay away like that.'

'You were grieving, Dad,' Nathan says. 'We understood.'

'But my place was here. You needed me. You've got your own work to do, son, and your own life to lead. You can't look after this place, keep it going, get all the work done that needs doing, on your own. Not that I'm not impressed by what you've already done – the Lodge and the holiday business – I've got to hand it to you, I never thought your gran would agree to it! But there's so much more to do. The patio, the grounds, the greenhouses – to say nothing of the inside of the house itself.'

'We can manage. Nathan and I,' I insist. 'We've managed so far.'

'But I need to come back.'

I feel the leap of hope in my heart, feel my breath catch in my throat – but I don't want it to show. I don't want to influence his decision. 'Only when you're ready,' I say firmly. 'And only if you're sure it's what you want.'

'Of course it's what I want.' He smiles. 'I just needed to . . . make myself come, this first time. I'll be OK now, Mum. I don't belong in the city. I'll work my notice and come back. For good.'

There's a silence that's so full of hope, and promise, and fragile, delicate possibility that for a moment none of us seem to want to break it. Even the two girls are sipping their drinks quietly, looking the other way, reaching a hand down to stroke Basil from time to time.

'Well, good!' Nathan says at last, and he gets up to give his dad a hug. 'Because we're not going to get any work done on that patio this weekend, are we, unless there's a sudden thaw!'

'Not much hope of that,' I say. We all turn to look outside, and despite the fact that the sky's still that threatening shade of grey and the snow's still piled deeply as far as the eye can see, with no sign whatsoever of any thaw, it has actually stopped snowing at the moment.

'I hope we're not going to get any more snow,' Julia says. 'I don't fancy driving home in this.'

'If you have to stay put, it's no problem,' I tell her.

'No, I need to get back!' she says, sounding quite panicked – so that even Lauren gives her a surprised look.

'Well, hopefully there won't be a problem. But if the roads *are* still dangerous, you've got the option. We haven't got any more guests booked in until the school half term next month.'

'Most people have probably got more sense than to book a holiday on Dartmoor in January,' Lauren says – and then she flushes and adds awkwardly, 'Not that it hasn't been lovely, as it's turned out, but –'

'But it was your ex who booked it,' I finish for her. 'And you'd have preferred a nice hotel somewhere hot.'

'Ah!' Stuart smiles at her and nods. 'I see. Well, we can't exactly take offence, then!'

'But he was a waste of space,' she goes on, firmly, with a decisive look on her face. 'And he didn't deserve me.'

There's not much any of us can add to that, so I offer the biscuits round and change the subject, asking the girls what they're planning to do today, in view of the weather.

'Well, I'm *not* going to get in Julia's car and drive off in a fit of temper again, that's for sure,' Lauren says, looking down at her feet.

'Thank God for that!' Stuart says, and we all laugh. She knows what she did was stupid – no point banging on about it, is there?

'I suppose it'll just be a quiet afternoon in the Lodge . . . perhaps another game of Cluedo?' Julia suggests.

'Well,' says Nathan, 'that sounds all very nice, but personally, I can only think of one sensible thing to do in weather like this.'

'What's that?' I ask him. I can see a gleam in his eyes. What's he plotting?

'Build a snowman, of course!' he laughs. 'Come on, guys. Coats on, boots on – have you girls got your gloves? Good. Race you outside!'

And I'm laughing as they jump to their feet, all talking at once, grabbing their coats, struggling into boots and hats and scarves and running to the outside door – the cats following them, meowing in consternation at all the fuss. And nobody seems to mind that I stay exactly where I am, sitting back in my chair, watching the two men I love more than anything else in the world, together with these two young guests of ours, laughing as they plough through the snow to make the most of this weather, to act like kids and not give a damn. And it's only for a fleeting moment that I wish I was young again. Then I'm laughing too, because from the window I see that they're leaving the embryonic snowman for long enough to scoop up handfuls of snow, chasing each other, forming themselves into two teams: the sisters against the father and son. And with shrieks of excitement, they begin a full-blown snowball fight. I close my eyes, smiling at the sound of their laughter, of young people enjoying themselves, as they should, while they can. And before very long, I'm falling asleep.

Lauren

It's been quite a while since I've enjoyed myself as much as this. I've been hit from all sides by snowballs, but I've given as good as I've got and all of us are screaming with laughter. Our pathetic attempt at a snowman is only about three feet high and hasn't even got a head yet, but by the time we've worn ourselves out with the snowball fight, none of us have got the enthusiasm to finish it off.

'Tomorrow,' Stuart suggests. 'I'll find an old scarf and hat for him.'

'It might have thawed by tomorrow,' Julia says, hopefully.

There's a silence as we all turn our eyes toward the grey, leaden sky. It's obvious to all of us that there's more snow up there. There's an unnatural frozen stillness to the air, now that we've all stopped laughing. A big old crow, watching us warily from a bare branch near the top of a nearby tree, gives a sudden loud caw and takes off, his wings flapping urgently to get himself airborne. A single large flake of snow lands on the sleeve of my coat, then another, then I feel one tickle my nose.

'It's starting again,' Nathan says, somewhat unnecessarily. He looks at us apologetically, as if he's personally responsible for the weather. 'It's forecast to get worse again during the night. Sorry.'

'Well, there's still time for it to thaw before Saturday,' I say, looking at Julia, trying to sound reassuring.

She doesn't say anything. She doesn't look reassured, either. She brushes snowflakes from her cheeks as we turn to head back inside, all of us a little more subdued now. It was fun while it lasted.

'I've got the kettle on again,' Betty says, to nobody's surprise, as we strip off our wet coats and boots. 'Sit yourselves down –'

'I'll leave you to it, thanks, Gran,' Nathan says. 'I want to get on with that work on the interior of the west wing, while I can.'

'And I'll help you, while *I* can,' Stuart tells him. 'I'm so glad to see you looking better, Lauren.' He gives me his lovely smile. 'I'll catch up with you both again before you leave, I hope.'

'Well, it looks like it's just us girls, then!' Betty jokes as the men head off. 'Sit down and get yourselves warmed up. I'll bring the drinks out.'

Julia and I have fallen silent now we're indoors again. We're both watching the snow – there's always something almost hypnotic about it: the dizzying flurries of white swirling out of the sky, falling, falling, in perpetual silent motion.

'Here you are, my lovelies,' Betty says from behind us, making us both jump. 'Get that down you while it's good and hot.'

'Thanks, Betty,' Julia says, taking a mug and holding it between her hands to warm them. 'I'm going to miss this when we go home.'

'I'm going to miss *you*,' she returns with a sad little shrug.

Strange, really, when we've only been here a few days – but it does feel like so much longer. With everything that's been said, and done.

'You're sure you're OK now, are you, Lauren?' Betty suddenly asks me, quietly, giving me a very direct look, and I feel myself reddening a little, with shame. It wasn't just Julia who worried about me, last night.

'I'm fine,' I say, wondering how to explain myself – because I think I should. One of the cats – Basil – is winding himself gently around my legs and I bend down to stroke him, so that I don't have to look at her or Julia as I go on. 'I'm sorry for all the worry I caused everyone. It was stupid, and childish, of me to storm off like that, and as for taking Julia's car – that was unforgiveable . . .'

'No it wasn't,' Julia says gently. 'Because I *have* forgiven you.'

'We had an argument,' I tell Betty, finally looking up at her. 'But it was my fault –'

'It usually takes two to argue,' Betty contradicts me mildly with a smile.

'Exactly,' Julia agrees. She's looking worried, like she doesn't want me to say any more about it, but I feel like I should. Betty's been good to us, and I've given her and Stuart a shedload of anxiety in return.

'It was . . . just going over old ground,' I tell her. 'From back when we were young. And it *is* my fault, because I've been carrying a stupid load of resentment around with me all these years about the fact that I looked after our mum when she was ill –'

'Lauren, don't let's go over this again,' Julia says, an edge to her voice, but I ignore her, because she needs to know this too. She needs to know I've realised I was wrong.

'I wasn't being fair,' I tell Betty. 'It's true that Julia didn't get involved with Mum, but it was inevitable. When they divorced, I stayed with Mum. I was only fourteen, you see, but Julia was older, nineteen and on the point of getting married –'

'I moved in with Phil,' Julia interrupts me. 'And naturally, you resented that.'

We're both silent for a moment, looking at each other carefully. We're not going to argue again. I'm going to make sure of it, this time. Anyway, it would be embarrassing to do it again in front of Betty. Perhaps that's why I wanted to say this now, rather than later, on our own.

'Yes,' I agree evenly. 'Of course I resented it. I was just a kid, I was jealous. But there was more to it than that, wasn't there? You took Dad's side in the divorce.'

Julia flinches as if I've slapped her. For a moment I think she's not going to respond; then she sighs, puts her mug down, and leans back in her chair.

'Yes,' she admits. 'Yes, I did. Well, let's say I sympathised with him, anyway. He put up with such a lot from Mum. She just didn't have time for him, Lauren – she was totally obsessed with *you*! She made you her life's work, her mission – looking after you, even after you didn't need looking after anymore. Fussing over you, watching your every move –'

'I didn't *want* her to! It wasn't my fault!'

'I know, I realise that – I've realised it more, this week, now we've spoken about it all,' she soothes me. 'But can't you see how it affected Dad? He felt left out. She didn't need him. Frankly, I understood why he found someone else.'

'Because *you* felt left out too,' I whisper – suddenly understanding. 'Is that it? That's why you understood?'

She shrugs. 'Never mind about me. I'd *found* my new life – with Phil. But Dad was lost. Lonely! When he met Pat . . . well, it was almost inevitable really. I'm not saying it was Mum's fault, but she had you: you were all she cared about.'

I feel tears threatening but blink them away. She's right. Mum was obsessed with my health – and although I hated it and pushed against it, I ended up staying with her and taking care of her. And after Pat, our step-mum, passed away, and Dad became ill and frail himself, he moved in with Julia and Phil. Well, they had a big enough house. It was no hardship for them. But all the same, I can't deny she did her bit, whereas I hardly ever saw him. I blamed him for Mum's decline into a lonely old age. Dad's in a care home now, and I can't blame Julia for making that decision for him; she told me at the time – in an email, we hardly ever called each other, any more than we do now – that he'd become incontinent as well as having dementia and was a danger to himself because he wandered out of the house while they were at work. Frankly, I just think it's sad that he's still alive, in his condition; he can't be getting any pleasure from his life.

'It wasn't that I didn't care about Mum,' Julia says. 'But –'

'But you were busy with everything else. Phil, Simon, the business. And Dad.'

'Yes. Although I can see, from your point of view, that it was no excuse.'

Betty's been silent through all this, but now she puts her own mug down with a thump on the table and says:

'It sounds like you've sorted yourselves out, then.'

We look at each other and smile. Put like that, it suddenly all seems so simple; so silly. So many years wasted in resentment and misunderstanding.

'I can't believe we've actually talked this over at last,' I say.

I feel, to be honest, like a weight's been lifted off me. But Julia's still looking a little wary, like she still feels we're on dangerous ground.

'You must be bored to tears with listening to us airing all our family's dirty laundry, Betty,' she says. 'Sorry. Why don't you tell us something about *your* life, for a change? I wanted to hear about the time you said you saw the Beatles.'

Betty laughs. 'Oh, you young things aren't interested in that, are you? Well, OK,' she goes on when we both urge her to. 'It was exciting, of course. I was a bit older than your average Beatles fan back then – there were lots of girls of about thirteen and fourteen in the audience. I was twenty-one. Old enough to know better, you might say, but it was . . .' She pauses, and looks away, out of the window at the snow, seeming suddenly to be miles away. 'It was probably the most exciting day of my life,' she finishes, so softly that I have to strain to hear her.

Julia and I exchange a glance. *The most exciting day of her life*?! Really?

'It was that good, was it?' I encourage Betty after a moment, as she still looks lost in thought.

'What?' She looks up quickly. 'Oh – the Beatles? The show? Well, yes, of course it was! It was their Christmas show. December nineteen-sixty-four, it was. At the Hammersmith Odeon.'

'You were in London, then?'

'Yes. I'd only been there a few months. I'd finished my teacher training and, like a lot of youngsters, all I wanted to do was get away from Devon and go in search of the bright lights! I took a job in a school in Fulham. That's west London – but of course, you'd know that, wouldn't you!' She nods to herself. 'I could only afford to rent a room. A bedsit, in a lodging house. The landlady was terrible, so strict, worse than my mother. I actually started to think I'd have been better off staying here at Deepcombe! But . . . then there was the concert, at Hammersmith.'

'And that made you feel happier?' Julia says, as Betty's fallen silent again, smiling to herself.

'Yes, of course – seeing the Beatles was, well – fab, as we used to say!' she chuckles. 'Although, to be honest, we could hardly hear a word of their songs because all these young girls were screaming the house down! Jumping up and down, screaming, crying, going hysterical!' She shakes her head. 'I was there with another girl from the lodging house; she was younger than me, about eighteen or nineteen but even she felt quite old that night.'

'It was obviously quite a memory for you, though, Betty,' I say, smiling. 'Very exciting!'

'Yes, it was. Exciting to be seeing them in the flesh, you know – up there on the stage, when all of us, at that time, were crazy about their records and had their pictures on our bedroom walls. Well, of course, I was a professional young woman by this time; I'd just done my probationary term as a teacher and however excited I was to be seeing the Beatles, I couldn't have shown myself up by jumping up and down and screaming like those young girls.'

'But it obviously made a big impression on you. To still remember it so clearly, after all this time,' I point out.

'Yes. I'll never forget it,' she says with another strange little smile.

'And did you stay in touch with that friend – the girl you went to the concert with?'

'What? Oh, Helen? No, I didn't. I lost touch with her . . . when I moved out of the bedsit.' Betty looks out at the snow again, a faint smile still playing about her lips. 'I lost touch with her that same night, to be quite honest,' she goes on after a moment, the smile twitching. Then she sits up straight, looking suddenly far more business-like, and says in a completely different tone of voice: 'Anyway, that's quite enough about me and my silly old memories, you must be fed up with listening to me droning on –'

'Not at all! It's fascinating, Betty – go on, please! Where did you move to after the bedsit? How long did you live in London for?' I ask her – but she's shaking her head.

'No, you wanted to hear about the Beatles, and that's it. I never got to see them again. Always loved their music, though.'

'Well, I expect we've tired you out quite enough for one day, Betty,' Julia says, and I nod agreement.

'Wrap up well, my lovelies, won't you?' Betty says as we get up to leave. 'It's looking like Siberia out there again now.'

'Well, at least we haven't got far to go!' I joke.

I know Julia's getting anxious about the weather for going home. So I can't admit to how I'm beginning, weirdly, to feel; and I know it's just because I'm on holiday. I'm relaxed – more relaxed, probably, than I've been for months. Maybe years. And I'm starting to feel like I don't care if I never go home at all.

Julia

We haven't been back in the Lodge for long, and in fact I'm just looking in the fridge to see if there's anything for lunch and wondering if we're going to have enough food to last us till Saturday, when there's a knock on the door – and it's Stuart and Nathan, stamping the snow of their boots and brushing it off their heads, faces red from the cold.

'We're taking the Jeep into the village for some shopping for Mum,' Stuart says, 'and we wondered whether you need anything?'

'Oh, I was just wondering the same thing!' I admit. 'I was going to use up the last of our ham for a sandwich for lunch, and then perhaps walk down to the shop –'

'You really don't want to be walking in this,' Nathan says. 'It's very deep in places.'

'Besides,' Stuart says, smiling at Lauren as she joins me at the door, 'there's room for us all in the Jeep. And we were thinking it might be nice to have lunch at the Duck and Partridge as well as doing the shopping.'

'They do sausage rolls and Cornish pasties,' Nathan says. 'But of course, if you'd rather have a boring old ham sandwich –'

My mouth's watering at the thought of a Cornish pasty. 'But are you sure we wouldn't be in the way?'

'Yes – you two have only got a few days together,' Lauren agrees. 'You don't want us crowding you, surely.'

'Well, it looks like Dad's only going back to London for long enough to work out his notice,' Nathan says, smiling at his father. 'So we're going to be seeing plenty enough of each other before too long.'

I'm so happy for them both, I almost feel like giving them both a hug, but after all, we still hardly know each other.

'That's excellent news,' Lauren says. 'Well, in that case, if you're celebrating with a sausage roll or a pasty, I think we should join you!'

The Jeep glides effortlessly through the snow as if it's melting beneath the wheels, but appearances are of course deceptive. Stuart's got snow chains on, and he's driving carefully, slowly, the wipers clearing fresh snow at every swipe. When he pulls in to the pub car park, I suddenly feel quite sick on seeing my car still stranded there.

'Will the battery be all right when we need to start the car?' I ask quietly.

'It might not be. But don't worry, we can jump-start it,' Stuart says, as he opens the rear door for me. 'It'll be fine. I'm more concerned about where your sister's shoes might be!'

At least he's managed to make me laugh – and Lauren, too, although she's hanging on my arm and whispering 'Sorry!' in my ear yet again, as soon as she's out of the Jeep.

We trudge across the carpark to the pub, and I'm stamping snow off my boots when Nathan touches my arm and says, 'Actually, let's all take them off here.' He points to a shoe rack in the porch, where several pairs of wellies and walking boots are already stacked, a plastic tray beneath the rack collecting the melted snow dripping from them. 'There's a good carpet in here. We'll be OK in our socks.'

In fact it's nice, treading softly in our warm socks across the thick carpet to the bar. Nathan and I get ourselves a glass of wine each, but Lauren looks slightly aghast at the sight of a glass of red wine, and says she's sticking to coffee today. And Stuart has the same, as he's driving.

'It might only be just down the road,' he says, 'but in view of the conditions –'.

'Yes.' Lauren nods at him. 'You're a lot more sensible than I was yesterday.'

'Don't keep beating yourself up now,' I remind her.

'No. We can do that for you!' Stuart teases her.

I watch the two of them, smiling at each other, as we take our drinks and go to sit at a table in an alcove near the fire. I'm wondering – as I always do, out of habit – if Lauren's taking an interest in him. To be fair, she doesn't seem to be. And I know I made a fool of myself for suggesting she was interested in Nathan, but the father is much closer to Lauren's own age than the son is! If anything, I think it's Stuart who's subtly watching Lauren, rather than the other way around. But perhaps it's just concern – after all, he was the one who found her last night and brought her home.

We've just started on our drinks, waiting for our various orders of sausage rolls, pasties, and chips to be delivered, when I see Lauren's own eyes suddenly light up in surprise as a couple of girls pass by our table on the way to the bar. They're both very striking; the bigger girl has really short hair, dyed a bright red, piercings, and a dragon tattoo on her neck that abruptly reminds me of the title of one of my favourite thrillers from years back. She has an arm casually resting around the shoulders of the shorter, slimmer, girl – who has dark hair, cut in an asymmetric style, and is wearing a black leather jacket and a massive purple scarf. She's also holding the hand of a little dark-haired toddler, dressed in a blue coat, yellow woollen gloves and a bobble hat to match.

'Hi, Fern!' Lauren calls out, and as the red-haired girl turns and sees her, returning the greeting, I realise who this is.

'Hi Lauren. Nice to see you again. This is Andy –' She indicates her partner, then smiles down at the child, 'And this is Ella. Say hello to Lauren, Ella.'

The child, evidently struck dumb with shyness, gives us all a fleeting glance and then covers her eyes with her fingers, making Fern and Andy both laugh.

'This is my sister Julia,' Lauren introduces me. 'And –' She turns to indicate Stuart and Nathan, but Fern is already saying hello to them.

'We know everyone in Deepcombe,' she explains with a grin. 'It's not exactly a metropolis! So you're back now from London, Stuart, is it?'

'Temporarily at the moment, Fern – but I'm planning on making it permanent as soon as I can,' he tells her. 'So how are you both getting on with this little one? Mum told me the adoption had gone through. When I left for London, you were still in the process of it all.'

'It was a long process, too,' Andy says. 'But it's all been worth it, hasn't it, Fern?' She smiles up at the other girl. 'Ella's a little angel, she's fitted right in with us as if we'd always been her mummies.'

They both look down at the child with such tenderness that I can't help feeling a tug at my heartstrings.

'How come you're in the pub like this on a working day, you shirkers?' Nathan teases them.

'Andy's on parental leave,' Fern explains. 'And I can't do a lot in this weather. Been up at the farm this morning to make sure all the sheep are safe but Paul sent me home till the snow lets up. So we figured we could treat ourselves to a little bit of lunch here.'

'Sausage woll!' little Ella pipes up eagerly, making us all laugh so that she smiles coyly and puts her thumb in her mouth, before realising she's still got her gloves on.

'Come on, Ella, let's get those gloves off, hat off, coat off and find a nice table while Mami goes and orders your sausage roll!' Andy says. 'And an orange juice, is it?' She turns to us as she's pulling the little girl's gloves off for her. 'I'm Mummy, Fern's Mami – the Welsh version. You'd think it might be confusing, but this little one's got the hang of it right away. Obviously highly intelligent, even if she hasn't inherited it from either of us! Catch you later, guys, have a nice lunch.'

Lauren's watching them walk away, a wistful look in her eyes.

'Glad it's going well for them,' Stuart says, and Nathan nods agreement. 'They're a nice couple of girls. Settled well here in the village, everyone seems to like them.'

'It must be tough, though – going through that long process, as they said,' I comment, giving Lauren a pointed look.

'I'm sure it was tough.' Nathan shrugs. 'But I guess, if you want something badly enough, you'll be prepared to wait for it. Worth it all now, for the pair of them, I'd say.'

'Yes, that little one's certainly a cutie!' Stuart agrees. 'Good for them.'

Lauren doesn't say anything. She's watching Andy settling Ella in a highchair and giving her some things out of her backpack to occupy her – a cuddly toy, a picture book, some paper and a couple of crayons.

'Anyone want some crisps while we're waiting for our lunch?' she asks suddenly – and before we've even had time to answer, she's on her feet, heading to the bar, where she joins Fern and starts up a conversation with her. It doesn't take a genius to know exactly what she's talking to her about.

Despite everything Lauren told me last night about how long she's wanted a child of her own, it's still all so new to me that I can't help the shiver of anxiety I feel. I hope she's not getting carried away by the vision of this perfect little family. Fern and Andy have each other for support; if Lauren's serious about this, she'll be taking on a child alone. I'm worried that she's idealising the whole scenario.

But I mustn't say anything. I've got to stop thinking of her as the little sister who was spoiled by our mum, who makes terrible life choices and even worse choices in men. The reality is that she's forty now, not fourteen, and I'm only just getting to know her properly after all these years.

She returns to our table after a few minutes with her phone in her hand. I presume she's exchanged numbers with Fern, that she's told her she's thinking of applying to adopt and they're going to keep in touch. Well, that can't hurt, can it? At least she's talking to someone who's been there, done that.

'What happened to the crisps?' Nathan asks, looking puzzled.

'Oh – there were too many people at the bar,' Lauren says casually. 'Anyway, look, here's the guy with our lunches.' She breaks into a grin and raises her coffee cup as the plates of food are put in front of us. 'Cheers, everyone!'

'Cheers!' We all raise our own cups or glasses in response.

'Here's to you girls – our first holidaymakers!' Nathan says.

'Yes. I hope you've both enjoyed your stay, despite . . . well, the weather! – and everything,' Stuart adds.

He gives Lauren a smile, then looks down at his plate as if he's giving his pasty his complete concentration. I wonder what he'd say if he knew that, I'm pretty sure, she's far more interested in Fern and Andy's little girl than she might be in him!

Friday

Lauren

Julia's looking anxiously out of the kitchen window when I come downstairs for breakfast this morning.

'It's stopped snowing,' I say, hoping to make her feel better. I know she was worried all day yesterday about whether we'd be OK for going home tomorrow. Personally, I'd be happy if we had to stay here for another day or two. But of course, her work is far too important for her to take more than a week off. I'm trying not to feel goaded into saying anything, but honestly, anyone would think she held an important position in the government or the Bank of England, the way she keeps looking at her phone, checking for emails or missed calls, going off upstairs to make a quick call herself every now and then, all secretively, as if I could care less what she talks about with her ex-husband or colleagues at the stupid car dealership.

'I know,' she says. 'But it doesn't look like it's thawed at all.'

'Well, if I have a look at the weather app on my –'

'I've already looked. It's not going to be any less cold today,' she snaps – then sighs and apologises. 'Sorry, I'm just so worried about what happens if it's still like this tomorrow.'

'Stuart said he could jump-start your car if the battery's flat.'

'I know, but driving conditions look terrible. It'll be OK once we get to the motorway, but there's a hell of a lot of these little minor roads to get through, before we even hit an A-road.'

'I know.' I relent. It's unfair of me to criticise her for worrying about it – she's the one doing the driving, after all. I have a sudden flashback to the day we arrived here, when I was still in such a state about Carl – crying nearly all the way from London, being completely ungrateful for what Julia was doing for me – and I warm to her slightly, thinking about how she's had to put up with me. Was it really less than a week ago? It feels like months. I feel like I've changed, completely, since we've been here. 'I'm sorry I've been such a pain in the arse,' I say.

She turns and looks at me in surprise.

'You haven't been. Well, OK, perhaps at first,' she concedes, with a little grin. 'But . . . I think you're feeling better now, aren't you? It's done you good, being here.'

'Definitely. You were right. It was the right thing to do, coming here, even though it wasn't exactly what we were expecting.' I pause, then go on: 'But I'm not sure it's done *you* good.'

'I'm OK. It's been OK here, apart from the snow. And I'm glad you and I have . . . I think . . . managed to get to understand each other a bit better.'

'Yes.' Perhaps. Although I'm not going to tell her I still don't understand *her*. Not at all, really. Even though we've said we straightened things out yesterday about why she took Dad's side in the divorce, it doesn't really account for her not even coming to see Mum when she was dying. Despite my view of Dad, I'd go and see him if *he* was breathing his last. Even if it was just to ease my own conscience.

'Hopefully the rest will have done us both good,' Julia's going on, evidently trying to convince herself it hasn't been all bad.

'But you've still been worrying about work!' There, I've said it, despite my best intentions to keep off the subject. 'You haven't really given yourself much of a rest – you're still making calls, looking at emails –'

'Only a few important ones,' she retorts. 'I . . . needed to.' She stops, looking down at her feet, sighing. 'Oh, all right: if you must know, I've been worried about Phil. He hasn't been well.'

'Oh. Well, I'm sorry to hear that. I suppose, if he's off sick, it has implications for the company. I suppose he would have wanted you back at work.'

'It's not just about my job, Lauren. It's about him. He's not well! Oh, look, forget I said anything –'

'OK. Well, I hope he soon feels better, then.' I can't really understand her level of agitation. It's obviously the business she's worried about, whatever she says, not her ex-husband having the flu or whatever! 'Come on, let's have some breakfast. Don't keep looking out of the window, it's only making you more anxious.'

I think we're both at a bit of a loose end this morning. Once we've had breakfast and cleared up, Julia settles down to read her book. I've finished all my magazines and I start wondering idly whether to attempt one of the jigsaws on the shelf in Julia's bedroom, where the board games are. But if I start it now, I doubt I'll be able to finish it by the time we're supposed to be leaving tomorrow. I'm just about to suggest we could try going for a walk, if only to see exactly how deep the snow is on the road now, and whether it's thawed even slightly, when there's a sudden clatter of the cat-flap in the kitchen and a loud howl.

'One of the cats is having a moan this morning!' Julia says mildly.

And then, all hell is let loose. The howl is repeated, at twice the volume; followed by a horrible, long, blood-curdling scream that sounds more human than feline, and then a thump. Julia throws down her book and we both run into the kitchen, where poor Rosie is lying slumped on the floor, bleeding from her mouth.

'Oh my God! What do we do?' Julia says, staring at Rosie in horror.

I kneel down next to the cat. She's conscious, but her breathing is very fast and shallow. I try to look at her mouth but she gives a deep growl of warning. She's obviously in too much pain for me to try to see where the blood's coming from, and I don't want to frighten her into running back outside.

'Lock the cat-flap,' I say quietly to Julia. 'And pass me the kitchen towel.'

At least I can try to make Rosie comfortable, as well as soaking up some of the blood.

'I'll call Betty,' Julia says as I'm covering Rosie with the towel. The poor cat's trembling, and I'm worried about her going into shock. 'She gave me her number the other night, luckily, when you . . . went missing.'

'Pity we haven't got Nathan's mobile number, or Stuart's. I'd rather have told them first,' I say. 'This looks serious, Julia. There's such a lot of blood. They need to get her to a vet quickly.'

Julia's talking on the phone now. And thank God, it sounds like it's Stuart who answered – I presume it's Betty's landline.

'Stuart's coming over right now,' she says. 'He's bringing the Jeep round so they can carry Rosie straight in. Nathan's coming with him so he can hold her, while Stuart drives.'

They're here almost immediately, Nathan carrying a cat basket, blanket and some more towels. He picks Rosie up with the utmost gentleness, but she growls again and cries out loudly with pain.

'I reckon the vet might have to sedate her, even to look inside her mouth and see what's going on,' Stuart says anxiously as Nathan lowers her into the basket.

'Come on then, the sooner we get there the better,' Nathan says. 'Thanks for helping her,' he adds to us as he carries the yowling cat to the front door. 'Maybe, if you're not busy, you'd like to go and sit with Gran? She's in a bit of a state. She loves these cats. She wanted to come with us to the vet's but we didn't think it was a good idea.'

'Just in case . . .' Stuart adds grimly.

And they're gone, the sound of the Jeep finally drowning out poor Rosie's cries.

'You did well, there,' Julia says to me as we both stand, slightly shaken, looking at the blood-soaked towel on the floor. 'I panicked a bit – it all happened so fast. But you didn't.'

'I've done a first-aid course,' I tell her. 'Although it didn't cover cat injuries, to be fair. Come on, let's go and sit with Betty, like Nathan said.'

'Yes. I'll just rinse the blood off that towel, though, before it's too late. And – oh!' she says, as she picks the towel up, 'there's some blood on the floor too. Oh, poor Rosie.'

'It might not be as bad as it looks. Mouths tend to bleed a lot – like scalps.' I grab a kitchen roll and clean up the floor while she rinses the towel in the sink. 'I always knew that first-aid course would come in handy.'

I don't know why I'm trying to make light of the situation; perhaps it's just easier than dwelling on the worst possible scenario. We both pile into our coats, boots, hats and gloves and head out into the cold.

'Perhaps it *is* thawing a little?' I suggest to Julia as we trudge through the snow towards the Manor. To be honest, I'm not sure that it is. The snow is still deep enough to go over the tops of my boots and my socks are already wet. Hers are probably the same, because she doesn't bother to reply.

Betty looks close to tears when we arrive at her kitchen door, having left our boots (and wet socks) outside the conservatory.

'What happened?' she asks, sitting down in one of the chairs and gesturing for us to do the same. 'Stuart said you just found her in a pool of blood. Poor little Rosie!'

We tell her, as gently as possible, what little we can about Rosie's condition, and try to reassure her that the vet will be able to find out what's wrong and do whatever's necessary to sort it out.

'Sit still,' I protest when she starts to get up from her chair, muttering about making us a hot drink. 'We're fine. We've only just had breakfast.'

'Let's talk about something else for a little while,' Julia suggests. 'Before we know it, they'll be back . . . or at least they'll call us to let us know what's happening.'

She nods. 'All right, then. Well, I bored you both to tears yesterday telling you about my Beatles concert. So how about you talk to me, now? Tell me what you're both going to be doing when you go home?'

Julia looks away, as if it's the last thing she wants to talk about.

'I suppose you'll both be back at work on Monday?' Betty goes on regardless.

Still nothing from Julia. It looks like it's down to me to make conversation.

'Well, yes,' I say, 'Back to work, unfortunately. Not that I get much pleasure from my job, to be honest – or much of a salary, either! In fact, I'm seriously thinking of handing in my notice when I get back.'

Where did *that* come from? I sit back in my chair, feeling shocked at myself. Am I really thinking of leaving my job? It isn't a decision I've made consciously, but yes, if I'm honest, while I've been here at Deepcombe I've gradually become aware of the fact that the life I'm living is shit, to put it bluntly. It's not the life I want, in the slightest.

'But I've got no idea what I *do* want to do,' I go on, quietly. I've almost forgotten I'm talking to Betty and Julia. I'm . . . kind of thinking aloud. 'But I want something completely different, from now on. A new life.'

'Where's all this coming from?' Julia asks, sounding a bit irritated. 'A new life? As *well* as adopting a baby?'

'A baby sounds like quite a new kind of life, in itself,' Betty says, without sounding particularly surprised.

'I know; but that's not something new. It's what I've wanted for a long time – I just hadn't told Julia before,' I explain, conscious that I'm sounding like I need to justify myself. 'But I've decided, now, to apply for adoption. For definite.'

'Well, I wish you all the very best.'

'Thank you, Betty.'

There's a silence, but finally Julia says, 'So do I, Lauren. I've always only wanted you to be happy. It was just – such a complete shock to hear about it.'

'There was such a lot we didn't know about each other,' I point out.

'Yes. And now you're saying you want a new job, too. Doing what?'

'I don't know!' I sigh. 'Come on, you did know I'm not happy, not satisfied, with my job. I never wanted to be a secretary – an *assistant* secretary, at that! I wanted to be a lawyer, originally.'

'But you dropped out of uni.'

I stare at her. '*Dropped out*? Is that really what you think? For God's sake, I didn't drop out, I never *went* to uni. I was offered a place, conditional on my A-levels, but in the event, I never even took them –'

'I thought you did? I thought you got fantastic grades and –'

'I was predicted to get good grades but there was a little blip along the road for me at that point, Julia, which seems to have somehow skipped your notice!'

Julia's looking stunned. I must look much the same – I can't believe she really isn't aware of this. She must have known, at the time. She's forgotten. Well, that shows how much she really cares, doesn't it!

'I don't know what you mean,' she says. 'I'm sorry, Lauren. What – were you ill, again? Honestly, I never knew. Nobody told me.'

I look at her more carefully. She does actually look shocked. Perhaps she really didn't know.

'No, I wasn't ill,' I say. 'It was . . . well, it was an *incident*. I brought it all on myself, if you must know.'

And suddenly, I get it. Mum was so ashamed. Dad was so angry. They didn't want anyone to know, not even my sister. And of course, who am I kidding? I was too ashamed, myself, to talk about it to anyone. It was a disgraceful chapter of my life. I don't even, really, want to tell Julia now, but I think I need to. I think I want her to understand . . . if that's possible. I take a deep breath, and prepare for her to be appalled.

Twenty-two years previously

Lauren

By the time I was seventeen, going on eighteen, I'd had to come to terms with my parents' divorce. I blamed Dad entirely, with the righteous indignation, and lack of understanding, of the young, and despite the fact that I could hardly blame him for being driven mad by my mother. She drove me even madder, but I put up with it, siding with her over Dad's infidelity, trying to forgive her for, even now, wanting to mollycoddle me as if I were still an invalid.

In fact, I was now a healthy teenager. I'd managed to slim down slightly, I'd made some friends, and now that Julia was married and living a completely separate life from me, I'd also shaken off my inferiority complex. I wasn't the sad, sick, lonely little sister anymore: I was doing well at school, I was confident, and I felt *normal*. During the first couple of terms of the sixth form I worked as hard as ever, anticipating good results in my A-levels in Law, English and History. I'd been predicted to get good grades in all of them.

I'd even had a boyfriend, of sorts. Raj was a boy in my English group. I liked him – and he obviously knew it – and I suppose it was only natural that he thought he was in with a chance, so he hung around with me, and came to my house so we could do homework and revision together. And inevitably, one day in the school Christmas holiday when Mum was at work, we had sex. It wasn't good, for either of us. I suspect it was his first time too, although he didn't admit to it. Anyway, I didn't like it, and I didn't want to see him anymore afterwards, but at least I felt like I'd got it out of the way. I could join in the chat and jokes about it with the other girls, and some of us were already agreeing that it was more fun to hang around with our friends.

And there was one particular friend I got closer to around that time. Her name was Callie, and she was the tough, loud, sweary ringleader of the girls who tended to get into trouble. Up till then, I'd steered clear of them. I couldn't understand why they'd stayed on for the sixth form if they just wanted to mess around in lessons. But for some reason, now, she latched onto me. Perhaps even her usual crowd were getting tired of her, finding her a bit too much. And looking back, I can understand now why I got in with her. I was flattered. After so many years of being unpopular, it felt unbelievably uplifting to be approached by the girl everybody was . . . wary of, but also a little bit in awe of.

It started gradually. She'd sit next to me at lunchtime and confide stuff to me, things the other girls had told her, things she'd somehow found out about some of the teachers. Stuff about the boys – always derogatory but hilarious. Her stories made me laugh, and I suppose they made me admire her. I admired how she didn't care: didn't care how many times she got threatened with suspension, didn't care whether she failed her exams, didn't care what anyone thought. It was liberating to be with her, to hear the casual way she dropped stuff into conversations that I secretly found shocking, but pretended not to. How many boys she'd had casual sex with; how she used to nick beer, and cigarettes, from the local shop, drink gin from the bottles that her mother – apparently an alcoholic – would leave carelessly lying half-full around her house before passing out. She told me she'd been pregnant and had an abortion. I wasn't even sure whether to believe it, because she shrugged it off as if it was nothing. If I'd been older, more mature, I'd have felt nothing but sympathy for her because of how bleak her family background sounded, compared with mine. But having been so cosseted all my life, all I felt was excitement.

For a while, I was just caught up with listening to her, being impressed by her. Gradually, I spent all my lunch breaks and study breaks with her, instead of my usual friends. I started to agree with her about opinions she expressed which would normally have shocked me. When she answered teachers back, I giggled, secretly admiring her cheek instead of raising my eyebrows about the waste of time, as I would have done before. When Mr Armstrong, our history teacher, told her to pay attention and she swore at him and got sent to the headteacher – a fairly common occurrence – I thought it was unfair. 'He picks on me', she complained afterwards. 'He got me suspended last term. He doesn't like me because I stand up to him. He's a bully.'

And I bought into it all. Yes, I decided, Mr Armstrong was a bully. When he picked on her again, another day, I raised my voice in protest. 'That's not fair, sir!' He stared at me, disappointment evident in his expression, and snapped at me to be quiet. I was incensed. How dare he? I was simply supporting my friend! And she loved me for it. From then on, we were inseparable.

I look back on the summer holiday that year with horror. I was never at home. Callie and I were out together every day, in the park, drinking, smoking, messing about with boys, being loud and annoying, acting like complete idiots. Mum was worried sick about me, of course, but that just made matters worse, because I'd had enough of being fussed over, and I'd finally found a way to shake off every restriction that had ever been imposed on me. The freedom was intoxicating. The bad behaviour became addictive. I stopped studying, promising myself, when I could be bothered to worry about it, that I'd get back to working for my A-levels in September. But I didn't. Being one of the class clowns had become too much of a habit by then.

The first major incident happened when we were both caught drinking alcohol from our water bottles at lunch time. We were sent to the headteacher; to be honest, I was a bit nervous at this point, but Callie stayed true to type and answered him back with her usual cheek and scorn. We were both excluded from school for five days. Mum was incensed. The head had told her the exclusion meant we had to stay at home and do work that would be set for us, and that she could be prosecuted if we went out of the house. He gave me a lecture, telling me he was disappointed in my behaviour and advising me to look for a different friend. I was a bit subdued by the whole thing and it could have been a turning point for me if only he hadn't said that, but it made me furious to hear him expecting me to be disloyal to the best friend I'd ever had. We called each other every day of the exclusion, of course, but when Callie suggested brazenly that we ignored the rules and met up, I chickened out. It was a step too far for me. I was frightened by the thought of Mum being arrested.

My second exclusion came at the end of the autumn term, when Callie and I (having again smuggled some alcohol into school and consumed it at lunch time) disrupted the Christmas concert by jeering insults at the cello and violin players. We thought we were hilarious. The head told us we'd made the young cello player cry. I felt a momentary pang of conscience, but Callie laughed. Again, I could have changed course at that point, seeing her show no remorse, feeling, secretly, slightly disgusted. But I didn't.

Inside, I was beginning to panic. I knew things were getting out of control. I was hardly doing any work. I was being warned by all my teachers that I was going to fail my exams. Everyone was exasperated by me, telling me I was throwing away my life, my chances, wasting everything I'd worked for. Mum nagged me constantly, tried to stop me seeing Callie. We were separated in the history classes, which were the only lessons we had together. Callie had already been told she was on her last chance before being permanently excluded, and the teachers had given up trying to persuade her to work for her exams. She didn't care. She had no intention of going to university, no plan for her future, no encouragement from her parents: according to her, they couldn't care less about her.

During the spring term, I started trying to catch up with my work, but it was difficult. I'd got so far behind, and forgotten a lot of what I'd learnt earlier in the courses. And Callie didn't want me to work, she wanted me to fool around with her. I'd alienated my original friends by now and didn't want Callie to drop me too. I tried to plough a middle course, but it never took much encouragement from her for me to join in with her troublemaking. There was a series of minor misdemeanours, including a hockey match with another school (obviously neither of us were on the team) where we both thought it would be hilarious to strip to our knickers and do a streak across the pitch. We were the only ones who found it hilarious, of course. There was another threat of permanent exclusion. By then, the Easter holiday was approaching and I promised myself I'd stay at home and do exam revision instead of getting drunk in the park with Callie.

But then it all came to a head. We did something so bad, we were both kicked out of school completely. We were spoken to by the police, and told we were lucky not to be arrested. Mum nearly died of shame. Dad was summoned to the house and I had the dressing-down of my life. Too late, I pleaded to be allowed to take my exams, promised to study hard at home and try my best to get the grades I needed for university, promised never to see Callie again – in truth, I didn't want to. It had gone too far, it had scared me, it was over.

No, Dad said. I'd never seen him so furious. 'You've had your chance, Lauren, and you've blown it. You'd better get yourself a job, because there's no way your mother and I are going to finance you through any more wasted education after this. Get a job, and bloody well grow up. You've been mollycoddled too long, that's your trouble.' He threw an angry, meaningful look in Mum's direction. 'You're not an invalid, and you're not a child anymore, so stop behaving like one and go out and earn your own money.'

So that's what I did. I got a job. And yes, I grew up. I was a failure, I've been a failure ever since – and of course, it's all my own fault.

Julia

I've been listening to all of this in silence.

'You're *not* a failure, Lauren!' I tell her now, and to my own surprise, I'm on my feet, going to her, giving her a hug. 'Don't say that.'

'How would you know?' she says. 'You don't know me, you don't know anything about me! You said you didn't even know about any of this. You weren't interested in me – you'd left home and got on with your own life.' She pauses and gives a little shrug. 'Oh, to be honest, that's not fair. If our parents never told you, it's hardly your fault.'

'It sounds like Mum and Dad were ashamed,' I say quietly, and she's nodding agreement. 'If the police were involved, well, you know what people were like back then. They wouldn't have wanted the neighbours talking. They'd have kept it quiet.' I stop, and then look back at her and add: 'What exactly *was* it that you and this Callie got up to, anyway – that last time? I guess it must have been pretty serious to get you both expelled.'

I'm thinking: drugs. Perhaps a fight. Theft of some sort? But Lauren's shaking her head, almost as if she knows what's going through my mind, then to my surprise she actually gives a little sheepish grin as she admits:

'We locked Mr Armstrong in a cupboard.'

'You – *what*?' I can't help it; I've burst out laughing. It sounds so ridiculous compared with thoughts of drug taking, or stealing someone's money.

'I know,' she says, the smile fading. 'It sounds funny, but it actually wasn't – even if it did serve him right. He really was a bully. I'm not saying Callie and I didn't deserve it when he yelled at us. We wound him up, deliberately. But there were other girls in the class who were really scared of him, the way he shouted and threw books around for the slightest reason, or for no reason at all – just because he was in a bad mood. Some of the boys tried to stand up to him but he had a nasty way of putting them down, making them feel small and stupid in front of everyone. And he deliberately picked on one boy who had a stammer. He was a big lad of eighteen but he made him cry, and the poor kid dropped history in the end.'

'I remember Mr Armstrong,' I realise. 'Luckily, I was never in any of his classes, but he was a nasty piece of work. I'm surprised he hadn't been kicked out by the time you were in the sixth form.'

'He was too intimidating for that. And the headteacher always backed him.'

'It sounds like you and Callie were the only ones prepared to challenge him. Good for you, really.'

Lauren looks surprised. 'I thought you'd be shocked. By the way I behaved. What we did.'

'You were a *kid*, Lauren! Yes, OK, you should've been old enough to know better, but honestly, you'd been overprotected and babied for so long, it's hardly surprising you went off the rails a little bit eventually. Loads of kids get up to stuff like that, and grow out of it. Anyway, you haven't said how it happened. The cupboard!'

'Oh, it was just an opportunity that presented itself!' She sighs. 'Mr Armstrong had kept Callie and me back at the end of class because we'd been messing around as usual. We were supposed to be doing the homework we hadn't done from the previous week. We were both in our usual seats at the front of the class where he could keep an eye on us, me on one side of the room, her on the other. There was no-one else around, everyone had gone home, and Mr Armstrong was tidying stuff up. He was an obsessive tidier: nothing was ever left on his desk. I looked up, and across the room, Callie was pointing towards the stock cupboard in the corner. He was in there; we could hear him moving piles of text books from shelf to shelf and muttering to himself. The door was half-closed behind him. It would only take a quick push; but we'd have to be quick. We nodded at each other, got up and silently moved towards the cupboard. *Slam*! It was so easy! We held on to each other, howling with laughter as the hated teacher began to shout and bang on the other side of the door. *Serves you right, Sir!* Callie shouted back. He yelled, he swore, he threatened, but we just went on laughing. It must have been a full five minutes before I started to panic a little. *When do we let him out? We'll have to run! He's going to kill us!* Callie looked at me like I was crazy. *Let him out? We're not letting him out. We're leaving him there. Come on – let's go.* And she grabbed my hand, pulling me out of the classroom. I tried to protest: *What if he dies? Is there any air in there? Seriously?* But she just laughed. She really didn't care. I felt a bit sick. For the first time, I started to have serious doubts about her. I should have refused to leave; I should have gone back and let him out, obviously – but by now I was scared he'd actually kill me.' She pauses, shaking her head. 'I was too frightened and too stupid to think it through properly, anyway. It was inevitable someone would hear him yelling; our classmates might have all gone home but there were still plenty of people in the school. After-school music lessons going on just along the corridor; sports practice taking place outside on the field; the headteacher still in his study; the cleaners yet to come in and do their rounds. In fact it was a couple of younger boys who'd been at Drama Club who were the first on the scene. They described in lurid detail how they'd let Mr Armstrong out of the cupboard, stunned by the red-faced, sweating, shouting, cursing state of him as he charged past them without so much as a thank-you, screaming *Where are they? Where are those filthy little bitches, I'm going to kill them, I'm going to hang them up by their fucking necks and kill them!* Apparently even the headteacher couldn't calm him down.'

Lauren pauses again and then goes on, quietly: 'So you can see why it wasn't really funny. Yes, he got out. But there *wasn't* any ventilation in that cupboard. It wasn't hot weather; he would have been OK even if he'd been in there overnight – but we didn't know that. We were prepared to take that chance. The head had to treat it seriously, had to call the police – I can't blame him. And anyway, he'd had enough of us. Everyone had. We were horrible.'

'You were led by someone else,' I correct her. 'And it sounds like she – Callie – was a very unhappy girl. Did you keep in touch with her, after it all happened?'

'No, I didn't. But I found her on Facebook a few years back, and we exchanged a few messages. And would you believe it? She's turned her life around. She said her parents threw her out after we got expelled from school. She spent a few years sofa-surfing with friends, then suddenly took stock of things and realised she needed to sort herself out. She got herself accepted onto an apprenticeship with a plumbing company; she'd never lacked confidence, and decided to be upfront with the boss about her lack of exams. He gave her a chance, and she never looked back. She's now a qualified plumber, married to a bank manager, lives somewhere in the Midlands and they have two kids.'

'Good for her.'

'Yes.' Lauren looks away, her silence speaking volumes.

'But you've done well too, Lauren! Don't look at me like that – you *have*. You've got your own house, a good job –'

'Which bores me to tears.'

'So you're still young enough to change careers. Train for something different, do a course of some sort!' Her negativity is irritating me now. 'You're fit and healthy, you haven't got to answer to anyone else, for God's sake put all that silly stuff that happened when you were young, behind you now and get on with your life!'

'I'm *trying* to, Julia!' she says crossly. 'I do want to do something different. You still don't really know me. You don't know what I've been trying to do, trying to change. Oh, forget it. I wish I hadn't brought it all up.'

'No, I'm glad you told me. I want us to get to know each other better. It's about time, isn't it?'

She sighs. 'Right. Yes, I suppose so. I suppose I am glad we've got a chance to get to know each other. Let's face it, we're not alike, at all; we never have been. But we ought to be grown-up enough now to try to get along together.'

'I'd like to think that's what we've been trying to do, this week.'

We just look at each other for a while. I'm conscious of Betty on her feet beside me, tending to one of her pots. I think we'd both almost forgotten she was here.

'Well, getting along together is worth a celebration, isn't it,' she says. 'I'll put the kettle on and see if I've got any biscuits in my tin.'

Lauren's staring after Betty as she plods off into her kitchen.

'Do you realise,' she says quietly to me, 'that it happened, this time, without her hot chocolate?'

'What are you talking about? What happened?'

'The thing we've been wondering about. Having these conversations – talking about stuff we don't intend to talk about, whenever we're here with Betty. I never wanted to talk about all that stuff – the school stuff, Callie, getting expelled – I had no intention of bringing it up, but I did. Just like the other things. We were blaming it on the soothing effect of the hot chocolate, but we haven't had any yet today.'

'So you don't think she puts anything in it, now? Or that there's any magic going on here?' I'm laughing. I thought we'd already agreed the whole idea was ridiculous. 'Come on, we didn't really believe that, did we? We thought it might just be the warmth in here, the calm atmosphere –'

'Calm? Hardly, today, with all that trauma with the cat!'

'But we've put poor Rosie out of our minds, haven't we?' I realise, suddenly feeling guilty.

'Exactly. How did we let that happen? Poor thing, I wonder how she's getting on at the vet's.'

'Betty wanted us to take her mind off it,' I remind her, then I drop my voice and add, 'And here she is.'

I take the tray of mugs from Betty and put it on one of the little tables. Along with the three mugs of chocolate, there's hunks of shortbread on a plate, and it looks home-made.

'I hope you're going to give us a bill before we leave, Betty,' I tell her, realising I should have mentioned this before. 'For all these extras you're providing.'

'Don't be daft!' She shakes her head. 'Charge you? For doing what I like – sitting here with nice people, enjoying your company, sharing a hot drink and a bit of my home-made kill-me-quick? I like baking, and it's nice to have a reason to do it –'

'You've got your grandson to bake for,' Lauren says. 'And your son now – permanently, soon! And Julia's right: if you keep doing this sort of thing for all your paying guests, you'll be out of pocket. We're supposed to be self-catering.'

'All my paying guests might not be as nice as you two,' she says. 'I might not want to offer them anything! Anyway, I've only got one more family booked in, so far.'

'I'm sure you'll get lots more,' I say. 'When the holiday season starts. Are you advertising online, Betty?'

'Online? I don't know anything about buggering online whatsits. Tweeting, Facebooking, Ticking-tocking, all that nonsense. That's why Nathan put it all in the hands of the agent.'

'And the agent's charging you. I hope he's doing enough to earn his commission.' I glance at Lauren. 'I suppose Carl must have found this place advertised somewhere, anyway.'

'I'll get Nathan to look into it,' Betty says with a shrug. 'When he's got time.' She picks up her mug, and then goes on, 'Talking of time, how long has it been since they took poor little Rosie to the vet's? Shouldn't we have heard something by now?'

'I'm sure they'll call as soon as they can,' I say.

But before we've even finished our drinks, we hear the Jeep pull up outside, and both men come in together.

'Never mind about that!' Betty calls out to them, when they stop to take off their boots. 'Where's Rosie? What happened? What did the vet say?'

'It's all right, Mum, don't panic,' Stuart says. 'They've kept her in, but she's going to be OK. The vet had to sedate her lightly, as we suspected, just to have a proper look. She's somehow got a sharp piece of glass stuck in the inside of her mouth – it's torn her mouth quite badly.'

'A piece of *glass*?' Betty repeats, staring at him. 'How?'

'How do cats do anything?' Nathan laughs. 'We need to have a good look around here and see if there's any broken glass lying around –'

'But the whole place is covered in snow!'

'I know. I can only think maybe she's found a broken jar or bottle somewhere, and licked it like cats do, and got a piece stuck in her mouth. And you're right, it must have happened somewhere where there's no snow covering it at the moment.'

'So what's the vet done?' Betty demands impatiently. 'Did he stitch the cut? Can you do that, with a mouth wound?'

'Yes: he was taking her into theatre to put her under a general anaesthetic so that he can get the glass out of the wound, clean it up and stitch it, and give her an antibiotic injection. He'll give us a call as soon as he's finished the surgery.'

'And then you can bring her home?'

'No, he'll keep her in overnight because of the anaesthetic, Mum,' Stuart says patiently. 'And to make sure there's no more bleeding, or infection.'

'She'll be fine now,' I say to Betty. 'She's obviously in good hands.'

'Yes. Thank goodness you two found her.'

Lauren smiles. 'In fact she came to find us! She was bleeding, crying and really in a state.'

'Poor baby,' Betty says. 'Will she be able to eat all right, Nathan, when she comes home?'

'I don't know, Gran, but I'm sure the vet will tell us what's best for her!' He chuckles. 'Come on, stop worrying. What have you ladies all been chatting about while we've been gone, anyway?'

'Oh . . .' I glance at Lauren, and she's looking back at me. 'This and that, you know.'

'Putting the world right?' Stuart suggests.

'Well, perhaps our little part of it. I hope so, anyway,' I say, still watching Lauren's face.

She smiles and nods. That's all it takes for me to feel a huge rush of relief – and something else. Something that feels strangely like sisterly love.

Betty

Poor little Rosie. I can't help it; I'm going to be worried sick about her until we get her back from the vet's. And worried about the broken glass, too – where she found it, whether she, or Basil, or any other animal, come to that, is going to find it and get injured again. Nathan says he'll go out and look around, and Julia and Lauren have said they'll look too.

I think they're going to be better together now. It's always good to get these things out in the open, in my opinion, better than brooding on them. And it seems they don't normally spend any time together, so this would have been their first opportunity to talk everything over. What a strange holiday it's been for them. I'd have liked them to be able to get out and about more, see all the lovely places on Dartmoor, and explore further afield in Devon. It's such a beautiful part of the world, and they've been stuck here, in the snow half the time, and with just an old woman like me for company. Perhaps they'll come back again at a nicer time of year. I hope so. I'll suggest it to them. I'm surprised at how much my heart lifts at the thought of it.

They're talking with Nathan now, about where they might look for the broken glass, every bit as if they're part of the family. How has that happened in just a few days? I suppose if the weather had been different – if they *had* been staying here in warm, sunny, summer weather, and they'd been out and about every day of their holiday, we wouldn't even have got to know each other. And the trauma of the other night, when Lauren disappeared, and Stuart brought her back, has helped to bring us together too. Thinking about this, I turn and smile at my son.

'It's so nice having you here,' I say. 'I wish you didn't have to head back to London so soon.'

'But I'll be back for good, before you know it,' he says.

'It was quite sudden, wasn't it – the decision to come down now for a few days.' I've been so excited about having him here, I haven't thought to question it before. 'Were you just in the mood for a visit, or were you actually considering coming back permanently and wanted to make sure you remembered the way here?'

I'm teasing him, obviously, but he doesn't respond in kind. He's looking down, as if he's weighing his words carefully.

'Well, to be honest, Mum, I wanted to talk to you about something,' he says finally. 'Something personal.'

He sounds very serious. I feel a shiver of foreboding. I don't think this conversation – whatever it's going to be about – ought to happen in front of the two girls. I start to ask him if it can wait, but they've already picked up on the vibe. They've both swallowed the rest of their drinks, put their mugs down and are nodding at each other and saying it's time they went. For once, I don't try to encourage them to stay.

'What is it?' I ask him as they're heading out of the door. 'Tell me.'

Whatever this is leading up to, he's looking so uncomfortable that I'm thinking he'll hedge around it, lead up to it awkwardly – but I'm wrong. In fact he comes straight out with it without a second's hesitation, looking up and meeting my eyes and saying it so quickly and loudly that I actually flinch.

'The thing is, Mum, I've found my father. I've met him.'

I can't speak. My ears are ringing, as if a bomb's just gone off or I'm about to faint. Like from a distance, I hear Nathan gasp, and start asking questions: how did he find him, who is he, what's his name. Then he's standing next to me, a hand on my arm.

'Gran, Gran, are you all right? Can you hear me? She's as white as a sheet, Dad, I think she's about to pass out. Do you want a glass of water, Gran?'

'I'm all right,' I mutter, struggling to pull myself together. 'Stop fussing, I'll . . . be fine. It was just –'

'– a shock, obviously,' Stuart says. 'I'm sorry, Mum, I really am. Sorry to blurt it out like that, but I've been trying to find a way to tell you, a way to lead up to it more gently, but in the end –'

'No, you're right. No good pussy-footing around it. Best to just come out with it,' I tell him as the dizziness starts to abate and everything swims gradually back into focus. But my voice is shaking, and I'm not even sure I believe what I'm saying. This is not just a shock, it's a disaster. I never wanted this to happen. He *knew* I didn't want it to happen. He's known that, since he first asked questions when he was a little boy. I don't know whether to feel hurt, cross, or . . . let's face it, just plain stupid for ever imagining I could have expected him to live out the rest of his time on earth without his curiosity getting the better of him. I suppose it was too much to ask. It's probably surprising enough that he's reached middle age without going against my wishes.

'I'm sorry,' he's saying again. Quietly, gently, looking at me with genuine apology in his eyes. 'I know you didn't want me to try to find out. But – the thing is, since I lost Janie . . .'

'Of course.' How selfish of me. He's lost his wife, the love of his life. He was so badly affected by that loss, he couldn't even bear to be around here, living in the home he shared with her, or even in the area. Let's face it, he ran away. But he must have felt so alone and lost, all that time in London, away from his family. It would have been only natural to try to find his roots. 'I understand,' I tell him.

I understand, but it doesn't make it any easier.

'We don't have to have this conversation right away,' he's saying now. 'If you need a bit of time to get over the shock, it can wait, we can talk later, or even when I move back again. But I needed to let you know I've found out. I signed up for one of these companies, that take your DNA, and look for matches, and they matched me with a half-sister –'

'Oh. His daughter,' I say in a whisper.

'Yes. She'd been looking too, just out of interest, she said. To see if there were any other relatives.'

'You've met her? His daughter?'

'Both of them.' He pauses, and looks me in the eyes before going on. 'And now I've met Dad. I talked to him, heard about – what really happened.'

'Yes. Of course you did.'

I sit up straight, try to get a grip of myself. It's too late now for regrets – this thing has happened. He knows. Now Nathan will know too. I can see how curious he is, and how can I blame him? He's perched on the edge of his chair, his eyes wide. It's his grandad we're talking about, the grandad I've always lied to them both about. I've always kept questions at bay by telling them he was an embarrassing one-night stand, a terrible mistake, such a drunken moment of stupidity that I never even found out his name, that I never saw him again and regretted everything about it apart from the gift of my wonderful son.

I take a deep breath. 'Tell me all about it, then,' I say. 'How was he, what did he say?'

And somewhere inside me there's a little flicker of something . . . something that feels suspiciously like joy. So: it seems Richard's still alive.

Lauren

'Well, that was a bit of a shocker, wasn't it?' Julia says as we crunch our way back to the Lodge through the snow. It's actually stopped snowing again now, and there's a weak watery hint of sunshine breaking through the clouds. I've got a feeling the snow might be starting to thaw a little.

'Yes,' I agree. 'But it's not right for us to speculate about it.'

I'm sure Stuart thought we were out of earshot before he dropped his bombshell. *I've found my father, I've met him.* But we'd had to stop to put our boots on; we were halfway outside, the conservatory door still open, and he came out with those words so loud and clear – as if he'd had to psyche himself up for so long to say them that they finally just burst out of him. Julia closed the door quietly after us and we've walked most of the way back without saying anything.

'I just assumed Betty was a widow,' Julia says.

'Me too.' I shrug. 'But it's not right –'

'For us to speculate about it. I know, that's true, but even so . . . well, I don't want to sound too nosy, but . . .'

'I know what you mean. It's hard not to wonder, isn't it? All these years, not knowing his father, poor guy.'

'Well, I hope it's worked out happily for him – finding him at last,' Julia says. And we both fall silent again until we get back to the Lodge.

'Basil's in here,' I say as I open the front door. He's jumped down from one of the chairs and come out to meet us, meowing loudly, his tail up, twitching. 'OK, boy, it's all right, what's the matter?'

'He's missing Rosie,' Julia says, bending down to stroke him. 'Oh, we said we'd go out and help look for that broken glass, didn't we?'

'Yes. In fact, I'm thinking it's quite likely to be around here somewhere, rather than nearer the Manor. Otherwise Rosie would have taken herself back there when she got hurt, wouldn't she? Instead of coming in here.'

We agree to have some lunch before we start the search, and by the time we go back outside afterwards I'm even more convinced I was right – there's a slow thaw going on. The winter sunshine may not be very strong but there *is* a change in the temperature.

'Hopefully we'll be OK for driving home tomorrow,' I say to Julia. I know how worried she's been about it. 'But if the roads are still bad, Betty has said it's not a problem for us to stay on for a bit longer. I can call my boss and explain –'

'We are *not* going to consider staying any longer, Lauren!' she snaps. 'I've got to get back. You're not the only one with a job to consider –'

'All right, all right, I know that!' I say quickly. But I'm shocked by how fiercely she reacted. She's red in the face, breathing fast like she's about to have a panic attack. For God's sake, it was only a week or so ago she was telling me blithely that she's a partner in the business so she can take holiday whenever she wants. Now, all of a sudden, it's like the world's going to come to an end, just because Phil's off sick with a cold or something and she's not there to take over. 'Well, let's just hope it continues to thaw,' I say to pacify her.

We poke around in the snow around the walls of the Lodge, neither of us having any idea what we're looking for or where to find it.

'If it's buried in the snow, I wouldn't have thought Rosie could have accidentally found it,' I suggest.

'No. You're probably right.' Julia straightens up. 'Well – unless Stuart or Nathan have more luck than us, looking closer to the Manor, I guess we'll just have to hope there *isn't* any more glass where Rosie came across that piece.'

'It's not bad out here at the moment, though, with that little bit of sunshine,' I say. 'And it *is* our last day. Shall we have a little walk, maybe just around the perimeter of the grounds? I'd like to take a few more photos before we leave.'

I'm trying not to sound too wistful. I'm not looking forward to going back to my boring job and my boring little house in its boring, dismal street of identical houses. It feels incomprehensible to me already now, that I was so utterly devastated and miserable when we arrived here. I've been happier this week than I can remember being for years – despite the various emotional outbursts between Julia and me. Or maybe even because of them?

'OK,' she says, amiably enough. Perhaps she regrets the way she took my head off just now. She probably wants us to part on good terms after this week's over, as much as I do. 'Come on, then. Before it gets cold and dark again.'

We set off to walk along the boundary of the property, following the old brick walls. They're taller than me, but Julia reaches up and runs her gloved hand through the layer of snow on top.

'I'd like to have seen the Manor when it was first built,' she says. 'It must have been pretty impressive.'

'Yes. Just like the big houses you see on TV, in historical dramas. I love those.'

'Me too. There, that's something we've got in common,' I say with a chuckle. I feel strangely pleased, and find myself wondering if we might start to find more things, if . . .

If what? What am I expecting? Do I really think things are going to be so different from now on, just because we've spent a week together and told each other a few home truths? Are we suddenly going to start calling each other every few days, exchanging WhatsApp messages, even getting together for evenings and weekends?

I hope so.

I give myself a little shake, taken aback by my own thoughts, and deliberately change the subject.

'OK, let's see if we can follow the wall all the way round.'

Before very long, we come to a tight little group of trees and bushes, where we need to deviate away from the wall rather than trying to push our way through them.

'Oh! Look,' Julia says in surprise as we round the trees.

We both stop and stare ahead of us. On the other side of the trees, there's a small brick structure built against the wall. It's octagonal, with an open front and domed roof, on top of which is an ancient-looking weather vane in the shape of a cockerel.

'What is it?' I wonder as we approach. 'There's no door – it's just open to the elements.'

'Yes. A little summerhouse, perhaps? It looks as old as the walls themselves – perhaps it was part of the original structure rather than being added on.'

'Yes. The bricks look the same. Oh – are you going inside? We shouldn't –'

'Why not?' Julia says mildly. 'It's not as if it's closed, or locked – and look,' she goes on as I follow her inside. 'The only thing in here is this wooden seat.'

'Broken seat.'

Two of the windows are broken, too, and the others are covered in cobwebs and years of grime.

'What a shame,' I go on, sadly. 'I bet it was lovely in here at one time – with those tall windows, and the trees on one side for shade.'

'*That's* not so lovely, though.' Julia points under the seat. 'I think our friendly cats have been in here.'

It's a dead blackbird, sadly – stiff and half-frozen, dusted with a little bit of snow that's blown in on the wind through the open doorway.

'Poor thing. That's the only problem with cats – if it *was* one of the cats. I mean, it might have just died from the cold . . .'

But Julia's not listening to me. She's crouched down next to the dead bird, reaching for something under the seat.

'What is it?' I ask as she straightens up, staring at an object in her hand.

'A little mirror.' She turns it over, and then shrugs and holds it out to show me. 'Well, that's what it *was*.'

'It's silver, by the look of it. Very battered and tarnished, though –'

'Not to say broken,' she points out. 'Completely smashed.'

'It's a handbag mirror. Mum used to have one a bit like it. Don't you remember?'

Julia shakes her head. Well, she wouldn't, I suppose.

I take the mirror from Julia's hand, brush the snow off it, and retract my hand quickly, looking as blood begins to trickle through my glove from my finger. 'There's still some of the shattered glass in the edge of the frame. Look, it's needle-sharp.'

'Are you OK?'

I've pulled off my glove and I'm sucking my finger. 'Yes, it's nothing, just a little nick.'

She's pushing snow to one side with the toe of her boot.

'I bet the rest of the glass is on the ground here, then.'

'Yes.' I sigh. 'Look, there are some splinters right by that dead bird. I think we might have found out where Rosie got hurt – and why. She's found this poor bird lying here and started turning it over, the way cats do –'.

'Yes.' Julia gives the dead bird a little gentle nudge with her boot. 'Oh, look. Bloodstains in the snow.'

'Could be from the bird?' I suggest.

'Or from Rosie. Look!' Julia says, and I turn to follow where she's pointing. 'How did we miss seeing that?'

More bloodstains, small ones like drips, leading from this gory death scene, out of the summerhouse and into the snow beyond.

'So much for your thing about nature being so beautiful. This is pretty gross!' I tell Julia.

She's busy collecting up the little shards of glass and wrapping them in a tissue from her pocket. I've used one of my own to wrap around my finger.

'You're right, nature has its gruesome moments, doesn't it! Well, I think I've got all the glass, anyway. I suppose the mirror was probably Betty's. Anyway, we ought to take it to her.'

'What about the blackbird?' I say sadly. 'Um . . . shouldn't we bury it?'

'And say a little prayer?' she teases me.

'No – I just think if we leave it here, it's going to attract the cats back again – or other animals – and if we've missed any tiny bits of glass –'

'OK.' She smiles at me. 'Come on then, pick it up!'

'Ugh. No!'

'And I don't fancy doing it either! So let's ask Nathan – or Stuart – if they'd like to come out and deal with it, shall we?'

'Good plan.'

We leave the summerhouse behind and head across the snow towards the Manor. We must have looked an odd little procession of two: Julia clutching her tissue full of broken glass, me holding the broken mirror in one hand and folding my cut finger into its tissue inside my glove.

'What have you got there?' It's Stuart who opens the door of the Manor to us. He's staring in surprise as Julia holds out her handful of glass splinters. 'Where did you find that?'

'It's from a broken mirror,' she says. 'We think it might be what Rosie hurt herself on.'

I show him the mirror. 'We found it in that little summerhouse building over on the boundary wall.'

'But there was a dead bird there,' Julia adds quickly. 'And we thought maybe you or Nathan might want to go and –'

'Get rid of it before one of the cats goes back for it?' he says with a grin. 'Sure. I'll tell Nathan! What is this, anyway?' he goes on, taking the mirror from me and turning it over in his hands.

'Be careful, there are sharp splinters of glass in the edges. It's a handbag mirror. We're wondering if it belonged to your mum.'

But we don't get any further – because right at that moment, Betty appears in the doorway behind Stuart.

'Oh, hello, my lovelies! Come in, come in out of the cold. What on earth are you thinking of, Stuart, keeping them standing there on the doorstep? I've just made a big pot of tea, girls, if you want to join us? Come in, come . . . oh!' She takes a step forward, staring at the mirror in Stuart's hand. 'What's that? Surely to God it's not –? My God, it *is*!'

She holds her hand out to take it, while we all try to stop her, warning her about the broken glass inside, but she's holding it carefully in her hands, staring at it, shaking her head.

'I never thought I'd see this again. I thought it was lost forever. I can't believe it! Where on earth did you find it?'

I repeat the story of finding it under the seat in the summerhouse, telling her about the broken glass, the dead bird, the bloodstains in the snow, the probability of it being the site of Rosie's injury – but she's barely listening, she's just staring and staring at the mirror as if it's a mirage and she half expects it to suddenly vanish into thin air.

Eventually she looks back up at us.

'I must have dropped it – out of a pocket or a bag maybe – when I used to sit over there sometimes in the summer and read my book. I've wondered so often what happened to it. Well I never! Thank you, girls. And come in, for goodness' sake,' she repeats. 'Come and sit down. Stuart, make these two young ladies a hot drink to warm them up.'

'No, honestly, we'll just get back to the Lodge,' I say. 'Thank you, but –'

'We need to pack,' Julia says.

I think we both feel that whatever's making Betty so emotional must be very private. We don't want to intrude.

'Are you all right, Mum?' Stuart's asking her as we're saying goodbye.

'All right? 'Course I'm all right,' she retorts, turning away.

But she hasn't looked away quite quickly enough. I couldn't help noticing the tears glinting in her eyes, and how she's clutching the handle of that battered, broken old mirror as if it's the answer to her prayers. I wonder if perhaps, for some reason, she feels like that's exactly what it is.

Saturday

Julia

It was already dark outside as we walked back from the Manor yesterday. The sky was clear, with a full moon, and now that the sun had disappeared, the air felt colder than ever. There was no wind, and there was something strangely spooky about the still, silent frigidity of the snow-laden trees in the darkness. We both had our phone torches on, to avoid tripping over roots and fallen branches as we crunched our way back through the snow, and the torchlight seemed to pick out the outline of every dry leaf, every bark pattern on every trunk, every blade of grass, as if they'd been frozen in time forever. Every now and then the stillness was disturbed by a soft scurrying or fluttering sound of a small creature disturbed by our footsteps, rushing back to the safety of its nest. I felt myself shivering beneath my warm clothes.

'So much for a thaw,' I said, my worries about the drive home resurfacing.

'Hopefully it'll continue as soon as the sun comes up,' Lauren said.

Our voices rang out in the frozen silence as if we were shouting. I half expected an echo. I knew Lauren was trying to make me feel better, but I was hoping to be on the road by the time the sun came up, or at least, to be getting my battery charged. Stuart had reminded us that he'd drive us to my car in the morning, with his jump-leads, and Betty had immediately assured us once again that we'd be welcome to stay another night if the conditions were no better in the morning. Lauren had looked at me hopefully but I shook my head. I need to get home. As soon as we got back in the Lodge, we packed our bags and I shut myself in my room to make the phone call confirming we'd be heading back as soon as possible in the morning.

And now here we are, at first light, staring out of the window. Instead of the sun coming up and continuing the thaw, we're faced with a sky the colour of ash, and every surface outside looking like a mirror. The night temperature must have hit a new record low; the snow-melt has re-frozen with a vengeance so that even to step outside, without wearing chains, could probably risk a broken bone or two.

Lauren's looking at me in silence as we eat breakfast. I realise she's not going to want to spell out what's obvious – even to me – but I don't want to admit it, either.

'It might improve a little later,' I begin – but I'm interrupted by my phone ringing.

'Julia, it's Stuart,' he says when I answer. 'Listen, I'm still happy to jump-start your car, but I'm afraid I don't think you're going to be driving it anywhere in these conditions.'

'I know,' I finally admit, on a long sigh. 'But perhaps it'll get better –'

'Sorry, but I don't think so. The forecast is for more snow – on top of this ice. It'll be deathly. There are already reports of serious accidents. Please don't risk it. I doubt the roads will be passable, anyway. You really do need to stay another night.'

'Right.' I'm not stupid enough to argue with that, however badly I need to get back. 'Thank you – and please thank Betty again for letting us stay. Should we settle up through the agent, or –'

'Don't be silly. We haven't got anyone else booked. And I've already told Mum to ditch the agent anyway. I'm going to take over running that side of the business myself, when I come back.'

'Thank you,' I say again. We'll have to repay them, somehow, for their kindness. Send them a present of some sort after we get home.

'I know you wanted to get back today, but –' Lauren begins as I hang up the call.

'This *sodding* weather!' I explode, cutting her off mid-sentence and dropping my phone on the table. I can feel tears threatening. 'Why the hell did we come somewhere like this in the middle of bloody winter?'

Lauren hangs her head, and I'd like to apologise, to reassure her that it isn't her fault, that I knew what I was doing when I agreed to bring her here on this so-called holiday, that I did it because I felt sorry for her and . . . well, because yes, I loved her. I want to say all this, but I can't, because my anxiety is choking all the kind words out of me.

'Want a cup of tea?' she asks in a little voice.

'No, sorry but I don't want a buggering cup of tea. I need to make a couple of calls, if that's all right with you,' I retort, wishing even as I'm saying it that I wasn't being such a bitch, that I wasn't perhaps risking the fragile new sibling relationship we've been trying to establish this week. But there's no time to take it back. I need to make the calls. I pick up the phone again and head back upstairs, closing my bedroom door behind me.

By the time I come back downstairs, Lauren's cleared the table, washed up the breakfast things and is pretending to concentrate on a jigsaw puzzle. She's tipped all the pieces out of the box and is moving them around the table, picking pieces up and staring at them listlessly.

'Sorry,' I say.

'That's OK.'

'No, it's not OK. I shouldn't have snapped at you. It's not your fault.'

'Julia, I'm just *worried* about you,' she says, turning to look at me. 'I know your job must be really demanding, I know you wanted to get back today, but surely another day won't make any difference? What's the matter? You've been on edge all week about your work.'

'I'm sorry,' I say again. I sink down onto the chair opposite hers. 'I . . . I told you. Phil's not well, and –'

I can't. I just can't tell her how worried I am, and why. I know I should, but I feel like if I start saying it out loud, it's going to overwhelm me, whereas if I keep quiet and just concentrate on getting home as soon as humanly possible, please God, everything will be OK.

'And obviously, he's not at work, so it's difficult,' I finish awkwardly, looking away from Lauren. 'I didn't know about it when I agreed to come away with you this week.'

'You should have told me. If it was difficult, we could have cancelled –'

'No. I'd promised you. And anyway, it . . . look, I'm sorry, but I don't want to go into it now.'

'All those phone calls. I could tell there must be problems. But surely –'

'I said I don't want to go into it now, all right?' I can hear the tremor in my voice. I'm in danger of losing my rag. 'Let's do this stupid jigsaw,' I finish, trying to make myself sound like someone who's in control of herself. 'You sort out the edge pieces. I'll concentrate on the sky.'

'OK,' she says, in a little, hurt voice.

I know she's upset that I'm not confiding in her. Considering all the stuff we've already shared this week, it must feel like a slap in the face.

'I will tell you,' I say, more gently. I reach across the table and lay a hand on hers, scattering jigsaw pieces in all directions. 'I will, but I just can't at the moment. I need to . . . hold myself together, and if I talk about it before I've managed to get home to . . . to deal with it, I might lose it completely.'

The truth is that I want to feel her arms around me. I want to put my head on her shoulder and cry my eyes out. I want to tell her what's gone wrong – not just this week, but since years ago. The mess I've made of things. The regrets, the shame, and now the terrible, terrible fear. I want her to tell me everything will be all right. But she can't, nobody can. So I've just got to grit my teeth and go back to pretending, the way I've pretended all week, that everything is fine and there's no deadline whatsoever for getting home and finding out if I've still got a life worth living.

Betty

'So are they staying?' I ask Stuart. He's called our guests to tell them the roads are even more hazardous than yesterday. I was worried sick that they might try to get home, in these conditions. I looked at the News on the TV this morning – accidents reported everywhere. It's even worse in the south-east, apparently, roads closed, motorway pile-ups, people abandoning their cars all over the place. And more snow forecast.

'Yes. Julia sounded pretty upset about it.'

'I gather she's got some high-powered job that she stresses about. That's what her sister says, anyway.'

'Poor woman.'

I hardly need to say I agree with him. What's the point of an important job, earning (I suppose) a huge salary, if you can't even take a week off without worrying yourself into the grave? Anyway, it's nothing to do with me, obviously.

'Are you going to pick Rosie up from the vet's now?' I ask him. 'Take Nathan with you, so he can hold her in the carrier while you drive –'

He laughs. I've mentioned this at least ten times this morning already.

'OK, OK, I had to call them first to make sure they're ready for us to collect her,' he reminds me. 'I'll give Nathan a shout – we'll go now.'

He's got chains for the tyres of his jeep, but even so, I tell him to drive slowly and carefully, and he gives me that look, the one that's meant to remind me he's a grown man and I'm just a daft old woman who hasn't driven anything anywhere for years. It's so lovely having him here, he can look at me, talk to me, however the hell he likes, I won't mind.

'Give those girls a knock and ask if they want anything from the shop, while you're out,' I remind him – if only for the pleasure of seeing him give me that look again.

I was so worried everything was going to be ruined between us, when he told me what he'd found out. When I had to talk to him, to tell him the truth about his father, the truth I was so determined he should never know. I was frightened he'd never forgive me for lying to him – and to Nathan – for keeping them both from knowing about Richard. But although he was upset, he understood why I'd done it. A promise is a promise, at the end of the day – and at least I can live with the knowledge that I never broke it. I should have known Stuart might try to find out the truth for himself, despite me having always told him not to. Despite all the lies I'd told him.

And now I'm living with this new truth for myself: the knowledge that Richard's still alive, and knows everything. To be honest, I haven't even been able to process this yet; I've had to put it to one side. It's too huge to deal with, and I've been far more consumed with the worry of what this all meant for my relationships with my son, and my grandson. Stuart says he's told Richard he was coming here to talk to me, to tell me he'd found out about him, before Richard did anything like trying to get in touch with me. The thought of this makes me feel such a mixture of emotions, I don't know quite how to describe them. Panic? Excitement? Fear? Confusion? I can't remember quite how long it's been since I felt anything like this. Or maybe I can: not since the last time I saw Richard. When I left.

I've been so lost in all these thoughts, that before I know it, Stuart's jeep's pulling up outside and as soon as I go to open the front door, I can hear Rosie meowing at the top of her voice.

'Bring her in, quick, let her out of that basket – you know she hates it,' I'm telling them before they've even got inside.

'All right, Gran, give us a chance!' Nathan says, laughing.

'Is she all right? Did the vet say her mouth's healed up OK?' I demand, bending down to pick Rosie up and check her all over.

'Her mouth's as good as new, Mum,' Stuart assures me. 'The vet says she's been eating and drinking fine, and he's completely happy with her now.'

'Completely happy now we've paid his bill, you mean,' Nathan says, raising his eyes. 'I wish I'd taken out one of those pet insurances –'

'Well, neither of the cats has ever needed treatment before,' I remind him. 'And let's hope they never do again.'

'Will she be all right to go outside if she wants to?' I wonder, putting Rosie back down and watching as she wanders off.

'Yes, Mum – don't fuss, she'll be perfectly OK now.' Stuart smiles at me. 'Incidentally, we took a pint of milk and some bread in to Julia and Lauren, and they asked if you'd mind if they came over for a little while to sit in the conservatory. I think they're a bit at a loss. You know, being stuck here for an extra day.'

'Of course it's all right. But you should have brought them round in the jeep, not let them walk across here in all that frozen snow –'

'We did. I dropped them at the conservatory door,' he says with a grin.

'Oh! Well, get your coat and boots off and get the kettle on, while I go and say hello to them.'

I'm glad they're here. Glad I've got another last chance to enjoy their company. I know they'd prefer to be on their way back to London, back to their real lives, but sometimes things are meant to be – and if this awful weather means they can relax for one more day before picking up their busy lives again, maybe they'll be grateful for it eventually.

'Rosie's back!' I tell them as soon as I see them.

'Yes, we know. She was in the jeep with Stuart and Nathan when they picked us up,' Lauren says. 'Is she OK? They said the vet was happy with her.'

'She seems fine. I think she's gone straight into the sitting room and she's probably already asleep on the sofa!' I smile at them both. 'Why don't you come and sit in there with us – Stuart's got the fire alight. It's cosier than in here, in this weather.'

'Oh, I don't know –' Julia says, looking a bit alarmed. 'I don't think that would be right. It's your personal space . . .'

'We're just the holiday renters,' Laura says, nodding.

'You're my *guests*,' I tell them firmly. 'And I'm inviting you. Come on. It's nothing fancy, mind you.'

I lead the way through the kitchen and down the passageway to the sitting room, where, sure enough, Rosie is already snuggled down on one of the sofas, her head on a cushion, snoring gently. I tell the girls to sit where they like – they choose to sit one on either side of Rosie – and I sit in my armchair facing them, looking around the room as I do. Seeing it through their eyes. It's quite a big room, with huge casement windows and French doors at the other end, and the old brick fireplace at this end, a fireplace you can walk into if you feel so inclined. The wallpaper is old-fashioned, a faded gold colour embossed with an outdated pattern; the curtains are heavy and drab, and the furniture's ancient and cumbersome. It's been in here since my parents' days, if not before, and it probably cost a fortune originally, but now it just looks shabby. The cats have scratched the fabric on the arms of the sofas and armchairs, and the legs of the little tables. But I love my cats, and the furniture doesn't matter. Or it didn't, until I saw these two young ladies from London looking around at it.

'Sorry, it's a bit . . . dated,' I say.

'What on earth are you apologising for?' Julia says. 'It's a beautiful room. Are those light fittings original? And the ceiling mouldings?'

'The carpet must have been so expensive,' Lauren says. 'I can see how old it is, but it's still retained its beautiful colours.'

'It's thin – going threadbare!' I laugh. 'Yes, everything in here is old. Nathan's plan is to update it of course – along with all the other rooms. A makeover, he calls it. But I doubt I'll live long enough to see the completion of it all.'

'Ah, don't say that!' they both say together.

'Not being morbid. Just stating facts. Anyway, I'm comfortable with the house the way it is.'

I'm watching Julia as we're talking. She looks worried, anxious, wiping her forehead as if she's hot, sighing and fidgeting. Is she *really* so worried about the job, or could it be something else?

'Here,' Stuart's saying to her, passing her a mug of chocolate. He's looking at her with concern in his eyes. He's like me; can't bear to see someone looking unhappy. 'Drink up while it's hot. A cup of Mum's special chocolate can make everything feel better, you know.'

'Special?' Lauren says. She hesitates, looks at me, back at Stuart, finally at Julia, then suddenly ploughs on with a little awkward laugh, 'To tell you the truth, Julia and I have been wondering all week. Is there something special in your hot chocolate?'

Stuart catches my eye and laughs. Nathan's already grinning at me.

'Are you going to tell them, Gran? Go on, reveal the big secret! It's not as if Lauren and Julia will be here long enough to spread the information around the village!'

I smile. I suppose he's right. It's silly, really, but I've enjoyed, for so long, keeping it a secret, knowing how everyone around here gossips about it. How they stare into their cups when I make them a hot chocolate when they come to visit me, to buy produce from my greenhouses and have a gossip. I encourage it – I admit that – it's company for me, and I don't really care what they think of me, what they'll say when they go back to gossip with the other villagers afterwards. I don't ask for their confidences but I must admit I enjoy hearing them, and it seems to help them too – talking things over, going away feeling better even though they look puzzled about it. Every time! Even those who come every week, and add more and more to their personal sagas of family rifts, neighbour disputes, relationship disappointments and so on – still they go away looking puzzled about why they've told me it all. I've seen it in the eyes of these guests this week too – the puzzlement, the slight disconcertion, a little bit of suspicion, despite the fact that they don't refuse another cup the next day! And despite the fact that the talking has helped them. Talking always helps. Sometimes tongues just need a bit of loosening.

'It's nothing,' I tell them, as they're both now contemplating the chocolate steaming in their mugs. 'Well, I sometimes add a little bit of chopped mint, if people like it, or ginger – things we grow here, you see? But only if people ask for it. Sometimes people want other things – like basil or rosemary –'

'Mum's favourite,' Stuart interrupts. 'That's why she named the cats Basil and Rosie – that's short for Rosemary. And Mum grows both of those here, in the conservatory.'

'Oh!' Lauren says. 'We just thought those were just, you know, um, *plants.*'

'They are plants – God, don't you Londoners grow anything?' Nathan teases, and they both shrug and laugh.

'So that's what you're adding – harmless flavourings? Mint, ginger, basil and stuff?' Julia says.

'But only if people ask for them. I haven't given *you* girls anything. Your chocolate is completely additive-free,' I say with a wink.

'The big secret,' Nathan explains, 'is just the fact that Gran encourages these visitors of hers – *customers* of ours – to believe whatever they want.'

'Like that she's the Wise Woman of Deepcombe!' Stuart says, grinning. 'Just because the hot drink, and the warmth in the conservatory relaxes them and makes them share confidences with her – gossip about their family and friends, that they probably regret even mentioning afterwards. *Wise Woman* indeed! More like the Wicked Woman!'

For the first time, I have a little frisson of doubt. Is Stuart right? Have I been hoodwinking everyone, telling myself I was actually helping people – giving them the chance to relax and unburden themselves of their worries, making them feel better, when perhaps I was having a little joke at their expense?

'Maybe you're right –' I begin, flustered. 'Look, I can't deny I like listening to them chat, but I don't repeat any of the gossip. But perhaps I shouldn't have encouraged them –'

But Lauren's laughing now. Even Julia's managing a little grin.

'Well, the thing is,' I go on, 'they all keep coming back. It gets us more customers!' – which seems to make them all laugh even more.

'OK, so perhaps it's been good for business,' Nathan admits. 'But you could do just as good a sales pitch if you push the sales of the herbs, the mint and the ginger, while they're relaxed sitting here chatting! And they'll spread the word.'

'I suppose so.' I think about this. 'But if we start expanding, we'll need more space in the greenhouses –'

'Don't worry, Mum.' Stuart reaches across and puts a hand over one of mine.

'No, don't worry, Gran,' Nathan echoes, with a smile. 'We've got plans.'

'What –?' I look from one of them to the other, puzzled. 'What plans? What are you cooking up?'

They look at each other and laugh. 'All in good time,' Stuart says. 'But for now,' he drains his mug, 'I think we should get back to work. It's my last day and I want to check all the greenhouse heaters are working properly before I leave.'

'And I want to do a bit more to the plastering in the west wing.' Nathan downs his own drink and they both leave the room, nudging each other and laughing as they say goodbye to the girls.

'I wonder what that was all about?' I say aloud – but of course, Julia and Lauren have no idea, and are too polite to speculate. Lauren deliberately changes the subject.

'We . . . hope it didn't upset you, Betty – finding that mirror yesterday.'

I notice Julia shooting her a look, quite obviously trying to warn her off the topic. I suppose my reaction must have startled them a bit. It was such a shock, seeing it again. Bringing back the memories. But I don't want them to think they did anything that distressed me.

'No. Not upset.' I put my cup down, lean back and close my eyes for a moment before going on: 'It just . . . brought back some memories, that's all. But they were nice memories. Would you like me to tell you about when I first got that mirror?'

'If . . . it's not too personal, Betty,' Lauren says.

So I do. I tell them about Richard.

Forty-eight years previously

Betty

Valentine's Day, nineteen-sixty-five. I'd been seeing Richard for nearly two months. Seeing him secretly, telling nobody, not even my flatmate. I knew it was wrong. I'd never done anything so wrong in my life, and it haunted me, night and day, knowing what my parents would think of me – what they'd say. The shame of it, on top of the disappointment they felt in me for abandoning my *place in the world*, and coming to live in London, which of course was known by everyone in small Devon villages to be a den of iniquity. It seemed they weren't wrong. I'd been sucked into it – that iniquity – me, of all people, a respectable young teacher whose only previous boyfriends hadn't been much more than platonic friends of friends, and whose sexual liberation had so far only amounted to a bit of kissing and cuddling. Quite apart from the fear of the consequences in those days when the Pill – a new invention – was only available for married women, I'd always been too shy, and too conservative, to go any further. Despite the determination to leave my so-stifling country upbringing behind and be a modern city girl, I still hadn't met anyone I wanted to take such a risk for. Until I was grabbed by the throat and shaken to my roots, by falling in love at a Beatles' concert.

If anyone had told me, before I went to that concert, that I'd have lost my heart before the Fab Four had left the stage, I'd have presumed they were talking about the obvious falling-in-love all the girls in that audience experienced for John, Paul, George or Ringo. We all had our favourites. Paul was mine, despite the fact that I shared John's famous surname. But no, instead of being carried away by the Beatles, I was carried outside by the guy sitting next to me – swiftly followed by my flatmate Helen, who'd been sitting on my other side and complained about missing *Love Me Do* as soon as I started saying I didn't feel well. It seemed she nevertheless didn't feel she could just leave me to my fate in the arms of a stranger and go on watching the show.

'You fainted.' The words seemed to come from a long way off. As I opened my eyes, I saw, through the mist of my dawning consciousness, Paul McCartney hovering over me, concern in his gorgeous big brown eyes. Except, of course, that it wasn't Paul McCartney at all but someone a little older, a little broader, but equally handsome – and he was giving me a tender smile of concern as I tried to sit up. 'Don't rush to get up,' he said.

'We're missing the *Beatles*,' Helen reminded me impatiently. 'Are you all right now?'

I looked around me. We were in the foyer of the Hammersmith Odeon, and I was lying on the carpet near the fresh air coming from the outside doors.

'Sorry,' I muttered to Helen. I tried again to sit up, but my head was still swimming. 'I think I was too hot. I'll be all right in a minute.'

'Stay where you are until you're not dizzy anymore,' the stranger said. He turned to Helen. 'I'll take care of her if you want to go back to the concert.'

She looked at me doubtfully. 'Better not,' she said, eyeing my rescuer up and down.

'Look, there are people all around,' he pointed out. This wasn't too much of an exaggeration. There was a bored looking girl at the ticket desk, who'd obviously had nothing to do all evening, as the event was sold out, and an usher looking after another girl who'd fainted and been carried out. And people milling around in the street outside, hoping somehow to get a glimpse of a Beatle. 'And I'm a respectable married man, OK? I'll bring her back in as soon as she feels up to it.'

A respectable married man. Even then, looking at him with hazy gratitude as Helen made no pretence of being sorry to leave me and go back to her seat – even then, weeks before I realised it was too late, that this was it, I'd found the love of my life and I couldn't, shouldn't, have him but I must – even then, I took in those words, swallowed them whole, and could never pretend to myself or anyone else that I didn't know.

He did as he'd promised: as soon as I'd recovered from my faint, he helped me to my feet, took my arm as if I were an invalid and escorted me back to my seat. The Beatles were singing their last-but-one number by now, and Helen was engrossed, carried away like everyone else, but my excitement had ebbed a little. Or . . . changed focus. Every now and then I sneaked a glance at that man sitting next to me, and each time, blushed furiously to find him looking straight back at me. As we finally got up to join the crowd of fans heading for the exits, some of them wailing and crying in disappointment that it was all over, I felt him tap my hand. I glanced up at him and he was smiling. And surreptitiously slipping something into my fingers. It was a piece of paper. I clutched it, feeling the deliciousness of its secret, as we left the cinema and said our polite goodbyes; as I headed back to the Tube station with Helen and what felt like half the population of London; and as we arrived back at our flat, where I made a dash for the bathroom and in its privacy, with every nerve of my body tingling in anticipation, finally opened the note.

Richard Cavenham he'd written – I imagined him scrawling it in the darkness of the concert, or perhaps while I was still lying dizzy on the floor of the foyer. And he'd added his phone number.

I waited for two whole days before I called, and even then, I'd stepped in and out of the phone box three times before I had the courage to use the phone. I knew what I was doing, knew it was wrong, knew I was starting something I was going to feel guilty about, that it would probably end in tears and I'd feel ashamed and sorry. But I did it anyway. I agreed to meet him the next evening. And the next, and the next . . . and by Valentine's Day, when he booked us a hotel room, and had champagne brought to the room, and gave me a present wrapped in gold paper with a pink bow and told me he loved me – it was far, far too late for regrets.

The present, of course, was a beautiful silver handbag mirror. 'So you can always look at yourself', he said as he kissed me, 'and see how lovely you are.'

And if you think that's cheesy, that I must have been pathetically naïve to fall for a line like that, to fall for a *man* like that – well, yes, you're right, I was. But whatever anyone thinks, he was the love of my life, and I've never fallen for anyone since. Or even regretted it. How could I? He was the father of my son.

Lauren

We sit in silence for a while when Betty stops talking. She looks up at us, apology in her eyes – I guess she's wishing she hadn't told us all that – but she doesn't say anything. So this Richard must have been – *is* – Stuart's father. I wonder why they broke up; why she kept him so secret. She'd been so determined not to let Stuart or Nathan to know who he was, but they seem to have forgiven her for all those years of deception.

Well, frankly he sounds a bit of a creep to me, if he made her promise never to tell anyone, just so that he could go on with his marriage, his deception of his poor wife. Did she even tell him she was pregnant? Did he care? And all that stuff about buying her the mirror so that she could look at herself and see how beautiful she looked – she's right, it's cheesy, to the point of making me feel nauseous. I'm sorry, but I'd have told him where to stick his present and his pathetic creepy lines, until he could come back and tell me he was free.

I look at Julia, wondering if she can see the irritation on my face, and whether she looks like she feels the same. But she's staring down at the floor, her eyes half-closed, as if she's in pain. As if she's been deeply moved by Betty's story instead of feeling cross for her, as I do.

'I'm sorry, girls,' Betty says finally, taking a deep breath. 'I never meant to bore you with all that . . . all my silly old ramblings –'

'That's all right, Betty,' I say. I give her a smile. Poor thing. It wasn't her fault she fell for a bastard, and perhaps things were different back in those days. I guess girls weren't quite as strong and independent as we are today.

I stop the thought in its tracks. *Strong and independent*? Who am I kidding? Julia would laugh out loud if she knew what I was thinking. She'd rightly point to the string of boyfriends I've loved and lost – or tried to convince myself I'd loved, anyway. I haven't ever managed to be independent, the way she has. I've wanted a partner and a child so much, I'd have convinced myself I was in love with anyone – yes, possibly even a married man. It's a sobering thought.

I glance at Julia again – and as I do, she finally looks up, but not before I notice her quickly wipe a tear from her eye.

'He must have been very special, Betty,' she says softly. 'Thank you for sharing your memories with us.'

Her voice sounds strange, like she's on the verge of crying properly. I'm surprised she's got so emotional about it all. I mean, it's sad for Betty – although at least she knows, now, that this Richard is still alive. I suppose they could get in contact if they really wanted to. But to me, it's surely just the old, old story – a married man taking advantage of an innocent young girl. It makes me sick to think she might have hankered after him all these years, maybe missing other opportunities to meet someone more suitable, maybe marry and have more children.

It's not like Julia to be so soft-hearted; she's always been made of sterner stuff. But, looking at her now, I realise once again that I didn't really know her at all. Perhaps it's all this worry about her job that's made her get upset. I'm just about to suggest that perhaps we should leave Betty in peace and go back to the Lodge, when my phone starts to ring.

'Oh – sorry, I'll just –' I begin to say, looking at the screen and planning to refuse the call. But a quick glance tells me the caller is Fern – the girl from the village with the adopted child. I have no idea why she might be calling me today, as she knew we were due to be going home, but something makes me feel I need to answer.

'Sorry,' I apologise to Betty as I take the phone out of the room. I feel a bit rude, but she waves it aside. I accept the call while I'm in the hallway, just outside the door of the sitting room.

'Hi, Fern,' I say cheerily. 'Are you OK?'

'Um . . . yes, we're fine here, thanks, Lauren. But I just needed to let you know, since I've got your phone number, and Eddie, the landlord at the pub, didn't know whose car it is –'

'What car?' I say, puzzled. Then, as the light beginning to dawn, I go on, 'Do you mean Julia's car? We know it's still parked at the pub – but because of the weather, we couldn't move it. Is – um, Eddie – upset about it? We're hoping to move it tomorrow –'

Julia's beside me, listening, now, frowning, looking like she wants to take the phone off me, but I turn away.

'No, it's not that, Lauren,' Fern says. 'But I'm sorry to say, I don't think you'll be moving it. There's been . . . a bit of an accident.'

'Oh my God. What kind of accident?'

Julia's actually trying to grab my phone now, but I shake my head at her, trying to listen to what Fern's telling me.

'A collision, it was,' she says. 'Not really the guy's fault, I don't suppose. He came off the road, he said – skidded on the ice, lost control completely, ended up in the car park with his bonnet halfway into Julia's car. I was in the pub at the time, and he came in, looking for whose car it was, wanting to apologise and do the whole thing with insurance details. But Eddie didn't know whose car it was, and I said I knew, but I didn't have a number for Julia. So he's written his details down for her, and Eddie's got them behind the bar. Couldn't put the note on the windscreen, with all the snow, you know.'

'*Shit,*' I mutter. I'm looking at Julia's face and I can see she's overheard some of this, as her mouth's dropped open and she looks like she's about to scream.

'It definitely isn't driveable. I reckon it might be a write-off,' Fern's going on, 'but on the other hand, it looks a pretty good car –'

It is, obviously. No point working for a car dealership if you don't get a brand new, posh car every year.

'So they might say it's worth repairing it.'

'Give me the phone! Give it to me! Let me speak to her!' Julia's trying again to grab it from me. 'My car! My sodding car! I can't believe it!'

'It's not Fern's fault,' I try to remind her as I hand the phone over. 'She's trying to help.'

'Who is he – the guy who hit my car?' she demands as soon as she's got the phone. 'I need his details – yes, OK, sorry, I didn't mean to be –. OK, yes, I'll talk to the landlord. I'll call the pub, yes. I know, but I need it sorted out right away! We've got to get home!' She takes a deep breath, apologises again and manages, at least, to thank Fern for her trouble, before turning to me, handing me back my phone, and saying abruptly: 'Well, this just about puts the lid on it, doesn't it? Honestly, can this week possibly get any bloody worse?'

I don't think she really wants an answer to that.

Julia

I feel sick. Not just nauseous, but actually like I might throw up.

'I've got to go,' I say, pushing past Lauren, looking around me like I'm not sure where I am or which direction to go in. 'I need to go and look at the car, right now. See how bad it is.'

'All right.' Sensibly, she doesn't try to argue with me. 'Just hold on a minute – I'm going to ask Stuart, or Nathan, to take us down there.'

'But I need to go right now. I can't phone the insurance company until I've seen how bad it is.' I can hear my voice shaking. My legs have gone weak, like I'm in shock. Perhaps I am. Seriously, it's just too much. Too much, on top of everything else. It can't really be happening, can it?

'Sit down,' she says, calmly. 'Just for a minute.' She's got my arm, and she's steering me back into Betty's sitting room, where Betty's looking at us anxiously, getting to her feet, asking if she can do anything to help. I suppose she's heard me talking to Fern about the car. I didn't mean to shout; I shouldn't have shouted. As Lauren said, Fern was just trying to help. But I feel too sick to worry about that right now.

'She's OK,' Lauren says to Betty as she pushes me gently down onto the sofa. 'But we need to cadge a lift to the pub car park. I'm sorry about this. Do you think Nathan or Stuart would mind? It's a bit of an emergency. Sit down, Betty. Just point me in the right direction and I'll go and find them.'

'No you won't,' she retorts firmly. 'I've still got a pair of lungs on me when I need to shout.' And to my surprise, she walks to the door of the sitting-room, holds her head up, opens her mouth and hollers at a volume completely at odds with her frail appearance: 'NATHAN! STUART! HERE! QUICK!' – ending on a series of rasping coughs that shake her whole frame to the point where I get up and run to grab hold of her, afraid she's going to collapse.

'I was a teacher,' she reminds us, on a wheeze of laughter, as she sinks back into a chair. 'You never forget how to raise your voice.'

Almost immediately, Nathan appears in the sitting room doorway, followed by Stuart.

'What the hell?' Nathan says, staring around us all in alarm. 'Are you all right, Gran?'

'What happened?' Stuart says, looking from Betty to us and back again. 'Did you have a fall or something, Mum? Are you hurt?'

'Sorry to worry you,' Lauren says, while Betty's still wheezing and gasping at the same time as protesting that there's nothing the matter with her. 'She shouldn't have got you running – it's not exactly an emergency, but . . . we just need a favour, if one of you wouldn't mind.'

'It's my car,' I explain. 'Someone's hit it. I need to see how bad the damage is. The pub landlord's got the details for the insurance.'

'Oh, right.' Stuart visibly relaxes for a moment, obviously grateful that there's nothing wrong with his mum, but then shakes his head and adds, 'God, sorry to hear about your car, though. Of course – I'll take you there right now. Nathan's in the middle of plastering a wall, so –'

'Sorry,' Lauren says again, to Nathan, who shakes his head and says he hopes my car's still driveable. 'I'll come with you, Julia.'

Even in Stuart's jeep, with chains on his tyres, it's a slow drive down the lane to the pub. Either side of the road, the banks are piled high with snow, the trees so laden with it that they look top-heavy. In the weak sunshine that occasionally finds its way through the blanket of low cloud, we can see the layer of iced slush glinting on top of the snow that's still lying thick in our path.

As soon as we turn into the pub car park, I gasp in horror. A white van, with *Eddies Electrical Services* emblazoned across the side, is resting almost casually with its front smashed into my poor car – as if some vindictive god had shoved them together for fun and just left them like that. I feel like crying.

'It doesn't look good,' Stuart says unnecessarily. He pulls up next to it and I get out of the jeep, immediately slipping on the lethal icy surface and only just managing to avoid falling over. 'Be careful!' he adds, following me, taking firm, steady footsteps in his sturdy boots. 'The whole driver's side is smashed. Damn it, I imagine it'll be written off, Julia.'

'But it's an S-Class Merc!' I hear myself wailing. 'This year's reg!'

'I know. Well, it'll have to be towed to whichever garage the insurance company wants to use for the estimate, anyway, but I somehow think . . .' He looks at me and sighs. 'Sorry, but in the end, that'd be a better result for you. You'll get a new car –'

As if that's ever been a problem. And anyway, it's not really the point. I wave aside the car, as if I'm not at all the sort of person who cares about luxury cars – and perhaps, I realise with a sense of shock, I might actually *not* be, anymore – 'the point is, I need to get home.' I raise my voice, wanting to scream it out to the world. 'I *have* to get home! It's really . . . I mean, it's really, desperately important. I've got to get home.'

Lauren, without me realising it, has slipped and slid her way to stand beside me, and now she puts her arm around me and says, quietly:

'Don't cry, Julia. We'll sort something out.'

'I'm not crying,' I retort – although I am. 'I just need –'

'I know. I don't understand why, and I wish you'd tell me, but I can see how important it is for you to get home. We'll find a way. We can get a courtesy car, can't we? If we call the insurers –'

Stuart's been tactfully silent while I try to pull myself together, but now he turns to look at me.

'It's not going to be possible,' he says, quietly but firmly. 'You can't drive home in these conditions –'

'I have to!' I insist, as Lauren, trying to calm me, starts to suggest to Stuart that perhaps tomorrow, all this ice and snow might have thawed, who knows, it might be a much better day, fine and dry.

'And even if that were to happen, which it won't,' he says gently, 'you know quite well that you won't get a courtesy car that quickly. I'll take you.'

'Take me where? To the insurance people?' I shake my head, confused. 'No, I'll call them, this afternoon, as soon as I've got this idiot driver's details from the publican –'

'I meant, I'll take you home.'

'What?' Lauren and I both stare at him. 'No, you can't do that. And anyway, I can't just abandon my car here and –'

'Yes, of course I can do that! I'm going back to London tomorrow anyway, so it's the obvious solution. And of course you can leave the Merc here. You have to say goodbye to it, Julia, you know that! You sort it all out with the insurance, they get it towed away. You'll get a courtesy car but not till you get back home.'

I do, obviously, know that's what will happen. I'm not completely stupid, and I haven't worked with cars all my adult life for nothing. I just can't think straight, the situation is too desperate.

'Julia, it's the only solution,' Lauren says. 'And if Stuart's being kind enough to offer us a lift – if you're sure you don't mind, Stuart?'

'It'll be nice to have company for the journey,' he insists. 'Come on. Let's pop into the pub and get this driver's details.'

And he links one of his arms through mine, the other through Lauren's, holding us both upright as he helps us across the glass-like surface of the carpark towards the pub entrance.

'Thank you,' I manage to mutter, but it comes out half-choked.

'Yes, thank you so much, Stuart,' Lauren says.

This is all her stupid fault anyway, I find myself thinking. If she hadn't gone off into the snowstorm in my car and got it stranded here in the first place . . .

But I somehow manage to shut the thought down quickly; I slam the lid on it, push it away, telling myself there's no point blaming her, she must feel bad enough about it already. She's my sister, and I love her. And despite the desperation of the situation, there's something ever-so-slightly warming about the realisation that I really mean it.

Lauren

I can't get over how kind Stuart's being. Well, OK, I suppose it's not putting him too much out of his way; he lives further east in London than Julia and further north than me. But he hardly knows us at all. I'm pretty sure the insurance company would have got us home somehow, in the circumstances, but he wouldn't hear of it.

'Mum says she already feels like you've become friends,' he says, 'which makes you friends of mine too.'

It doesn't take a minute to get the driver's details from Eddie in the pub, in fact it takes us longer to slip and slide across the carpark and back. I glance at the compacted snow and ice around Julia's car and can't help wondering, fleetingly, where my shoes might be, beneath it all. I shake my head at myself; in comparison to the wreck of the car, it seems ridiculous to care about a pair of old shoes.

As we head back to Stuart's jeep, I hear someone calling my name. It's Fern – she's standing at the door of a cottage just along the other side of the road, waving at us.

'All right, Lauren? All right, Julia? Did you get the details from Eddie?' she shouts, her voice carrying clearly through the crisp, cold air.

'Yes! Thanks,' I yell back.

'Are you still hoping to get home tomorrow?' She's crunching confidently up the lane towards us now, leaving the cottage door wide open. I can see

Andy inside, holding onto Ella's hand to stop her from running out. 'Will the insurance people –'

'I'm taking them both back to London, Fern,' Stuart answers for us. 'I'm going back tomorrow myself anyway so it'd be daft not to.'

'Tidy.' She smiles at us. 'Well, I hope everything works out for you both. The car. And –' She gives me a nod, '– the other thing.'

'It's OK, Julia knows about it – the adoption plan,' I tell her.

'I was surprised,' Julia admits. 'I had no idea Lauren was even . . .' Then she breaks off, pausing for a moment, before going on quickly: 'But I understand. I hope it works out too, obviously.'

'Cracking,' Fern says, nodding.

'Fern and I – and Andy – are going to keep in touch,' I tell Julia, although I think she's already guessed that.

'We are,' Fern agrees. 'We want to give Lauren a bit of support, share our experiences. I'm not being funny, Julia, but it won't be long before Lauren's complaining about how long it all takes, all the waiting, all the questions, all the paperwork –'

'I realise that,' I reassure her. 'I'm prepared to wait. I've waited this long.'

'It's very kind of you to want to support her,' Julia says. She looks around, to see Stuart waiting, passing his car keys from hand to hand. 'Well, it's been nice to meet you, Fern. Perhaps we'll see you again one day, who knows.'

She looks shocked as soon as the words are out of her mouth, almost as shocked as I am at hearing them! Can she really be serious? I didn't think she'd ever want to come back to this part of the country again! Even Fern's looking from one of us to the other in surprise.

'Well, I hope so, Julia, I do,' she says. 'Come in the summer next time, won't you! We'll show you the farm.'

She gives us both a hug. It feels odd. We've spent even less time with her than with Stuart, but I feel sad about parting from her.

'I'll see you again,' I promise. 'Soon. Definitely.'

Julia and I are silent in the back of the jeep for the short drive back.

'You're coming back? Soon?' she challenges me eventually as we turn in at the gate.

'You said you were, too,' I point out. 'But I suppose you were just being polite.'

'I guess so. Anyway, I can't think any further at the moment than getting onto this insurance company and then getting home.'

'I know,' I sympathise. 'Thanks so much, Stuart,' I add as he pulls up outside the Lodge.

'No problem. Now, do you need any help, Julia, with getting this insurance claim underway? Not that I'd imagine you're anything other than completely competent,' he adds quickly. 'But I know it's been really upsetting for you.'

'Thanks, Stuart,' she says. 'But I'll be fine. I want to get on with it right away.'

'And while you're doing that, I'll be finishing the packing ready for tomorrow,' I say. 'And cleaning and tidying the place up, of course –'

'No, you don't need to do that – that's our job,' he says immediately. 'Well, sorry: it's going to have to be Nathan's job, for now at least. Cleaning is included in your rental charge.'

'Poor Nathan, he's got enough on his plate!' I protest. 'Well, the least I can do is leave it as neat and tidy as it was when we arrived.'

A week ago. Is that really all it was? It feels like a month, at least. I feel like London is a long-distant memory. I'm struggling to remember what my own living room looks like. Or what my office at work is like.

'If I don't see you before,' Stuart says, as we're getting out of the jeep, 'I'll pick you up in the morning at half past nine – or is that too early?'

'That's perfect,' Julia says quickly. I know she'd go sooner – right now, probably – if she could.

'But we can't leave without coming to say goodbye to your mum!' I tell him, a strange kind of panic suddenly coming over me at the thought of perhaps not seeing her again. She's eighty years old – as she says herself, life's short. I can't bear to think about it.

'Well, come over later. I'm sure she'd love that. How about joining us all for farewell drinks after dinner?'

'Oh no, that's surely going to be your family time,' I protest. 'You'll be saying goodbye yourself –'

'Not goodbye for long,' he reminds us, smiling. 'Come over at seven. In fact I'll pick you up and drive you round the road way. Too icy underfoot to walk through the woods in the dark. I won't be drinking anything alcoholic anyway because of driving tomorrow.'

He's starting the engine before we can begin to argue – and reversing back onto the lane, with a wave and a smile. I'm going to miss that smile, I realise. As well as everything else.

Once inside, I make Julia a cup of tea as she immediately settles down with her phone and her insurance policy open on her laptop. I know she needs to concentrate so I take my own tea upstairs, tidy the bedrooms and give the bathroom a quick wipe round before coming back and doing the same in the kitchen. Despite what Stuart said about cleaning being included, it feels only courteous to leave it looking nice.

'Right,' she says eventually in a weary voice. 'They're getting the car towed to a garage in Okehampton. They'll get in touch with me. I suppose I've just got to wait.'

'Yes. There isn't any more you can do for now, is there. Have you told Phil? What did he say?'

'No, I haven't told him!' she snaps.

'Oh, OK.' I suppose she wouldn't, if he's been off work sick. And she probably reasons that it's her car, so she'll sort it out herself, fair enough. Although, after all, it *is* a company car, and he *is* the boss. I'm wondering if perhaps they've been having some arguments. Maybe that's why she's got herself in a state this week. I always did think it was weird the way they've still been working together, running the company together, but I presumed they've managed to keep the working relationship strictly professional.

A little later, as we're tidying up in the living-room, there's the sound of the cat flap rattling in the kitchen and the two cats come tearing in, one after the other like kids playing Chase.

'It looks like Rosie's back to her usual self!' Julia says.

'Yes.' I bend down to give them both a stroke. 'Oh, I'm going to miss them, Julia! I really think I'll have to get myself a cat –'

'As well as a baby?' She gives me a pointed look. 'You'd better check with the Social Services people.'

'Yes, I suppose that's true. Don't worry, I'm going to look into all this stuff, get all the advice I can, do it properly. Whatever you think, it isn't something I've rushed into. Meeting Fern and Andy has just helped me to make the final decision. But I know there are still lots of hurdles to clear. I might not be considered suitable, for a start.'

'I'm sure you will. Why wouldn't you? You've got a good job, a nice home –'

'So you keep saying.'

She gives me a quizzical look but, probably wisely, drops the subject. The thing is, this is what worries me. I'm more certain now than ever that I want to try to adopt a child. What I'm *not* certain about anymore are my job or my home. It sounds ridiculous, flaky, though, to say so, just because I've been away on holiday for a mere week and started feeling like I don't want to go back to normal. So I know; I know perfectly well that before I can even think any further about applying for adoption, I need to sort myself out. Get home, take stock, and either

have a reality check and get on with my real life
again, or . . . or what? I have no idea.

We don't stay with the family for too long this
evening. Stuart pours us out a drink, while Nathan
offers plates of Betty's home-made biscuits, and we
all raise a glass.

'To the next time?' Betty says hopefully. 'I'd
really love you both to come back again in the
summer.'

'I hope so,' I say.

'Well, you'd better book early!' Nathan teases.
'We're hoping to get lots of holidaymakers here –'

'Oh, take no notice of him!' Betty says
dismissively. 'It doesn't matter how many others we
get booked in, we'll always find room for you two
somewhere.'

'In the potting shed?' Stuart jokes, winking at me.
Then he holds my gaze for a fraction of a minute, and
I have to look away, a bit taken aback. Is he *flirting*
with me? But he's already turned back, to talk to
Nathan, and the moment has passed. I probably
imagined it. Anyway, I'm too busy watching Julia,
who's already on her second drink, having downed
the first one far too quickly for someone who
normally rarely has more than one small glass.

'Are you OK?' I ask her very quietly as she's
taking another large gulp.

I know she's stressed, but if she drinks more than
she's used to, she's might make herself feel ill for the
journey home.

'Yes,' she says, shortly. Then she looks into her
glass, like she's surprised that it's already half-empty,

and puts it down on the table next to her. 'Thanks,' she adds.

When it comes to saying our goodbyes, I'm surprised at how emotional I feel. It seems ridiculous. I've only known these people for one week! Betty gives us both a hug and looks a bit upset, herself.

'Take care, now, won't you, girls,' she says. It's funny how she thinks of us as girls. I suppose anyone under sixty might seem that way to her. 'Stuart's going to give me a call when he gets home, and he'll let me know he's dropped you both off safely.'

'Thanks, Betty – for everything,' I say. 'We'll keep in touch.'

I intend to, anyway. And Julia's nodding agreement. We both give Nathan a quick hug too, and he gives us a peck on the cheek.

'Hope to see you both again,' he says. Then he adds, with a little grin, 'Maybe I'll be married again by the time you come back!'

'Nathan, for God's sake, you've only just started seeing this chap!' his gran rebukes him, but he's laughing, and telling us that of course he's joking, he's got no intention of making another mistake, but he *has* had a first date with a guy who works on the local farm.

'I've known him for years. He's a friend of Fern's, too.' He shrugs, looking sheepish. 'I just never realised he would be . . . interested.'

'Well, I hope it goes well,' I tell him. He's such a nice guy; he deserves to be with someone who's right for him.

And with that, all too soon, it feels like the holiday is properly over. Stuart drops us back at the

Lodge and we go to our rooms for our last night's sleep here at Deepcombe.

But maybe not forever.

Sunday

Julia

I feel a bit better now we're on the way home. Now that Stuart has successfully negotiated the frozen wastes of the Dartmoor lanes and we're on an A-road – although even this has been affected by a fresh, but lighter, shower of snow during the night. But it's been gritted and looks relatively normal if you ignore the mounds of snow beside the carriageway and on the central reservation. I've sat in the back seat because I want to keep my phone in my hand, looking for messages, alert for any further calls. Stuart and Lauren are chatting about his mum – how she managed on her own before Nathan moved back in with her, whether the veg and herb business has been successful over the years. I'm half-listening, but all the time the pressures of what I'm going home to are taking up too much space in my head to concentrate properly or contribute to the conversation.

'It was a thriving business at one time,' Stuart's saying. 'When Mum was a bit younger and fitter, and Janie and I were living and working there with her. But on her own, with Nathan gone too, she obviously couldn't do it. She had to let it go, really, apart from the herbs she grew in the conservatory. She could have employed somebody to help her, but by the time we'd all recovered . . . from losing Janie . . . the business was already going downhill.'

'Was that when Nathan suggested starting the B and B business?' Lauren asks.

'Yes. And then he moved back in, and literally took over. Thank goodness he did, too – while I was selfishly hiding myself away in London refusing to get involved.'

'I don't suppose it was selfish at all. It sounds like you were . . . pretty traumatised,' Lauren says softly.

I look up, just in time to catch them exchanging a glance. Stuart quickly looks away, back at the road, but I saw something . . . in fact I kind-of *felt* something . . . in that quick glance. I suppose it's just sympathy, from Lauren. Kindness. She *is* a kind person, a nice person, and it's taken me too long to recognise that.

'Yes. It was a tough time,' is all Stuart says in response. Then he shrugs and goes on: 'Anyway, Nathan and I have got plans, now. We want to get the business re-established. Deepcombe Market Garden – that's what we traded under before. And we want to run the guest accommodation alongside it, of course.'

'But you'll need more staff, surely? To run both sides of the business? Especially if you're still trying to renovate the house at the same time,' she points out.

'Yes. We will.'

'That's what you were hinting at, the other day? You and Nathan – you were talking about having plans, looking . . . kind of excited,' she says.

'Yep. We're both feeling really fired up about it now. Nathan's had enough of doing odd building work here and there when the weather's OK – which it often isn't, in Devon! And – as you know – I can't wait to walk away from my job in the city. So Nathan and I are going to get a couple of new greenhouses built, start up the market gardening again, and employ someone to run the B&B side. We're doing up rooms in the west wing with a view to using them for more guests. They'll have their own kitchen; it used to be the servants' quarters back in the day.'

'It sounds really exciting,' Lauren says. 'You must keep us updated.'

They both fall silent for a while. We're all watching the countryside out of the windows. The snow is still lying thick beside the road as we get onto the M5 motorway. We leave Devon, passing the Somerset county sign and heading steadily east. I glance at my phone again. No more messages. I don't know whether that's good or bad. I send off a message myself, but I have no idea whether it'll be answered. I'm finding it hard to breathe for thinking about what might be happening.

'Will you be meeting up with your father again?' Lauren suddenly asks Stuart, and I can't help giving a little gasp of shock.

'Lauren!' I say. 'That's a bit personal –'

The thing is, we're not even supposed to know about it. We only overheard him telling Betty he'd found his father, but nothing's actually been said to us, and why should it?

But Stuart's laughing. 'It's fine, it's not a secret, and yes, of course I want to meet him again. The first meeting was quite . . . overwhelming, for us both. I didn't know if he'd be angry for tracking him down. I presumed he didn't *want* to be found. But it wasn't like that at all.' He pauses, takes a breath, then goes on in a rush: 'The fact is, he didn't know about me. He didn't know Mum was expecting. She never told him.'

'Oh.'

There's a silence for a few minutes. Lauren obviously doesn't know quite what to say to this. I find myself thinking about how Betty described meeting Richard at that Beatles' concert, how they fell in love, how he was *the love of her life.* I wonder how long the relationship lasted, and whether he ever left his wife. Why wouldn't she have told him about the baby? Whatever else we might think about it, surely it was his right to know he had a child? And her right to have his support? But after a minute Stuart goes on:

'I suppose I always assumed he must have been a nasty piece of work. That he was some bastard who got Mum pregnant – back in a time when it could have really wrecked her life – and didn't want to know. I guessed that was why she never mentioned his name, never wanted me to try to find him.' He pauses, and when he goes on again his voice is softer. 'But it wasn't like that at all.'

He's shaking his head now, changing the subject, and I'm sure even Lauren knows better than to ask any more questions.

'Anyway, look, we're making pretty good progress, we're just about to join the M4, so –'

And then, almost as if he'd tempted fate by mentioning it, as we leave the roundabout where we join the M4, we come to a complete standstill.

'There must have been an accident,' Stuart says after we've crept forward about two yards and stopped again. 'Let's hope it's not too bad . . . if it's just a shunt, we should soon get going again.'

But we don't. I feel the panic rising as the situation sinks in. We're on a motorway. We can't just turn around, or get off unless we're able to get to the next exit, and how far is that? If this is a serious accident we could be here for an hour. Longer. Who knows how long? I glance at my phone, close it, open it, look at it again. I feel myself fidgeting, getting hot, while Lauren's calmly reassuring Stuart, telling him 'Oh well, we just have to sit it out, don't we, at least we're not the ones involved in the accident,' and although I know this is her being who she is – nice – I want to scream at her that it isn't as easy as that! I've got to get home. I *need* to get home.

'Are you OK, Julia?' Stuart asks. He's probably heard me hyperventilating. They both turn round to look at me, and Lauren's face creases in concern.

'Oh God, what is it?' she says. I realise I'm holding my phone in a vice-like grip, staring at it, willing it to beep with a message.

'I need to get home,' is all I can manage to say.

They look at each other, then back at me.

'Julia,' Lauren says in a different tone of voice now. Calm, but firm. 'Tell me what's going on. Is it an emergency? Has something happened – something serious?' She pauses. 'It's not Simon, is it?'

'No.' My son's OK, thank God. But I desperately need to hear from him.

'Hang on, we're moving,' Stuart says.

We start to inch slowly forwards, a few yards at a time, then suddenly get a spurt on. Lauren's still watching me anxiously, but I shake my head, go back to my silent staring at my phone. Still no message. Should I try to call? Will it just make things worse?

'I think it's just that everyone's driving more carefully than usual,' Stuart says as the traffic begins to slow down again a couple of miles further on. It's snowing again here – still quite lightly, but enough to need the wipers on, and it's evident that the snow here over the past few days has been even heavier than it was on Dartmoor, if that's possible. Another *Beast from the East*, the weathermen are saying. I worry about how bad it might be, the further we go east.

Suddenly, Stuart pulls off the motorway into one of the services.

'I need the loo anyway,' he says. 'And unless you are literally in a life-or-death situation, Julia, I think we ought to have a half-hour break for a coffee or something.'

I feel bad now. He's doing us such a favour, and the least I can do is let him have a break from driving, especially in this weather. If he gets so tired that he has an accident, I'll never forgive myself.

'Of course,' I say.

We park up, and Lauren takes my arm as we follow Stuart away from the car. It's bitterly cold outside, the sleety snow stinging our faces and we keep our heads down until we enter the warmth of the service building.

'I need the loo too,' Lauren says. 'Come on, Julia. Meet you at this coffee area, Stuart.'

It's not until I'm washing my hands that I realise I'm crying. I'm staring at myself in the mirror, trying to stop the tears, when Lauren arrives at the adjacent sink and sees me. Without even drying her hands, she grabs hold of me in a tight hug.

'Would it help to tell me?' she says. 'I'll just listen. I won't say anything, if you don't want me to – whatever it is.'

That's how we end up in a quiet part of the Costa outlet, Stuart, seeing the state I'm in, having brought us each a mug of coffee and then discreetly going to sit a little distance away. I've stopped crying, because I know she's right. Perhaps I'll actually feel better when I've said this out loud.

'It's Phil,' I say, trying to stop my voice shaking. I take a deep breath. 'I told you he wasn't well –'

'Yes. Oh . . . Julia, it's not something serious, is it? You just made it sound like a cold or some kind of virus –'

'He's having major surgery. He could have died.'

'*What*?' She nearly drops her mug. 'Julia, what the hell? What's happened? What's wrong with him?'

'Oh,' I shake my head. 'He's been ill for a while, but I didn't take it seriously. Nor did he, unfortunately. Always busy, you know how it is. How it *was*. Both of us, married to the business, never taking a break. He's had problems for years with his stomach, but he just put it down to stress. When it finally got bad enough for him to get it checked out, they said he had a gastric ulcer. He didn't seem overly worried. He had to take medication and he was supposed to go for a further investigation later to make sure the ulcer had healed, but of course, he cancelled the appointment because he was too busy. Then it was Covid, and nobody was getting appointments. His symptoms had flared up again but he said he was OK. He didn't *look* OK, he looked anaemic, and I was worried the ulcer was bleeding – I'd Googled about it, you know, about the side effects. But of course, it wasn't easy to see a doctor at the time and he kept saying he'd be all right. And he did seem to get a bit better eventually. So of course, he's never been back to the doctor.'

I pause, take a gulp of my coffee. Lauren waits for me to go on.

'But now,' I say, and my voice starts to tremble again, 'He's ended up in hospital. Having a major operation.'

'What happened?' She's put her hand over mine, lightly, starting to stroke it. 'Is it the ulcer, then?'

'Yes. Simon called me, soon after we came away. He was worried about his dad. Phil had been getting severe stomach pain again. Simon wanted him to go to the doctor, but of course, he wouldn't, he just kept taking more of his tablets and trying to carry on. Simon was getting more and more worried –'

'That's what all the calls were about. You just said Phil was off sick. You made it sound like it was trivial. I thought it was the work situation worrying you. Why didn't you *tell* me it was serious, Julia?'

'Because at first, I kept trying to persuade myself Simon might be panicking unnecessarily. It seemed so sudden – to have been OK before I left, and then suddenly in excruciating pain . . .'. I look away, swallowing. 'I even wondered if Phil was just making a fuss because he hadn't wanted me to go away.'

'Oh, Julia,' Lauren whispers.

'But then,' I go on, 'in the end, Simon told me Phil had been rushed into hospital. There's another ulcer, and it's perforated, and he's been in agony but somehow, he's ignored it until he's now got peritonitis. It's serious. And they've been trying to treat him with intravenous antibiotics, but the call last night was to say it's gone too far now, his stomach lining is too seriously damaged, and he's got to have surgery – a partial gastrectomy. The operation's today. Simon's in the hospital with him. He said he'd message me as soon as he knows any more.'

'You *should* have told me then!'

'I couldn't. I just couldn't – I was so worried, I couldn't talk about it. And let's face it, we hadn't exactly been sisters who confided stuff – emotional stuff. Anyway, I didn't want you to think I was looking for an excuse to go home. Then, of course, when the snow came –'

'You were stuck.' She sighs. 'But if you'd told me, we could have got home somehow – a train, a taxi –'

'Well, I thought as long as I got home in time to see him before the operation – and then, the car got hit, and Stuart offered to drive us, so . . . this had to be the best option.'

'Well, that's true, it is. And we're well on the way now, so there's nothing else you can do.' She pauses, then goes on: 'Of course you're upset. It's such a shock. Especially for Simon – it's his dad, he must be so worried. And a shock for you, too; even if you *do* hate each other, he's still the owner of the company. Your job –'

I stare at her. 'My *job*?' I retort. 'Lauren, I don't give a *shit* about my job right now. And I don't hate Phil! Of course I don't, I've never hated him, never!'

'Sorry, no, bad choice of words, but you know what I mean. You divorced him, so obviously you –'

'I didn't.' I look down at our hands. Hers is still stroking mine. They're so similar, our hands – long fingers, wide nails. She's my sister, but she doesn't know the first thing about me. And that's mostly my fault. 'I didn't divorce him,' I say again, more softly. 'He divorced me. I never stopped loving him. Why on earth else would I have carried on working for a bloody car dealership all these years? It's all been for Phil. I still love him.'

Lauren

We're silent when we're back in the car. Whenever I look round at Julia, she's watching her phone constantly, as if she's willing it to ring, or beep with a message. She's upset, of course, because she'd still hoped to see Phil before he went down for surgery, but Simon called her this morning to say his operation was first on the list. She said she's consumed with the fear that something will go wrong, that he won't wake up after the surgery and she won't have said goodbye to him.

'I'm sure that's not going to happen,' I told her. 'If it was literally life or death, they'd have operated straight away, last night, in the middle of the night if necessary, wouldn't they. They wouldn't have just scheduled him for the morning.'

But she hasn't calmed down much. She's like a cat on hot bricks – I can see her literally twitching, unable to sit still.

'Why don't you call Simon now?' I suggest. 'The op will probably be over by now.'

'He's promised to let me know immediately it's over. I don't want to hassle him. He might have had to turn his phone off, anyway.'

I wonder if, really, despite everything she's said, it's because she's afraid to ask. Afraid of the answer. I want to say come on, Phil's a fit, strong, man, only in his mid-forties, he'll come through this, no problem, he'll be fine, it's just a warning, he needs to slow down, cut out the stress . . . But I don't. Because

I've just found out that she still loves him, she never stopped loving him, so I can understand why she's in such a state. I don't know why he divorced her, of course – I presume he wanted someone else, at the time. I'm not asking; but it changes almost everything I thought I knew about her.

'Not too far now, Julia,' Stuart says, and I see him glancing at her in the mirror. He's been so kind. So tactful and discreet. He could obviously see that Julia had been crying when we left the motorway services; I saw the concern clouding his eyes, but he said nothing, other than asking her very gently if she was sure she was ready to set off again.

As we head slowly east, we talk quietly together in the front, sparing Julia the effort of joining in. He tells me how pleased he is to have seen Nathan these last few days, to see with his own eyes that he's definitely recovered from the break-up of his marriage, to the point where he's ready to start dating again.

'The thing is, Nathan always wanted a life partner,' Stuart says. 'He didn't want to be that stereotypical gay man, playing the field. So he convinced himself Ben was right for him. I was worried about it – so was Gran. But he's not a child, it wasn't for us to tell him he'd got it wrong. However much we both loved him, we had to respect his choice.' He pauses, then adds, 'I've told him now: you can't fool yourself into being in love. When you *really* love someone, you'll know it.'

'As you did? With Janie?'

'Yes,' he says, and he smiles. 'Absolutely.'

'I think I've been a bit like Nathan, in a way,' I admit. 'Julia must have seen it quite plainly, but I resented her telling me. Every man I met, I convinced myself I was in love with them – that they were *the one.* But it was only because I was so desperate to settle down; to have a marriage, and a family life. Does that sound really shallow?'

'Not at all. In fact I'd say it sounds the opposite of shallow,' he says without any hesitation. 'Shallow relationships are surely those where someone is actively avoiding settling down! It sounds like you were . . . looking for something, Lauren. Something that sadly kept eluding you.' His voice is soft, as if he cares. As if he knows me, as if he can see me – who I am. He gives me a quick glance, turns back to the road and adds, 'You deserve to be happy. And there's nothing wrong with wanting that for yourself.'

'Thank you,' I say, so quietly I'm almost whispering. 'I'm not looking anymore, though – for a relationship. I'm going to sort out my life, first.'

'That sounds like a bit of a task!' He chuckles, then goes on: 'Which aspects need sorting out? Or would you rather not say?'

'Oh, just about all of it. My house, my job, my . . . life in London.' I stop, shocked at myself. What am I saying? I was going to think about all this gradually, calmly, rationally, after I've got home and got settled back into the routine again. I wasn't supposed to be talking about it yet, and definitely not to someone I've only just met, however much he seems to be acting like he knows me!

He nods. 'Some might say that's normal, though – after a holiday.'

'I know. That's why I'm not rushing into anything. I'm going back to my house, going back to work tomorrow, carrying on as before. And taking my time over any decisions.'

'Including the decision about adoption?'

'Yes. That's too important to be rushed into – even though I have been considering it for quite a long time. Even though I've . . . pretty much . . . almost definitely . . . completely made up my mind.'

He's laughing now. 'Pretty much almost definitely completely?'

'Yes.' I laugh too. 'Completely.'

We fall silent again. I look out of the window, watching the countryside flying past without really seeing anything, my thoughts miles away, so it's with a shock that I eventually realise we're already approaching the Heathrow turn-off. Stuart's got Julia's postcode in his Sat Nav and we're heading towards it now, and faster than I'd expected.

'The snow seems to have disappeared here, after all,' he says. 'Although there might be more on the minor roads, of course.'

'Stuart,' I say, dropping my voice almost to a whisper, 'Could we take Julia back to my place, please? My car's there. Phil's in hospital and I want to drive Julia there. I'm closer to it, anyway.'

'No!' Her hearing's even better than I thought. 'I'll go home. I need to drop my luggage off. And I can get a taxi. I'll be wanting to take Simon home too – afterwards. He hasn't got a car, he goes everywhere by tube and bus, but he'll be tired –'

'I can take you both home. We'll pick up your luggage on the way back from the hospital. Please,

Julia – you don't want to be messing around with taxis at a time like this. Let me take you. I want to.'

'OK,' she concedes, in a tired voice. 'OK, if you insist.'

I put my postcode into Stuart's Sat Nav for him, and we head north, towards my part of London. My road. My house. We're nearly there. The roads are clear, with just piles of slush at the sides and the occasional icy patch. It's not snowing anymore, here. It must have come from the east and cleared from the east.

'Next turning on the left,' I tell Stuart, even though the Sat Nav is doing a perfectly good job. I feel strangely nervous about being back, as if I might not like what I see. In truth, I don't, already. The narrow straight streets of identical terraced houses, so different from the winding country lanes we've come from. 'It's just along here on the right. Number thirty-two. Here – with the grey door.' Grey, like the street, like the whole area, like the way I feel about it. I need to stop this and buck up, be positive, for Julia's sake if not my own. 'Yes, this is it. Thanks, Stuart – thank you *so* much.'

'I'll help you in with the bags.' He turns off the ignition, gets out and has a stretch. 'Home sweet home, eh?'

'Hmm,' I respond, catching his eye. 'Oh, it's OK. It's not a bad area. Not as nice as where Julia lives, but –'

'It's nice,' he says. 'Quiet.' He opens the boot and takes out a suitcase in each hand. 'Go on,' he tells me as I try to take one from him. Julia's taken the cool bag that we took some food in with us, when we headed off on our holiday, and I grab the bag with our boots in and lead the way up the path to the front door. I unlock it and let Stuart go in ahead of me.

'Go straight through,' I say, awkwardly, as he carries the cases down the narrow hallway. 'Through to the living room, just dump them there. Thanks. Um – would you like a cup of tea or something? A sandwich? You haven't had anything to eat.'

'No. Thanks, but I haven't got far to go, anyway. I'll be home in five minutes. And you want to go straight to the hospital.' He turns to Julia. 'I hope everything's OK. Please let me know. You've got my number, haven't you?'

'Yes,' she says. 'Thank you, Stuart. And I'm sorry – sorry for being, well, for seeming ungrateful. I'm not, I really appreciate what you've done for us –'

'But you're worried. I'm not going to ask what it's about, but it's obviously really important.' He puts a hand on Julia's shoulder and kisses her on the cheek. 'I really hope everything will be OK.'

He turns to me. 'Lauren. I'm going to wait while you start your car. Just in case . . . you know, with the cold weather, and it sitting there all week.'

'Oh God, yes, the battery! I didn't think of that. Thanks Stuart. It's always started all right so far, but –'

'But let's just make sure.' He follows us back outside. My six-year-old Vauxhall Corsa is parked in the road, in front of his jeep. It's got a scratch and dent on the driver's door where I opened it into a lamppost a couple of months ago and haven't got around to having it repaired. But to my relief, it starts first time and I leave it running just for a moment to open the door again, reach up on tiptoe to kiss Stuart on the cheek and thank him again for everything.

'Stay in touch,' he says, leaning down to give me a return kiss. He looks down at me, holding my gaze for a full minute before adding, 'I want to know what you decide. About sorting out your life!'

'I will,' I promise.

We pull out past Stuart's jeep as he's getting into the driving seat, and we give each other a wave. I feel like I'm saying goodbye to a friend. Did I really only meet him when he found me outside the village pub in a snow drift? I feel like I've known him forever.

But there's no time to think about that – or anything else. We're off to the hospital.

Julia

He's OK. Oh, thank God, he's OK, he's come through the surgery, he's in recovery, he's going to be fine. I feel so shaky with relief, I can hardly talk. One of the surgeons has come to speak to us in the relatives' room. Lauren's sitting on one side of me, holding my hand, while Simon sits on the other side, looking completely exhausted. The surgeon's looking at me in surprise, as if he can't quite understand why I was so worried. He tells me there was actually very little danger to Phil's life, that yes, he'd definitely needed the surgery but once the decision to operate had been made, he was always going to be all right.

'Of course, if we'd continued to defer surgery in the prolonged hope of the antibiotic therapy working, it might have been a different story,' he concedes – but then sees my face and stops. He glances at the records in his hands. I wonder if he's taking note of Simon being listed as the next of kin, rather than me, or of Phil's marital status being listed as *divorced*. He looks back up at me and I think I see sympathy in his eyes. 'He's going to be fine now,' he repeats. 'He's going to be transferred to the HDU – the High Dependency Unit – but probably only for tonight, and only so that he can be carefully monitored overnight. So I suggest you all go home and get some sleep now, and –'

'No, I want to see him,' I insist.

'If you come back first thing in the morning, he'll have slept off the anaesthetic by then and hopefully we'll have him back on the ward.'

'I'll sleep here.'

The surgeon looks at me wearily. He's exhausted too, I realise. He doesn't want to have to argue. He shrugs, and begins to get to his feet.

'OK. I'll let the staff know you're here. They'll come and tell you when you can see him.' He gives us a smile as he leaves. 'Try to get some sleep, if you can.'

Lauren touches my arm. 'I'll stay here with you,' she says.

'But you've got to go to work tomorrow.'

'I'll call my boss. It'll be fine.' She turns to Simon and says, 'I'll drive you home first, though. You look absolutely shattered.'

'I've been here all day,' he admits. 'And all yesterday. But it's OK, I'll get an Uber.' He pulls out his phone. 'It'll be here by the time I walk outside.' He bends down to give me a kiss. 'Bye, Mum. You sure you're all right?'

I nod. I'm almost too worn out with worry and relief to speak. Simon looks across at Lauren and adds, a little diffidently: 'Thanks, Lauren.' I notice he doesn't call her *auntie*.

'I haven't done anything,' she says.

I notice, too, that he doesn't disagree.

'I haven't seen him for so long,' Lauren says quietly after we've both sat in silence for a while. 'I don't even know him now. It's my fault.'

'It works both ways,' I say. 'He's an adult.'

But she's right, really: the situation between her and Simon is mostly her fault. She hasn't bothered to keep in touch, she hasn't even tried. She's never shown the slightest interest in him. But somehow, after this past week, after everything that's happened, I feel the need to defend her. I know, now, that nothing is as black and white as I'd managed to convince myself. Our estrangement has been my fault too; I've made no more effort than Lauren has. I've excused myself that I was too busy with work, with Dad, with Simon, whereas all Lauren had to worry about was her interminable succession of failed relationships.

'When Simon was a little boy,' she's saying now, 'I thought he was the most gorgeous thing I'd ever seen. I was at that difficult stage of my life – all my own fault, of course. I'd ruined all my prospects and had no idea where my life was going. It was then that I first started fantasising about having a child of my own.'

'You used to come and see us back then. Occasionally,' I remember. 'But it got less often, and then you just stopped. You never came anymore.' I turn to look at her; she's dropped her head and she looks like she might cry. 'Sorry. I'm not criticising.'

At the time of that conversation back in Deepcombe, when she told me she stayed away because she was jealous, because she always wanted a child of her own, I wasn't sure I believed her. But now, I suddenly get it. She was very young. She'd had to give up on her dream of being a lawyer, and never revisited it. She never found a job she really liked. She couldn't keep a boyfriend; perhaps they sensed her desperation and beat a hasty retreat.

'I'm ashamed of it now, Julia.,' she says quietly. 'But . . . it hurt too much. I couldn't bear it. Couldn't bear seeing you in your perfect house, with your perfect husband and perfect little boy. I was jealous, and I'm so sorry now. And I was angry that you left it to me to look after Mum, but I was just as bad, I didn't help with Dad, I still don't. I've been a crap sister, a crap daughter and a crap auntie! And I didn't know Phil had divorced you, I always assumed it was the other way around, and I didn't get it! I thought you must have been mad, to throw away what you had, that perfect lifestyle. It drove me nuts just to think about it.'

'Don't cry,' I say softly, putting my arm around her. 'It's OK, Lauren. I understand. And it's been my fault too. I'm just as much to blame.'

I pause now, wondering if the time might have finally come to admit to it. To tell her what I promised myself I'd never speak about. It would be a relief, in a way, to get it out in the open between us, but on the other hand I dread to imagine what she might think of me once she knows. I take a deep breath.

'That perfect lifestyle that you thought I threw away?' I begin. I can hear my voice trembling slightly. I think, fleetingly, of seeing the magpies when we were walking together in the grounds of Deepcombe Manor. Nobody ever sees seven magpies together. But this is it: my *secret never to be shared.* 'You were right, Lauren: I did. I threw it away. But not in the way you thought.'

Julia

Fifteen years earlier

Simon had been a difficult baby: colicky, difficult to get to sleep, difficult to feed. We had sleepless nights with him until he was turned two, and temper tantrums until he was four, when he started school and slowly settled down. I'd found those first four years so exhausting, I told Phil I didn't want any more children. But by the time I was thirty, my life had settled down into a calm and fairly straightforward routine. Simon was seven now, and was doing well at school. He'd made friends, and our house and garden often echoed with the excited voices of little boys playing. I only needed to be around for the school drop-off and pick-up, so I was able to work from nine till three most days; but Phil and I agreed it made sense for me to be based mostly at home, so that I could be around during the school holidays and if ever Simon were to be off school, ill. He set me up with a home office, including phone line, computer, internet, access to all the company's systems so that I could work on the accounts and correspondence in between doing the housework, child care and cooking.

But I resented it. I was bored. Working at home in that big, empty house, with no real constraints on my time, I managed to overlook the fact of my immense privilege. Did I ever give a thought to how lucky I was, in comparison to other parents who perhaps had to commute to badly-paid jobs, giving up much of their salary to pay for child care? No, I resented the lack of adult company. I resented having to be responsible for all the housework, while Phil came home late in the evenings, tired but full of satisfaction, mentally energised by the increasing success of the business.

'We made a couple of great sales today!' he'd say, flopping into an armchair with a glass of wine while I stirred a saucepan or turned a steak. 'What have you been up to, Jules? Did you finish that invoicing?'

'Yes,' I'd mutter ungraciously. 'After doing the school run, the supermarket shop and cleaning the bathrooms.'

'Great,' he'd enthuse. 'Thanks, darling. What would I do without you?'

'Do you think we should have had another baby?' I asked him one evening.

He looked at me in surprise. 'I thought you didn't want any more? You never wanted to go through it all again?' he reminded me, as if I needed reminding. 'I respected that decision: I still do. I agree, it was a real struggle, those first few years. Why? Do you regret it now? Simon's happy enough, isn't he? Plenty of friends?'

Yes, he's happy enough, I wanted to scream. *But what about me?*

Even in my most selfish moments, though, I knew that to have another child to keep me from confronting my own boredom, would definitely not be the answer. I needed to find myself; I'd been Phil's girlfriend from the age of fifteen, Phil's wife from twenty-one, Simon's mummy from twenty-three. I had no idea who I was, without those tags of possession. Perhaps turning thirty was the wake-up call. All I knew was that I'd reached a point where I wanted to do something for myself, to be something other than a clerical worker for a car dealership, however much that may have been glorified by Phil making me a director. But I also knew I couldn't just give up that position to work elsewhere. I owed Phil, and the business, my support, and I knew the job inside out. Besides which, I wasn't qualified to do anything else.

One day, taking a coffee break from my work, I started idly Googling adult education classes. There was a centre just a ten-minute walk from our house, and the list of possibilities was impressive, from O-level courses in English and Maths, to Needlecraft, Painting, Creative Writing, Car Maintenance, First Aid . . . I spent far longer than I should have done, that day, studying the list of subjects, carried away by the thought of learning to play the guitar, or joining a drama group, or taking up photography.

When Phil came home that evening, I was more cheerful than I'd been for months.

'Phil,' I began as I carried our plates of casserole to the table, 'I'm thinking I might like to take French lessons. For beginners. At an adult education class.'

He looked at me in surprise. 'French? Really?' He thought about this for a minute, then guessed: 'To help Simon? When he starts learning it at school?'

'No,' I said, a little more sharply than I intended, 'That didn't cross my mind, actually. I'd like, for once, to do something just for me. Not for Simon. Or for you,' I added, picking up my fork and stabbing a piece of meat with it.

There was silence for a few moments. Then he laid down his own cutlery, smiled at me across the table, and said:

'Of course. Yes, you should do something for yourself, Jules – great idea. Something to get you out of the house. And also, next time we go on holiday,' – we'd rented a *gîte* in France during the previous two summers – 'you'll be able to help me and Simon, won't you. Talking to the locals. Ordering for us in the restaurants.'

Call me churlish, but I couldn't help noticing that even now he'd given his blessing, he was turning my new hobby into something for him and Simon, after all.

'I'd just like to . . . *challenge* myself,' I tried to explain. 'I didn't get any qualifications at school, and I'd like –'

'A break from the housework. Fair enough, babe – go for it. If you need to take a day off from the business once a week for it, you could catch up with the work during the evenings, or at the weekend.'

Well, thank you, I'm sure, I felt like saying, but I didn't. We had a good relationship, but our roles were different. I'd accepted my position: I was the supportive one, the one who provided the back-up service, kept the laundry done, the paperwork in order, the fridge full, our son happy. It wasn't fair to kick against it when it was all I'd wanted, all I'd asked for. Until now. No, I just nodded and smiled. I enrolled at the adult education centre, and from that

September, every Thursday morning at ten o'clock, I went to my French class.

'*Voulez-vous un verre de vin rouge?*' I asked Akin, the guy sitting next to me in the classroom. We'd done nearly a whole term on basic grammar and vocabulary, and today we were having a conversation lesson. 'Accent is everything!' our teacher, Monsieur Duval, kept reminding us. 'Get the accent wrong and no-one will understand you.'

'*Voulez-vous,*' I began again.

'Julia, Julia, it's not *voolaise,* the teacher said with a sigh. 'The *z* isn't pronounced. Try again.'

'*Voulez-vous . . .*' I glanced at Akin, who was smiling at me, his eyebrows raised suggestively. I felt a giggle welling in my chest. '*Voulez-vous un verre de vin rouge?*'

'Not half!' he whispered to me, and I burst out laughing.

M. Duval shrugged. '*Eh bien, Julia. Pas mal.* Not bad!'

He moved on to the next couple to be tested. I nudged Akin to stop him teasing me. His accent was good. He'd done some French at school but forgotten most of it and needed to improve it for his job, so he was on day-release from his company. French class in the morning, practice at home online in the afternoon. He was about the same age as me and we'd sat together from day one, as most of our classmates were retirees. And . . . by now I'd admitted it to myself: I really fancied him.

I thought I could handle it. So he was good-looking, so he was charming, so I found myself looking forward all week to the class, dressing a bit differently on Thursday mornings, making an effort with my hair and make-up. So what? I was only human, only thirty and couldn't help being attracted to a sexy man, could I? But I was married, I had no intention of being unfaithful, it was just a bit of innocent flirtation over the *voulez-vous*. It made me feel good about myself for a change.

For the last lesson before the Christmas break, M. Duval suggested we each brought a packet of biscuits or cakes to the class to share, and he kindly provided *vin rouge, vin blanc*, and *jus d'orange* for those who were driving. I wasn't driving, so I was able to ask, in my best accent, for *un verre de vin rouge*.

'*D'accord, la classe*,' M. Duval began when we were all settled with our drink and snack. And he asked us to discuss what we were going to eat over Christmas. *En français, naturellement.*

The room echoed with attempts at the French for turkey, roast potatoes, mince pies, Brussel sprouts. We made pathetic guesses at Christmas pudding and giggled over stuffing. On the whiteboard, M. Duval wrote the translation of the lyrics to *We Wish You a Merry Christmas*, which we all copied down and tried, with some hilarity, to sing. It was lively, and fun, some of the pensioners at the back of the class were getting jolly and giggly, and I . . . was looking into the gorgeous brown eyes of the man I'd dreamed about the previous night, and fantasised about kissing for the past few weeks, and seeing him smile back at me, his lips every bit as inviting as they'd been in my dreams. And thinking dangerous thoughts.

We walked back along the road together afterwards, as usual, as far as Akin's Tube station.

'*Joyeux Noël*, Julia,' he said with a grin as we were parting – and kissed me. It was just a peck on the cheek, but he lingered for a moment longer than necessary, his mouth close to my face, his breath warm, his hand lightly touching my arm. It would have looked completely innocent to anyone watching, but to me, it felt almost illicit in its unspoken suggestion of more. I could feel my heart beating madly the rest of the way home. I sat down at my computer, with the intention of doing some work, but my thoughts, my feelings, were all over the place.

You have to stop thinking like this, I told myself. *He's just a friend, a classmate. You're married! You have a child! You're thirty years old! Behave yourself!*

Oh, it was stern, that inner voice, that voice of reason. But the reply from my heart was louder. *But I love him!* it said. Just that. Just those four words. As I heard them, in my head, coming from my heart, I felt a shiver of shock. Did I really mean those words? Was that really me, thinking I was *in love*? No! That couldn't be what this was. I loved Phil! This was just . . . what? I didn't know. It felt too big and scary to be just an infatuation. Too serious to be just lust. And it was nothing, nothing at all, like I'd ever felt for Phil.

No wonder I was confused. I'd never had any other boyfriends before Phil. I was eleven, fresh into Year Seven at school when I first met him, fourteen when we became friends, fifteen when he asked me to be his girlfriend and took me to the cinema on a proper date. I'd never felt this trembling, earth-shattering excitement before; Phil and I had simply liked each other, been attracted to each other, grown slowly to love each other. Now, I had doubts, for the first time in fifteen years. Had I ever really been in love with Phil at all? It had never felt like *this*. Was it just a habit, a comfortable, easy habit? Had I, in fact, been missing out, all these years, on how it felt to fall properly in love?

That Christmas, I forced myself to concentrate on my family. I watched Phil unwrap the expensive new iPhone he'd wanted; laughed with Simon as he squealed with excitement over his X-Box; tried to swallow the fear and sadness as my dad, his mind already becoming confused even back then, looked from his presents to the Christmas tree and asked in a puzzled voice whose birthday it was. And told myself this was my life. A handsome fellow student at a French class was just that. But still my heart kept on repeating those treacherous, enticing, elicit four words. *But I love him*!

On the first Thursday of the new term, I purposely sat next to one of the retired ladies at the back of the classroom. Akin turned, from our usual place, and looked at me, puzzled. He waited for me afterwards, outside the centre, even though I'd purposely lingered, talking to the lady I'd sat next to, pretending to be interested in her opinion of the new local supermarket.

'Was her French better than mine?' he teased, falling into step beside me. 'Or have I suddenly developed body odour? Or halitosis? You can tell me, I won't mind.'

I tried not to smile. Tried to avoid looking at him. I kept it up for all of three more steps. Then I laughed. I couldn't help it, he'd looked so crestfallen.

'Idiot! Your French is the best in the class and you know it.'

'Is that the only reason you normally sit next to me?' His smile was back. I loved his smile. *I love him*, said that little voice.

'What's the matter?' he asked more seriously. 'Are you OK?'

'Yes. No. I don't know.' I looked back at him again and felt my heart lurch. 'Oh, shit, Akin, I think I'm going to have to stop coming to these classes.'

'Why? Don't!' He stood still, grabbing my arm so that I stopped walking too. 'I've only kept coming because of you.'

'What are you talking about? Your firm's paying for you to come –'

'Yes, but M. Duval thinks I should move up to the intermediate class. I didn't tell my boss. I don't want to move classes. I want to come to this one. Because of you.'

I felt myself shiver, quite literally from head to toe. It was frightening, and at the same time, it was exhilarating.

'But we're . . . just friends, aren't we. I've got a husband. And a child,' I said. My voice sounded weak. It sounded unconvincing. 'I can't . . . I can't ever . . .'

'Don't tell me you haven't felt it too,' he said, softly. We were standing on our own in the street, standing still, looking into each other's eyes. 'I'm not asking anything of you, Julia. I know you're not . . . free. But I can't help how I feel.'

'I feel it too,' I whispered. The words were too monumental to say out loud. I shivered again, and he tried to put an arm round me, but I shook it off. 'I should stop coming to the class,' I repeated, but even as I said it, I knew I wasn't going to.

I'd like to say nothing really changed for a while, but of course, it did. It changed as soon as we'd both admitted how we felt. We started having coffee together after the French class. Sometimes we continued into having lunch together. Sometimes we just went for walks. He wasn't just handsome, I'm not that shallow: he was funny, he was kind, he was interesting, he was patient and considerate. We talked endlessly, we laughed, we looked at each other and we did a lot of sighing, a lot of wishing things could be different. We shared little kisses and hugs that we told each other were only how we'd kiss or hug a good friend – but of course, they often went on for longer than that, and were far more addictive. At times I felt like I was flying. Other times, the knowledge that this was forbidden fruit just made me cry. I couldn't consider leaving Phil. How could I? I still loved him, despite *this*. I had my son to consider. My home. My dad. The business. My real life. I made a deal with myself. I'd keep seeing Akin until either of us found it too difficult to go on like this any longer.

What a fool I was. Even at thirty, I was too naïve to understand that when that point came – when neither Akin nor I could bear the frustration of our *friendship* any longer – we didn't immediately agree to stop seeing each other. Of course we didn't. We went back to his flat.

It was *after* that, that we did stop seeing each other. Afterwards, when I told Phil what I'd done.

Lauren

There's only the two of us in this hospital waiting room, and when Julia finishes talking and wipes away the tears, you could hear a pin drop. I've listened to this entire story in silence and I can still hardly speak, because I'm absolutely astonished. Not shocked – everyone makes mistakes, I don't think I've ever been one to judge. But *astonished*.

'You had an affair?' I say, trying to keep my voice level. 'And that was why Phil divorced you?'

'It wasn't an affair,' she says. 'It was . . . just one afternoon, one stupid afternoon when I gave in to temptation. I thought I was in love. Like an idiotic, pathetic schoolgirl –'

'Julia,' I say softly. 'You're only human. It happens. We all know it shouldn't, but it does.' I pause, shake my head. 'Would you have carried on seeing him – this Akin – if Phil hadn't found out?'

'No.' She closes her eyes and sighs. 'Oh, to be honest, I don't know, but I don't think so. The guilt was horrible – and not just for me, for Akin too. His parents came here from Nigeria, they were apparently very traditional and religious: they'd have been appalled that their son was seeing a married woman. He said he couldn't regret what happened between us for himself, but felt ashamed because of the values his parents had instilled in him.'

'But how did Phil find out? You said you *told* him – why? Did he guess? Was he suspicious?'

'No.'

'So why? I'm not being funny, Julia, but honesty *isn't* always the best policy, is it? I mean, if telling him was going to hurt him – as it obviously did – and you weren't going to go on seeing Akin . . . wouldn't it have been better to keep quiet and –'

'And bear the guilt. As my punishment. Live with it.' She nods. 'I know, and perhaps I would have done. But . . .' There's a long pause; Julia's looking at me, steadily, like she's weighing up whether to continue. 'This is why I've never told you the reason for my divorce, Lauren. That day,' she goes on eventually, her voice shaking slightly, 'the day I made the biggest mistake of my life – it was also the day our mum passed away.'

I feel like I've been hit over the head with something. *That day*? The day I tried to call her about twenty times – on her home phone, her dedicated work line, her mobile – leaving messages on all of them? Eventually I gave up calling and text-messaged her, even emailed her. I was considering leaving my dying mother's bedside to drive frantically to her house – anything, rather than feel guilty for not letting Julia know, while there was still time to see Mum, even though she hadn't bothered much up till then. But I didn't; I couldn't risk not being there for Mum myself in her last moments. So eventually I called Phil, at his work.

'I know she was going out this morning,' he said, sounding puzzled. That would have been the French class. 'But she should have been back by lunchtime. She must be so caught up in her work, busy on the phone, she hasn't been able to answer you. I'm sorry to hear about your mum, Lauren. I'm sure Julia will want to come and see her. I'll see if I can get hold of her – I'll go round to the house if necessary. I'll pick her up. We'll come to the hospital together.'

But they never came – either of them. Julia didn't even call me. Mum passed away peacefully just before six o'clock that evening, and despite everything – despite the resentment I felt – I knew I had to let Julia know. When I called her, she sounded shaky and upset. I snapped.

'If you're that upset about Mum, why didn't you come to see her? Why didn't you answer any of my calls, or my messages? Why didn't you come when Phil told you?'

'I'm sorry, Lauren,' she said. She was actually crying. I couldn't understand it. She'd never cared much about Mum. Was it a guilty conscience? 'I . . . was . . . busy. So much work . . .'.

I'm afraid at that point, I just hung up on her. I didn't call her again for weeks, and when I did – only to tell her the details of the funeral, which I'd arranged on my own – she told me she and Phil were getting divorced. She didn't say why, but I guess I just automatically assumed it was her decision – that even with all her advantages in life, she wasn't happy, wasn't satisfied. It irked me to hear she was keeping her position in the company, her income, and even the house until Simon was eighteen. So she wanted all those privileges but not the man who'd given them to her? What was wrong with her? I compared her lifestyle with mine: single following the latest break-up, struggling to pay the mortgage, at the time, on a one-bedroom flat, lonely, unfulfilled. And I suppose I couldn't even be bothered to talk to her anymore.

'When I got home, late that afternoon,' she says now, looking down at the floor, 'I was already regretting what Akin and I had done, promising myself it would never happen again. When I saw Phil's car outside, I was shocked. He never used to come home during the day. *Where the hell have you been?* he demanded. *Didn't you get my calls? Your sister's been trying to get hold of you all day. Your mother's dying*! I felt my legs go weak. It felt, ridiculously, as if this was some kind of punishment: almost that Mum was dying because of me, because of what I'd done. I started crying – and of course, Phil was then really worried, concerned that I'd been in an accident or something else horrible had happened to me. That made me feel even worse! He was being nice to me, I didn't deserve it, I'd just been unfaithful to him. And I told him. I couldn't lie – not at that moment, with Mum dying and him being so concerned about me – I couldn't bear the guilt. I told him the truth, that it was just the once, that it was a stupid mistake, that it was never going to happen again, that I still loved him.' She tails off, tears in her eyes again, still looking at the floor. 'I'm sorry, Lauren.'

I reach out and hold her hand, lean my head against her shoulder.

'I wish you'd told me. When we had the argument about our parents, back at Deepcombe. When I walked out and took your car –'

'I nearly did. I wanted to. But I thought – when you heard exactly what I was up to, why you couldn't contact me while you were sitting with our dying mother – you'd hate me . . . even more than you already did . . .'

'I don't hate you, don't be stupid, I've never hated you. You're my sister and I love you. Oh – don't cry! Look, we've just had too many misunderstandings between us, haven't we? We've both made mistakes, we're grown-ups, it's time we had all this stuff out in the open and moved on. Didn't we say that, just last week?'

She nods. 'Thank you. I thought you'd be disgusted with me – and furious.'

'No. In a way, I'm glad there was a reason for you not responding that day, not coming to the hospital. I was furious to think it was just your work, that you believed your work was more important than Mum. I presume there was an almighty row with Phil after you told him about Akin?'

'No. He's never been the type to lose his temper. He just went completely silent – shocked – and cold. He walked away from me, went upstairs and when I tried to follow, he told me to just leave him alone. I was blubbing like a baby, wishing I hadn't told him, wondering if he was going to walk out on me. I poured myself a drink and knocked it back, much too fast. Suddenly, Phil came back downstairs, and without looking at me, said in this really tight, strained voice that we'd have to discuss what we were going to do about it later, but for now, I owed it to Mum to pull myself together and go to the hospital to say goodbye to her. *I'll drive you*, he said. *You can't drive in that state.* So I washed my face, got myself ready, we got in the car and – and then I had your call to say Mum had died. I made that stupid excuse to you about being busy and I knew it wasn't good enough, but I couldn't think straight, I was still crying too much. *It's too late*, I said to Phil. He turned off the ignition. *You're right*, he said. *It is.* I knew, then – knew he wasn't talking about Mum, I knew he was going to leave me. I should have still come to the hospital, for your sake, I know that. But I couldn't drive, I'd had a large neat gin, and –'

'And you were too upset. You'd have had an accident. And there was nothing you could have done, once Mum was gone,' I say. 'Poor you – what a mess. Has Phil never forgiven you?'

'Oh, yes: it took a long time, and I can't blame him for that. But we were still colleagues, we still had our son to consider, so we were . . . civilised. And eventually we became friends again.'

'And you've never stopped loving him.'

'Never. Never wanted anyone else. But I've never told him that, of course. He's made a new life for himself, without me.'

'He's never remarried, though, has he? Does he have . . . somebody else?'

She shrugs. 'I think he's had various girlfriends, over the years. But –'

We both start, suddenly, as the door to the visitors' room opens and a tired-looking doctor who looks almost too young to be qualified, comes in, stethoscope dangling.

'Mrs Davis?' he says, looking from one of us to the other.

Julia scrambles to her feet. 'Yes?'

'I'm Henry, I'm one of the doctors on call tonight; I've just popped into HDU to check on your husband. He's awake and pretty anxious to see you. Would you like me to take you?'

'Go on,' I tell her. 'And . . . talk to him, Julia. Tell him.'

She nods at me and leaves the room with the doctor. I don't have to spell it out. She needs to tell him what she's just told me: that she's never stopped loving him. It's never too late to tell somebody that, is it?

A week later

Betty

It's been a few days now since the last of the snow disappeared here at Deepcombe. There's a cold wind up here on the moor, cold enough to have kept patches of the snow lingering in the shady areas that the sun doesn't get to, for quite a while after most of it had melted. Now I can get out to the greenhouses again, at least, and check on my herbs and my tomatoes. I've had the usual visitors from the village coming to buy their rosemary and basil, their ginger and mint, have their usual moan about their lives, over a hot drink, and go off looking like I've helped them in some way that they don't quite understand.

But I'm feeling strangely lonely. I've got Nathan for company but he's busy, so busy it worries me. He's working on the west wing here, he's got jobs for customers in the village, and nearly every evening I hear him talking on the phone to his father about their *plans*. Plans for *the business*, as they've started calling it again, plans for when Stuart's worked his notice in London and comes back to take up the running of *the business* with him. They don't tell me what's going on; if I ask, they just laugh and say 'Nothing, nothing for you to worry about, nothing's going to change, it'll just be better, that's all.'

So I keep quiet, sit here keeping quiet, listening to the villagers' stories of marital discord, household debts, family bust-ups, and so on, and so on, and I miss the two young ladies who were our first guests in the Lodge, and wonder how on earth I felt so close to them in such a short time, and I think about Richard, and wonder what I'm going to do about him.

Richard's alive. For so many years, I convinced myself he must be dead by now. It isn't that hard, at my age, to accept that people older than myself have died. I didn't feel grief, because the grief came years ago, decades ago, back when I left him, left London, never to return. It was the hardest thing I've ever done, and the wound of that grief was constantly being reopened, every time I heard anything about him – where he was, what he was doing, what he'd become, without me. Then, gradually, I stopped hearing anything, and I purposely stopped trying to find out any news of him. It was, grotesquely, somehow easier to tell myself he must have died, than to reopen that wound all over again.

I wouldn't have believed I was going to feel this . . . *joy* . . . on learning he is, after all, still alive. He must be eighty-nine, nearly ninety. I wonder what he's like now; wonder what his circumstances are, where he's living, whether he's in good health. Whether he's on his own now, and perhaps lonely, like me. I keep giving myself a little shake when I find myself wondering about this. I haven't spent all these years refusing to give in to silly, pointless, ponderings – ignoring the dreams, the daydreams, trying to forget the memories, refusing to search the bloody Internet or the bloody Google or Face-thing, in case there's a mention of him somewhere – just to fall into the trap of it all over again now at the age of eighty, when I'm past it. Past everything, never mind stupid adolescent fantasies, never mind straining a poor old heart that ought to know better, by giving it skipped beats over a stupid old broken mirror. I ask you! I shake myself, crossly, and go back to tending my herbs, keeping myself busy, closing my mind again.

There aren't any more holiday visitors coming until next month. A family: mum, dad, and two boys, Nathan says, coming for the February half-term holiday. It's nice to think there's a family who would choose to book a holiday on Dartmoor in the winter instead of jetting off somewhere hot. Costa Fortune, they call it. They queue for hours at the airport, getting delayed, losing their luggage, getting sunburn and diarrhoea and coming home broke – well, I suppose some people think it's worth it. I've never bothered, never wanted to. I used to take Stuart down to Cornwall, to the coast, for a week or two every year. We had such a lovely time together, just the two of us. Well, I hope this family with the boys will be nice people, hope they'll enjoy our countryside. But I can't expect to make friends with all the people who might come here for holidays. They won't all be like Julia and Lauren.

I've had a couple of calls from them, since they left. And some flowers by Interflora, and a nice letter, thanking me for their holiday – 'despite the snow and everything'. It was Lauren who sent it, but she signed off 'from Julia and Lauren'. It'd be good to think they're getting along together now. When Julia called, she told me her ex-husband had been ill. She'd gone straight to the hospital to see him when Stuart took her back to London. It sounds to me like he might be more than just an ex-husband to her, and that's obviously what she was so stressed about, all the time she was here. She said Lauren had gone with her to the hospital, and stayed there with her all night. So that's good.

But I can't expect them to carry on keeping in touch with me. Their holiday's over, they've got their lives to get on with, and really, I was just part of a very short interlude for them. So I need to get over this odd, restless feeling, move my tired old bones a bit more to help my grandson in the house, forget about Julia and Lauren and just look forward to my son moving back here in a few more weeks. And . . . decide what I'm going to do about Richard. What I'll do if he decides to contact me. Which he probably won't. And I probably shouldn't be hoping he does. And . . . oh, for God's sake, it's exhausting. I'm far too old and tired to put myself through this kind of stuff all over again!

Early February

Julia

Phil's been home for a week now. He's fine; he keeps telling me he's fine, anyway, but I can see he's not, not really. He's tired, obviously – that's only to be expected after a major operation. But I think, too, he's been very frightened. He was always one of those stoical males who rarely even had a cold, and he'd never before had to confront the idea of his own mortality. Now he's had such a scare, he's realised he was playing fast-and-loose with his own health and it's left him feeling shaky, less sure of his own ability to judge what might or might not do him harm.

'It'll pass,' I tried to reassure him when he was trying to explain how he felt when he first came home. 'You'll soon be back to your old self again.'

'But that's the point,' he said, looking away from me, with a self-conscious little shrug. 'I don't think I *want* to go back to my old self. I think, possibly, my old self was an idiot.'

I've moved in with him for now. Only for this first week or so, only to help him settle, and help with his shopping and cooking and so on, until he's got his strength back properly. I'm in the guest bedroom, obviously. It's not the house we used to live in together – that was sold several years ago, after Simon grew up. We split the proceeds and Phil was generous, as ever, with my share. But while I was more than happy to buy a smart, detached new-build on a nice estate – which Lauren nevertheless refers to as my *big posh house* – Phil seemed to want to make a point by splashing out on this rambling Victorian three-storey townhouse, set on a swanky square in a far more affluent area than the one where we lived together. He used to have a housekeeper; I thought he still did, but he's been telling me he's had to let her go.

He's been telling me a lot, this week, a lot of things I had no idea about.

'I'm up to my eyeballs in debt,' he said, that first day when he was discharged from the hospital. He was propped up on the sofa, his face still pale from the effort of being helped in from the car, his voice shaking with the enormity of his decision to confide in me. 'I've made a complete mess of everything.'

'What? How? What are you talking about? The business is –'

'Oh, the business is doing OK.' He nodded, giving me a brief flicker of a smile. 'I couldn't try to fiddle the books and leach money out of the business to save myself, could I? You're the one looking after all that.'

'Well, only up to a point. The accountant –'

'Yes, exactly. Theo wouldn't have even let me get away with pinching the odd pen from the office, never mind trying to –'

'Phil, you're scaring me. What's going on? How are you in debt? How much?'

'I'm going to need to sell the house,' he said bluntly. 'I've re-mortgaged it already, and I can't afford the payments. The business might be doing fine, but it wouldn't be, if I gave myself another increase. And . . .' He closed his eyes. 'It wouldn't be right for the rest of the staff – including you – to pay for my mistakes.'

'What mistakes?' I was practically whispering now. 'How have you got into debt, Phil? Is it drink? Gambling?'

'No.' He sighed. 'Well, not drinking, anyway. And not exactly gambling, although I suppose you could say that's exactly what I've done. Gambled it all away. But that wasn't how it was meant to be; not how it started off. I thought I was being clever. Investing – you know – putting my money somewhere it would grow, grow *properly*. I didn't bother with safe markets, I thought I was too clever for that. I took risks, and at first, they paid off. The trouble was, when that happened, I got carried away. Thought I was some kind of expert, kept taking more and more risks, putting more and more of my capital into the markets that had given me a good return before, instead of diversifying. I was already starting to lose money, starting to panic and wonder what I was doing wrong, when the pandemic hit, and the bottom dropped completely out of everything I'd put the money into.'

'Couldn't you have asked for advice? From some kind of financial expert? Or even from our own accountant, wouldn't he have helped?'

'Theo?' Phil shook his head. 'Poor chap's more hard-up than I am, he's got three kids and a sick wife. I doubt he's ever been in a position to invest anything anywhere in his life. And I couldn't risk spending out more money to pay a financial advisor, not at that stage. I should have done that from the start, instead of thinking I knew it all. All the advice I read online said you should 'sit it out', but after a couple of months of watching all my shares sinking lower and lower in value by the hour, I lost my nerve and bought them all out at rock bottom price before they crashed. I needed money to pay my mortgage. I'd depleted what I had in my bank accounts, just to pay the bills.'

'Oh, Phil. And all this must have coincided with the lockdowns?'

'Exactly. When all the car dealerships were closed for those three months during the pandemic, it was always going to be tough, even without my own personal situation. Fortunately the business picked up again as soon as we were allowed to reopen. But it was too late for me.' He hung his head and I saw the glint of tears in his eyes. 'I've been such a bloody fool, Julia.'

I sat down next to him, on the edge of the sofa, and took hold of his hand. It didn't feel odd, or inappropriate. It was just what I'd do for a friend, any friend, who was upset.

'Don't talk like that,' I said softly. 'You haven't done anything wrong, Phil – not anything illegal or wicked or unkind. You've just made a mistake –'

'I kept on making mistakes. I didn't learn from them,' he retorted. 'That takes a special kind of stupidity.'

'No. It just makes you human.'

Looking back on that conversation now, I realise it was the turning point. I'd already poured out my heart to him, back in the hospital, at his bedside in the high dependency unit. Julia hadn't needed to tell me what to say to Phil; the words just rushed out of me. I'd been so scared, felt so powerless, knowing he was ill, having urgent surgery, while I was stranded in Devon by the weather and a smashed-up car. Scared I was going to lose him, lose him even as a friend, before I'd been able to tell him what he meant to me. So no, I didn't need any prompting – I sat there at his bedside with my face resting on his shoulder, and I told him I'd never stopped loving him. I told him again the next day, when he was back on the ward, in case he hadn't taken it in properly the first time, and I repeated it every day until he finally seemed to believe me. And that was when he told me about his financial situation – told me as if he thought it was going to make a difference. As if I was going to stop loving him just because he's made mistakes.

We're talking about it all again today. Calmly, objectively, discussing options together. Almost like a couple.

'How much would it upset you, to sell the house?' I ask him.

'Not at all. It would be a massive relief, to be honest.'

'Would you be able to buy something else, then, after you've cleared the mortgage debt?'

'Yes. Something a lot smaller. Why do I need a big house anyway? It was an ego trip, that's all.'

'Something to impress the ladies?' I suggest. I'm smiling, chuckling, to show I don't care how many women he's succeeded in impressing over the years. And he's shrugging, looking down, looking away.

'Yes, I guess it helped. It helped attract a certain kind of woman, the type I got bored with quicker than you could imagine. The type who's after a rich man to give her the lifestyle she doesn't want to have to work for –'

'*I* was never after that,' I say, quickly, my smile gone. Does he think that of me?

'I know you weren't; I didn't mean to imply that you were.' He turns back to me, grabs my hand, honesty raw in his voice. 'You were never interested in the money, the power, any of it. That was me! You were . . . when we married you were just a kid, just a girl who wanted –'

'You. That's all I wanted, Phil! You. You, and our son.'

'I know.' He sighs, hesitates for a moment, and then goes on in a rush: 'And I took you for granted.'

'No, you were busy, you were –'

'I just expected you to be there, to look after the house, and Simon, and I thought I was such a great husband for providing you with a job that meant you could stay in the house the whole time, working for me. It was all about me, what I wanted. I wasn't just stupid, I was selfish.' He pauses, then adds very softly: 'No wonder you wanted a little bit of excitement.'

'*I* was selfish too. Selfish enough to go after that excitement, even at the risk of hurting you, killing our marriage.'

'You made a mistake, Jules, that's all. I was an idiot for ending our marriage over it. It was my pride, stupid male pride – I was so hurt and angry to think that you wanted someone else. But why wouldn't you? I was never there for you. I never gave you my company, or even my attention.'

'And I was an idiot too. I thought I loved him – Akin.' I say. 'But you're right, of course, it was just the excitement. It only happened the once; I was so ashamed. I should have walked away from it, before it got to that stage. I knew that, but being desired was . . . kind of addictive.'

'Like gambling on the stock exchange, I suppose.'

And amazingly, ridiculously, we're both laughing.

'We've both done stupid things, Jules,' he says softly.

'Yes. Of course we have.' I pause, and then go on, quietly, 'Do you think you'll ever be able to forgive me?'

'What? Don't be ridiculous! Of course I've forgiven you, years ago. Years that I've regretted acting like a self-righteous prick and insisting on divorcing you. Can *you* ever forgive me for that? Because I still love you too, you know. I just haven't wanted to say it because I don't think I deserved you, after everything that's happened.'

And I don't need to answer that, really. I just kiss him.

A Saturday in February

Lauren

Who would have believed it? Julia and Phil are back together. She's moved in (*actually* moved in, now, not just to help him with his recovery anymore), and they're apparently talking about selling both their houses and looking for something smaller together. I'm pleased for her, obviously. We've been speaking on the phone every couple of days – who would have believed that, either? – and she sounds . . . just completely different. Not stressed anymore. Happy.

'We're not rushing into anything,' she tells me. 'Well, I suppose we are, in a way: I've put my house on the market already. If we sell that, it'll help with the finances until we've had a chance to look around for a new property.'

I don't know the whole story about the financial issues. She says she'll tell me one day, but I get the impression it's a kind-of sensitive issue so I'm obviously not going to push her. I've been round a couple of times to see Phil. He seems to be making a good recovery. He looks happier, too. They keep smiling at each other, like they're newly-weds who can't take their eyes off each other. And although I'm so happy for them, it gives me an odd kind of heartache, too, that I just have to ignore. I'm not jealous. They deserve to be happy. And I've come to terms, now, with not having a man myself.

For a week or two, though, I did think I'd made a friend. Stuart had started calling me occasionally. It started off with a call on the day after he dropped me and Julia at the hospital – to ask how Phil was. He'd phoned me instead of Julia because he didn't want to intrude on her at such a stressful time, but said he really wanted to know how everything was going. Then he asked if he could call again later in the week for an update. I thought he was such a nice guy, he seemed very caring, and so easy to talk to. He asked if I'd settled back down at home and at my work, since coming back from Devon, and I had to admit I was finding it a struggle.

'I never really liked my job much,' I found myself admitting. 'Or my house. I can't really understand why I put up with them both for so long.'

'So are you still thinking about making some changes?' he asked.

'I don't know. Yes, I think I'd like to, but I feel too unsure, at the moment, about exactly what I do want.'

'So, probably still best not to rush into anything.'

'Exactly. I'm just . . . kind of coasting along at the moment, taking stock, thinking about my options – all of which I should have done years ago.'

Instead of focusing on finding a man, I wanted to add, but didn't, obviously. I didn't want to come across as a desperate, sad case.

When, at the end of the second week back, and following a few more chats on the phone, he asked if he could call round to see me, I was a bit unsure. I didn't want to give him the wrong idea. I liked him, but I was determined not to look for another boyfriend or even date anyone for now. I'd already started making enquiries about the adoption process and this, at that moment, was my main focus. Anyway, I knew Stuart was going to be moving back to Devon very soon, so it would be a waste of time even beginning to think like that. But he explained that he just wanted to talk to me about his flat. I wasn't sure what to make of that. Was it just an excuse – some trumped-up reason to come and see me? I hadn't seen any real evidence of him being attracted to me, though – he simply behaved like a really kind, caring sort of man.

'Well, OK, then,' I agreed. 'Saturday afternoon?'

He came with a selection pack of biscuits. A good choice, I thought; flowers, or a box of posh chocolates would have freaked me out and convinced me he was after more than just a friendly chat.

'Thanks. I'll put the kettle on,' I said, smiling. 'How's it going? How much longer at your job now?'

'Another two weeks.' He nodded. 'And I've asked the landlord if I can terminate my rental early. He's being a bit sniffy about it. I'd only recently signed up for another six months.'

'Surely he can find another tenant? There's such a shortage of rental property in London.'

'Yes, there is. But . . . it's not a very *ordinary* property.' He shrugged. 'It wouldn't suit everyone. It'd be no good for a young family, for instance, or anyone elderly, or with any kind of disability. It works best for someone on their own, like me, but the rent isn't particularly cheap.'

I laughed. 'Why? Is it made of gold, or something? Or did someone famous live there once?'

'Not quite! But I guess you'd say it's . . . quirky. It's a converted church. Not a big church, but it has a lot of stairs – up to the bedroom and bathroom in the steeple.'

'Wow.' I turned from the kettle to raise my eyebrows at him. 'That does sound quirky!'

'Yes. I've liked living there. I'd have wanted to stay, at least till I'd found a place I could afford to buy. But everything changed after I went home to Deepcombe.'

Of course, I could understand that. As he'd already told us, it had only taken a couple of hours back in his real home, for him to realise that he'd never really belonged in London.

I poured the tea, put some of his biscuits on a plate and brought everything into the lounge, where we sat for a moment, looking at each other. I wasn't sure what to say. Why was he telling me all this, about his flat? And why did he then give a little cough, obviously feeling awkward, before he went on to say:

'So that's why I thought maybe I should tell you about it.'

'Me? Why?'

'Well, because . . . I thought . . . I'm sorry if I've misunderstood but I've got the impression, talking to you, that you were looking for a change. You said you were bored with this house, and – of course, I realise you own the property so you'd be looking to sell it, but I think you could sell it so quickly, probably to a first-time buyer – and maybe by then I'll be ready to move back to Deepcombe, and my flat would be available. While you look for somewhere to buy, I mean, obviously,' he added quickly, going a bit red. 'I realise it would only be a . . . temporary thing . . . but –'

I felt myself suddenly getting hot. I stared at him.

'So you thought it might be handy to use me as a solution to your problem?' I said.

'What? No – of course not! What do you mean?'

'Well, it's pretty obvious, isn't it? What a convenient solution for you: silly little me, complaining about being bored with her life, just the right person to ask to take over your *quirky* flat for you, so that your landlord lets you foreclose on your rental agreement. Never mind that I'll be paying rent and a mortgage at the same time –'

'No, no, I meant that you could use it temporarily, between paying off this mortgage and looking for a new place.'

'Yes, always supposing I can sell this at the speed of light, that the whole thing goes through at record speed, never mind estate agents and solicitors and all the months of legislation – do you really think I'm such an idiot that I'd actually think that could all happen in the next couple of weeks?'

'No, of course not!' He put his mug of tea down, pushed it away as if he suddenly couldn't face it anymore. 'I'm sorry, it was probably a stupid idea, I just thought – if you'd sold the house first, you'd be in such a good position to buy something else. I'm not intending to leave London in two weeks, just my job. I'll be working from home here, working for the family business, taking over getting the holiday accommodation side up and running, taking it away from the agent. Yes, I want to go back as soon as I can, but . . .' He stopped again, spreading his hands, looking miserable. 'I'm sorry, honestly, I didn't mean any offence, I wasn't trying to make use of you or anything like that. I just thought it might help you. But I got it wrong, obviously.'

I wanted to believe him, but the shock of having thought he was trying to manipulate me, take advantage of me, thinking me naïve and . . . all right, not caring about me as a friend after all – it had shaken me and I wasn't ready to back down.

'Apart from anything else,' I said a bit frostily, 'I told you I'm hoping to adopt a child. As you said yourself, your *quirky* flat isn't suitable for a family. I suppose you just presumed I wasn't really serious about it. Is that it?'

'Lauren, honestly, what on earth are you talking about? Of course I didn't think that. I know you're serious about it, I just didn't think it would happen for quite a while. You've said yourself that you're not rushing into it, and that you know how long it takes! This was just a short-term suggestion, I honestly thought it might help, but –'

'I don't need help, thank you.'

'OK.' He got to his feet, looking thoroughly miserable. 'OK, well, look, I'm just really sorry I seem to have offended you. I would never have wanted to do that. I don't think any of those things about you – I don't think you're an idiot at all, far from it, you're an intelligent, kind, sensible person, I really like you, and I'd never try to manipulate you or make use of you in any way. If that's how this has come across, it's my own stupid fault for approaching it badly and wording it all wrong. Whatever; I've said too much already and I'd better go.'

Say something, I told myself. *Stop him from going. Tell him perhaps it's just a misunderstanding, tell him to forget it, say you overreacted.*

But I didn't say anything. I sat there, staring at the floor, listening to him walk across the room, down the hall, and open the front door. I heard his car start up and pull away.

So it seems like even when I try to just have *friendship* with a man, it goes wrong. I've got the strangest feeling it's my own fault again, as always – and yet, when I think through what he was proposing, I still don't get it. It still sounds like, once again, I'm being taken for a mug by a man who tells me he likes me. And I'm furious with myself for having to admit that it hurts.

Monday

Julia

I can't remember when Phil and I last talked so much together. Probably not since before Simon was born; perhaps not even since before we were married. The honesty between us now is almost tangible, as if the air around us has become purified by it. We're telling each other everything. I've told him all about Lauren, how we quarrelled, in Deepcombe, about our childhoods and about our parents, and then made up when Lauren went off in my car in the snowstorm. And he's told me how running the business has slowly gone from being a pleasure, a pride and an excitement, to being an exhausting, debilitating grind of anxiety and stress.

'Then we need to give it up,' I tell him today.

I've been wanting to say it for about a week now, listening to how – together with the increasing worry of his debts – it's been wearing him down, ruining his health. But I've reined in my own feelings and opinions, feeling that I should just let him talk. Today, though, it's just burst out of me. It seems so obvious that I can't hold it back any longer.

'Give it up?' he says, staring at me. 'How can I do that?'

'How can you *not*? We need to start again, Phil. We need to sell up – as you've already said, sell this house as well as mine – and sell the business too. It's still doing well, it'll be snapped up, you know that.

And just like that, your stress levels will be down to zero and your health will be –'

'Hang on,' he says, shaking his head but smiling at me. 'Aren't you forgetting one rather important little point? We'd both be out of work as well as homeless.'

'We are *not* going to be homeless. We've already talked about finding ourselves a smaller place together. I've already got a potential buyer for my house, and when we put this one on the market, we'll be able to start looking at properties. The sale of the business will help us get on our feet again –'

'Sorry, love, but I think you're being a bit naïve. It'd be a long process, we wouldn't just suddenly be out of debt, like magic –'

'No, of course not, and we'd obviously both need to find new work.' I smile at him. 'We can think about doing something completely different. Something – I don't know – something calm and gentle, like –'

'Like stroking little fluffy kittens or sitting in our armchairs knitting babies' bonnets?' he teases me. 'Come off it, Jules! I love that you're trying to take a positive attitude to all this, but I think you're being just a little bit *too* optimistic. We're both pushing fifty –'

'Hey, I'm only forty-five!'

'And we have to face it, our employment opportunities are *not* as good as when we were in our twenties. Neither of us have degrees. Neither of us have any work experience outside of the motor trade.' He pauses and looks at me sadly. 'Nice daydream, but we've got to be realistic.'

I shrug, and pretend to concede. But I know – I just know from the way he's fallen silent, and from the way, when I go to the kitchen to make coffee, and come back to find him scribbling figures on the back of an envelope, which he hastily puts behind a cushion – I know I've made him think, however much he might pretend otherwise.

This afternoon, we've got a follow-up appointment for Phil at the hospital.

'Well, I'm pleased to see everything's healing up very nicely,' says the consultant surgeon after he's examined him. He leaves Phil to adjust his clothes while he sits back behind his desk and gives me a sympathetic look. 'I understand you've been looking after him during his recovery.'

'Yes.' I nod. 'In fact, we're back together. So –'

'That's good to hear. Well, he's doing well but it'll be at least another four weeks on the strict diet. No fatty food, no spicy food, no sugary food, plenty of protein. He needs to keep to several small meals per day, but he can gradually build them up a little.'

Phil has joined us now, sitting next to me with his head down as if he's being told off by the headmaster. In fact, we've both made sure he's been sticking to the diet completely rigidly, we were so afraid something would go wrong if he didn't.

'No eating during the last couple of hours before bed,' the consultant goes on, ticking off his list on his fingers, 'Eat slowly and carefully. And most importantly, no heavy lifting or straining, only gentle exercise, nothing strenuous.' He looks from me to Phil and back again. 'No stress.'

'No stress,' I find myself repeating, without looking at Phil.

'We don't want you developing another ulcer.' The consultant's voice is surprisingly gentle now. 'I'm sure you don't want to be on and off medication for the rest of your life, and I certainly don't want to have to be doing any further surgery on you. You might not be so lucky next time.'

I shudder, and have to blink back tears. Phil looks up at me and takes hold of my hand.

'No stress,' he agrees, and the consultant nods.

'Good. I'll see you again in four weeks' time and hopefully then I'll be able to sign you off. Take care and keep up the good work.'

He shakes us both by the hand and we leave in silence.

Lauren calls me later, while Phil's having a nap.

'How did it go?' she asks, and I describe this afternoon's appointment to her, having to pause and swallow a couple of times when I get to the part where the consultant mentions not being so lucky next time.

'There won't be a next time,' she reassures me softly. 'I think he's learnt his lesson. If he *did* get another ulcer, he wouldn't ignore it, he'd go to the doctor and he'd take the medication –'

'But I don't want that to happen. The consultant says the evidence for stress causing gastric ulcers isn't conclusive, but he definitely sees a link in his patients. I don't want Phil to have that link anymore. I don't want him to get stressed anymore.'

'I know, Julia, I get that. And if you do what you're planning – sell both the properties, pay off all the debts –'

'I certainly hope that'll help. But I don't think it's the whole answer. I've told him we should consider selling the business. Doing something less stressful, for both of us.'

'Really?' She pauses. 'Like what?'

'I don't know. And I'm not sure I can convince him, anyway.'

There's silence between us for a moment. Then I have to ask, because I've asked her every time she's called me recently, but I still haven't got a straight answer:

'How are *you* now? You're still sounding . . . a bit down.'

'Oh, I'm OK.' I can almost see the shrug, almost feel the gloom.

'Just still a bit fed up about being back at work? Have you thought any more about looking for a new job? Thought any more about the adoption?'

'No. I . . . like I said, I want to give myself a chance to settle back down, first, before rushing into any decisions.'

'Yes. Of course.'

I know there's something she's not telling me. Something's happened to upset her – to burst that bubble of excitement about changing her life, that she talked about so enthusiastically when we came back from Devon. I just can't put my finger on what it might be. We'd started to confide in each other, but I feel, instinctively, that she's not going to talk to me about this, whatever it is, until she's ready.

'Well,' she says, putting on a too-bright tone that doesn't fool me, 'I'm really, really pleased to hear the appointment went well today. Keep up the good work, Nurse Julia!' Then she pauses and adds more quietly: 'Maybe we could have a little chat together one day soon?'

'Of course! Oh, Lauren, you don't have to ask, you can pop round any time. I've been missing you! I've just been so concerned about Phil, I haven't –'

'I know. I've missed you too, but I didn't like to bother you. I knew how worried you've been. I didn't want to . . . add to your burdens.'

'You're not a burden, you idiot! Come this evening. I'll leave Phil in front of the TV and we can have a catch-up.'

I sit for a while after we've ended the call, staring into space, thinking about the chats, the arguments *and* the making-ups, the new understandings of each other that we achieved during that week in Deepcombe. Even while I was struggling with my anxiety about Phil, I was so glad to think that Lauren and I had begun to forge a new, better relationship. I don't want that to slip away now that we're home. The phone calls have been good, but now I've suddenly become aware of how much I need to see her. I need to find out what's worrying her.

And I wish I wasn't finding myself hoping that it's *not* anything to do with a man this time.

Betty

Richard called me. Yesterday, just as I'd sat down and given myself a stern talk about forgetting it, not putting my life on hold – what's left of it – and wasting my time and energy fretting about whether, and what if, and what if not. Stuart's been filling me in, anyway. He's seen his dad a couple more times since he's been back in London, and he's been speaking to him quite a lot on the phone a too. Just *filling in the gaps*, as he puts it to me. The gaps in what, I wonder – as he had no history of his father whatsoever to begin with, and yes, that's my fault, I know that now. I was wrong to deprive him of the knowledge of his father. Even if I did do it with what I thought was the best of intentions.

Richard's voice, on the phone, was just the same as I remembered. Does that sound completely potty? After all, it's been fifty years. Do I *really* still remember his voice, or is that just a romantic notion on my part? But I knew. Of course, I knew as soon as he said *Hello*, that it was him, and all I could do was mutter *Hello* back, and in the ensuing silence, without meaning to, I went on in what I can only describe as the sulky tone of a spoilt child: 'What took you so long?'

And he laughed – and I laughed too, and then ridiculously I started crying. So that was a good start!

'I never thought I'd hear from you again,' I said, after I'd blown my nose.

'And whose fault was that?' he said, chuckling.

'Mine. I know. But you know why I did it. Why I stayed away.'

'Stayed away? You just vanished. Quite literally, vanished from my life! I knew you must have gone back to Devon, but you'd never told me whereabouts your family home was, and Devon's a big county, Betty! I did look in the phone directory –'

'I went ex-directory.'

'So I had, eventually, to accept that you didn't want to be found. You'd chosen to leave me –'

'Leave you?' I echoed. 'I never *had* you, Richard! And . . . oh, look, you understand, now, don't you. Why I had to go. I had to disappear, cut all ties.' I paused, then went on, quietly: 'I never looked for news of you, you know. I deliberately turned the page in the paper if you were mentioned. Turned off the TV news. In the end, I stopped buying newspapers altogether because for a while, you were all over them, and I couldn't look. Couldn't look at photos of you or read anything –'

'But you would have heard how things panned out in the end. You couldn't have missed that.'

I didn't answer. I didn't need to.

'And Elaine left me. In the end,' he said, quite matter-of-factly. 'When the kids were older.'

She left him. I've wondered – of course I've wondered. I won't say I hoped, because by then it was too late for hope. I'd given him up, made a conscious decision to make a life for myself and Stuart without him, so I had no right to hope, no reason to hope. But still. She left him.

'I'm sorry,' I said.

'Oh, don't be sorry. I wasn't.'

'So . . . how have you been?' I asked, to change the subject – and he laughed. So did I, because yes, it's a ridiculous question, after fifty years. As if we'd spoken only a couple of weeks before. 'What have you been doing, I mean. With your life. All this time, after – what happened.'

'Oh, this and that. Speaking engagements. You'd be surprised what people will pay for that. And I've written my autobiography – it was published last year.' He paused, then, and added quietly: 'But I missed out a big chunk of it. I couldn't write about that part, without asking your permission. And . . . anyway, I didn't know I had a son that I'd never met.'

His voice broke on those last few words.

'I'm so sorry,' I said. 'I . . . did what I thought was best. For *you.*'

'I know. I do realise that, and I'm grateful. But I wish . . . Oh, there's no point wishing, is there, Betty? Not at our time of life. We have to just make the most of every day, that's all we can do.'

'Yes.'

'So; it's taken me long enough to pluck up the courage to make this call, and every day I'm inching closer to my ninetieth birthday and I don't want to waste any more time shilly-shallying around, so I'm just going to ask you, and you can say no if you want to. Can I come and see you?'

'Oh, of course you can! Why would I say no? Absolutely, no shilly-shallying, Richard, we've got so much to talk about, and . . . as you say,' I added more quietly, 'so little time. But – are you sure you're OK to travel all the way down here? I don't mean to be rude, but –'

'Ha! You're not being rude, you're quite right, I'm an old crock and of course, I don't drive anymore. My elder daughter took my driving licence away from me a year or two ago because she said I was a menace on the roads! So I've thrown myself on the mercy of . . . my new son.' His voice wobbled again slightly as he said this. 'Stuart says he'll bring me down. He wants to come back for another weekend anyway. He said he was hoping to be moving back down before long but he's had some kind of hiccup with his landlord here, so it might take a little longer.'

'Oh. He hasn't told me that.'

'But would that be acceptable? Next weekend? I'll be on my best behaviour. I promise not to clutter up the place, scare the local inhabitants or throw any noisy drunken parties.'

'Actually, a noisy drunken party would liven Deepcombe up no end!' I joked. 'Of course, I'd love to see you next weekend, Richard. I'll look forward to it.'

I'm thinking about all this again, this evening. It's Monday today, and Richard's supposed to be coming on Friday evening with Stuart. And Stuart still hasn't said anything to me himself about this, so I'm slightly puzzled. I'm going to have to call him to make sure it's all OK, and there's no point waiting till the end of the week.

'Hi, Mum!' He answers straight away. 'How are you?'

'I'm fine, Stu, but – are *you* all right? I've heard something about you having problems with the landlord there?'

'How did you . . . oh!' He gives a little laugh. 'I suppose *Dad's* called you.'

The word *dad* sounds odd from his lips. I smile.

'Yes, Richard called yesterday. It was lovely to hear from him. And he mentioned you'd offered to bring him down . . . this coming weekend. Is that right?'

'Yes. Oh, sorry, Mum – have I not told you? I thought I did.' I hear him sigh. 'I've been . . . a bit busy, with . . . stuff . . .'

He tails off, and I realise that, despite the cheery start to the conversation, he doesn't actually sound very happy. My maternal concern flares with a vengeance. What's going on in bloody London to upset my son?

'So what's been happening? Something to do with the landlord?'

'Oh, it's nothing, just that he's being awkward about me wanting to get out of my tenancy agreement here. It means I won't be able to move back yet, unless I can –'

'Surely he can find someone else to take it over!' I interrupt crossly. 'I thought people were falling over themselves to rent properties up there? Don't you know anyone – at work, or whatever – someone who might want the chance of a nice flat?'

'I thought I knew someone who might,' he says more quietly. 'I suggested it to her, in fact, but I seem to have just ended up offending her. And I . . . well, I liked her. So unfortunately, I've messed things up, now. Never mind.'

'*Never mind*?' I hear myself squawking. 'Since when have you been such a defeatist? If you like this woman, you're surely not just going to leave it like that, are you? I can't think why she'd be offended by you offering her the chance of a flat, but well – if she is, you need to apologise, that's all! What's the problem?'

'I've tried to apologise, but she quite clearly didn't want to hear it. And when I say I like her, I mean it's just that I thought we were friends, not anything else. Anyway, Mum, it's not the end of the world, I'll have to just keep trying to persuade the landlord . . . and meanwhile I'll see you with Dad on Friday. Looking forward to it.'

I'm not fooled, and that isn't just because he's my son. I know the sound of rejected hope when I hear it – I haven't been the *Wise Woman of Deepcombe*, listening to people telling me about their disappointments in love for so many years, for nothing!

'I'm looking forward to it too,' I tell him. 'But I'd like you to turn up looking a bit happier than you sound right now, so for God's sake, son, give that woman, that *friend,* whoever she is, another chance to forgive you, even if you haven't done anything wrong! Ask her out for a drink or something. Talk it over and do a lot more apologising. It can't hurt, can it? Don't just give up on a . . . *friendship* . . . at the first hurdle. Well, that's my advice, anyway.'

'And you *are* the Wise Woman, after all,' he says, finally laughing and sounding more like himself.

'OK, I'll try. No harm, I suppose, as you say. And I'll see you on Friday.'

I wonder about it after I hang up – of course I do. Yes, Stuart's an adult, a middle-aged man, not that I can quite think of him as such, I don't suppose one can ever accept their children being middle-aged! – but he's been through a lot. He's told me several times that he's not interested in looking for another relationship, that he'll never find anyone else who can possibly mean as much to him as Janie did. And I understand that, of course. How could I not? I've never found anyone else since I left Richard – never tried to, never wanted to, and that was a hell of a lot longer ago. But Stuart's not like me. He's sensitive, and lonely, and he needs someone in his life, someone other than me and Nathan. And besides . . . I suppose I should admit it: I do sometimes regret having been so dogmatic about remaining on my own all these years. Perhaps I should have made more of an effort to be completely happy. So I'd like my son to be happy again. Perhaps it's true that this woman, whoever she is, was only ever going to be a friend. Perhaps she won't forgive him for whatever imagined slight he's inflicted on her – and I have to say, if that's the case, then he's better off without her! – but I hope he's at least going to give her another chance.

Whoever she is, she'd be lucky to have him.

Tuesday

Lauren

I went to Julia and Phil's place last night, and had a long chat with Julia. I kept apologising for talking about myself. She's had this terrible worry about Phil, and the financial issues she's alluded to. And yet, she seemed calmer than usual, and insisted I tell her what was bothering me; she said it was obvious something was. There was so much I needed to talk over, I hardly knew where to start.

'I called the adoption agency last week,' I began, once we were sitting at her kitchen table with a cup of tea. 'They're sending me an information pack.'

'Oh good! That's exciting!'

I sighed. 'Yes. Well, it should be. But I'm not sure.'

I saw her face fall, and I knew what she was thinking. Her flaky, pathetic sister was changing her mind already!

'I'm still sure about wanting to adopt,' I assured her. 'But I might need to apply to a different agency.'

'Right.' She nodded. 'Well, I suppose there are quite a few?'

'Yes. Lots, in different parts of the country.'

Julia was going to think it now anyway – that I was flaky and indecisive, and never seemed to know what I wanted or where my life was going. And she'd be right – until now. It was when I called this London adoption agency, and they said they'd send the information pack, that I suddenly knew it wasn't going to be right. I knew I'd already made up my mind but hadn't had the courage to admit it, even to myself. So I took a deep breath, looked my sister in the eyes and just came out with it:

'I don't want to bring up a child in London. I don't want to live here anymore. I want to go back to Devon. I want to live there.'

I watched her face, waiting for her to start talking to me in the tone I'd become so used to over the years, telling me not to be so silly, to be grateful I had a home and a job, to grow up and stop chasing rainbows.

But she didn't.

'I'm not rushing into it,' I went on quickly. 'I've thought it over and over, ever since we came back. I've tried telling myself I could look for a new job here in London, and that once I start the adoption process, I'll settle down and be happy. But –'

'But you know you won't,' she said quietly. 'I see.'

'You do? You don't think I'm being stupid, that it was just the holiday that's unsettled me?'

'No. I think we've all only got one life, and we need to take a risk sometimes, do what we think might make us happy. I don't think your life has fulfilled you or made you happy for a long time, Lauren. If ever. And I'm sorry I hadn't realised that. You *deserve* to be happy, and you should go after whatever it is that calls you.'

I felt tears rush to my eyes.

'Thank you, Julia. For . . . for believing in me,' I managed to get out.

She smiled. 'Well, I suppose it'll take quite a long time, anyway, to find yourself a job in Devon, and somewhere to live . . . does it have to be Devon?'

I shrugged. 'I suppose not. It could be anywhere quiet and countryfied, I suppose. But I've kind of got my heart set on it now – Devon.'

'What sort of job will you look for? Secretarial work, or something completely different? There might not be much available down there.'

'I'm not sure. I know I'll need to be in settled employment, earning regular wages, before I'll stand any chance of being accepted for adoption. So I don't want to waste time. I'm looking online at jobs, and housing, every evening. I don't know whether to put my place on the market yet or whether that's too hasty.'

'I wonder . . .' Julia looked at me carefully for a moment. 'What about talking to Betty? I'm sure she'd love to help. I bet she'd even offer to put you up for a time, while you look for something –'

I hung my head.

'I can't,' I said in a squeak of embarrassment. 'I did think about asking her, to be honest, but I can't now. I've messed everything up.'

'What? How?'

'Well, it's going to sound really silly. But . . . I've fallen out with Stuart.'

'Really?' She looked at me curiously. 'I know you said you've been talking to him. Were you . . . seeing each other, then?'

'Not like that!' I exclaimed quickly. 'No, it was just chatting on the phone. Then he called round to see me on Saturday, and he started talking to me about his flat. Apparently, he can't go back to Deepcombe yet because his landlord's being difficult about him getting out of his tenancy agreement, so he thought I might like to sell my house and move into his rented flat!' I could feel the indignation rising. 'He said it was only really suitable for a single person. I suppose I can't blame him for thinking I'm your stereotypical lonely singleton, never likely to need more than a one-bedroom flat –'

'Hang on, why on earth would he think you'd want to give up your own house, to rent a flat?'

'Exactly!' I blinked, looked down again, and conceded, 'Well, I'd already told him I'm sick of my house and looking for a change. He said he thought it might help if I put my house on the market, to sell it quickly so I'd be a cash buyer when I found a new home. But frankly, it stinks. It just sounds like he wants to make use of me so that he can get out of his tenancy and go back to Deepcombe.'

'It does sound a bit odd,' Julia agreed, frowning. 'But I thought he was so nice!'

'So did I,' I muttered. 'I really liked him. Just . . . as a friend, of course.'

'Of course,' Julia said. 'Well, never mind, love. Friends come and go, but your big sister will always be here for you. Better late than never!'

So we managed to have a little chuckle over it together, and I came away last night feeling better for talking to her. And now it's Tuesday, it's my lunch break, and I've finally plucked up the courage to call someone who might be able to help me.

'Hello, love,' Fern says as soon as she recognises my number. 'I'm in the middle of a field of sheep, look you, but if it's urgent, I'll listen while I'm herding them into the next field.'

'Oh, sorry – no, it's not urgent. I just wanted to tell someone, someone down there. I've decided to move down. I want to look for a job, and a place to live, and I'm going to contact the adoption agency there. I've made up my mind.'

'Tidy! Leave it with me, OK? I'll talk to a few people. I suppose you've told Betty? She'll be glad!'

'Um . . . no, I haven't, not yet. I didn't want to bother her. Until it's definite.'

'Right, well, I'm not gonna lie to you, Lauren, I'm up to my arse in mud here and half the sheep are going the wrong way so –'

'Sorry, I should've called in the evening, –'

But she's hung up, of course. What did I expect? I feel a rush of embarrassment. I shouldn't have called Fern at all. I should have spoken to Betty. Or – and here I have to struggle with myself all over again – I should have told Stuart. If I'd explained how I was thinking, what I was planning to do, we wouldn't have got into the whole argument about his flat. Why was I so reluctant to tell him? He'd have offered to help!

And of course, I know, really, that this is exactly why I didn't tell him. I'm too afraid of giving away too much of myself. Afraid of where it might lead. Because this time, I'm *not* making the same old mistake. I'm not falling into the trap of turning into someone's girlfriend, giving up my own life, ending up making a fool of myself for someone else's benefit. This is the new me, with my own hopes and dreams, and I'm determined to make them come true. On my own.

When I arrive home this evening, there's an envelope on the doormat with just my name on it. Hand delivered. I don't recognise the writing. I rip it open, and have to sit down to read it, even though it's short and to the point.

Lauren. I haven't called, or come round, as I guess you won't want to see me. And if you don't want to speak to me again, fair enough. But if you'd let me buy you a meal or a drink just to show I'm sorry and would still like us to be friends, give me a call.

Stuart. PS. I'm free tonight.

And I think: oh, what the hell. I probably do owe him an apology too for jumping down his throat and pretty much chucking him out of my house. An hour out of my life, to call it quits, will probably make me feel better. I call him. And he's on his way.

It's a Tuesday evening, early, so we're surprised when the first restaurant we try is already fully booked. It's not until we're being turned away from the third, that we notice the red hearts hanging up in the window, and the penny drops.

'Oh, shit!' Stuart starts to laugh. 'It's Valentine's Day!'

'Oh.' I'm *not* laughing. 'How embarrassing.'

'Yes.' He tries to straighten his face but is having a struggle. 'In the circumstances, it is, a little, isn't it. Well, we're obviously not going to get a table anywhere, and all the bars are full of loved-up couples. Um . . . want to come back to my place for a ready meal out of my freezer?'

'With an offer like that –' I begin, a little ungraciously, and he adds:

'Or would you rather just write it off?'

He sounds disappointed, and I start to feel mean. I agreed to come out with him. The least I can do is make an effort.

'No. OK, a ready meal would be perfect. Well,' I add with a shrug, 'maybe not perfect, but exactly what I'd have had at home anyway.'

Ten minutes later we come out of the Tube and turn down a quiet road with a mixture of properties on both sides and – there, on a corner, a church, with a steeple. Except, of course, that it isn't: it's Stuart's flat, and I have to admit, it's different, it's quirky, just as he said. I try to ignore my annoyance, remembering his suggestion – and as he opens the door to let me in, perhaps he's trying not to think about it too.

It was obviously a small church. The whole ground floor's taken up by an open plan sitting, dining and kitchen area. There are two doors to the back, one of which he explains is a downstairs toilet, the other a walk-in cupboard where he keeps his coats and shoes. He takes my coat and hangs it in there, pours me a drink and gets two individual lasagnes out of the freezer.

'Let's just enjoy our drinks while they're microwaving,' he says. 'Sorry it's not much.'

'It's fine.' Actually, it makes me feel more comfortable than if he'd spent the evening trying to placate me with an expensive meal. 'And you're right,' I feel I need to say, 'it's a very quirky flat.'

'Yes.' He takes a gulp of his wine and looks up at the ceiling as if for inspiration. 'Lauren, I won't try to make excuses for what I said the other day –'

'No. Please, let's just forget it.'

'But I want to explain why I suggested it at all. I wasn't entirely truthful –'

I stare at him now. Please don't let him come out and admit he just wanted to use me for his own advantage. I might have suspected it, and been hurt by the thought of it, but I really don't want to hear him say it.

'Honestly, I did suggest it to help you, because I knew you were fed up with your house,' he goes on. 'But there's more to it than that. From everything you've said, I've gathered it isn't just your house you want to change. It's your job, too, and London, and your whole way of life. But maybe I got that wrong – perhaps it was just a post-holiday-blues thing –'

'No.' I'm watching his face. He's trying so hard to explain himself, he almost looks in pain. 'No, you're quite right.'

'So the thing is, it occurred to me, that perhaps I could help with that.'

'By moving *here*? I'm sorry, but that isn't what I want.'

'No! I mean *yes,* but that's only part of it. And only temporarily. I thought it might help you to move more quickly –'

'But I don't want to live in London anymore!'

'I know. And I could see how much you loved your time in Deepcombe. If you thought I was being selfish, yes, I was, in a way – because I was hoping you could get out of London more quickly and move down to Devon.'

'Why did you think I wanted to move to Devon?' I ask a bit shakily. 'How did you know? I haven't said anything about that!'

'Well, it was a guess. You said you missed it, you wanted to go back, and OK, I'll be honest, I was hoping so. I'm not being creepy, or coming on to you, honestly, Lauren, but I thought we got along together, so . . .' He pauses, wiping his brow as if the effort of saying all this is making him sweat. I think it actually might be. 'I thought,' he goes on more quietly, 'I might eventually persuade you to come and work for us.'

'What?' I'm so startled, I have to put my drink down. I don't know what I expected, but it certainly wasn't this. '*Work* for you? What – at the Manor? The market gardening? But I don't know the first thing about –'

'No. On the holiday bookings side. We're going to need more staff on both sides, but for this, we need someone who's good with admin, and tech, who loves the area and can promote it. You can live in at the Manor – unless you prefer not to. That's one of the reasons we're renovating the west wing – in case any of our new staff want to live in. And more importantly, for more holidaymakers. Nathan and I have talked endlessly about all these plans.' He's sounding enthusiastic now, looking less awkward. 'We want to make the business successful, so Mum can retire at last. But –' He pauses and shrugs. 'You're probably looking for something completely different –'

'Why the *hell*,' I ask him, 'didn't you say all this on Sunday instead of letting me think you were . . . just *using* me, to appease your landlord so you can get out of here yourself?'

'I wasn't sure if you're ready yet to think about moving to Devon; I didn't want to rush you, so I thought, if this just encourages you sell your house, and be in a position to think more clearly about the next step, I could suggest it then. But I messed it up, said it all wrong, and . . . didn't want you to think I was making assumptions.' He sighs. 'Anyway, I'm sure you'll be looking for something more high-flying and professional, and maybe not even in Devon, and certainly not in the back-of-beyond in Deepcombe –'

'Stop talking,' I tell him.

'OK. I know I've said too much. I'll just go and check on the lasagnes, now –'

'I'm saying *yes,* Stuart! Yes, I'd love to work with you and Nathan and Betty. I'd love to live in Deepcombe. I can't think of anything I'd like more! Thank you, thank you so much, and I'm sorry I took it all the wrong way but you're an idiot, you should have spelt it out to me in the first place!'

'Really? You really want the job? You mean it?'

'I really do. I'll put my house on the market tomorrow! But – I'm sorry, I *won't* need to move into this flat. I'll want to move straight to Devon as soon as I've sold the house.'

'Of course! It doesn't matter, I'll find someone. I'll persuade the landlord –'

'But you made it sound like I'd be doing you a favour by taking it over.'

'No, I just wanted to give you first refusal, before asking anyone else. I really did make a mess of it, didn't I?'

'You did! But it doesn't matter now. I'm *so* thrilled about the job!' I pause. 'I want to hug you, but I don't want you to think –'

'I don't think. I promise I won't think.'

And the next thing I know, we're hugging, and I'm laughing with happiness, because we're still friends, and I've got a plan for my new life, and it's all just turned out so unbelievably well.

'Quite a good Valentine's Day after all, then?' he says when we break apart, smiling at each other.

'Definitely! The best!'

'Can I tell my mum? I'm going down to Deepcombe on Friday to see her. Taking my dad.'

'Ooh, that's great! You must let me know how it goes, I'll be thinking of you all.'

He gets to his feet. 'Well, the lasagnes should be ready.' He pauses, smiling. 'My mum's told me that it was on a Valentine's Day that my dad gave her that mirror. Horrible thing – I can't imagine why she even liked it. And he used some terrible line on her –'

'About looking in it and seeing how beautiful she was! She told us, too. Yuck!'

'You're right, yuck!' He shakes his head. 'People in love can be ridiculous, can't they?'

'Yep!' I agree, and I'm laughing again, enjoying the fact that we both find it so ridiculous. 'Valentines' Day, huh! What a joke!'

But somehow, I think I'll always remember this one.

Wednesday

Julia

I had the strangest phone call from Lauren late last night. Apart from anything else, I've never heard her so excited, so positive and enthusiastic.

'I don't know where to start!' she squawked, all high-pitched and laughing. 'You see, I went round to Stuart's place tonight for a meal out of his freezer, and –'

'*What?*' I said. 'Where did this come from? I thought you were really upset with him!'

'Well, I was. But he asked me to go out with him to explain himself, and I thought I owed him that at least, but it's Valentine's Day, everywhere was busy, so we just went back to his place, and –'

'Right. And you've made up?'

I must admit, I was thinking: *Please* don't let this be that same old thing: Lauren believing she's in love with him, getting hurt all over again despite everything she's been saying.

'Yes. We're friends again. He'd just made a hash of what he was really trying to suggest, and I'd got the wrong end of the stick . . . but never mind all that, Julia – the thing is, I'm definitely moving to Devon – it's all on, it's all agreed!'

'Um . . . agreed with *Stuart?*' I said.

Oh, God, I was thinking. *Please, please don't say she's moving in with him.*

'He's offered me a job! I can live in, to start with, but of course, I might want to look for somewhere of my own. I've got to sell my house first, of course, but that shouldn't be a problem, so –'

'Hang on, slow down!' I said. 'What job? What are you talking about? You're going to be living at Deepcombe Manor – really? Are you sure? This all sounds . . .'

I managed, just, to stop myself saying it all sounded like another one of her flights of fancy. What had happened to the adoption plans? What was she supposed to be doing at Deepcombe – picking tomatoes? Feeding the cats?

'I know how it sounds,' she said, calming down a little. 'But honestly, Julia, it's like I've finally got the chance to do something I really want.'

'And the adoption?'

'I'll be contacting an agency in Devon. I've been looking online already. I can't really do any more until I've sold this house, worked my notice here, and got a date for moving down.'

'You're serious, aren't you,' I said, a lump suddenly coming to my throat. When she mentioned moving to Devon the other day, it just sounded like something she might do in a year or so. Not yet! I've only just got to know this sister of mine, and she's moving away from me.

'Absolutely.' She paused, and the tone of her voice changed. 'But I'll miss you. Now, I will.'

I had to swallow. *Now*, she'd miss me. Before the holiday, she wouldn't have done. But of course, I couldn't blame her. The holiday had changed everything – for us both.

'Tell me about it, then – the job,' I said, more gently. 'What are you going to be doing?'

And as she told me, all about how Stuart and Nathan are going to be building up the business – both sides of the business – so that Betty doesn't have to work anymore, how they're going to need more staff, and particularly someone to manage the holiday lettings, which is what Lauren's going to take on, I felt a strange feeling coming over me. It was partly relief – because it didn't sound like a madcap idea after all; it sounded like a proper job prospect, a sensible plan, something she could get her teeth into and enjoy. And it was partly . . . only partly . . . just a tiny, strange, little touch of envy.

After we finished the conversation and hung up, I told myself to ignore that strange little flutter of a feeling; it couldn't possibly be envy, because I don't have any room in my head at the moment for sudden urges to move out of London, look for a new job, or do anything impulsive like that. I've got enough to think about with helping Phil with his recovery, never mind trying to get our finances back on track: seeing through the sale of my own house, and then putting *this* house on the market and looking for something smaller we can move into. And keeping the severity of this crisis from our son and his girlfriend – they're so happy that we're back together, they know we're selling the properties but they don't need to be worried by the details, the scale of the problem. The enormity of all this responsibility – on top of continuing to work at my own job, while Phil's still on sick leave – is as much as I can handle right now.

I sat down with Phil and told him all about Lauren's news.

'I'm so pleased for Lauren,' he said when I'd finished. 'She's never really seemed happy, or satisfied with her lot, has she?'

'No. You're right, I'm pleased for her too. I just hope –'

'Look, she's young, single, intelligent – even if it doesn't work out, she'll find something else. Find some*where* else. I think she's needed to do this for a long time: to . . . spread her wings, fly a little. We both think she'll make a great mum and I hope the adoption process works out for her too, but it can sometimes take years. She knows that. In the meantime, she really needs to . . . find herself.'

I had to swallow. He'd put it so well; it struck me that he might have known Lauren better than I did – or at least, understood her better.

'You're right. She does need that. And she deserves it,' I acknowledged. 'And she's insisting she and Stuart are just friends.'

'OK. Well, let's see how it all works out.' He gave me a sympathetic smile, then, and added, 'Devon is only a few hours' away, Jules. It's not as if she's going to Australia. We can visit her – all the time. And it won't be for a while. She has to sell her house, and tie things up here. Don't be sad. Be happy for her.'

So I wake up this morning feeling better, more positive, determined to be encouraging and helpful, and not to think about what might go wrong. Or think about my own feelings.

I'm just getting ready for work when my phone starts ringing. I smile to myself: I suppose Lauren's forgotten some exciting aspect of the story. But it isn't Lauren's number on the display. It's Dad's care home.

'Hello?' I answer. I feel a flash of guilty conscience. I haven't been in to see Dad since we came back from Deepcombe. Not that he'd know: he doesn't recognise me anymore, and it's not as if we can have a chat as he's lost most of his language. But nevertheless, normally I try to go, once a week, just to make sure he's as comfortable as possible.

'Mrs Davis? It's Sue at Parkdean Residential Home –'

'Yes – hello, Sue. Is Dad OK? I'm so sorry I haven't been in recently. I've had a few –'

'Mrs Davis . . . Julia. I'm so sorry to have to tell you: your father's passed away.'

'Oh!' I gulp, and tears spring to my eyes. I've been expecting this phone call, anticipating it every day for the last few years, and yet, somehow, it's still a shock. 'Has he . . . had he been unwell, or –'

'Not at all. He was just his usual self. He was still asleep this morning when his carer went into his room with his usual cup of tea in a beaker. She opened the curtains to wake him, he stirred a little and she told him his tea was beside his bed and that she'd come back in a few minutes to help him sit up and drink it. When she went back, he'd simply stopped breathing. He was completely peaceful. I don't think any of us could wish for a better ending.'

'Oh.' I'm having trouble speaking. 'Oh. Well, thank you.'

'The doctor is here now, to sign the death certificate. Would you like to come –'

'Yes. Yes, of course. I'll . . . come right away –'

But I need to do something first. I need to call my sister.

'I'm coming with you,' Lauren says immediately. 'I'll pick you up.'

'There's no need.' I hesitate, then go on, my voice wobbling: 'After all, I didn't come when Mum –'

'We're not going to go over that again,' she says very softly. 'We've put it behind us, haven't we. I feel bad too, as you know – I haven't been to see Dad for ages.' There's a pause; I can hear her swallow and sniff, then she goes on, quietly but firmly: 'Let's do it together, this time, Julia. Let's make up for . . . everything that went before. We'll do it all together.'

So we do. We go to the home, we see how peaceful Dad looks – at last, having not been at peace for so long, in his struggle with dementia – and we hold each other and cry together, then we go, together, to the funeral director and make the arrangements, and finally to the café right next door to the funeral director, where we both get a big mug of hot chocolate and finally manage to smile, thinking immediately of Betty.

'Shall we take the rest of the day off?' she suggests, looking at her watch. 'It's nearly lunchtime anyway.'

'I shouldn't,' I say. 'With Phil being off –'

'Is everything all right – with the business?' she asks me gently. 'Only you seem a bit . . . stressed whenever we talk about it. And you've talked a lot about the financial difficulties. I presume it's the business. I didn't want to pry, but, well, obviously I'm concerned.'

I sigh, and for a moment I don't answer. I sit, looking into my cup, stirring my drink until eventually Lauren touches my hand and jokes that I'm going to make a hole in the bottom of the mug.

'The business is all right,' I say, finally. 'But we're not. Financially, we're not, we've got some debts. But it's . . . nothing to worry about. It's all in hand.'

'Is that why you're selling your house? I presumed it was just because you've moved back in with Phil.'

'We're selling his too.'

She looks at me, concern etched in her face. 'So it *is* something to worry about.'

'It won't be, once we've sold both properties and moved to something smaller.'

'OK.' She nods. 'OK, I'm not going to ask what happened. But I'm here for you, all right? Even after I'm – not here. I'll do anything I can to help.'

And she reaches across the café table and touches my hand, grasps it, rubs my fingers with hers. I can't reply. So far, I've coped; once I knew Phil was going to be OK, I was OK too. I had to be strong, because he couldn't be. And I'll continue to cope, I know I will – but right at this moment, having just arranged my dad's funeral, and with my sister squeezing my hand and looking at me like she'd fly to the moon and back if she could, to help me, I feel like I just want to bury my head against her shoulder and cry my eyes out.

'You'll be fine,' she says softly. 'You and Phil – now you're back together – you can take on the world. You'll get through this.'

And I just nod, and wipe my eyes. And we sit like this for half an hour or more, just drinking our chocolate and remembering our conversations and arguments in Betty's conservatory. And we do take the rest of the day off; we go to the park, walk round the duckpond, have lunch in a cheap sandwich bar, buy a paper and do the crossword together, talk about Deepcombe some more, then get more maudlin and talk about our childhoods and how we drifted apart. Finally she drives me home and we hug and kiss and shed a few tears, and I go indoors feeling absolutely exhausted.

'Are you OK, love?' Phil asks anxiously. 'I'm glad you took the day off. It was bound to be stressful, arranging the funeral –'

'I'm all right, Phil – just tired,' I reassure him, throwing myself down in an armchair and giving him a smile. 'It was all OK. I had my sister with me.'

Saturday

Betty

They arrived last evening – my son, and his father. I told myself not to think about Richard at all – what he might be like now, whether I'd even recognise him from the young man he was all those years ago – and just concentrate on the excitement of seeing my son again. But of course, that was easier said than done. And in the event, it was strange. I'd like to say I looked at Richard and felt the passage of time melt away, that nothing had changed, we were both just the same. But of course, I'd be lying. He's eighty-nine, and he looks it. And I could see in his eyes that he was thinking the same about me, even if I am a few years younger. I don't suppose I've aged well. As for him, he's got arthritis; he walks with a stick, stooped and unsteady, and his breathing's bad – he told me later that he has COPD. He talks a lot about his health, and his anxieties about it. I suppose that's what you get for living in bloody London, and working in a stressful environment.

Stuart, on the other hand, seemed so much better than when I spoke to him on the phone recently. He was happy, and I was pretty sure it wasn't just about being with his father.

'I've got some news,' he told me quietly while he was helping me dish up the dinner.

'And would it be, by any chance, something to do with the girl who's only a friend?' I asked him. 'Did you manage to make up with her?'

'Yes. And not only that – she's going to be moving down here, Mum. She's going to be working for us.'

'Oh – to take over running the holiday lettings? Good! I thought you were going to advertise, but it's even better if it's someone you know.' I pause, frowning. 'But I thought you were hoping this girl was going to take over your flat?'

'Um, no, that was just supposed to be a means to an end. So that she could sell her house, and – then I'd try to talk her into –'

'Talk her into it?' I looked at him in surprise. 'A means to an end? It sounds like you were pretty keen to have her move down here.'

'Well, yes, I thought it would work well – for us both. And I thought you'd like it too.' He gave me a grin. 'It's Lauren.'

'*Lauren*? The Lauren who stayed here with her sister –?'

'Yep. I knew she was looking for something different, and frankly, she'll be perfect for this job, she's a bright girl but she's never found anything that satisfies her. And she wanted a new start. She's going to apply to adoption agencies down here too. So –'

'So it could all work out really well. For you both,' I said, giving him a knowing look.

He didn't meet my eyes. 'Hopefully, yes,' he said.

So we had dinner, and Richard and I looked at each other now and then over the table. Assessing the damage. When he smiled, I got a glimpse of the man I once knew, the way his eyes widened, the dimples at the side of his mouth. He said he'd never forgotten my voice – my West Country accent – and that my eyes were exactly the colour he remembered. But mostly it was just polite conversation. I don't know what I'd imagined I was going to feel . . . a rush of the old passion? A flood of precious memories returning? No. I felt nothing. We were strangers, complete strangers. Stuart had more to talk to him about than I did. I left them to chat over their drinks, and took myself off to bed, tired out from all the anticipation and . . . anti-climax.

This morning, I'm laughing at myself. Silly old fool! What on earth did I expect? It all happened in another life, a life I left behind half a century ago, and I've been ridiculous for ever imagining it would still feel the same if we met up again. We're both too bloody old for all that hearts and flowers nonsense now, anyway.

After breakfast, Stuart and Nathan take him on a tour of the house and the greenhouses. I watch from the conservatory, smiling to myself at the pride evident in my son and grandson, showing off their work, talking about their plans. When they come back, I make him a cup of coffee and we sit together in the warmth of the winter sunshine in the conservatory. Stuart and Nathan leave us to it, saying they want to discuss the rest of the plans for the West Wing.

'I think they're being tactful,' he says, smiling at me.

'Yes.' I don't know what to say, now we're on our own. It feels awkward.

'We've got a lot of catching up to do,' he goes on.

'Yes. It . . . must have been a shock for you. When Stuart contacted you.'

'You're right, it was. Finding out I had a son – *your* son. Well.' He shakes his head, like he still can't quite believe it. 'I'd . . . always assumed you just left me, back then, because you'd had enough of me. Not because of . . . a baby.'

'I promised you, didn't I. Promised I'd never let you face a scandal. So I was never going to tell you, even though I know you'd have supported me if I did, maybe left your wife –'

I stop, looking at him now and suddenly feeling stupid. *Would* he have left her? *Would* he have supported me, supported his son? We'd carried on our affair for nine years; nine years of clandestine meetings, hotel rooms where we arrived separately and left separately – until he bought me the flat – phone calls from public call boxes, never being seen together in public, never being a proper couple. I'd believed he loved me. Believed everything he ever said. Accepted the loneliness of the weeks that went past without seeing him or hearing from him. Refused offers of dates with other men – single, available men. Living half a life, at an age when I should have been having fun, and promising, always promising, that I'd never do anything to ruin his life – to destroy his marriage, his family, his all-important career.

I shake my head, push the negative thoughts away.

'I couldn't have stayed in London and managed on my own with a child: with Stuart,' I go on. 'I had to come back to . . . where I belonged. And I kept my word. I never tried to contact you –'

'No.' He smiles. 'Nor I you, not after failing to find a phone number for you. I reasoned, then, that there was no point searching for you. It was for the best, I suppose.'

I freeze, shock hitting me so hard it makes me shudder inside. *No point searching for me.* I should have realised, of course. They say that anybody can find anyone, these days, if they try hard enough. If they really want to. What an idiot I am. All these years, while I disciplined myself not to look for him, even in the media, I always imagined him trying desperately to find me.

'For the best,' I repeat shakily.

'Yes. After all, we both had to get on with our lives, didn't we,' he goes on, blithely unaware of how his words are stinging me. 'I mean, we were great together, you and I, we couldn't get enough of each other!' He laughs. 'What memories, eh? What it was to be young and lustful! But at the end of the day, I reasoned you'd decided to move on – probably found someone else, someone free to be with you properly, and I couldn't blame you for that.'

'I didn't. I told you why I left. It was because I was expecting Stuart.'

'I know that *now*. But, well, you were better off without me, clearly. Look what a nice life you've got here, with Stuart, and your grandson.' He pauses. 'Did you have any more children?'

'No. I never married.'

'Just enjoyed yourself, eh? Good for you!' He laughs. 'Oh, it's good to see you again, Betty, it really is. Still the same old Betty –'

'No, I'm not,' I retort, suddenly angry. 'I'm not the same old Betty at all. I didn't *enjoy myself*, as you put it, after I left you. The reason I never married is that I never met anyone else I was remotely interested in. I had a few casual boyfriends, but they didn't want to take on a woman with a child, and anyway, I didn't love them. I didn't love anyone else, ever, Richard – I was still in love with you.'

'Oh, steady on, old girl! I mean, yes, we had a bit of a fling, I was always very keen on you –'

'A *bit of a fling*? We had a nine-year affair! You were lucky your wife never found out!'

'Well, she did in the end, of course. Not about you. You were too decent about it all – you played the game, kept it quiet. But not all women are like you.'

'You had other affairs, after I left?'

'Well, be fair, a man has to live!' he chuckles. 'You'd gone, so –'

'But you had a wife! A family!'

He just looks back at me, his eyebrows raised, and I sigh, deflated. I'm hardly one to complain. I knew perfectly well, throughout the nine years I was seeing him, that he had that wife and family.

'I got caught out, in the end,' he says, with a shrug. 'My own fault. Picked a girl young enough to be my daughter. She didn't follow the rules.'

'How many more affairs did you have?' I ask dully, beginning to feel that I wouldn't care if he said a hundred.

'Oh, a few.' Another shrug. 'You know how it is. Being a public figure, you get . . . pursued.'

'Poor you.'

We look at each other for a few moments. I'm wondering whether to just get up and leave the room. Then Basil wanders in, meowing, and I automatically lift him onto my lap and start stroking him to calm myself.

'I did love you, Betty, in my way,' Richard's saying. 'Don't let's fall out; I've been looking forward so much to meeting up with you again.'

'Why?' I ask bluntly.

'Well . . .' He looks taken aback, almost embarrassed. 'You're my son's mother, and I'd kind-of hoped –'

'Hoped what?' I persist. 'To be part of the family?'

'Yes. Yes, of course – well, I consider I already *am* part of the family, now I've met Stuart, and Nathan – and you again –'

'And how do your daughters feel about that?'

'Oh –' He gives a dismissive shake of his head. 'They've got their own lives. They take their mother's side in everything, of course. Never forgave me for the break-up. They want me to move into a care home now – can you believe that? I mean, they've both got nice homes, plenty of room –'

'You were expecting to move in with one of them, were you?'

He shifts a little awkwardly in his chair. 'Not *expecting* it, but, well, family is family, you know? I'd have hoped they might like to . . . But no, they're turning their back on me, now I'm old and decrepit!'

'As you turned your back on them when they were little girls,' I say softly – so softly he doesn't hear me, and I don't repeat it, because I know, of course, that I was just as guilty as he was, of choosing to ignore the existence of those children, when it suited me.

I know I'm being unfair. I can't blame him for *getting on with his life*. It's my own fault for harbouring, all these years, the ridiculous notion that he might have stayed true to me, searched for me, grieved for the loss of me. And that he ever really loved me.

But disappointment can make us bitter. And the scales have finally fallen from my eyes. I think I'm realising, now, where this is all heading: this visit, this whole charade of wanting to see me again, and be a part of our family.

'I suppose when Stuart told you about where we live – this house – our business – the plans to cater for more paying guests . . . it must have sounded appealing to you,' I say, looking him straight in the eye.

'Well, of course, I was interested to come and see it – see *you*,' he blusters.

'Let's face it, it must seem like a better proposition than a care home.'

'Oh, come on, that's not –'

'I'd like you to be honest, Richard. Please. You've been hoping to move in here, with us, haven't you?'

He swallows and looks away.

'Well, look, this *is* a big house,' he says finally. 'And, well, Stuart is my son. Nathan is my grandson. Naturally I'd like to be nearer to them. And I have a good pension – I'd contribute, of course –'

'Contribute to what, exactly? Your *care* costs? You're expecting us to look after you, aren't you. You've already told us about all your health conditions.' I feel my throat tightening. I'm stroking Basil so hard, there's fur flying off him. 'Listen, Richard, I'm glad my son's found his father. And that Nathan's got a granddad. I'm happy for you to be part of their lives, obviously, but your daughters are your real family. Maybe you should follow their advice. Use your bloody pension to pay for a care home, because Deepcombe Manor isn't going to be it.'

He doesn't try to respond. I put Basil down carefully on the floor and walk out of the room with the cat following me. It's funny, but I don't even feel sad about Richard. I can almost laugh at myself for the fool I've been, all these years. How strange that, at eighty years old, I seem to have only just grown up. So much for being the Wise Woman of Deepcombe.

A Saturday in April

Lauren

My house is cleared, most of the furniture ready to go into in storage, the sale virtually a *fait accompli* apart from the solicitors doing their usual job of dragging it all out. I've given in my notice at work and I'm finding it almost impossible to sit still at my desk. Stuart's landlord finally gave in and agreed to let him find someone else to take over the flat, and that happened so quickly that he's already back at Deepcombe. And I'm almost ready to move down there myself now. I can't wait!

Julia and I have got into the habit, since Dad's funeral, of having lunch together every Saturday. Dad's passing was in many ways a gentle blessing; Julia told me how confused, frightened and unhappy he'd been for so long now, not even knowing who he was, let alone who she, or anyone else, was. But the very process of dealing with his affairs and his funeral was probably the final stage of bringing us together as sisters. We're closer now than we've ever been. It's sad but true to think that even in our childhood we didn't have much time for each other; but we've moved on from all that, now.

'Have you been in touch with the adoption agency in Devon now?' Julia asks me over our lunch today.

'Yes. They've taken all my details and told me to get back in touch as soon as I have an address –'

'But you've got it already, haven't you? Deepcombe Manor!'

'Yes; but it needs to be my *official* address, so once I've moved in, I can tell them I'm ready to start the process. I'll be renting the first one of the new flats in the West Wing –'

'Flats? Wow, I thought they would just be rooms.'

'No. You know how big the Manor is, Julia! Each flat will be two bedrooms, a living room with a little kitchen area, and a bathroom. There will be six of them eventually – three upstairs, three downstairs. There's only one finished so far, and that's what they're letting me have.'

'But what about the holidaymakers?'

'We haven't got any booked in yet for the summer, because Stuart's finished with the agent and taken the website down temporarily. I'm going to start off by getting that all up and running. We'll only have the Lodge on offer this summer. The other flats next year.'

'You sound like you're already part of it all. Already there,' she says, suddenly sounding a bit wistful.

'I know. I'm *so* excited about it all.' Then I pause, look at her face, and go on more quietly: 'About all of it, apart from missing you. Missing these lunches, and . . . well, just *you.*'

'I'll be calling you all the time.'

'You'd better. I want to know . . . what you decide.'

She and Phil are selling the business. Julia's former house already has a potential buyer, but before they put Phil's house, where they're living now, up for sale too they want to make some decisions.

'Phil wanted us to carry on with the business at first,' she explained when they'd first started to discuss the situation. 'It's doing OK . . . but perhaps that's the best time to sell.' She sighed, shook her head, and admitted: 'But I don't want Phil to go back to working the way he was before. He really needs to avoid stress now.'

'So what will you both do for work?'

'Not sure yet. It won't be easy for either of us, having never worked anywhere else. It'll be starting all over again. In some ways, that could be quite exciting; but after all the worry of Phil's health, and the debts, I'm not so sure.'

'It sounds like you'd be better off not to rush into anything. Give it some more thought, maybe look at job opportunities?'

'Yes, that's what we're going to do. I think even Phil realises, now, that he needs to cut his anxiety levels. After we've moved to a smaller house, and we're completely out of debt again, we can think about it all properly. And we won't need such a high level of income. Meanwhile, I've warned Phil he has to let other members of staff – including me – take some of the load, and some of the strain, off him.'

'How's Simon doing?' I ask her now. She's told me how badly he took the whole business of his dad being so ill, swiftly followed by the shock of his parents' financial difficulties.

'He's OK now. It was all such a worry for him, and I felt bad about that, obviously. I suppose children always expect their parents to be all right. It scares them if the status quo suddenly changes – so a health wobble *and* a money wobble must have frightened the life out of him.'

'He must be glad you and Phil are back together, though?'

She smiles. 'Yes. I think that's made up for everything else we've put him through! And anyway, he and Freya are talking about getting engaged, so –'

'Oh, that's wonderful!' I give her a grin. 'Next thing you know, you'll be a grandma!'

'Ouch! Am I really old enough? No, I doubt they'll be in a rush for kids. They're both building up their careers. They're pretty settled, though – they've been together for over three years now. And Freya's lovely. We're happy for them.'

'And so am I. I must give him a call – and pop round and see them again, before I move.' I've been making a conscious effort to be a proper auntie to Simon recently. I bitterly regret not having a relationship with him before. 'I've already suggested that they might like a holiday at Deepcombe later in the year,' I add. 'And – obviously – it would be lovely if you and Phil could spare the time to fit in a week in the summer . . . but I know you're probably going to be busy.'

Julia looks at me, thoughtfully. 'Do you know what, Lauren, that actually might be lovely. Once everything here's been sorted out – however long that takes – I really think we'll both be ready for a break. And let's face it, we're not going to be able to afford to go abroad.' She gives me a smile. 'Should I book it with you now, though, in case you get a flood of bookings as soon as you start working on it?'

'I've got to get the website up and running first!' I laugh. 'Although . . . I have started working on it in my spare time.'

'You *are* keen!'

'Yes. I am. But don't worry, if we're booked up, you can always have the spare room in my flat.'

'I'll take you up on that,' she promises. 'Have you spoken to Betty recently, anyway? How is she now?'

Julia knows about the drama back in February, when Stuart took his dad to Deepcombe: Betty called me the following day. Julia and I were both worried about her – how upset she must have been to have all her happy memories of Richard dashed. But I've realised there's a lot more to Betty than meets the eye!

'I've still *got* my happy memories,' she insisted when I asked her about it, 'because they're memories of how happy I was back then – in the Sixties, when . . . it all happened. I know I didn't deserve to be happy, because he was married, and it was wrong. But I loved him then, and I thought he loved me –'

'I'm sure he did!' I tried to reassure her.

'Hmm. Perhaps, in his way, as he says now. Anyway, my lovely, look: the fact that he's a selfish old bugger now – and perhaps he always was – doesn't change how I felt back then. I'm just glad I haven't got to go to my grave wondering how it might have all worked out, if I'd stayed with him: whether he'd have left his wife, whether we'd ever have got married. I know now that none of that would have happened, but I don't feel bad about it. He wouldn't have been a good husband. And I've had a nice life since, so I'm glad, now, that I left him, before I let him hurt me.'

'Ah, Betty, are you *sure* you're not upset?' I pressed her.

'I'm *absolutely* not upset,' she retorted. 'I was angry, when I realised that all he wanted was to take advantage of us. But I'm over it now. Stuart's still in touch with him, of course. And I'm not saying anything to spoil his relationship with his father. I kept them apart for too long.'

'Stuart says he's still talking to him on the phone a couple of times a week, but he –' I began.

Then I stopped, embarrassed, realising I was making it sound like I knew more about what Stuart was doing, what he was feeling, than his mother did. It was true, he'd talked to me about it after he returned to London at the end of that weekend, told me how disappointed he felt that his mum hadn't seemed as thrilled to be reunited with his father as he'd hoped. But Stuart didn't know the reason – Betty had only told him Richard 'wasn't quite how she remembered him.' And now, rather awkwardly, I was in the position of knowing more than he did.

Stuart and I were meeting up regularly before he moved back to Deepcombe. We needed to make plans, discuss my new job, of course, that's all, although it was quite nice to have a friend to have a drink and the occasional meal out with in the evenings. Now he's gone back, we've obviously stayed in touch too. Phone calls, texts, WhatsApp messages. Emails about the business. Because of the business, we've got a lot to talk about, a lot of decisions to make. The different sides of Deepcombe

Manor Ltd will inevitably overlap somewhat. I'll be reporting to Stuart once I start work on the holiday lettings, but he'll mainly be running the market gardening side. He's started work already on building that up: two big new greenhouses are going up, and he's bought a lot of new stock – plants, fruit bushes and so on. He's joking that he'll have to give me a crash course in gardening – because until the holiday business starts to really take off, I'll be helping him outside whenever I'm free. They're going to hire a couple of temporary labourers, too, who can help inside or out. After this first summer, we'll have a better idea of how much permanent staff we'll need. There's so much work to do, and Nathan's entire time, this year at least, will be taken up with the renovations to the Manor.

'I don't want to rely on you for garden work long-term, though,' Stuart told me recently. 'Because once you've got a child to look after –'

'That might not happen for a long time,' I remind him.

'I know. But I also know how important it is for you.'

He's right, it is – that hasn't changed, but I'm glad I've got so much else to keep me occupied, now, while I wait for that slow process to go through. I've never felt so motivated before, ever, in my entire life. And it's all getting closer by the day. I'm nearly ready to go. Finally, at the age of forty, I feel like my life is going to begin.

Betty

Lauren's arriving in two weeks' time. I'm looking forward to it: to seeing her, and to knowing my son's life is going to be easier for the rest of the season. Not only easier, but better in another way, too, although I'm not allowed to even hint about that. He's keeping very quiet about it, insisting he and Lauren are just friends, that they're just going to be colleagues, that they get on well, and that's the end of it. So I'm saying nothing.

We've had nobody else here, staying at the Lodge, since the family with two little boys who came at the end of February. Nice couple, they were, and nicely-behaved children: one was seven, one was five. The weather wasn't bad, for February, and they went out most days, driving around Dartmoor and further afield. But every afternoon when they came back, the mum brought the boys over to the swimming pool. The younger one used a floatation thing but he could swim a little bit without it. The seven-year-old was quite a good little swimmer. He was practising jumping in, and doing handstands in the water. I asked their mum if she'd mind if I sat and watched them, and she was very nice, happy to sit with me sometimes and chat, if she wasn't going into the pool herself. Of course, we soon got into the habit of having a cup of chocolate together! But I behaved myself. There was no sharing of family secrets. I guess the shrieking of little boys enjoying themselves in the pool doesn't result in the same atmosphere of quiet, warm, cosiness that lends itself to that kind of thing, and it's probably just as well. I get enough of that with the villagers who come to buy their herbs and vegetables. Anyway, Stuart says I've got to start charging for all the hot drinks and cakes and biscuits and so on. We argued over it a little bit.

'Not for the holidaymakers!' I protest when he brings it up again today. 'They're already paying us, and I don't want to charge them for a couple of little extra treats – especially as I'm *offering* them to them!'

'OK, maybe not, for now anyway,' he agrees, smiling and giving me a hug. 'But the thing is, Mum, I want, eventually, to make it another part of the business.'

'What? Making cups of coffee and chocolate? Surely not!'

'Not yet. Probably not for a while, maybe not till next year. But eventually, if the market garden business takes off the way we hope, we're going to need a place to serve customers. Somewhere they can come inside to pay, instead of just settling up in one of the greenhouses, and us writing paper receipts if they don't want an emailed one – it's all a bit antiquated –'

'It's how I've been doing things for ever, it's worked perfectly fine,' I say sniffily.

'I know, Mum, and you've done brilliantly. I don't know how you've managed it all on your own, all this time. But we're getting bigger, aren't we, and we'll need to be . . . a bit more professional . . . in due course.'

'Huh.' Of course, I'm proud, really. So proud of what he and Nathan are doing, what they're planning. They're right, I couldn't have kept going on my own for much longer, even though I was only growing a few things and not making much money. And of course, they're not old fogies like me, they do everything on the Internet, take payments out of thin air with no cash changing hands, they use card machines and something on their phones, it's all completely beyond me.

'So what we're thinking is,' Stuart goes on, watching me carefully, 'We'll start with just a counter somewhere – probably at the window of the old breakfast room, where that table is, that we never use?'

'I do use it. I keep some of the pots of herbs on it –'

'They can go elsewhere, Mum. It's not as if we haven't got plenty of room.'

I shrug and nod.

'So that can be our counter, for now,' he repeats. 'And what we're thinking is, in due course the breakfast room can be extended. And converted.'

'Into what?'

'A kind of reception area,' he says, watching my face. 'Where the holiday guests can come – again, it's all a bit unprofessional, them having to knock at the front door, or go straight to the Lodge and let themselves in. And we can serve the produce customers there too, and – we thought it might be nice – to have some tables and chairs.'

'What for?'

'A little café,' he says. He laughs. 'I can see it now: Deepcombe Manor Special: hot chocolate. With or without a little extra of your choice!'

I have to laugh, despite my reservations. It all sounds . . . so *grandiose*. Not just a holiday business and market garden, but now a café too?

'We'll need *so* many more people working here,' I say, doubtfully.

'A few more, yes. But we're going to take this all very slowly. We can't afford to do it all at once, and we want, eventually, to take on good, loyal staff who'll stay with us for years. It's not going to happen overnight.' He smiles at me again, seeming to understand my reservations. 'It's still going to be your home, Mum, first and foremost. And if there's any of this you don't agree with, we won't do it. I promise.'

'No. You're right.' I smile back. 'It's a huge big place, and all these years, most of it's been empty, wasted space. If you do make all these changes, there'll still be plenty of room for an old girl like me to totter around in, won't there? And, more than anything,' I add – and I have to pause for a moment because there's a lump in my throat now – 'Most of all, Stuart, it's wonderful to see you so happy again. I thought that might never happen.'

'Me too,' he admits. 'It's helped me more than I can tell you: having these plans to get my teeth into. Having a future to dream about.'

'And possibly someone to share it with you?' I tease him gently, but he immediately shakes his head.

'She's just a friend,' he says, as always – even though I hadn't said who I was hinting at! 'I keep telling you, Mum, I can't envisage having another relationship. It's too soon after Janie.'

'I know,' I say, and I leave it at that.

I shouldn't tease him about Lauren. It's probably true that he doesn't want to think about any romantic relationship. He's had enough emotional upheaval recently anyway, with his new relationship with his father.

It was only the week after Richard's visit here, that Stuart called me to say they'd had dinner together back in London, and something awkward had come up.

'What happened between you two over the weekend while Dad was at Deepcombe?' he asked me, a bit hesitantly. 'I mean, I sensed that the reunion wasn't exactly a case of hearts and flowers, but –'

'Oh, it was all right, really,' I said, trying to sound nonchalant about it. 'But of course, it had been a long time, we've both changed, and –'

'I could tell he upset you.'

I hesitated, unsure how to answer. But Stuart suddenly rushed straight on:

'Did he ask to move into the Manor?'

I sighed. 'I didn't know whether to tell you this. He didn't ask directly, no, but he was definitely making hints that it was what he wanted; and when I asked him, he didn't deny it. Stuart, I'm sorry – he's your father, and if it's what you want, I suppose we have got the room, and he's said he'd contribute his pension, but he'd need looking after –'

'No, it's *not* what I want,' he retorted, to my surprise. 'He's hinted about it to me, too, and I think he's got a f – sorry, Mum – a *bloody* cheek. Yes, he's my father, and I'm glad I found out who he is, but I've already got the measure of him, and I'm not altogether sure I even like him.'

'Oh!' I was flabbergasted. 'I thought you and he were –'

'We've met up a few times, and no doubt we'll stay in touch occasionally, but I don't owe him anything, and you *certainly* don't. It's funny: Nathan actually took a bit of a dislike to him right from the start, but he didn't want to say so. But he admitted it when I discussed it with him this week.'

'Oh!' I said again. 'He hasn't said anything to me about it.'

'No. He wouldn't. And I didn't want to, either. I didn't want to spoil it for you, if you were still hoping to . . . be friends with him. But I gathered that he upset you at the weekend, and it seems you're getting the same vibes about him as I have – so, well, I can be more honest now. I think he's a selfish, self-obsessed old man who's only ever thought about himself and doesn't care about anyone – only what he can get from them.'

'Oh!' I seemed to have lost most of my vocabulary apart from that one exclamation.

'Sorry.' He paused, and amended his tone a little. 'Sorry to sound so harsh. It's just – such a disappointment. After finding him, you know. And – I've been worried about you. Whether you were disappointed too, whether he hurt you.'

'He did, a little,' I conceded. 'But only because he told me the brutal truth, and I'd been hanging onto a . . . little fantasy, all these years. But I was angry, more than hurt. And now, I'm just upset that he's hurt *you*, too.'

'Oh, he hasn't hurt me, not at all. Like you, I'm just angry. Do you know what I did, after that conversation where he talked about the possibility of moving into the Manor? I talked to one of his daughters, the one whose DNA mine was matched to, you know? We'd only met once – I'd been too keen to meet Dad, to spend much time talking to her, originally. Anyway, I asked her if she thinks her father's still fit to live on his own. "Yes, at the moment, he is," she said. "But he's lonely. And that's his own fault." She went on to say that he'd never been interested in her or her sister, never bothered with them when they were children, and still never calls them, or even sends them birthday cards or takes any interest in his grandchildren. She thinks he's suddenly realised he hasn't got many years left, and that there's nobody still alive who wants to know him, now that he's not famous – or, as she put it, notorious – anymore. And he wants someone to spend his last few years with. I don't blame her, or her sister, for telling him no.'

Stuart paused. I could hear him swallow before he went on: 'She said she didn't like saying this to me, because it seemed we were half-siblings even though she hadn't been aware of my existence, and she didn't want to hurt me, but went on to say: *The truth is, I doubt very much whether he really cares about you. Or your mother. He's a user, and always has been.*'

'Oh, Stuart,' is all I can say.

'Mum, I really don't care. Look, I'll do the decent thing, as I said: I'll keep in touch occasionally, from a distance – distance will be easier once I'm back at Deepcombe. I've already told him he should move into sheltered accommodation if he's lonely. I'm not sorry I found him, or I'd always have gone on wondering about him. But I can't think of him with any affection. He's still a stranger to me, and I hope I'm nothing like him. I hope I've inherited my whole personality from you, Mum, to be honest. You were all I needed, after all, growing up. And you and Nathan are all I need now.'

I'd be lying if I said I didn't shed a few tears after that conversation. But Stuart's back here at Deepcombe now, with me, and he's happy. And if he's happy, so am I. He and Nathan can build their business, their little empire here, whatever they like, they have my blessing, because I'm finally taking a back seat now; all I want to care for are my indoor herbs, and my cats. And it'll all be theirs anyway after I've gone. If they hadn't wanted it, this place would probably then have been sold to developers, knocked down, and a monstrosity of a modern hotel or something built here instead.

Deepcombe Ltd. I'm getting used to the sound of it. I rather like the idea of it being my legacy.

A Friday in mid-July

Julia

Phil and I are here at Deepcombe – we've had a week's holiday here, staying with Lauren, in her flat, as she promised. It's been wonderful to see her – and not just because I've missed her, but because I've never, in my whole life, seen her so happy, so fulfilled. She's busy: there are holidaymakers staying in the Lodge every week now, and all through the rest of the summer, and when she's not dealing with that side of the business she's helping at their new reception desk, taking payment for produce. But Stuart's insisted she takes most of this week off to spend with us, and we've driven out across the moor, seeing it, of course, in completely different colours from when we were here six months ago – the greens and yellows of summer – and heading further afield, too, to the coast, to pretty villages and bustling resorts, ancient castles and busy riversides. We've packed a lot in.

And now it's Friday evening, we've got to head home tomorrow, and we're sitting quietly with Betty in her conservatory. It's still warm, the evening sunshine intensified by all the glass, Lauren and I have got a cat each on our laps and we're drinking a glass of wine each. And although it's nothing like the chilly days when we sat here pouring out our life histories, back in January, I guess we're both remembering them. This evening, of course, Phil's with us, and so is Stuart. Nathan's out with his boyfriend, Jack – the guy he'd started seeing when we were here before. Apparently it's going well, and there's talk of them moving in together, but he's ruled out getting married this time!

I think this break has done Phil good – and me, too. He looks so relaxed, and the fresh country air has put colour back in his cheeks. I'd like to think the improvement will last, now he's calmer, now that we know the sale of the business should be going through OK. We're both staying on, working there, until the new company's taken over, then we'll be out, looking for new jobs for ourselves – we're already on the lookout for opportunities. We've got our house on the market now, too, but we haven't found anywhere new yet. It's difficult: property in London being so expensive, and the combination of downsizing, moving to lower-paid jobs *and* paying off the remaining debts will mean that all we can afford will be a small flat. Not that we mind; we both realise we've been very fortunate all our lives and there are only the two of us: we can make do, and be comfortable, anywhere, really, as long as we're together and have our health. Recent experiences have focused us on those priorities.

'I've got such memories of sitting here with Lauren, going over all our resentments and disagreements from childhood, while you pretended not to listen, Betty!' I comment as I sip my wine, and she laughs.

'Well, I think it helped, didn't it?' she says. 'Getting all that stuff off your chests?'

'It did,' I say, smiling at Lauren. 'But seriously, I think it's amazing, what you've all done here. What a transformation, in such a short time.'

The garden produce business is booming; the holiday renters have been leaving fantastic reviews on the new website – and on Trip Advisor – and Lauren's been telling us that the breakfast room, where they serve customers at the moment, is going to be extended to make a little café.

'We've applied for the planning permission for that, and hopefully Nathan can start work on it after he's finished the flats in the West Wing,' she explains now.

'I don't suppose he needs to take on any work elsewhere, now,' I realise.

'No. He's so busy here, he's got another guy working with him.'

'I'm surprised you don't all look worn out. There's such a lot for you all to do, but you all seem . . . full of energy!'

Stuart laughs. 'It's because we're so motivated – so excited about it all. We're all pulling together. Even Jack's been helping Nathan with a bit of labouring when he's got any free time. That's the beauty of a family business.' He glances at Lauren, and adds: 'Lauren's practically one of the family now – the way she mucks in and helps wherever she's needed!'

'I love it,' Lauren says with a smile and a shrug, and something about it – the way I can tell how much she means it – tugs at my heartstrings for a moment. 'I've got more friends here already then I ever had in London,' she goes on. 'I've been seeing a lot of Fern and Andy – and Ella, of course. They've been so supportive – helping me settle down in Devon, and about the adoption process of course.'

She's told me that's all going well too, and she's hoping she could be accepted for adoption by the end of the year. Then it'll be a question of waiting to match her with a suitable child. She's been babysitting Ella for Fern and Andy sometimes. 'To get a bit of hands-on experience!' she says.

'God knows how we'll manage, now, when she finally gets the child,' Stuart says, and I can tell he's only half-joking. 'I'll have to get cover for her parental leave, of course, but after that, there's no way I'm going to let her do anything apart from running the website and the bookings – from her own flat. Lauren's wanted this for so long, I'm not letting her miss a moment of her child's first few years.'

'You're a good boss!' I say.

'He's a good *friend*,' Lauren corrects me. And the smile she's giving him is – like sunshine.

She loves him, I suddenly find myself thinking. *And I don't think she even realises it.*

Perhaps they're both simply too busy to analyse the friendship right now. Perhaps that's the best way to build it into . . . whatever it might become. Whatever I *hope* it becomes.

We're on the second glass of wine when I find myself telling Stuart – while Lauren's deep in discussion with Phil, explaining how much she's learned about market gardening – how many different flats we've looked at in London, without getting any feeling of enthusiasm about any of them.

'Of course, we haven't completed the sale of our house yet,' I add. 'But we might end up renting, if we haven't found anything we really like by the time it goes through.'

'What a shame my old flat's not still available,' he says. 'It could have worked for you, in the interim.'

I shrug. 'I don't know, Stuart. Phil and I both feel ... kind of in limbo. I suppose it's inevitable. We're between jobs, as well as between homes! We're trying not to be fussy – we know we've been spoilt, living in nice houses. But nothing we look at seems worth the money they're selling for!'

'London prices are ridiculous,' he agrees.

'For God's sake!' Betty suddenly explodes. She's sitting on the other side of me, and she's been listening to this exchange in silence, taking it all in but without making any comment – just tutting and sighing in exasperation. I thought maybe she was just getting tired. We both turn to look at her now.

'What's the matter?' I ask her.

'For crying out loud, Stuart,' she says, giving him a despairing look and ignoring me completely. 'Just ask her! Just say it! You've been talking to me about it all week. I've already said it's a good idea. What are you waiting for? Christmas?!'

'All right, Mum, calm down. I just wasn't sure whether –'

'And you'll never be sure if you don't ask! Nathan's said it's a good idea, *I* think it's a good idea, even Jack thinks it's a good idea and it's nothing to do with him! And Lauren thinks it's the best idea ever in the whole history of good ideas and she's only holding back because she says it's not her place to ask, it's yours, because you're her boss!'

Lauren, by now, has stopped talking to Phil and is looking at us. Smiling at me.

'Go on, Stu,' she says. 'Ask them.'

He nods. Looks at me, then at Phil, and grins. 'I was leading up to it,' he says. 'Listen: property prices in Devon are much more reasonable, obviously, than in London. I'm not saying it has to be permanent. I realise you're both at . . . a kind of crossroads, deciding what you want to do, and I get that. But – if it would help – we'd love to offer you a flat here. The second one – next to Lauren's – is almost finished. In fact it only needs the paintwork doing, so if you're interested, you can choose your own colours! But I'm jumping the gun a bit. What I'm saying is, you'd be welcome to rent the flat, temporarily, while you decide what you're going to do with your lives. If you were to decide to stay in Devon, of course, you can buy it. But I don't suppose you'd want to live in Devon – why would you?'

I'm too astonished to speak. But Phil's ahead of me – he's looking at me, smiling, his eyes wide.

'Why *wouldn't* we?' he retorts. 'The only tie we'll have left in London will be our son, but he's young, he's got his career and his girlfriend – sorry, fiancée! – and London is what they love, what they need.'

'They can visit you, whenever they want!' Betty says, the edge of exasperation still in her voice. 'What's the problem?'

'All right, Mum – let them have a little while to think about it!' Stuart says.

Phil turns to me, the smile still on his face. *He looks excited*, I think. *For the first time in months, maybe years – he's excited about something.* I feel a similar feeling rising up in my own chest. Could this really be something that might work for us – even temporarily?

'I love it here, Jules,' he says. 'I was going to talk to you about it when we got home – the idea of maybe moving out of London. Somewhere like this. We want a fresh start, don't we? How can we do that while we're still in the same old area where everything happened?'

Everything happened. Yes, everything: good and bad. All our history. All our successes, all our mistakes. Why would we want to hang around there any longer? There's no need. We can do exactly what Lauren's done: reinvent ourselves. It's not too late.

'Perhaps we should let the two of you talk it over,' Stuart suggests.

'No!' I find myself saying firmly. 'There's nothing to discuss. We'd *love* to accept the offer – to rent the flat next to Lauren.' I smile at her, and she smiles back. 'Next to my sister,' I say, softly. 'For as long as it takes us to decide what we're going to do next.'

'Good!' Betty says in her usual business-like manner. 'And if you can't decide on anything else, you can stay here and work for us. He's too polite to say so, but Stuart's going to need more staff here if we're going to be opening a café, a gift shop, and whatever the hell else he's secretly planning and hasn't dared to mention to me yet –'

'How did you know I was thinking about a gift shop?' he squawks in surprise, and we all laugh.

'I just know you,' she says smugly. 'I guessed.'

We have another drink to celebrate – I'm on lemonade now as I'll be driving home tomorrow – and by the time we're all ready to go to bed, it's settled. We'll be coming back, as soon as the sale of the house has gone through and the money's in our account. We'll help out here however we can, until we've decided what our future plans will be. And I think we both know there's a possibility – a fairly strong possibility – that we might stay.

Lauren and I sit in the kitchen of her flat, talking it all over, after Phil's gone to bed.

'I could be here when you get your child,' I realise happily.

'Yes! It'll be great, having you here – Auntie Julia!'

'And maybe if you and Stuart . . .' I begin, but she gives me a look.

'I know what you've been thinking,' she admits after a moment. 'And yes, I do really like him. And . . . he's told me he'd like us to be more than friends.'

'Oh, I *knew* it!' I squeal, but she holds up her hand to stop me.

'But I'm taking it very, very slowly. You, of all people, know what my track record with relationships is like. I don't want to make another mistake, not now I'm hoping to have a child. And I'll be honest – I was amazed when Stuart told me how he feels about me: that he's cared about me ever since that night he found me stumbling around in the snow outside the pub! I've been so busy, concentrating on starting my new life here, and at the same time filling in all the adoption forms and going for all the interviews and meetings about it – I really hadn't given any thought to how close we've become. It's been gradual. And nice.'

'Probably the best way,' I say softly. 'I'm so proud of you, sis. You're making such a success of your life –'

'At last!' she says, raising her eyebrows.

'Yes. But you've done it. Started over. And it's all going to be great. Oh, come here – give me a hug, before I start crying!'

'Daft cow!' she laughs, but she comes and hugs me anyway. 'Who'd have believed things would turn out like this – back in January when we arrived here?'

'Snapping at each other and both as miserable as sin!'

'Thinking it must be a mistake because the place looked like such a dump!' she chuckles.

'We were both different people then, weren't we, in a way.'

'Yes, we were. It seems almost unbelievable that one week here, in the middle of winter, could have changed both our lives so completely.'

'As if there was some kind of magic in the air here.'

'Some kind of magic in Betty's hot chocolate, more likely!' I said – and we both laughed.

Christmas Eve

Betty

I've had some good Christmases in my life, and some not so good. Those years when I spent Christmas completely on my own in London because Richard was with his wife and children and I was too proud to come home to my parents – they obviously weren't the best. Then my parents passed away and – until I had Stuart, I was even more alone. But having a child changed everything: Christmas was wonderful when he was little, of course, and even better when he grew up and brought Janie into the family. When Nathan arrived, I had the pleasure of seeing a little boy opening his presents, all over again. Recently I was beginning to think Christmas would never be the same again now that Janie's gone – but look how things have turned around now. Here I am, surrounded by family – yes, family, all of them, because that's how it feels, being with Lauren – and Julia and Phil, who arrived here in the autumn and have fitted in as if they've always belonged here. I know it's supposed to be a temporary arrangement but I'll be surprised if they end up going anywhere.

By *next* Christmas, if all goes to plan, we'll have another little child here to buy presents for and make a fuss of. Lauren got the all-clear last week, to become an adoptive parent, so in the new year, the process of matching her with a child begins. She's been warned it could still take some time. But I couldn't be more pleased for her, and we're all sure she's going to make a great mum. After all, she's got so many of us here to support her! And if I'm not mistaken, my son in particular is going to be just as involved in parenting this child as Lauren is! They might think nobody's noticed them holding hands and sneaking little kisses from time to time, grinning at each other like it's a secret, when it's so clear to everybody from a mile off that they're in love! But sooner or later they're bound to give up the pretence, as well as giving up the waste of a flat when it's quite obvious they might as well be sharing! I'm so pleased for my son. I understand why he's taking so long to commit; he always swore he'd never love anyone again after losing Janie. But I just want him to be happy. And although Lauren's child won't be his, I know how much he'll enjoy being involved with a little one again, too.

We've got friends calling in later for Christmas Eve drinks: Fern, Andy and little Ella, and a few other people from the village. Then in the morning, Jack's joining us for the rest of the celebrations; he and Nathan are now officially *an item*, as they keep calling it, which I presume means they're a proper couple. Jack's another lovely addition to the family. So we'll all be here together, and it's going to be a wonderful Christmas. Despite what we learned a few days ago.

It was Saturday evening, and it had been a busy day, with lots of customers for our new Christmas lines. We've got into the habit of having dinner all together on Saturday nights, and we'd lingered over the table, talking business, talking Christmas, all of us in cheerful moods. So it was late by the time we all collapsed in the lounge together, watching the late evening news. I was only half concentrating, trying not to fall asleep over the dregs of my wine. Then suddenly I heard his name. *Richard Cavenham.*

I sat up, with a start. Did I dream that? Or was the news presenter really talking about Richard? I tried to sit up and listen properly, but already the news flash had finished and the presenter was talking about shortages of turkeys, and certain children's toys being out of stock all over the country because they were so popular. I looked around the room, to find everyone staring at me.

'Did he say *Richard Cavenham*?' I asked.

'Yes, Mum.' Stuart got to his feet – I didn't know why. And Julia, sitting next to me, put her arm around me. Nathan's eyes were wide with shock. So then, I knew. There could only be one reason for Richard to be mentioned on the TV news now.

'He's dead, isn't he.'

'Yes.' Stuart came to take my hand, squatting down in front of me. 'Passed away peacefully in his sleep, apparently. Found by his carer this morning.'

I nodded. So he'd got himself a carer, in the end.

'Died on his own, then,' I said. I felt detached enough to recognise how strangely calm my voice sounded.

'But in his sleep. Peacefully.'

'Yes.' I swallowed, but it wasn't the onset of tears I was choking back. It was the words I'd nearly uttered, but common decency wouldn't allow past my lips: *More than he deserved.*

So we all sat in silence for a while; I saw glances exchanged, understood that nobody knew quite what to say, so I stroked Stuart's hand a little absent-mindedly and told him, and Nathan, how sorry I was that they'd found their father and grandfather only to lose him so soon.

'It's OK, Mum,' Stuart said. 'It's not as if we developed a close relationship, is it.'

'I'm glad we found out who he was,' Nathan agreed, 'but that's as far as it went.'

'And he was ninety. A good age. Not exactly a tragedy for *us* – but it must be . . . a shock . . . for you, Mum,' Stuart said.

I shook my head. 'Not a shock. A peaceful death at ninety can hardly be called a shock. It's more like . . .' I struggled for a moment to think of a suitable way to express how I felt. Then I recalled a word I'd heard them use sometimes. And I looked up and smiled. 'Closure,' I said firmly.

And that was it. All I could honestly manage to feel, after all those years of remembering him, dreaming of him and wondering about him, was a sense of closure. No sadness. no sorrow. How could I mourn someone of ninety who'd died peacefully in their sleep, especially when, let's face it, for most of my life, I hadn't even known him. The Richard I thought he was, was really just a figment of my imagination.

'You're sure you're all right, Betty?' Lauren asked me softly.

I smiled at her. 'Yes, of course I am. I've got all the people I love around me, and it's nearly Christmas. I'm fine, my lovely.'

'But . . . that's who he was, then.' She frowned. 'Richard Cavenham – I don't remember the name, but it seems –'

'He was a politician,' Stuart said. 'You wouldn't remember him, Lauren, any more than I did. But he told me all about his glory days –'

'Yes, he was quite somebody, at the time,' I said, nodding. 'Oh yes. Quite a catch. Perhaps that was the trouble. I was too young, too impressionable. And of course – I thought he loved me.'

And finally, one treacherous little tear trickled out of my eye. I dashed it away quickly, but not quickly enough to prevent an avalanche of sympathetic exclamations and hugs that I tried pathetically to bat away.

'I'm fine,' I kept insisting, but nobody seemed to believe me. And more than anything else, it was their love, so evident on all of their distressed faces, that moved me to more tears.

'Richard, you bastard!' I managed to splutter eventually. 'Look what you've done – you've upset everyone now!'

And fortunately, finally, I'd made them all laugh. So then I told them the whole story.

1965

When I first met Richard, he was working for the local council. At least, that was what I understood. It didn't sound like a particularly important job, and I suppose I was less interested in what he did there than what he did when he was with me. It was a while before he explained: he was actually a Borough Councillor. I knew he was a member of the Conservative party, and that he lived in a Conservative borough. Out of loyalty to him I voted Conservative instead of Labour in the 1966 election, for the first time in my life, even though I really liked Harold Wilson and was secretly glad that his Labour government got back into power. Richard and I didn't talk much about politics or his career. We didn't talk much about my career either. Looking back, I wonder what we did talk about, but I suppose our hours together were so rare and precious that we didn't waste too much time talking!

One of the few things I did quickly learn about him was that he was never happier than when he was name-dropping. He was fascinated by celebrities: when I'd asked him why he was at the Beatles' concert – he was older than the average fan and he went on his own – he looked at me in surprise and said he wanted to meet them. He hadn't actually met them then, of course – he'd just seen them on stage, and missed some of the experience while he was helping me recover from my faint! So at the time, I just laughed about it.

I make no excuses for myself. I knew when I met him that he had a wife, and a baby daughter. I don't suppose I was the first silly, innocent young woman to be taken in by the sort of promises he made me, and sadly I'm sure I wasn't the last. I believed him when he said he and his wife never made love anymore, that he couldn't possibly do that with her because I was now his only true love. So when, a couple of years later, he let it slip that she'd had a second baby girl, I was beside myself. How could he do that? How could he go from my bed to hers? How could he make her pregnant, when I was the one he really loved? I almost finished with him then, but he begged me not to, showering me with flowers and gifts and promises, explaining that he really couldn't leave his wife now because of the children – surely I must see that he couldn't hurt two tiny little girls, it wasn't their fault that their parents didn't love each other anymore? One day, he promised me, we'd be together properly and he'd make it up to me then.

In 1968, there was a by-election in the London borough he represented, and to my surprise, he told me he was going to stand for election.

'As an MP?' I said. 'Really? You'll go to parliament?'

'Of course – if I'm elected!' He laughed. 'You must realise that's always been my ambition.'

I felt too silly to admit that no, I'd never realised it at all. He'd never talked to me about his ambitions, or asked me about mine. His borough on the western fringes of Greater London was a Conservative stronghold, and he was young, handsome, appealing, popular. He won the by-election with a huge majority, and I soon started noticing changes in him. He'd always had an air of confidence about him; that was one of the attractions, to a shy young teacher from the countryside like me. Now, week by week he was becoming more sure of himself. Dare I say it? A bit more arrogant. If anything, it made him even more attractive to me, and made me feel even more privileged to be his lover.

He bought me a flat in a nice part of central London, and would come to me whenever he could manage it, sometimes late at night after a long-running debate and vote in the House of Commons. From what little he told me about his career, it seemed he was making a good impression within the Conservative backbenches. He was a good speaker, well-educated, smart, opinionated.

'They like my ideas,' he used to tell me smoothly.

He was making a name for himself, and finally he was mixing in the circles he'd always dreamed of. Money was no problem – he'd come from a well-to-do family – and he'd started frequenting clubs and bars where he knew the rich and famous hung out. As his career gradually took off, some of these celebrities became his personal friends. I remember having a proper tantrum when he casually mentioned partying with two of the Beatles and one of the Rolling Stones. I demanded that he take me along with him the next time – but of course, he wouldn't. He couldn't.

He continually assured me that he'd leave his wife and be with me, once the girls were older. He never specified how much older the girls needed to be, and I didn't ask. I was living rent-free in a beautiful flat with a view over the Thames; I reasoned that he must really love me, to treat me so well. I just had to wait.

And then, at the June 1970 general election, the Conservatives under Edward Heath ousted Harold Wilson's Labour government, and the up-and-coming Richard Cavenham was picked for a minor position in the new cabinet. From then on, I saw him less and less often. But how could I complain? The country needed him, he explained: he had to put duty before pleasure. From what I now know, I don't suppose it was just the country that needed him but no doubt God-knows how many other women, and I don't suppose for one minute he went without any of the pleasures on offer to him. I can't believe how naïve I must have been.

Over the course of the next couple of years there were several cabinet reshuffles, and with each one, Richard gained a more senior role. He was a favourite of every shade of Tory, from the heart of London to the outer shires, always in the news, supporting underrepresented minorities and outspoken in his views in favour of populist policies. It wasn't long before he was being tipped to be the next Prime Minister. I was bursting with pride every time I saw him on TV, or saw his picture in the national papers, and wished more than anything that I could tell everyone he was my man. But I knew the rules. Yes, I played the game. I promised him, promised him faithfully, I'd never do anything to break his trust in me. Never do anything to hurt him or ruin his career.

It was in the summer of 1972 that I realised I was pregnant. I'd been on the Pill – Richard had made sure of it – but I'd had a stomach upset one day after a fish curry takeaway we'd shared, and the nurse who confirmed my pregnancy said the Pill probably hadn't been absorbed by my system because of it.

'It's really bad luck,' she said calmly. 'Quite unusual.'

'Bad luck is putting it mildly,' I said, fighting back tears.

'You're not married, I take it?' she said, glancing at my naked left hand. 'Will your boyfriend stand by you?'

I shook my head. 'He's . . . not in a position to.'

'Well, you need to think fairly quickly about what you're going to do,' she said.

Abortion had been legal for a few years by then, but I'd put off having the pregnancy confirmed for longer than I should have done, hoping it was going to be a false alarm, so I had very little time left to make a decision which I knew would haunt me for the rest of my life. I couldn't do it. And becoming pregnant had suddenly, finally, brought everything into sharp focus for me. I'd never have Richard to myself now. His career was too important to him; leaving his wife and children and shacking up with a pregnant girlfriend would cause a scandal, and it would be all over the papers. He'd never make Prime Minister; he'd be relegated to the back benches again and he'd always be known as the Cheating Tory. I told myself I couldn't let that happen to him – I loved him too much. I'd have to sacrifice my own happiness on the altar of his success.

It was almost like self-flagellation. Almost as if I *wanted* to suffer, to feel genuine heartbreak, to prove how much I loved him. Or, perhaps, underneath it all

I'd just had enough. I was going to have a baby now: someone of my own, who would truly belong to me and love me in the way I'd craved. I even wonder now whether I actually knew, deep down, that Richard never had, and never would.

Stuart was born in March 1973, and a year later, the country went to the polls again and Edward Heath's Conservatory government was ousted by a minority Labour government. From the moment I arrived back at Deepcombe to live alone in the Manor I'd now inherited, and bring up my baby on my own, I'd been determined not to follow Richard's career anymore. I'd stayed away from newspapers and the TV news, and imagined him becoming more and more successful and powerful. I wondered, of course, whether he missed me, and assumed – wrongly, as I now know – that he'd tried, and failed to find me. But this news that the Labour party under Harold Wilson was back in power would have been impossible to miss – everyone was talking about it. I wondered how Richard must be feeling. Defeat wouldn't have come easily to him; I presumed he'd have a major position on the Shadow Cabinet, that he'd possibly even become Leader of the Opposition. Perhaps he'd finally achieve his ambition and become Prime Minister at the next election.

In time, concentrating on my child and trying to earn a living as a single parent, I was able to move on. Sometimes, I even forgot to think about Richard for several days at a time, so that I found myself watching the News one night and seeing his face pop up on the screen before I had time to turn it off.

Top member of the Shadow Cabinet Richard Cavenham has been arrested today on charges relating to possession of illegal substances. Mr Cavenham, who has enjoyed a successful and colourful political career, often pictured in the company of celebrities from the entertainment industry, once counted members of the Beatles and the Rolling Stones as his friends. He has often argued vigorously for tougher sentences for drug dealers and traffickers. Approached by journalists today, he refused to comment on the allegations against him –

I turned off the TV abruptly, and sat in the sudden silence, my head spinning. *Drugs*? It wasn't possible – was it? I used to listen to him, often enough, describing how strongly he felt about the dangers of even experimenting with them. But despite all that, I somehow knew it was true. His habit of cosying up to celebrities had finally been the undoing of him. In due course, he was convicted of possession of Class A drugs and – because of his position and in recognition of the betrayal of public trust – sentenced to five years in prison.

I'd started following the news again, up until the point of his sentencing – it had been too difficult to avoid mention of him. But afterwards, knowing his career would be over, and disgusted with myself for still feeling a terrible sympathy for him despite his hypocrisy, I tried harder than ever to forget him. In time I could even smile to myself when I did occasionally think about those years. I smiled at my own foolishness, but also because of the memory of how it felt to be so much in love. I never felt that way about anyone else. Perhaps I held back, remembering how much it could hurt.

When Stuart started asking about his father, I had no problem about withholding the truth. I'll be honest: I'm not sure, now, which was my strongest motivation: protecting Richard's reputation from further damage, not that it could have sunk much lower, at that point; protecting Stuart from finding out his father was someone so notorious; or protecting myself. I couldn't risk having to meet Richard again – not then, while I was still so emotionally vulnerable, so likely to feel that same pull of attraction and desire. After all, even at the ridiculous age of eighty, I had wondered how it was going to affect me, seeing him again. I'm glad to say that I needn't have worried.

I wish I could say I've got no regrets, but of course, I have. I regret having been the mistress of a married man, having been complicit in his cheating, hurting his wife and daughters. I regret not having been mature enough to have moved on from that situation much more quickly. And I regret the fact that the whole experience spoiled, for me, the chance of meeting someone who might have really loved me. My fault; my loss. But of course, I don't regret having my wonderful son, and my lovely grandson. I don't regret coming back to Deepcombe and making my life here, instead of staying in London.

I've made mistakes; but haven't we all? I hope it's helped me to understand other people better – to sympathise with their weaknesses, their own worries and regrets. So I suppose you could say it's made me who they all say I am: the *Wise Woman of Deepcombe*!

A Sunday afternoon, the next Summer

Lauren

She's three years old, with blonde hair, blue eyes, the face of an angel, and a smile to melt your heart. Her name's Molly, she's going to be legally my daughter, and I adore her. She's been, since her birth, with the nicest foster parents you could imagine, who've showered her with love, and who've spent the past three months bringing her to visit me, allowing our relationship to develop slowly, naturally, until Molly was ready to come to me without any coaxing, to show me her toys, chat to me, let me hug her, and finally, to spend time with me on my own. She lives with me full-time now, and I'm hoping she'll soon start calling me *Mummy*. I know I can't rush that; she has to feel ready. But she has an amazing vocabulary for someone so small; she knows, and understands, so much more than I expected. I'm constantly in awe of her. In awe of the fact that she's here, she's real, she's perfect.

I was wary of introducing her to Stuart too soon. I explained the situation to the foster parents; explained that we won't be moving in together yet, because I applied for adoption as a single parent and we don't want to do anything to upset or delay the process. Stuart feels as strongly as I do about this.

'Let her get used to him as naturally as she's doing with the rest of your family and community here,' they advised me. 'Just let it all happen gradually, she'll see him as your special person, then it won't feel strange to her once you're both ready for him to be a permanent part of her little world.'

She'll take my surname, of course, once the legal process is finalised, although perhaps one day, if things work out for us, she might be calling Stuart *Daddy*. But we don't want to risk upsetting her by introducing too many changes too soon. She's a happy little girl and we mustn't let anything happen to spoil that.

This afternoon she's playing with her little friend, Ella, on the lawned area behind the Manor, while I chat to Ella's mummies Fern and Andy and we all keep a constant watch over the two little girls.

'It's lush, it is, seeing them together like this,' Fern says. 'Just think how cute they'll be, starting school together, growing up and being best friends, hanging out together as teenagers –'

'Hey, slow down!' I protest. 'Don't wish it all away: I've waited so long for this!'

'Yes, you're right, too.' Andy smiles at me. 'This is such a perfect age. They're so innocent.'

'But learning so fast!' adds another voice, and we all look up to see Julia walking towards us, bending down to kiss both children on their heads before joining us on the blanket we've laid on the lawn. 'Look how clever they are with those bricks. They're building a house.'

'They've been watching Nathan working on the extension!'

The extension's almost finished, and Julia's been helping the guys order and store the internal fittings for the café we'll be opening in time for the Bank

Holiday weekend: tables, chairs, counter and cabinets, as well as fridge, microwave and all the other necessities for the little kitchen area at the back. We won't need a chef. We'll only be serving hot and cold drinks, sandwiches and cakes; maybe cream teas – that's quite a must in Devon! Julia and Phil have taken on the management of the café between them and they're so excited about it, so committed to it, it's hard now to believe they ever lived in London and ran a car business.

Julia leans back on the blanket now, shading her eyes against the fierce August sun, and as she does, there's a sudden chorus of meows as Basil and Rosie chase each other across the grass towards us. Basil jumps straight onto Julia's legs, while Rosie sits down carefully on the other rug, next to the two children.

'Hello, Rosie cat!' says Ella, stroking her gently.

'Rosie's *my* cat,' Molly says.

'She's not just yours, Molly,' I say, laughing. 'Really, she's Gran's. Although I must admit,' I add quietly to Fern, 'Rosie does seem to have taken a particular liking to Molly.'

'Does Betty mind you calling her *Gran*?' Andy asks – and Julia and I both laugh.

'No,' says Julia. 'It was her idea! She loves it. She's used to it from Nathan, anyway.'

'Aw, tidy,' Fern says. 'I think she's got a new lease of life, that woman, since you all moved in here. Some people her age might have been looking forward to peace and quiet – but not her! She's lapping it all up, and good for her.'

'Yes.' Julia and I exchange a smile. 'You're right – good for her. She spent too much of her life alone, and now she's making up for lost time. She can shut herself away if it all gets too much for her, but mostly she just likes to sit in her conservatory, watching us all take our dips in the pool, enjoying seeing everything going on.'

'Chatting to people, like she's always done, eh?' Fern says.

'Of course. And listening to their problems. She thrives on it. And let's face it, there will always be people with problems for her to listen to.'

'That'll never change,' I agree. 'And it's . . . what makes Betty who she is, after all. The *Wise Woman of Deepcombe*. She fits the title.'

'She earned it,' Julia murmurs.

'Oh-oh!' says Molly suddenly. 'Rosie's been sick, Mummy!'

I jump up quickly. 'OK, girls, move off the blanket a minute. Let me clear it up – there you go, you're fine, she's just eaten grass, silly cat, that's all.' I turn back and grin at the others. 'Did you hear what she said?'

But I can see they did, because Julia's got tears glinting in her eyes and Fern and Andy are both smiling back at me.

'She called you *Mummy*,' Julia says softly.

And I think, as I turn back to my little girl, that life couldn't possibly get any more beautiful than it is right now; and even if anything bad should ever happen to me again, I'll always remember this moment: here on the lawn at Deepcombe Manor, with my sister looking at me with such love in her eyes, and this trusting little person calling me *mummy* for the very first time.

There's definitely something magical about this place. It's still hard to believe how much has happened to Julia and me, since we first came here. Since we spent that one cold week together – mostly arguing! – here on Dartmoor in January last year. Perhaps I should thank Carl, after all, for my birthday present. That one week in winter was worth so much more than any five-star hotel somewhere hot and exotic. It changed our lives.

COMING SOON from SHEILA NORTON:

Four brand new books, to be published by Boldwood Books from Spring 2024.

Follow Sheila Norton on Amazon or at www.sheilanorton.com to keep up-to-date.

Previous books by Sheila Norton:

Also set in Devon, published by Piatkus
The Secret of Angel Cove
Winter at Cliff's End Cottage
(Winner of the Christmas/Winter category of the RoNAs 2022)

Feel-good stories, featuring pets – published by Ebury
Oliver, the Cat Who Saved Christmas
Charlie, the Kitten Who Saved a Life
The Vets at Hope Green
The Pets at Primrose Cottage
The Pet Shop at Pennycombe Bay
The Lonely Hearts Dog Walkers
Escape to Riverside Cottage

Novels set in the 1960s
Yesterday
Ticket to Ride

A series about sisters
Sophie Being Single
Debra Being Divorced
Millie Being Married

Originally written as Olivia Ryan and published by Piatkus:
Tales from a Hen Weekend
Tales from a Wedding Day
Tales from a Honeymoon Hotel

Romantic comedies, originally published by Piatkus:
The Trouble with Ally
Other People's Lives
Body & Soul
The Travel Bug
Sweet Nothings

Short story anthologies:
Travellers' Tales
Let's Get the Kettle On!

**For more information about the author and her books please visit:
www.sheilanorton.com**

Printed in Great Britain
by Amazon